Also by Judith Rossner

Looking for Mr. Goodbar
Any Minute I Can Split
Nine Months in the Life of an Old Maid
To the Precipice

JUDITH ROSSNER

SIMON AND SCHUSTER   NEW YORK

Attach-ments

PUBLISHED BY SIMON AND SCHUSTER
A DIVISION OF GULF & WESTERN CORPORATION
SIMON & SCHUSTER BUILDING
ROCKEFELLER CENTER
1230 AVENUE OF THE AMERICAS
NEW YORK, NEW YORK 10020

DESIGNED BY ELIZABETH WOLL
MANUFACTURED IN THE UNITED STATES OF AMERICA

1   2   3   4   5   6   7   8   9   10

LIBRARY OF CONGRESS CATALOGING IN PUBLICATION DATA

ROSSNER, JUDITH.
    ATTACHMENTS.

    I. TITLE.
PZ4.R834AT   [PS3568.O848]   813'.5'4   77-6421
ISBN 0-671-22591-X

FOR DANIEL ROSSNER

In experiments in which animals are confined for relatively short periods of time and their behavior and physiological responses observed, the findings seem to be inconsistent with an instinctive notion of territoriality. The most important result is that being in a cage with other animals produces effects regardless of the size of the cage.

—JONATHAN FREEDMAN,
Crowding and Behavior

HERE is the first time I saw them:

1956.

Their home in Beverly Hills.

For years I've known about them, dreamed of them, clipped articles about them, wanted to meet them.

Now I park my father's car on the road outside the high bordering bushes and walk up the driveway, expecting to be stopped by a guard or a housekeeper or a dog. But the place is silent. The house is one of those standard white-stucco jobs with red tile roof, small for the area but set beautifully into the hillside. Lovely winding paths lead away from the building, one of them, presumably, to the pool I know is there.

I feel weak. I haven't eaten all day; my mouth is full of my heart. I can't breathe, either; oxygen must be seeping in through my ears and other small places.

Still no sound.

I walk to the front door but instead of using the bell or the knocker I rap lightly with my knuckles and call hello in a soft voice. Nothing. I walk around the house to where the ground slopes down toward the facing hills. In the distance the sun is setting rose and gold. Closer to me, just down the slope and past some bushes, I can see a round section of what I would swear was a pond had I not known that a pond was virtually impossible in this high, dry area. As I walk down the path the pond illusion diminishes although it's obvious that the illusion was planned. I can see cement sides on the perfect circle but bushes are planted unusually close to the water and the pool lining is painted a dark greenish brown instead of the universal turquoise.

It's so quiet that at first I think the ripples in the water are being caused by the wind. Except there is no wind.

A moment later their heads surface, facing each other, and I can see them moving around the pool. I shiver. There is no noise, even now. Their limbs haven't surfaced, only their heads, facing each other, silent, as far as I can see, unsmiling. Moving, moving, never needing to speak, each understanding without words where the other is going. The scene is eerie and unspeakably beautiful. I am engulfed by sexual feelings and frightened lest someone stumble upon me and force me to move when I feel that I can't.

Slowly the fear passes and I settle down on the grass to watch them. It might be another hour (or five minutes) before they make their way to a small semicircle that extends from the large circle and appears to have steps. At which point I scramble to my feet and flee back up the path to my car.

I am twenty-one years old. I have been aware of the existence of the Siamese twins for six years; Dianne has been my closest friend for five.

FRIENDSHIPS, like marriages, have their myths: the myth of the easy and the difficult one, the active and the passive one, the needy and the self-sufficient one, the villain and the victim and so on. Having had the distinction of being the difficult one in a marriage of four I developed a strong interest in this question. After all, I asked myself, if the poor little German peasant hoeing his potatoes twenty miles from the tracks that guided the trains that carried the Jews to Buchenwald is now understood to have had some complicity in the murder of those Jews, then how can any married person be innocent of the crimes of his or her spouse? I lean toward the theory that where there are two hearts that beat as one, the one who gives the beatings is generally doing it for two.

It was the myth of Dianne's and my friendship that she went along for the ride. If we built a fire it was because I got cold; if we went out to eat it was because I was hungry; if we cruised, so to speak, it was because I felt like getting laid. If in the process she happened to have a good meal or a good lay, well, why not? Although she often made it a point to tell me later that she would have been just as happy if she'd stayed home with a good book.

For many years the myth didn't bother me. That's a subtle lie; I grooved on it. On the image of myself as the kid with the greatest needs of all. Number One in the Miss Hungry Lusty America Contest. I'm not sure when I got tired of representing the spirit of furious need, although I may remember as I write. Maybe it was a gradual process—live a little, learn a little. Or maybe I just woke up one day knowing that furious need, by definition, couldn't be satisfied.

The latter doesn't seem too likely. The truth is, I've been a slow learner. The truth is that during the first twenty-five or thirty years of my life I was too agitated to learn much. Too busy trying to keep myself from falling.

My mother, who had once taken third place in the Miss America Contest, was tall but delicate—a word almost meaningless to an adult who knows the variety of truths and lies it can conceal. To a child its meaning is extraordinary and explicit: Don't touch. She will break. Having had two abortions and then three miscarriages before my conception, my mother conceived me, remained in bed for the last seven months of my incubation, gave birth to me as the clock struck four on a snowy March morning, and not too many weeks later was diagnosed to be suffering from acute tuberculosis. A postpartum depression of the throat.

Home from the hospital she recuperated gradually from TB only to be dogged by a series of ailments which varied greatly in gravity although they were uniformly terrifying to me. The welts, for example, which swelled through her skin when she ignored an old allergy and ate an avocado provoked no less anxiety in me than the stomach pains which turned out to be from a ruptured appendix. Or the attacks she had on the rare occasion when she tried to eat grapefruit, beginning with a mere "tickle" in her

14

throat, developing into a choking cough and ending with convulsions that racked her entire body. Or the skin disease of the groin which forced her to lie in bed on and off for months at a time during the early years of my childhood with her knees raised and her legs spread, her very position a perpetual reproach to me for having put her through the ordeal of childbirth.

Someone who might herself be eradicated at any moment. Hardly the sort of person you ran to for comfort in the middle of the night because you'd dreamed that you'd gone off the diving board and the pool wasn't there and you were falling . . . falling . . . you would have died if you hadn't awakened in time.

My father was an ex-swimming coach (UCLA), now the owner of a pool company franchise, who traveled inner space on a sea of alcohol whose volume increased over time until eventually no land could be sighted. But that was when I was already grown up. I remember him during my childhood—tall, terribly handsome, loving to putter around the house, to swim, to garden. The house (and the pool) were always full of his friends, whom my mother gently disdained. She had won first place in the talent part of The Contest, as it was always known in our house, and felt she had been destined for a more meaningful life. She often said that she would have been happier living in New York, if only it had a climate like Los Angeles'.

My father loved my mother more than life itself.

My mother wanted my father, the sturdy son of Irish, German and Polish immigrants, to take care of her, to make her *happy*, to support her in a style appropriate to a singer of Olde English folk songs, although she didn't know precisely what that style might be.

My father was uncomfortable with childish demands. He sometimes really liked to give, but asking for anything was a cardinal sin. My mother never asked but only got depressed when she didn't get something because he hadn't known she wanted it. When she was depressed he drank more. This turned her depression to illness which in turn made him drink even more.

In other words, there was nothing extreme in my background—

15

only in the way I reacted to it. Some people spend their lives falling and never notice. I not only noticed but screamed the whole time.

Dianne never screams. Dianne was a child prodigy—a prodigy among prodigies, you might say, for she was born and bred in New York and only came to Los Angeles as a teenager. At nine Dianne composed a sonata; at twelve she directed herself in *Under Milk Wood*; at fourteen she won the Westinghouse contest and at twenty-two she was admitted to the bar. It's all there in her head; she doesn't let it leak out of her mouth like other people.

Must I tell you about Dianne's childhood? I will have to battle with myself to fairly represent its horrors because I want you to be on my side when we separate. Can I trust that if I let you feel for her now you'll switch sympathies later when I need you? It's a risk I wish I didn't have to take.

Her father is a behavioral psychologist, her mother a Freudian analyst. There are twenty-seven, hardcover, black-and-white notebooks covering the first ten years of her life. In these notebooks are celebrated the dates of her teeth, sounds, words, the width of her smile, the texture of her bowel movements—along with profound explanations for each of these phenomena. Letters and childish drawings are neatly pasted in. The first letter to her parents from the first school she attended mentions a tendency to be secretive. (The next twenty or thirty pages are full of carbons and originals of furious letters to and annotated replies from the teacher and school administrators, ending with an excruciatingly reasonable explanation, signed by both parents, of why Dianne is being withdrawn from the school.) Dianne's parents always seemed to me pleasant and eminently sane, but to glance through those notebooks is to wonder that she did not physically as well as emotionally metamorphose into a gigantic, hard-shelled clam.

She took little or no pleasure in her achievements of talent and intellect. They apparently represented in her mind primarily a way of fending off her parents—particularly her mother. Meat

16

thrown to a two-headed beast to keep it from devouring her. Sometimes I've thought that for Dianne our marriage represented the ultimate piece of raw meat. The piece her parents would forever choke on, which would therefore save her from them.

I myself was nonacademic from some point in my preadolescent years, doing just well enough on high-school tests to ensure that each year I would be discovered as an underachiever. Then I'd be called into the guidance cubicle where some social worker type would smile beguilingly and ask me what I did with my brains when I wasn't taking annual achievement tests, and I would say that I kept them in a cushioned box so they wouldn't get hurt when I fell. Since this reply was never taken at face value it invariably brought an end to the interview, but a week or two later I would drop a teaser in the guidance office mailbox:

My name is Nadine
My station is WHYS
The call letters of the falling stars . . .

Then I would receive some ecstatic response (mawkish adolescent verse going further at Beverly High than it did in New York, where it was even then a drug on the market), and satisfied that I was known, I would lapse back into underachievement.

This was not the way it was supposed to be.

From the day that I was two years old and it had been discovered (accidentally, by my father's sister who was visiting from Minnesota) that I was acutely farsighted and needed glasses, it had been ordained by my mother that I should at least be Very Intelligent.

It would be difficult to exaggerate the anxiety this whole eyeglasses business created in my parents, who were both born in California and had eaten nutburgers twenty years before lysergic acid was invented and never wore glasses and didn't know about things like poor eyesight, a strange *Eastern* kind of defect. They looked at little Nadine, two and a half and all wide smile and big thick glasses, and saw a thirty-year-old blind spinster, dependent on them for life. She didn't even have a waistline. Or breasts!

Actually, they didn't look. They looked elsewhere, even when I was talking.

Help! Mommydaddy! Look at me! I'm fallllllllling!

My father sold Dianne's parents a swimming pool when they moved to Beverly Hills to become Dynamic Duoshrinks to the Stars. Teaching behaviorism in the movie colony is something like teaching sequins not to sparkle but the Shapiros had this idea, a pretty advanced one for the time if you don't look at where they chose to do it, of working in different modes with the same patient. They didn't do too well with it, perhaps because each secretly despised the other's method, and they eventually developed separate practices, but that's not to the point, not at this moment anyway.

My accident-prone father had sprained his wrist coming out of our pool one night and I was driving for him (illegally) when I didn't have school. On this Saturday we were going to take Dr. and Mrs. Shapiro (my father would never call Di's mother Doctor) to the pools of some satisfied customers to get a sense of the possibilities. Dianne wanted a round pool while her mother liked simple rectangles and the doctor went for kidneys. Dianne couldn't swim.

I liked her right off. I generally went for the type, in males as well as in females, the pale, bland-looking ones whose volcanoes were nowhere near the tops of their heads. It was the reason I went for Eddie, not Amos, when I met them, and doubtless why I married Amos, not Eddie.

"Mmm," Dianne said when she saw the first lush, turquoise kidney.

"You should see the heart-shaped one," I said with a grin. "That'd really knock you out. It was built by an eighty-year-old director for his twelve-year-old girlfriend as a Valentine's Day present."

18

Whatever I had in the way of taste had been acquired by inference from reading Nathanael West, given to us by a freshman English teacher who was fired at the end of the year over that and other taste-related questions. Growing up in Los Angeles, for the obvious reasons, I never knew the difference between an artifact and an eyesore. Any more than I knew the limits of normal human behavior or whether I was a normal human and should be guided by them.

Dianne looked at me. Not with visible interest, but in the type, if you're familiar with it, the fact of bothering to look conveys greater than normal interest.

It was 1950. We were both fifteen. I was about to enter my sophomore year of high school and she would be a senior.

I spent most of that summer indoors with her. I could swim any year but this year I'd found a friend. She let me talk about the twins until my intensity made her uncomfortable. I showed her my file—TWINS, SIAMESE. They'd been discovered less than a year before and everything I had on them fit into a lingerie box from Magnin's. She read through without comment—everything from the first *Life* picture spread to the encyclopedia article I'd found and copied out in my chaotic scrawl:

DOUBLE MONSTERS—SIAMESE TWINS

Individuals partially or wholly double but joined together are represented by the rare occurrence in man of Siamese twins. This type of monster, so called from the famous Siamese pair exhibited for many years in the 19th century, consists of identical twins joined by a bridge of tissues through which the circulatory system communicates. They probably arise by the incomplete separation of a single fertilized egg into two parts. The experimental production of such double monsters in newts was accomplished by Hans Spemann by constricting the egg in the two-cell state with a Lair loop . . .

. . . Chang and Eng, born Siam, May, 1811, died North Carolina, January, 1874. They were of Chinese extraction . . . They grew to be about five feet two inches in height, could walk, run and swim. In April, 1829, they were taken to the

19

United States and exhibited throughout that country and later in Europe. They became American citizens, married two sisters in 1843 and fathered nineteen children. They finally settled at Mount Airy and lived there until their deaths.

Then there were the first sensational pictures from *Life*: the sixteen-year-old twins swimming in the pond near the state home where they'd been raised, fixing a car engine, eating at a long table in the home, Amos's right leg slung over Eddie's left one. And dozens of articles, the same sparse details relayed over and over again:

When they were approximately four years old they were deposited on the doorstep of a home for retarded children in Dixonville, New Hampshire, along with one change of clothing (homemade, of course, with the holes cut out in the proper places in the shirts) and a note saying, *ther mother hev died and the father dont want them.* They were joined at the abdomen by a thick band of cartilage which was three and a half inches in circumference and not very much longer than that when they were found, and which turned out to contain a bridge of liver. By the time they were adults the band's length had stretched to a point where they could stand almost back to back.

The four-year-olds could not or would not speak and it was presumed by the matron and the examining doctor that the home was the proper place for them to be. They were given a name, Edward Smith, and a birth certificate. Only later when they began to communicate with each other verbally did it occur to anyone that they needed two names, and no one bothered about the second birth certificate for years.

They didn't attempt to walk until they'd been at the home for many months but they sat comfortably facing each other for long periods of time. They slept on their sides, facing each other. They began to experiment with speech when they were five. Their words always had a strange, somewhat thick quality, they (particularly Eddie) were slow spoken and neither would ever be verbose, but gradually they learned to speak well enough so others could understand them and then, when they were nine or ten, they

20

began to read and write. They were well behaved. Certain problems—in toilet training, for example—which were common among the other children never arose with the twins, who used the toilet consistently within a few weeks of entering the home. The fact that they were well behaved and not retarded, while it didn't move the personnel to examine whether they should be living there in the first place, did spur the matron to some effort at education. They were patient students, seldom restless, although Eddie's concentration was never as good as that of Amos, who eventually became an omnivorous reader.

They were happiest in the pond that lay nestled in the back lands of the home. The lake, a pond, any water they could find. They swam from the first time they were left near the pond's edge. The clumsiness that characterized their movements on land disappeared in the water, where they moved swiftly and gracefully, a two-headed human fish.

Of the doctors who served the home during the twelve years the twins were there, at least two raised the question of surgical separation and at one point Amos and Eddie were taken to Concord for examination by the surgeons there. Of these two, one thought the twins should be taken to Boston and that probably surgery should be undertaken no matter what the risks. But others pointed to the fact that there was no history of successful surgery on twins conjoined at the liver and thought it best to leave them as they were. Their legal guardians at the home decided against further investigation.

They were particularly adept at certain of the skills that country boys have, while togetherness made others too difficult. They were skilled electricians. They were fair carpenters but severely limited by the physical size of their project. They could take apart and put back together the engine of any car.

In the summer of 1949, when the twins were sixteen, some tourists who'd gotten lost looking for a garage where they could have their faltering car engine repaired stumbled upon the home. The boys were summoned to aid them. The man was a *Time-Life* stringer. Two weeks later the *Life* spread appeared and in another month they had a five-year contract with Ringling Bros. Barnum & Bailey.

There were few clippings after that; they'd been with the circus for just a few months when their names virtually disappeared from the papers. I told Dianne that I wanted more than anything to know them; she smiled as though I were being whimsical but there was nothing whimsical about my desire.

I introduced Dianne to my crowd. The pretty, suicidal teenage girls whose mother's milk had been tales of faces and boobs discovered by SHEER ACCIDENT at soda fountains on Wilshire Boulevard. The fey sixteen-year-old Judy Garland-loving tap-dancing boys with whom I had my deepest friendships, knowing, as I did, that it wasn't because I wore glasses that they didn't love me.

None of my friends could stand Dianne. Not only was her indifference to them visible but they would have perceived it even if it weren't there. They knew about New Yorkers, about Eastern Types, Communists controlled by Rockefeller and a handful of other rich Jews . . . gray from reading books . . . disdaining Hollywood, Sunshine and Senator McCarthy. Slowly Dianne taught me the facts of life as they had been revealed to the Eastern Establishment. I tried passing on my new knowledge to the others, who were furious with me. Not only was I turning into a crazy Communist whose talk was dangerous but furthermore, next year when Dianne was off in college and I had only them again, I'd be sorry, so I'd better watch my step.

I watched my step. I was constantly aware that Dianne would be leaving me with them, and I was frightened on other grounds, as well. I had grown up blind to the world as it really was and as it ought to be. Dianne had taught me how to see. I felt unsure that my vision would survive her departure. Maybe I would slip back into primordial ignorance. I'd never heard the phrase lobotomy, if the procedure even existed then, but something like it was what I feared. I would forget what it had been like to know the way things really were. I would assume once more that Senator McCarthy was a vehicle of the truth; Alger Hiss was a traitor; everything that glittered was gold.

22

Dianne didn't think so. Dianne thought her teachings would survive her absence. (She was going back East to something called Radcliffe I'd never heard of.) Dianne thought that I was Basically Extremely Intelligent. She gave me reading lists (I hid the books under my bed where my friends wouldn't see them) and wanted me to come East to college in two years when I graduated. I was jealous if I saw her talking to anyone in the halls, which was seldom enough, for she actually never made any friends but me in the Glittering West.

I dreamed about her all the time after she went. In my dreams there was always something she was supposed to have given me or told me before she left that would have guaranteed my safety, but I'd forgotten to ask her and now it was too late. Actually, the dreams were confusing because often I couldn't be certain that it was me in them and not Dianne. Physically we weren't exactly the North Pole and the South Pole. We were both around five feet four inches tall, she had long dark-brown hair and I had long light-brown hair, I had tits and she had an ass but details like that don't always show up in dreams.

Two years later, through the machinations of Dianne's mother, whose dearest friend was a friend of the president, I was admitted to the East Coast—not the Radcliffe branch but the Bard College twig, which had a weakness for artsy underachievers long before they dominated the culture, and hadn't gotten many other applications from Los Angeles that year.

My mother was very depressed. She wanted me to go to UCLA, although she wouldn't stand in the way of my going East. A couple of months before I left she got a Pekingese to replace me but then she couldn't stand the way it yipped. She replaced the Pekingese with a cat but then it turned out she was allergic to cat dandruff. They got rid of the cat and my father erected a beautiful aquarium in front of the living room window but within two weeks every fish in it was dead. She went to a doctor and got tranquilizers. She drifted around the house with a weird near-

23

smile and licked her lips all the time. My father's drinking got worse and when he was sober enough he kept telling me how worried he was about my mother. I almost caved in and went to UCLA (I was scared, anyway). I wrote to Dianne asking whether she'd be mad at me, after all the trouble she and her mother and her mother's friend had gone to, if I went to UCLA so I could be close to my parents. She wrote back that she wouldn't be mad BUT—BUT she would grieve—nay, mourrrrrrrrnnnnnnn—for me, forever lost to the Nadine who might have been. She had plenty more to say about what would happen to my brain if I didn't escape the cultural vacuum of Los Angeles, but it was the *forever* lost that convinced me. Anything that was forever was too frightening to be faced.

THE East. The Yeast, as I'd always referred to it in my letters to Dianne, thus conveying, quite unconsciously, both my awe of it as a mysterious place of feverishly fermenting intellects and my fear that I would not readily find a place in this mass.

My arrival in the Yeast was a simple, low-key nightmare, blurred in retrospect. I remember mainly how hideous, how dark, how *old* everything seemed. The dark, old, littered streets between the bridge and Dianne's uncle's apartment; the dark, old, book-filled apartment on West End Avenue; the slow, creaky ride on the train up the Hudson to Bard (I'd never been on a train before). It was the last week of August, a typical, ghastly, hot New York August, and all I could think about was how I wished I'd never left Beverly Hills and our pool.

What I remember much more distinctly than I remember my arrival in New York is the first time I heard someone say, "It just isn't done."

The quality of Dianne's I'd always most admired was the ability to make sense of a variety of facts that seemed to me meaningless. She appeared to possess a kind of system, a way of looking at things, that made the world seem reasonable—if not in its actions then in its possibilities. If I had any conscious intellectual aim it was in the direction of that kind of understanding. If I understood the world's order I would know its limits, and understanding the limits of the world I might find my own. I had been raised by parents who were fearful of everything but forbade me nothing, in a place that was at once parochial, restrictive and utterly permissive. I wanted not simply to know right and wrong as abstractions but to *experience* them in such a way that my disorderly impulses would be controlled by my knowledge.

It just isn't done.

It was one of those meetings intended to bring new students and faculty together in the days before everyone knew that this was less of a problem than keeping them apart.

A tall melancholy youth was speaking to me but I was staring at another speaker, a slender beautiful woman of at least fifty with white hair gathered into a loose bun at the nape of her neck. She had startling blue eyes set in a high-cheekboned face that would have been more striking had one's full attention not been commanded by the eyes. She wore a wine-colored knit dress, delicate silver earrings and a somewhat heavier engraved silver pendant. The boy who'd just been speaking to her dwarfed her in height and seemed to be trying to push himself down from the shoulders in order to look at her directly. She—Dr. Marianna Story, professor of Romance (and various other) languages, looked amused but firm as she said the magic words. (I would discover that she always looked amused but firm.)

I stared.

The young man who was speaking to me followed my gaze.

"Do you have a class with Dr. Story?" he asked in a low voice, for she was standing less than two feet away from us.

I shook my head.

"I *know* it isn't done," said Dr. Story's companion, quietly insistent. "I just don't understand *why*."

"You will," she promised. Smiling. And slipped away from him with a graceful gesture that managed to deny that she was doing just that.

There goes a woman who knows what isn't done.

I continued to stare at her. Transfixed. As one morning years later I would stare at a screen where Eddie and Amos and Dianne and I were doing our number for a young documentary filmmaker and think: *My God! It just isn't done!* One simply does not marry men who are Siamese twins! What insanity had ever led me to believe for a moment that I could commit such an act? And having believed it, proceeded to persuade myself that it was possible by doing it?

I would major in Romance languages. I cursed the day I'd settled on Spanish as my foreign language because that was what all my high-school friends were taking. Dr. Story wasn't teaching Spanish that semester. I resolved to start a new language at midyear. In the meantime I followed Dr. Story all over the campus, stopping several feet behind her when she got into a conversation, straining to hear what she was saying. She knew I was there but she didn't mind; I wasn't the first, although I might have been the first from Los Angeles.

In the spring term she gave a course in Don Quixote. I fell in love with Don Quixote because he belonged to her. I got an A in the course as I would later get an A in psychology because I'd fallen in love with my psych teacher. If I'd been in love more often I might have had a more distinguished academic career. There was always a person between me and the subject, which I couldn't absorb unless I loved the person.

Meanwhile I cultivated the boy Dr. Story had been talking to,

27

who was in my English class. His name was Shlomo and he liked me. He tried to explain Dianetics to me and I laughed. I tried to find out what he'd been asking Dr. Story that made her say it just wasn't done, but he would never tell me, sensing that his secret was his main strength with me.

For two years when I had a good dream it was about her. I was looking for her in a series of corridors, except the corridors weren't the dry ugly corridors of an institution but wide beautiful spaces lined with ferns and moss (neither of which I'd ever seen until I came East) and rich fabrics. I opened many doors before I finally found her in a room lined in shimmery satin, wearing a pale-blue-satin nightgown (Los Angeles was rooted in my dreams more firmly than in my everyday existence). Her hair was long and loose and wine colored, like the dress she'd been wearing that first day. She was talking to someone I couldn't see but when I came in she rose from the bench at her dressing table and came toward me. I was flooded with pleasure as I anticipated what was to come. I woke up still feeling wonderful although I wanted the dream to have continued so I could know what was going to happen that made me so happy. Sometimes when I felt myself awakening I tried to halt the process but I never could.

In another dream she was instructing me in the matter of what was done and what simply wasn't. The most interesting quality of this dream was that the list of Not Dones was always more vivid as she spoke the words—and made me happier. In the dream the words she spoke were all crystal clear but they began to fade as I struggled against consciousness and by the time I was fully awake they were gone.

At first I spent frequent weekends with Dianne, meeting her in New York where we stayed with her aunt and uncle, who left us pretty much on our own. This arrangement didn't work as well, though, when I began traveling with Shlomo and Dianne with a tall, bearded poet named Berry. It wasn't so much that the men disliked each other, because their dislike wasn't active enough to keep Dianne and me apart, but Dianne didn't care for Shlomo. She found him superficial. She barely pretended to listen when he talked. (Unlike me, who found him too deep to understand but pretended to listen because I was growing fond of him.)

There was little the four of us could talk about. Shlomo was ardently political and had been active in the Campus Democrats for Stevenson. He believed Stevenson to be the closest thing to a saint that our electoral system had seen. Eisenhower was a Republican, than which nothing more need be said. Berry, who was several years older than we were and had been in the Army and after his discharge bummed around Europe for a couple of years, was a Beat Poet, although it was years of course before we'd hear that phrase, nor did I ever see any of his poetry. When Berry wasn't around Dianne might deign to argue with Shlomo that Stevenson was worse than Eisenhower just because he was so much better that he would have delayed the inevitable end of the whole rotten system. But when Berry was around, Berry who claimed not to know the names of either Ike or Stevenson and didn't give a hot damn for socialism or capitalism or any other government, my mentor laid down her intellectual arms and smiled as her friend laconically asked Shlomo, in accents, learned from the Southern jazz musicians he'd met in Paris and still saw in New York, "Hey, man, can't you see it don't make no never mind?" Through those same musicians, incidentally, Berry had also developed an intimate acquaintance with marijuana, which Dianne told me she had smoked on several occasions. I don't remember ever hearing the name before then.

"Maybe," I said to Dianne after our first disastrous weekend together, "if we really need to talk we should meet without the men."

She smiled. It would be accurate to say that her smile was condescending but I didn't think of it that way, then, or if I did condescension seemed appropriate. If I was beginning to meet enough smart Eastern types to take the edge off my awe of her, I still knew that Dianne's brain was vastly superior to mine and that I was lucky she let me be her friend.

"*Need* to talk?" she repeated. She was amused. "I don't know if I *need* to talk."

"I do," I confessed quickly. "I need to . . . I miss having you around to sort of check things out on. I'm in a whole new country, you know. Sometimes I just wish I could call you long distance and talk for an hour, but then I think it's not worth it, it's much better to see you." When I talked to her on the phone I found her silences nearly unbearable, while looking at her I felt reactions even when her expression didn't change.

"Mmmm," she said now.

Mmmm was Dianne's basic remark and now at the beginning of our tale it might be just as well to give you a partial list of its meanings.

> *Partial List of Meanings of Mmmmm*
> 1. You may be right.
> 2. You're probably wrong but I haven't the energy to explain why because to do so I would have to disabuse you of 372 other cherished notions which are also wrong.
> 3. Okay, but it was your idea.
> 4. Yes, it might be fun. Or at least you'll think so.
> 5. That's the dumbest statement I ever heard out of the mouth of someone who is allowed to be my friend.
> 6. That's the dumbest statement ever uttered by anyone anywhere.

"What do you think of Shlomo?" I asked.

"He's all right," she said cautiously. "For his age."

Neither of us was eighteen yet but she'd been in college for two years and Shlomo for just one. Since Berry, who was twenty-six, she had let it be known that younger men bored her.

"I think he's sweet," I said. "And very smart." I was proud, with her, of having a Jewish boyfriend, but she didn't seem to notice.

"Mmmm," she said.

After that Shlomo and I stayed with his parents, who lived on the Grand Concourse, in the Bronx. His mother was a dentist and his father taught history at a nearby high school.

Shlomo and I had started out as mutually suspicious pals. I was suspicious of him because I didn't understand why he liked me. He was suspicious of me because he (rightly) thought that I wasn't particularly drawn to him. Neither of us had many friends. He was fiercely into ideas as people—to be latched onto, delved into, seduced, overwhelmed and finally abandoned because they'd been replaced by something better. I was convinced that my safe path lay in keeping my mouth shut in company so others could only *suspect* that I knew nothing and didn't belong in the Yeast. I was assumed to be acutely shy.

When we finally began sleeping with each other it was in the most casual way. A virgin when we met, I had once considered myself the possessor of some marvelous buried treasure that no man had the initiative to take off my glasses and dig for.

"It's here," I'd often wanted to call out to the young men in L.A. who drove by and whistled at us but seldom stopped their cars. "It's here waiting, damn it. Why do you whistle and drive on?" Not understanding that they whistled instead of stopping. By the time I was seventeen my treasure had become a burden, yet it never occurred to me that I might lose this particular burden in the East, where I was going, after all, to improve my *mind.*

Anyway, Shlomo and I progressed over the weeks from holding hands to necking to petting, as it was then known (while the more obvious *grooming* seems to have been universally ignored), and then one day, in the carriage house on the Zabriskie estate, which had been donated to Bard and was half converted to a theater, we found ourselves, having worked later than everyone else, lying on our coats and some tarps on the cold floor and slowly, heating up, taking off the rest of our clothes. Neither of us was terribly anxious, perhaps because we were such pals, perhaps because it was only 1954 and performance standards of sexuality hadn't hit the mass consciousness yet. Not that we were totally at ease. Virgins both, we fumbled and giggled and certainly we never reached anything resembling what the sex technologists would call the hot center, but we didn't have that sense that seems to pervade so many sexual transactions of the seventies, that our entire selves were at stake. And as I write this only one thing strikes me as strange, that I should feel the need to explain why this was so. We were friends.

Afterward we put Shlomo's parka over us and fell asleep together,

31

eventually awakening because the temperature in the unheated carriage house had gone down to freezing and the parka didn't cover our legs.

"Give me one good reason why you won't tell me."

He smacked his forehead and groaned. "Jesus Christ, I thought we were finally over that one."

"Why? Because you're making me?"

"Anytime you're ready to tell me why you care so much, I'll tell you."

"Don't you understand, Shlo, I can't know why I care until I know what it is?"

"AAAAAAARRRRRRRAAAAGGGGGHHHHHHHHHH!"

He had many traits that endeared him to me. Or maybe they became dear to me because they were his.

When I teased him and he couldn't find an immediate riposte his nose got itchy and he had to scratch it.

He had a lot of dandruff. I don't recall any trace of self-consciousness over his bony, intense Jewish looks, his ugly clothing, his awkward manners or anything else, but every time he took off a jacket or shirt he shook off the dandruff.

When explaining to me, or rather talking out for his own benefit in my presence, some major idea he'd stumbled across in a book, a class, or maybe just his own head, he'd slowly count my toes (or my fingers, toes being unavailable) with his thumb and index finger in a way that reminded me of my father doing *This little piggy went to market*, when I was little.

In the middle of the school year Berry took off for California and then for a while the three of us met in New York. Each of them talked almost exclusively to me, although their tastes were much closer to each other's than to mine. Once the warm weather came it was Shlomo and Dianne who wanted to endure the stone steps of Lewisohn Stadium for the rare Varèse concert, and I who could sit still for Gershwin. They could have seen *The Bicycle Thief* every time it was revived while I craved the M-G-M musicals and Errol Flynn epics on which I'd been raised.

In my second year I found within myself—invented might be a better word—an interest in a group of modern Latin-American poets for a project on which I requested weekly tutorials with Dr. Story. The tutorials were held at her home, which was one of the reasons I wanted them so badly. She would initiate me to the mysteries which I not only was far from solving but could not yet even identify.

Her home did indeed contain a clue, if only in its contrast to that of my parents, with whom I'd just spent a desolate summer. Here all was beautiful, ornate, tiny yet more than large enough for one person. This home was a refuge and what this home was about was the past, which was smaller, prettier, and at once more complex and more orderly than the present. The clue, then, had to do with the past. I lost overnight my aversion to small dark rooms full of books and knickknacks. We sat in the drawing room facing each other on teal velvet Victorian love seats and talked about the poets I'd selected for my project. The most modern of whom it turned out she had known for many years. (Perhaps he had been her lover?) In discussing interpretation she would often settle a point through her personal knowledge of his intentions. If I later had doubts about this as a method of discovering what was actually contained in a work of art, it seemed to me at the time a most powerful method of scholarship.

My second summer at home was more disastrous than the first. My parents were the same and everything else was worse. Redwood houses with glass walls were too big, the light was blinding. The chlorine in the pool was too strong. And the ocean was awfully goddamn noisy. I left on some pretext in the middle of August, vowing that I would never again come home for more than a week at a time. In my valise this time as I headed back to the nearly deserted Bard campus was the lingerie box marked TWINS, SIAMESE.

33

The following spring Dr. Story had a breast removed because there was a lump in it which turned out to be cancerous.

It was May. I was lying on the grass with Shlomo. The sky was particularly blue and masses of cottony clouds were moving above us in shapes we identified in poetic (then, embarrassed, humorous) ways.

"Did you hear about Story?" my friend Ellen asked disconsolately, dropping down beside me on the grass.

"She said she'd be out this week."

"This week. Ha."

That made me sit up. "What?"

"She's in the hospital."

"Where?" Not *why*, the answer to which may be more than I can handle, but where?

"New York. Columbia Presbyterian."

"When's she coming back?"

Ellen shrugged. "It almost doesn't matter, it's . . . she won't be in school for the rest of the term."

"All right. What is it?"

"Mastectomy."

"I don't know what that is." Flatly. *Angrily*. I don't want to know what it is and in the fifties, when lopped-off boobs have not yet become the mainstay of the six o'clock news, it's still possible to not know.

"She had a breast removed. Cancer."

"No."

Not Dr. Story. There are people things like that happen to but she isn't one of them. I stood up, slapped the dirt and grass off my jeans and began running around the lawn.

"Where is she? Never mind. You told me. What room is she in?"

I want to see her! No! I don't want to see her! I can't see her!

"I don't know. Linda Bernbaum has the number."

"How come?" In the midst of anguish, pause for a little jealousy of Linda Bernbaum. I have not been close to the whole thing.

I don't want to be close to the whole thing!

"She was in the office. Someone was talking on the telephone and repeated it."

"I'm going." To Shlomo, still lying there. "You want to come with me?"

"Okay," he said after a moment. "But first let's find out if she can have visitors. And when."

"I don't want to find out, I just want to go."

He sighed and squinted at the sky.

"Now?"

With a mother who's a dentist, after all, you don't spend your life trying to figure out women.

"Yes."

"Should we try to get a car?"

"I guess." Instead of being grateful for his flexibility and practicality I am irritated by his failure to grasp the urgency of the situation, his willingness to get bogged down in details.

With a grunt he drags himself up and to his feet, picks up his books.

Larry Hopkins walks by and Shlomo negotiates with him for the use of his beat-up Studebaker.

"He needs it tonight," Shlomo tells me. "We can have it early tomorrow morning."

I shake my head.

"Come on, Nady, we probably wouldn't even be able to get in today."

"Forget it," I say bitterly. "You just don't . . . I'm going to hitch. You don't have to come. It'll probably be easier for me to get a ride by myself." And get raped or murdered and it'll be your fault.

"Oh, yeah," he says sarcastically. "Much easier."

Half an hour later we were on the road, thumbing a ride, and at seven that night we were at Columbia Presbyterian, where we were told that Dr. Story's condition was satisfactory but she could not have visitors today. Her brother was with her. Advised that we were there, he came out to speak with us. He looked just like her and had similar speech and mannerisms. I couldn't stop staring at him. I must have been gaping like an idiot, as a matter of fact, because he avoided my eyes and spoke only to Shlomo. I loved Dr. Moore Story because he looked like his sister and I hated him because he was keeping us from seeing her. Shlomo asked if he thought we'd be able to see her tomorrow if we stuck around. I flinched at the colloquialism. Shlomo's language didn't change according to whom he was with, a quality I'd often admired as unpretentious and now disdained as uncouth. Dr. Story said he couldn't promise although he would certainly mention our visit to his sister, who would be touched by our concern.

Fuck you. Touched.

We took a bus over to the Bronx and walked up to Shlomo's parents. He tried to talk about other things but I wasn't having any. I was furious with him. He was part of that vast male conspiracy that thought you could get through times like this by pretending they were normal. His mother was the one I really wanted to talk to, except that I was intimidated by her. It was quite different from what I felt for Dr. Story—an awe that was nearly religious but didn't incorporate fear. Shlomo's mother inspired fear not only because she was so accomplished and very down to earth but because she was the first Terribly Busy Woman I'd ever known. She had her dental practice. She had a husband and two sons, one of whom was just beginning high school. She cooked and cleaned and shopped, albeit with considerable help from her husband, with whom she also had subscriptions to the opera and various other cultural events. And beyond all that she painted beautifully in the style which I later learned was called primitive, although it appeared anything but primitive to me. Marvelous, intricate pictures with hundreds of people in them of life in the Bronx—in the park, on benches along the Concourse, at a wedding in the Concourse Plaza. There was a great deal of color in them, but never bright red. She leaned to the earth colors and her people seemed to have sprung directly from that earth without going through Customs or any of the other gross ordeals through which peasants normally passed into the New World.

36

This was the person I wanted to be with now. That she was Jewish, that these people had in some way incorporated the history from which my parents had fled to California and seemed realer and richer as a result, was part of it, but only part.

She was small and compactly built. She sometimes had to stand on a stool to reach the mouths of particularly tall patients. She was homely without being ugly. Both of the boys resembled her more than they did their father. She made no secret of her desire for Paul to grow up and leave home so she could use as a studio the room he had once shared with Shlomo and now had to himself.

When I was with Mrs. Becker my mother was always with me; they were such direct opposites that one instantly conjured the other.

At home that summer I'd been more aware than ever of my mother's inactivity.

"You really ought to develop an interest in something, Ma," I'd say when she told me how happy she was when I was there and how miserable when I was away. "It's only that you're bored. If you were doing something you liked you wouldn't care if I was here or not."

It wasn't that she hadn't tried. She'd taken a course in art history, and one in yoga, and one in Spanish, having fuzzy ideas about doing some kind of social work with Chicanos, which one of her friends was enjoying. I asked her why she didn't go back to singing, find a chorus someplace, and she said she couldn't. I was irritated with the answer but it was true, and no amount of saying she should have or if she'd had to, she would have, could change that. She didn't have to do anything and therefore she couldn't. I told her about my boyfriend's mother in the East, how she was happy because she did so many things. Painted. Dentistry. Concerts. All this with one of her sons still at home. She seized on the last—a child still at home—as the explanation for this strange woman's happiness. I felt confused and guilty but it never occurred to me, until I was on the plane heading back to New York, to point out to her that she'd been no happier than she was now during the years when I was still at home.

37

Shlomo wanted to eat in a Chinese restaurant near his parents' house but I couldn't wait to see his mother and made him get containers that we could carry there.

"Maybe tomorrow you'll be able to get in to see her," Mrs. Becker said as I beat out Shlomo for the last sparerib, then scraped the bottom of the chow mein container and looked around the table for anything else I might be able to devour.

"You haven't had enough to eat," Mrs. Becker said, watching my eyes scour the table.

"Yes, I have," I said. "I've had too much, I just—"

But she understood. She was at the refrigerator, already, bringing covered dishes to the table. Cold chicken. Cheese. Cherry tomatoes. A carton of milk. I kept eating and eating. One by one they became infected by my voraciousness and began nibbling in self-defense. From the cupboard Mrs. Becker brought Fig Newtons and Lorna Doones and chocolate-covered grahams, which we had with milk or tea. I had a vision of cleaning out the apartment like a vacuum and then going on to the next door neighbor's. I was embarrassed but not too embarrassed to continue. Afterward I did the dishes with Mrs. Becker, not just because it was polite but because I thought it would give me a chance to talk with her. I was exasperated because at first Shlomo hung around in the kitchen, but finally he joined his father in the living room. (Paul, not a loner like his older brother, had gone down to the yard at Taft High School to play softball with his friends.)

Now we could talk. I looked at the bustly, no-nonsense little lady who was drying the silver as I washed it, although if I ever tried to dry she would tell me it was unnecessary work, everything drained. I searched her face for some indication that she was ready to receive my confidences.

"I guess I've been acting crazy," I said. A ploy and a fake. I want her to tell me it's the natural way to act at a time like this.

"You're upset."

"Shlomo's been very practical about everything." A feeler.

"When we found out, I nearly had a fit but he stayed terribly calm and made all the arrangements."

"Mm. It doesn't do any good to get hysterical."

The magic words: *Don't get hysterical now, Nady.* The words of a father most likely to create hysteria within the breast of his otherwise merely frantic little girl.

"Males are different than females about these things." One last attempt at communion.

"Mm. Thank God."

Tears came to my eyes. Of course I should've known better, to begin with. Who was I—the half-crazed *shiksa* who was lucky enough to have engaged the attention of their brilliant son? And now I not only dared to complain but complained about what was essentially his marvelous ability to bring his intellect to bear on the anguish of real life and in so doing, reduce it!

I finished the dishes and wiped my hands on my jeans. I went into the bathroom and cried for a few minutes. I came out.

"I'm going to take a walk."

"Want company?" Shlomo asked.

"No."

On the way out of the building I met Paul coming in. It was after nine, too dark for softball.

"Want to come for a walk?" I asked.

"No," he said.

By the time I got back to the apartment the others had gone to bed. The curtained French doors that sealed us off in the living room were closed and Shlomo had opened up the sofa and put on the sheets and blanket. I got into bed with my clothes on. Under an unspoken agreement, we slept on the sofa together and in the early hours of the morning Shlomo removed himself to a sleeping bag on the floor.

"What's with you?" he asked.

"Nothing," I said.

"Why aren't you getting undressed?"

"Don't feel like it."

The following year I would take my first psychology course and lose the ability to offer simple answers to simple questions.

He turned on his side, facing me, and tried to put his arm around me but I moved away.

"I think I'm getting my period."

He didn't like to make love when I had my period and I assumed for some time that this was a universal.

"You had it two weeks ago."

The mathematician. Maybe that was what math was originally invented for, to count the days between periods.

"Well, I feel all bloated."

"That's because you ate like a pig."

"Drop dead." (We're not in the Fuck-you Sixties, yet, this is the Drop-dead Fifties; still they are strong words. I may not have voiced them since I came from the West, where they were diluted by frequent use and Pacific breezes.)

He kisses me and I burst into tears.

"Is this all because of Story?" he asks.

"No," I lie, sobbing. "Why don't you stop me when I'm being bad?"

"Why don't you stop yourself?" he asks.

"I can't!" I wail. "I never even know until after I've done it!"

"Done what? You're just a little crazy, is all, you haven't actually *done* anything."

I stop crying. I stare at him thoughtfully. I am at once the most ingenious and ingenuous of nineteen-year-old women.

"What," I whisper, staring into his beautiful, myopic Jewish eyes, "what did she tell you wasn't done?"

He sighs. "If you let me tell you, you'll be disappointed."

"I *want* to be disappointed." I am a child wanting a goody so desperately she will sign away the rest of her life for it.

A minute or two of silence. Another sigh. Then a brief tale of a young Bard student who the year before wanted to carry a political demonstration on an important local issue to the homes of the individual trustees of the college instead of just fighting out the issue on campus with the administration.

More silence. I look at him and wait for more.

"And?"

He shrugged. "And nothing. That's it. She said you couldn't do that sort of thing."

I stare. I can't believe that's all there is although I have to believe it because it's Shlomo and he never lies. He doesn't *think* that way. He never conceives of himself as being on the defensive and thus doesn't feel the need to lie.

Shlomo is watching me. I have a sick, crumbling feeling inside of me as this new information combines with the groceryful of food I've consumed. I wonder, almost idly, if I can get to the bathroom in time or if I'm going to throw up on the sofa bed.

"What is it?" he asks, his face inches from mine.

I lurch to my feet and toward the French doors, stagger down the hallway, almost but not quite making it to the bathroom. Less than a foot from the threshold I begin heaving it all up, huge wet mounds full of gray Chinese food, undigested chunks of bright orange American cheese, pink bologna, red tomatoes. Shlomo, behind me, supports my head then guides me over the puddle into the bathroom, where I kneel at the toilet, rest my chin on the seat and stare gloomily into the bowl, remembering my childhood fantasy of a snake that would rear its head from the watery depths for just long enough to bite off some valuable piece of me that hadn't already been stolen for the starving children of China.

In back of me Shlomo is cleaning the puke from the floor. Feet pad down the hallway.

"It's all taken care of," Shlomo says. "Go back to sleep."

The feet pad away.

I can never come back here.

The next afternoon we got in to see Dr. Story, or at least some person in a hospital gown with a ravaged face who pretended to be Dr. Story. She was wearing Dr. Story's makeup but it didn't work on her. She smiled Dr. Story's smile. She was in a half-reclining position, pretty much covered by hospital sheets. She didn't move at all.

"How lovely of you to come, Nadine," she said. "And Shlomo."
She moved a fraction of an inch in the bed and pain stabbed at
her face.

So it was all true. Even God didn't know where to stop.

In the absence of any coordination between my brain and my
tongue Shlomo and Dr. Story conversed for a while, after which
Dr. Moore Story said he thought perhaps it was time for his sister to rest again. I mumbled good-bye and followed Shlomo out
of the room, down the corridor, into the elevator and out onto
168th Street.

"So," he said, "what now?"

"Isn't there anything *you* want to do?" I asked irritably.

"I'd just as leave go back to school," he said.

"So go."

"Without you?"

"Why not?" I was exasperated beyond belief. "You think I
can't manage without you?"

"How much money do you have?"

I blushed furiously. I didn't have a penny. I wheeled around
and walked away from him without knowing where I was going.
Broadway. I started down Broadway. Shlomo followed me by a
few steps, as though he just happened to feel like going in the
same direction.

Ah, Shlomo, where are you now? Married no doubt to some
wild-eyed hysterical girl—now woman—very much like me, whom
you've never divorced although God knows you've had enough
reason. She asks if you don't hate her for getting fat and you tell
her it doesn't particularly bother you but she should lose it if it
makes her unhappy. She asks how you can put up with her on
her shrew days and you say the same way as she can put up with
herself.

"I suppose if I keep walking you'll keep walking."

"Sure. Why not?"

Anger at him for his uncomprehending patience vies with pity
for myself, the victim of his kindness.

"Don't you even *want* to understand me?" I shout at him, so that three black men, standing on the corner, unaccustomed to seeing whites exhibit on their turf, cease their conversation to gaze at us.

"You want a Coke?"

"OF COURSE I WANT A COKE! I'M DYING OF THIRST!"

"C'mon."

Farther down we found a luncheonette where we ordered two Cokes and one grilled cheese sandwich. He did not seem to have any strong sense of unfinished business between us.

"I know I've been acting crazy."

He was silent. If he'd denied it I would have been furious but I didn't like his accepting it, either. I knew damned well I wasn't crazy.

"Don't you care why?"

"I know you're upset, Nady."

"Why am I upset?"

"Oh, for Christ's sake, you practically went nuts the minute you heard about Story."

"Why? I mean, the truth is I hardly know her. It's not as if it was happening to me. Or my mother. Or . . . so why?"

"All right. I'll bite. Why?"

"I don't know," I said, bursting into tears. "But at least I *want* to know!" I buried my head in my hands, waiting for Shlomo to comfort me, but he was silent. Finally I looked up at him.

"You really don't want to understand, do you?" I said.

"You know I care about you, Nady," he said.

"But you don't want to understand me."

"No," he said. "I don't see why I have to."

"Without any money," I said, "we better start hitching back while there's plenty of light."

That night I wrote to Dianne that if I could get the money from my parents I would accompany her on her planned graduation trip to Europe in the summer. She'd been talking about the trip ever since Berry's departure. She wanted me to go with her and I hadn't refused yet I'd felt no real desire to go. Now I started getting my parents used to the idea of my not coming home for the summer, and trying to wangle the money to go with Dianne instead. I also fucked every available male on the Bard campus and one or two who weren't generally considered available. I'm not sure what I was doing but it seems that whatever else was involved, hurting Shlomo was at least a fringe benefit. I would show him what he could do with his blind love!

Dianne adored Europe and was happier there than I'd ever seen her. I was miserable the whole time. England, where I had the language, was bearable, but we were only there for the first week and it took me that long to recover from the flight. Then we went to Paris because Dianne knew that was the place to be. The place I wanted to be was on the grass in back of the dormitory with Shlomo.

I hated the French, not for any of the rational reasons that the normal sensitive tourist hates them but because they spoke their own language and wouldn't even try to speak mine. They kept insisting that I try the little French they knew I must have. As though there were no way anyone could have been born and lived for nearly twenty years without it. I wanted to strangle them. The knowledge that I was wrong because I was in their country made no difference at all.

At night I cried into my pillow and chewed the ends of the case. I wanted to go home early but Dianne was having a marvelous time and in my paranoid state I was afraid to fly back by myself, as well as ashamed to think of the questions I might have to answer if I spent the month of August on the Bard campus or at home.

I wrote to Shlomo. I told him I knew I'd been crazy and I hoped he'd forgive me. I said he could write to me care of American Express if he felt like it but I would understand perfectly if he didn't. I didn't really expect him to want to have anything to do with me. Four days after I sent the letter I began haunting the American Express office but I never heard from him. When I got back to Bard his friend Alex told me with a straight face and a monotone voice (neither of which was yet obligatory on college campuses) that Shlomo had transferred to the University of Chicago. I was stupefied.

"But why?" I cried out. "How come? All of a sudden?"

Sardonic amusement replaced indifference. Alex was one of Shlomo's friends I'd seduced during my sexual rampage the previous May. One of the "older" men, a veteran of the Korean War at Bard on GI benefits plus a scholarship, he lived in a barracks that was farther from the school buildings than the other men's housing and affected a certain emotional distance from most of the goings-on. His relation to Shlomo (and to most of the other boys) was that of teacher to student; whenever I came upon them, Alex was the one who was talking.

On this night a bunch of us had been at Mike's drinking beer and eating hot sausage sandwiches. Alex had just broken up with a girl named Libby. She'd gotten pregnant and pressured him to marry her and let her have the baby. He'd raised the money for the abortion, made sure she was physically okay afterward, then told her he never wanted to come that close to getting trapped again and they were through.

Shlomo hadn't come with the crew that night, maybe because he was really concerned about an unfinished paper. Or maybe because he'd gotten tired, in the days since our return from Dr. Story's bedside in New York, of having me spread my legs whenever one of his friends entered the room while perpetually finding excuses for not going to bed with him.

It was a beautiful night. We walked with our arms around each other, singing the German beer-hall songs that in 1954 still had a strong tinge of the forbidden to them. In between songs most of us giggled but Alex never did; he was already at home with the forbidden. His arm was around my shoulders, mine was around his waist. When he veered off toward the barracks I veered with him. I thought we were heading for the grass in back but he took me inside instead. I was high, with that strange, excitingly weak feeling at the base of my spine that I still get when beer hits me.

My heart pounded at my chest as though it were trying to get out.

He led me through the dark room, cursing softly as he banged his toe on an iron cot leg. Then I tripped over a pile of clothes someone had left in the middle of the aisle and giggled nervously into the quiet. At his cot he lay down on his back, his arms under his head, and waited to see what I would do. I felt rather than saw him grinning at me like the Cheshire cat. A few feet away from us, on either side, were cots occupied by sleeping men whose faces would be familiar to me if I could see them. It was a dare. I loved dares. They terrified me because I didn't know how far I would go in response to them but then that very terror excited me further. I waited as his face became increasingly discernible to me, the grin a fact in reality as well as in my imagination. I yawned and stretched, consciously sinuous. I took off my sneakers, feigned a yawn, stretched again. Then I unzipped my jeans and slithered out of them, like a seasoned stripper in the Jersey City burlesque house I'd been to the year before with Shlomo. My tight jeans, then my baggy sweat shirt, then my underpants. (I'd stopped wearing brassieres a week or two earlier. They didn't feel good. They cut your skin. For all I knew they gave you cancer.) Then I stretched out on top of him and kissed him passionately, already more excited by the situation and my performance than I'd ever been at the height of my real-life lovemaking with Shlomo. He returned my kiss without moving his arms out from under his head. I began undressing him. I opened his shirt, his belt buckle, his fly. I tried to get out his penis but I couldn't because I was on top of it. I sat up, straddling him, and lovingly removed the bird from its cage. I curled over and kissed it affectionately. My face had never been within a foot, so to speak, of Shlomo's—of *any-one's*—penis. I liked it. I did some tribal rites over it and then I mounted him. His arms never moved from his pillow but his eyes were closed and he wasn't smiling anymore as I squirmed and writhed and bounced on top of him. Occasionally he moaned softly and that spurred me on to greater efforts. When he came I came with him—the first time it had ever happened to me, and the last, in point of fact, for some time to come. So to speak.

Alex was watching me again. I was cold. Into the dead silence of the room a voice several feet from us said, "Academy Award." There were a couple of guffaws. Alex grinned at me. I got off him, picked up my clothes with a show of nonchalance and walked out of the barracks, not stopping to get dressed until I was twenty yards away and behind a tree.

For the remaining weeks of the term Alex had treated me with exactly that degree of friendly condescension that he always displayed toward me and everyone else.

Now the sun was shining in my eyes, giving his sardonic grin some extra power.

"It wasn't because of me, was it, Alex?" I wasn't the sort of female men loved so desperately that they had to leave a place. "Why?"

"He felt that he required," Alex said deliberately, "a broader academic environment."

"Ohhhh. . . ." I was on the verge of tears. Why wouldn't he just confirm that I was as evil as I'd always feared I was? "What'm I supposed to do now, slit my wrists?"

"Do whatever you want to do, chicken," he said, turning and walking away. I followed. The girl he'd gotten the abortion for and then dropped had committed suicide over the summer but I didn't know that. No one was talking about it. Suicide wasn't fashionable yet. "What you do is what you do, it has nothing to do with me."

"I didn't say it *did*," I pointed out, breathing hard as I struggled to keep up with him.

"Then don't give me this slit-my-wrists shit."

"It's just an expression," I said. "You think I'm going to do it, for crying out loud? It's a disgusting idea. I never think about things like that."

He stopped walking and looked at me as though he was trying to decide if I was telling the truth. After a moment or two he began walking again, but in his usual relaxed way. He wasn't trying to shake me anymore.

"How was Europe?" he asked after a few minutes.

"Disgusting," I said. "Everyone spoke foreign languages."

He laughed. He looked at me for the first time with what seemed like simple friendliness. Something had clicked between us.

"Especially the English," he said.

"It wasn't as bad there as everyplace else," I told him.

He put his arm around me. A wave of sexual feeling passed through me. Toward the end of August I'd finally gotten into the sack with some Italian who picked us up as we got off the boat in Naples, but it was the same old story. He not only talked the whole time but he talked in Italian; I was so dry it hurt.

"Want to go to the movies tonight? I'm seeing *Bicycle Thief* in Poughkeepsie."

"Ha-ha."

"All right. I'll get to Mike's around ten thirty, eleven. Meet me there."

"Okay."

So there it was. Our Yalta Pact. The simple agreement that set up the terms for our relations over the next couple of years. The limits were there; I never had to go scratching around for them.

I didn't see much of Dianne in those years. She'd graduated from Radcliffe and gone to New York to Columbia Law School, so she was closer to Bard than when she'd been in Boston, but among other things the antagonism between her and Alex was stronger than it had ever been between her and Shlomo. Alex couldn't *stand* Dianne; she made his skin crawl and his asshole tighten, or so he claimed. Strange, when as with Shlomo their tastes and views were closer to each other's than mine was to either's.

On the other hand, Alex made no claims on me that would have prevented me from seeing her on my own; the reverse was true. On the rare occasion when I disappeared without explanation for any length of time he was inordinately affectionate upon my return. On at least one of those occasions I know he knew I was being unfaithful to him with a camp follower of his who'd been hot for me ever since he found out I was now considered Alex's girl. (A designation which, needless to say, irritated Alex, who didn't want to own anything, most particularly a female.) Anyway, he was particularly warm and cuddly with me after my weekend in New York with his "friend." He chose to believe I did it out of a sense of freedom, while in reality of course I only did it to get a rise out of him. And then he was relieved by his belief. Even more than he didn't want to own a female Alex didn't want to owe an obligation to another member of the race.

The funny thing was that he was never unfaithful to me. If you could use the words faithful or unfaithful, which were actually irrelevant, not even part of his conceptual vocabulary, to describe the fact that he didn't happen to put it to another female during my amorphous tenure.

"If we have no obligation to each other," I once asked him, "how come you never go out with anyone else?"

"I don't feel the need," he said.

"Is that a compliment?"

"No. I don't need much from women. I'm not sure I need *anything*, but obviously there're one or two things it's pleasanter to have than not to have."

"Obviously." I was upset because I believed him. He was always convincing because he never cared if you believed him.

"What would you do," I asked, "if some lunatic female fell madly in love with you and hounded you to marry her?"

"I would remove myself from her vicinity," said Alex, a lover of Shaw and Mencken.

"And if she followed you?"

He shrugged. "Enter a monastery."

"No women at all."

"Masturbation."

I was silent. This was only the year 1955 in the evolution of surfaces and most of us still knew when we were shocked.

"It's not the same thing," I finally ventured.

"It's only a matter of degree," he assured me.

Yet he was a marvelous lover. What he lacked in passion I made up for in imagination and he was skillful, flexible and considerate. Determinedly considerate. Much more determined than I myself was to ensure me full satisfaction with each round. I think he never wanted to leave feeling as though he owed me something. He got me onto pot by insisting that I smoke it when I didn't come after that first time. Pot was still the realm of the most sophisticated few on any campus and I resisted it, thinking it would make me crazy. When it turned out not to make me crazy I continued to resist like a kid resisting cough medicine. I felt he was trying to force me to have a better time than I wanted. Trick me into coming to him. I wanted to be loved before I was conquered. Obviously. (The word obviously comes up most often in discussions of the relation between men and women, upon which nothing has less bearing than the true or the obvious.)

He cultivated my philistinism as though it were a rare orchid, speaking to me at great length on subjects he would have been dismayed to find that I understood. His major fields of interest were philosophy and political science, with particular emphasis on Russian history since the Revolution. He would address himself for hours to the questions involved in some esoteric struggle in the politburo and then I would sigh and ask how the world could ever be better before the people who ran it got nicer and he would pat me on the head and make some remark about women, or Los Angeles, or brain damage.

What Alex couldn't stand was when I talked about my psychology courses. I loved my psych teacher and I loved my psych classes, the first ones I'd ever taken where it seemed the right answers might be good for something beyond points on an exam. Once I'd thought I would major in languages but psychology was the only language which interested me now, one year after the last time I'd looked directly into the eyes of the woman I'd once loved, the woman who'd had the bad grace to let a team of surgeons in New York hack a breast from her body and throw it in a garbage can someplace.

It probably goes without saying that Alex had no such interest in questions of human behavior, instinctively resisting anyone else's transgressions and being unperturbed by his own. The mere mention of the possibility that someone might be motivated by forces beyond conscious control was enough to make him walk out of a room.

Although she denied feeling anything but indifference, Dianne was the only person I knew whose hostility to Freud and his followers was as great as Alex's. During this period conversation between us was nearly impossible. I was pleased to finally have some personal system of comprehension and made the standard error of assuming that the unconscious substructure was the only way of understanding anything and everything, while Dianne's response, when I dragged psychological issues into our conversations, was that it was all very well for me to play around with that silly stuff but I mustn't make the mistake of thinking it had any relevance to real life. We went to a lot of folk concerts at Cooper Union during this time, as well as poetry readings at the Y, neutral grounds, both. Dianne was in her second year at Columbia Law School and apparently had many friends and dates but I never met most of them. If we doubled it was usually friends who came in with me from Bard or a couple of males I'd struck up a conversation with at Cooper Union.

Shortly Alex will graduate. I have a year to go. Alex will attend the School of Russian Studies at Columbia. With each passing week I become increasingly the kind of girl he will not mind having left behind. I am coy and hostile, sometimes not even bothering to alternate.

"If you lift one little finger of your left hand I'll visit you in New York."

He lifts a limp finger.

"I'm not asking you to pretend that you'll miss me, Alex, but at least you could treat me as if I'm more than a . . . a . . ." I have to flail around looking for what I mean because the rhetoric hasn't been born yet. ". . . an object for your convenience."

51

"To me, you're an object of convenience. To you, you're a subject and I'm the object."

"All right, it's true," I lie. "Forget the whole thing."

The truth being unacceptable. The truth being that I'm sure I love him madly, that I want to be with him forever and have babies who'll grow up knowing instinctively what I'd needed to be taught, that the Russian Revolution couldn't be dismissed just because it had been run by Communists; that I would, if it would serve that end, follow him to the ends of the earth, hurtling through monastery walls, vowing to kill myself if he didn't marry me. Neither taste nor sanity prevents me but only the knowledge that such a pursuit would be futile.

I have a recurring nightmare in which I run into him when he is with another woman and betray my feelings to him. Sometimes the woman is Dianne and they are both so repelled by the way I am carrying on that they turn their backs and refuse to look at me.

In point of fact I am allowed to visit Alex in New York as often as I wish, provided only that I call first to see if he's free. He always seems to be free but the dream in which he's with someone else has a greater reality to me than his actual freedom. I'm convinced that if he hasn't found someone else he soon will.

I develop a crush on my psych teacher and stick him into my fantasies where Alex had once been. I go to a party at his home and flirt with him whenever his wife isn't in the room. But when I go to the bathroom he follows me, still holding his wineglass, and backs me against the wall, giving me a stunning, long, warm, wet kiss, pressing his body against mine. My response is to squirm and run for my coat instead of the toilet, hightailing it out of the house so quickly that the next day I have to make up a whole story to cover myself. I couldn't tell the truth because it was so obvious to me that I'd encouraged him to do what he'd done.

I started convincing myself that I was falling for some other male creature at Bard. I can't even remember his name. I took him into New York with me. I wasn't going to be caught alone by that son of a bitch Alex. I called Alex from New York, then slipped away from my companion for one night with some dumb excuse, slipping away from Alex the next day with an even dumber one. The third time I did this a girl answered Alex's phone and I decided not to call him again. Why should I hang around waiting to get hurt?

In the early spring of my last term at Bard Dr. Story went back to the hospital for the second of her bouts with the cancer that was spreading through her. Someone tried to explain to me that they'd known all along it was going to happen because by the time they took her breast the disease had been found in the lymph nodes. But I wasn't going to stick around for long enough to find out what a lymph node was, much less to have her die on me. I left Bard with my last few courses incomplete and hit the road for California, where my natural mother clung to life by a thread of misery too straggly for cancer to bother eroding.

My father was bewildered (and drunk) when I showed up at the door but my mother seemed to find it perfectly natural. As though in her mind as well as my own it was the first three and a half years of my college career that had been the aberration, rather than the few dropped courses. She'd sensed all along in her dreamy, uncritical way that my mutation to an Eastern Intellectual was a lot of horseshit.

"It's good to have you back, dear," she said.

Back.

At first my father sort of kept his distance. He was uneasy. Unlike my mother he had an instinct for what was crazy and he knew that my arriving back home when I was fifteen-sixteenths through my college career was not a sane or simple act. I caught him looking at me thoughtfully over his glass. After a week or two, when nothing seemed to be happening, he began inviting me to join him for his late night swim. I'd get on my bathing suit and go out to the pool, where he would be standing on the board, waiting to dive. He always waited there until my mother and I, or just I, came out to watch him. I think he wanted to be admired as he had been admired when he was young and beautiful and in swimming competition, and indeed even now there was much to be admired. My father was a different man from the time he got within a few feet of a swimming pool. Uncertainty, even drunken uncertainty, vanished, and with it that irritation which comes from not being able to settle the problems of life for once and for all. The thirty or forty pounds that had thickened his body and altered his athlete's gait to a businessman's stride seemed to fall away as he stood at the end of the board, not so much surveying his domain as prolonging the exquisite anticipation of climax.

The whole thing made me nervous.

I cracked jokes to my mother if she was there and called them out to him if she wasn't. But he didn't hear.

For a while after he slid almost silently into the water in one of his perfect dives we would swim in silence, both of us stroking effortlessly around the huge pool. Then we would dog-paddle for a while, and chat. The pool was where we had our chats.

"What are your plans, Rosie?"

He'd called me Rosie since he first heard the phrase Rosie the Riveter during the Second World War, a name superficial in its charm and actually referring to the way my childish voice pierced his eardrums.

"Plans? I guess I don't really have any yet."

"You're not in any kind of trouble, are you?"

Did he think I was pregnant? Should I tell him that so awful to me was the idea of becoming pregnant that I used a diaphragm every evening whether I had a date or not—just in case I got waylaid on campus?

"Not that I know of, Dad."

"I guess if you were in trouble you'd know it."

"I guess."

Paddle, paddle.

"Do you have any ideas about what you want to do?"

"Do?"

"Well, I mean, you can't just hang around here doing nothing."

How come he'd never said that to my mother?

"I can't?"

"Now be reasonable, Nadine," he said uncomfortably. Was he uncomfortable with the ironic contrast or because I was being crazy?

"Maybe Mom and I could go into some kind of business together."

"I don't know if your mother's cut out for that kind of thing."

"I don't know if I am, either."

"You know you can do anything you really want to do," he said.

"So can she, Dad."

"Now that's not true, Nadine. You're a much stronger person than she is."

I was furious. Much too furious to trust myself to answer. I always got furious at the suggestion that I was much stronger than my mother and certainly more than strong enough to take care of myself. How would I ever find a man to baby me, to coddle me into passivity, if I radiated health and strength? At moments like this I felt strong enough to kill but not strong enough to do anything else! I needed a man powerful enough to stop me from killing him but crazy enough to want to take care of me the rest of the time!

In the third week my father said that the girl who ran his office was out sick and asked if I would answer his phone and take care of the bills for a few days. I said sure, ignoring my suspicion that he'd gotten rid of her just to make me do *something*. I was bored stiff anyway. I hadn't thought it would take Dianne so long to find out that I was gone and start looking for me.

One wall of the trailer that was the office of Challenger Pools held the aquarium that had killed fish in our home. (They flourished here.) Against another wall were the desk and file cabinets.

56

On the wall over the desk and cabinets, and stuck in at various points on the other walls where there were two or more inches of space, were hundreds and hundreds of pictures of satisfied customers in front of and in their pools. Movie stars in the most conspicuous spots, then, ranging out from there, faces you knew but it took a minute to remember why. The starlet everyone had told her producer wasn't gorgeous enough to make up for what she couldn't do, like speak English, but he'd said that with tits like that no one would ever listen to her, and in this particular case he'd been mistaken. The actor who hadn't waited for the House Un-American Activities Committee to summon him before he'd called a press conference to discuss a past he wasn't famous enough for anyone to be interested in. A couple of years earlier my father had taken down the photos of his two or three clients who'd crossed the path of Senator McCarthy or any of democracy's other vigilantes. Now in the spring of 1956 when he understood McCarthy to have been just a trifle overzealous in his work, one or two of the most famous ones were back up. Some of the pictures had been there since I was a child; others were new. I spent long hours looking at them in between phone calls. It wasn't until my second day there, when I reached the second wall, that I saw the twins.

At first I wasn't sure of what I was seeing.

Two men, business-looking types in sport shirts and slacks, standing very close to each other, one's arm about the other. One seemed to lean slightly forward as he grimaced at the camera; the other, a little straighter and taller, was smiling. I'm not sure that I ever would have understood who they were without asking my father had it not been for the space they'd occupied in my fantasy life all along. Dreams of falling through infinite amounts of space had been replaced by dreams of being permanently attached to someone else so I could never fall. Sometimes these were good dreams and sometimes they were bad but in some way the idea of them had been incorporated into my existence. So that now, as I stared at the photo, the match in my mind was set not to paper but to a mass of oily rags that had been smoldering for years.

Frantically I went through the files: SMITH, MR. AMOS AND
MR. EDDIE. Their address was above Sunset in a house that might
have cost less than a quarter of a million but probably hadn't.
There was nothing of interest in the files. I called home but my
father wasn't there.

Cool it, Nadine. Cool it.

I'd been thinking about closing the office and driving right over
there.

This is too important to blow.

I didn't know why it was so important, but it was. I didn't
know why I needed to see them but I did. I didn't know what I
wanted beyond seeing them but I knew how much I wanted that.

Be careful.

I didn't want to be just another one of the freak-seekers. In-
distinguishable from the autograph hunters who thirsted for
celebrities the way film thirsted for the chemicals that would
bring it at least halfway toward being a positive.

Slow down.

"You made a pool for the Siamese twins."

"Oh. Yeah." He seemed uncomfortable. As if I'd accused him
of doing something vaguely obscene.

"When?"

"Last year."

"How come you never mentioned it?"

"You weren't home."

"I've been home for weeks."

"It didn't occur to me."

"Tell me about them."

"There's nothing to tell."

"Nothing?"

"Look here, Nady," he said irritably, "I don't know what you're
so excited about, they're just a couple of . . ."

He was angry with me. It reminded me of my childhood, when
so many questions conceived in simplicity had turned out to be
charged with issues I didn't understand.

58

"I'm sorry, Dad, I'm not excited, I'm just curious. I'd just like to know . . ."

He was somewhat mollified but not about to volunteer any information.

"Didn't you like them?" I asked cautiously.

"No, of course I didn't like them. You don't like some . . . something like that, it's unnatural."

"But it isn't," I pointed out patiently. "They were born that way, they didn't have it built on or anything, so it's natural to them."

"You know what I mean."

"Weren't they nice?" I asked quickly, sensing that he would use any pause to get out of the conversation. "I mean, when they talked to you, what were they like?"

"I don't know," he said. "One of them was all right. Friendly. The other one I didn't like."

"Which?"

"How'm I supposed to remember that?" he demanded. As though the request that he briefly view them as separate human beings were totally unreasonable.

"It doesn't matter, I just thought . . ."

"One of them, the other one, kept changing his mind," my father said suddenly. "The one that didn't smile. Shape, size, where we were going to set it, he changed his mind a dozen times. The other one, the one that smiled, he just went along. He didn't care what kind of pool they had as long as it made the first one happy. But you know, Nady, there's no making some people happy."

I looked at him sharply but there was no indication from his expression that he had in mind anyone of our mutual acquaintance.

"So you liked one of them but not the other," I said.

But he got uncomfortable again. "You can't really say that. How can you say that? It's not as though they were two people. You can't be friendly with just one of them. You can't ask just one of them to come over for a drink."

"That doesn't mean you can't like him," I argued.

He shrugged. "To me it does."

End of conversation.

Sleep was out of the question that night. My only conscious fear was that I would be so taut with controlled hysteria that I would careen into their presence like some overwound, life-sized, key-operated toy and get myself banned from the grounds forever. I eyed my mother's tranquilizers wistfully but I was afraid to use them. I read through the file in the lingerie box, one of the few possessions I'd bothered to pack when I returned to California. It was all as familiar to me as a daily catechism although I hadn't looked at it in years. Finally I had a few shots of brandy so I could sleep enough to put in a full day at Challenger Pools before I went off to find them.

So here we are, reader, back spying on the beautiful couple in the beautiful pool that looks like a pond.

Slowly the fear that I will be discovered passes and I settle down on the grass to watch them.

I think of a night when I was little and awakened from a bad dream to sit at the foot of my bed, looking out of the window. My parents were swimming in the moonlight, embracing and then moving away from each other, swimming softly around the pool, coming back together again. I was flooded with delight, with love, with a desire to be down there between them; only a strange but pleasant weakness prevented me from moving or feeling unhappy that I couldn't be there. I wet my bed that night although I was too old and hadn't done it in years.

But with this memory comes guilt over my intrusion. I don't belong here. It is something that hasn't actually occurred to me, that I might be intruding. Now I am unable to go further or to retreat. I wait until they swim to the steps, then quietly scramble to my feet and make my way back to the car.

IT also hadn't occurred to me that if Dianne called Bard no one would tell her anything except that I'd left. I knew I should have written to her if I couldn't call. (I was afraid to call because I didn't want her to try to talk me out of leaving.) It didn't occur to me that she'd hold back from calling my parents on the sensible grounds that if they didn't know she might be frightening them unnecessarily.

Memorial Day weekend she flew to L.A. and called one of my old high-school friends, who told her he'd heard somewhere that I was working at a drugstore on Wilshire, which indeed I had been from the day I was no longer needed at my father's office.

We saw each other at the same moment. The BLT Down I was about to serve flew out of my hands, landing on the sundae fixings in back of me. Dianne burst into tears. I stared at her. Dianne never cried in those days.

"My God!" she cried. "I thought you might be— You just disappeared!"

"Di, Di, I'm sorry!" I wailed.

"What exactly do you think you're doing?" demanded the incredulous manager, surveying the scene we made, Dianne and I and the BLT Down pieces in the sundae fixings.

"Oh, go fuck yourself," I said joyfully, and walked out from behind the counter and out of the drugstore with Dianne, forfeiting two days' pay and maybe another fifty cents in tips lying around on the counter.

She persuaded me to write a note to Bard saying that emotional problems had compelled me to leave and expressing the hope that they would keep my case open, or whatever. What she really wanted me to do was room with her in New York and complete my last year at Columbia. I said I wouldn't go back to school but I might go back to New York. My father was willing to give me plane fare. One of his friends had seen me drawing coffee in the drugstore and asked how come, wasn't I supposed to be in college? At the age of twenty-one I was still embarrassing him. Soon he would put a stop to all that.

I told Dianne there was just one thing I wanted to do with her before we returned to New York. I asked her if she remembered about the Siamese twins. She nodded yes and pulled back inside her skin at the same time. I told her about my discovery and about going to see them; the expression on her face was identical to that on my mother's when years ago she'd finally allowed the little Nadine to stay up and have dinner with company and I'd farted and spilled my milk at the same time.

"It's not the way you think, Di," I said hastily. "It was beautiful. The pool looks just like a pond and they—"

She didn't want to hear about it. She thought they were freakish but I thought *they* were beautiful and *I* was freakish. What made them freaks, anyway? That they'd been born to a condition I was spending my life trying to achieve? She didn't want to argue about it.

"I'm not going to New York until I see them again," I said.

Finally we compromised. We were leaving the following evening. We would stop off on the way to the airport and if they were there we would see them.

Dianne didn't tell her father exactly why we had to leave for the airport half an hour early. I think she said I had to pick up something from a friend. She got out of the car with me, though, and followed me up the front path and around the house, not really hanging back until we reached the path down to the pool. I beckoned her on without turning. I couldn't see any heads in the pool but my fingers were crossed. Then I saw them, not in the pool but on the grass nearby. They sat wet and naked, facing each other—no, they weren't actually sitting, they were squatting. Their buttocks weren't touching the ground although there was no air of exertion around them. They were playing checkers. I turned around, expecting to have to urge Dianne down the path, but she was staring at them, transfixed.

I smiled.

She felt my smile and started. Her eyes met mine and slid quickly away. Then she turned and ran back to the car so swiftly that I couldn't catch up with her until we were in her father's hearing.

She wouldn't let me talk about them again.

An hour later we were on the plane and a few hours later we were three thousand miles away. Just in time to spend summer in New York.

Dianne was sharing a three-room apartment on Riverside Drive with a Barnard undergraduate named Maya whom she couldn't stand. Maya didn't mind if I moved in; Dianne hoped that shortly Maya would move out.

Not your typical 1956 Barnard undergraduate, Maya led an extraordinary social life, being as likely as not, in the warm weather, to run around naked, take showers with whichever man or men were around and have living room picnics in the buff. I shared Dianne's room while Maya had the living room. Dianne complained that Maya's behavior confined her to the bedroom but Maya said Dianne was free to be anywhere in the apartment at any time. This, of course, infuriated Dianne, who was no more capable of lolling around in a room where people were eating in the buff or screwing than of admitting there was magic in Siamese twins.

Maya had ropy, waist-length black hair and a slightly crossed eye. She had what would have been a great body had it not been set on legs that were too short and stubby to do it justice. She never wore a brassiere and I once saw her smelling her underpants when she took them off. I was fascinated by her. If I went around in a cage I occasionally burst out of, Maya didn't even seem to know that people like us needed cages. I don't know how I would have reacted to Maya if I hadn't known Dianne's feeling about her before we met. If I hadn't known that we were planning to share an apartment while Dianne finished her last year of law school and I worked. But of course that's what this little Maya tale is about, how I took care of Maya for Dianne and myself.

I felt for Dianne, so quiet and self-contained, going crazy as Maya spilled all over the apartment. I felt a little for Maya, too, who didn't understand what she was doing that was wrong, and who just wanted to go her own way and have a good time, preferably with witnesses.

But Dianne and I were so close now. Dianne had come three thousand miles to bring me back to New York. I had to be with Dianne; where would I ever find another person who cared that much for me?

It was a hot sticky night around the end of the second week in June. We were dying to go to a movie and didn't have a cent to our names. Literally. I didn't have a job yet and had used up my money; Dianne's check from her parents was late. Maya would have lent us money but Dianne refused to ask her or to let me ask. I was spaced out, incapable of action, and had been since my return to New York. Maya had the only fan in the apartment; it was whirring away in the living room. The bedroom fronted on an airshaft through which no air moved. I was stretched out on my cot, wearing bra and pants. Dianne sat on her bed in a cotton smock reading aloud to me from one of her texts in preparation for her last exam. The ice water we drank seemed our only direct line to a bearable future.

As Dianne reads she pulls the sticky cotton away from her sweating body. I blow down the valley between my breasts and drink water. The cubes are rapidly vanishing. Dianne drones on. I fall into a light stupor.

"I'm going to get some more ice water," Dianne says.

"Maybe we should . . . go . . . out . . . there." Even through the closed door I can hear the inviting drone of the big fan.

Tight-lipped Dianne collects my glass and her own and opens the door. The hint of a breeze comes through the room but I don't bother pressing again because Dianne has told me more than once that it will be impossible to work with the door open. Maya sends out what we will later be able to identify as bad vibrations to Dianne. I drift off into one of my box dreams (in the summer I'm always trying to get out and in the winter I want to get in) from which I'm awakened not so much by a noise as by a feeling. Dianne is standing over my bed, staring at me—or through me. She is white as a sheet and if her body isn't actually shaking, the general effect is of fear and trembling. I bolt to a sitting position, thinking that there has been some terrible accident.

"What?"

Dianne forces out the words, her eyes wet with tears, her lips twisted with the effort to speak.

"She. Used. Up. All. The. Ice. Cubes."

I am astonished. Relieved. Amused. Disbelieving.

And then, slowly, the reality of the situation is borne upon me. That is to say, I cease to be amused by the force of Dianne's reaction and begin to focus on the ice cubes. We haven't got a quarter to get more ice cubes.

"How?" I ask. "How could she have used up all three trays we left? I filled four this afternoon."

"Take a look." Quiet. Tragic.

I drag myself off the bed and into the living room. Maya is sitting in one of the armchairs, which she has covered with towels so the material won't stick to her naked body. Her arms are spread on the chair's arms and her legs are spread out in front of her, her feet propped on two stacks of books on the steamer trunk that is the coffee table. The fan, the kind of model that can stand on the floor or fit in a window, is at her feet, on the trunk. She flaps her breasts to get the breeze under them and grins at me.

"How do you like the air conditioning? Why don't you come in and cool off?"

She isn't drinking anything and I am briefly at a loss to understand what has happened to our ice cubes but then I realize that between the fan and the books her feet rest on stands the crockery bowl we normally use for salads. The bowl is filled with the precious cubes, cooling the air that passes through the fan on its way up Maya's vagina and around the rest of her.

I am speechless. Dianne is absolutely right. Maya is proven to be not simply carefree and fun-loving but selfish beyond belief. Still, I might not have spoken at all, I might have just grabbed a few cubes and left, had I not felt Dianne standing behind me, waiting for me to do something to make things right. I'd always had that feeling with my mother, that she was waiting for me to do *something*, except I never knew what and so I just ran around screaming. Now, by comparison, the task seemed clear. All Dianne wanted, after all, was for me to take care of the Maya problem; my mother wanted me to change her *life*.

"For Christ's sake, Maya, did you have to use every ice cube in the house?"

"They're right there," Maya said cheerfully. "Take 'em if you need 'em."

"That's not the point."

"I thought you said you wanted some ice cubes."

It was deliberate, then. Nobody could not understand.

"Not from your crotch."

66

She grinned at me. She saw the part of me that was being silly but not the part of her that was wrong.

"I know what that sounded like," I said, "but don't you know how demoralizing it is, living with someone who doesn't give a shit for anyone else?"

"It's too hot to give a shit for anyone or anything," Maya said.

I felt waves of gratitude emanating toward me from Dianne. United we stood.

"You're taking pretty good care of yourself," I pointed out. "It's only everyone else you don't care about."

"Ohhhhhh. . . ."

It was the first time either of us had gotten to her. People like Maya and Nadine do not take lightly to the accusation that we are being good to ourselves.

"What do you want from me?" she yelled suddenly, drawing in her legs and in the process knocking over both the books and the bowl of ice cubes. She stood up, pulling her breasts away from her body and making a platform for them with her hands so there'd be no flesh against her torso. "You act as if you're going to feel better if I feel worse! I thought you were going to be better than Dianne! You didn't seem like such a fucking wet fish!"

All the jolly-casual exterior was gone now, all the fake phlegmatic stuff and the what's all the fuss about, the attitude that would become the universal plea for No Hassles. Why wasn't Dianne making any move to get the ice cubes off the floor while I was holding the enemy at bay?

"You're not even paying any rent!" Maya shouted. "Dianne asked if I minded if a friend shared her room for a few weeks and I said no, of course not, why should I, and now the next thing I know—"

Dianne, say something! You got me into this, now get me out!

I turn around. Dianne is staring past Maya at the window with a sad, fixed smile on her face. Why should she get involved? Nadine had entered the fray, why should both of us yell and scream? Another few minutes of restraint and she can pick up her merit badge for getting shat on.

67

Maya left us, bag and baggage, announcing that she could live with one crazy but not two and we could sue her if we wanted her to pay her share of the rent. I was surprised to find that Dianne was depressed, rather than elated, at my surgery to remove Maya from our midst. It took a while for her to confess the truth to me. She had been seeing her old boyfriend Berry again on and off. Maya had gotten to know him and now Maya had moved in with the Beat Poet of Dianne's choice. This only really became clear to me because the names of Maya and the poet Berry began to intrude into our conversations frequently in unexpected places. "Like Maya and her ice cubes," became Dianne's most oft-used reference point for any outrageous act, and she was given to frequent discourses on men like Berry who let themselves be taken over by women they didn't even like.

One year later, having graduated from law school, passed the New York Bar and gotten a job with the Civil Liberties Union (she'd tried the NAACP first but this was during the height of the excitement over the changes in the South and the NAACP was overstocked with applications like hers), Dianne found Berry in the Village and married him. He allowed her to support him in Eastern-vegetarian splendor for about two years before he took off for what he told her was Argentina but turned out to be Venice. California.

Having moved out of the apartment on the Drive to make room for Berry, I moved to the Village and worked as a waitress in a series of coffeehouses and hash (remember corned beef?) joints. I never stayed in one place for too long. I slept with the owners. If they ended the affair I was hurt and embarrassed and found it difficult to face them. I myself didn't know how to nicely end an affair, to say it was great fun but it was just one of those things. So I dropped trays and got myself fired. Or collected my paycheck and went to the nearest phone booth to say I'd had a phone call from my mother that my grandmother was dying in Minnesota . . . or Wyoming . . . or Detroit . . . and I had to take off. By the third time I'd done this I began to fear that someone somewhere was keeping track of my grandmothers and I decided to initiate a series of false names for myself so it would be harder to keep track of me and my lies.

I kept wishing someone would ask me to marry him and let him take me away from all this nothingness. I assumed I would say no, I couldn't get married because I hadn't lived yet, but that having an alternative would make the rest of my life more acceptable to me. No. More than that. I assumed that once I knew for sure what I *didn't* want (to marry the first any-old-person who asked) then what I *did* want would come into clearer focus. I read a lot of psychology books. Everything in them seemed to be about me but nothing told me what to do about that. I couldn't believe that I'd ever had the gall to think someone as helpless and crazy as I would be able to go into a field where she could help others.

I saw very little of Dianne that first year or so that she was married. I assumed she was terribly busy, leading a life full of civil and other liberties, and didn't have time for someone as ordinary as I'd become. In point of fact, Berry, who hadn't been all there to begin with, had been drifting further and further from her since they'd married and by a year or two later she didn't have a marriage. Dianne's way of dealing with this painful reality—had I only been willing to understand what this boded for the future —was to work very hard at concealing it from the outside world, including me, by which perpetual effort she apparently managed to convince herself for a long time as well.

Berry had a friend, a poet somewhat younger, wilder and prettier than himself, Omu. Omu moved in with them, which was apparently all right with her, although Berry often wound up sleeping on the second foam rubber sofa in the living room instead of in the bedroom with her. She never faced their being lovers until she stumbled across them making love and then she thought of him as bisexual, swinging gently both ways, though in point of fact he'd long since stopped swinging even gently in her direction. In short, she never faced the fact that she didn't have a marriage until Berry and Omu took off together for the Coast, and then it

69

was a month before she told me, her best friend in the world if she had one, that she and Berry had decided to separate for a while so he could work out his problems.

Meanwhile I'd married Joe Tumulty, the owner of the Unoriginal Joe's, the last Village joint I worked in. His wife had left him with three kids and the restaurant. His cook quit the second weekend I was waiting tables there. I had to learn fast. Next thing you knew the kids were coming by Unoriginal's for snacks after school because they liked me. Joe told me their real mother hadn't liked them as I did. I was a treat for them. They loved me. I felt honored. I assured him that I loved them, too, which was true. Joe wasn't handsome but he had thick, wavy red hair, a bushy mustache and a wry sense of humor from which I was exempted during our first six months together, when he was amused by my jokes and grateful to me for taking care of his kids, but not during our second and last six months, when he was irritated by my mothering instincts and bored by my tendency to wake up every day in the same body.

I remember with every fiber of that body his slyness, his indifference, his betrayals; I remember only with my brain the crimes I committed against him. We made ourselves dumb, insensitive and one-dimensional, then fought over the petty details of our petty lives with all the passion and imagination of Maggie and Jiggs. As a matter of fact, if my life until then had been a simple drift in collegiate existentialism, my new existence had a distinctly comic stripe.

What made it worse was that Dianne had begun dropping by and every time she was there I could see my life through her eyes, which I knew had to be ten times as critical as my own. It never occurred to me that she wouldn't be coming down to the Unoriginal Joe's after a hard day's work instead of going home if everything were okay *chez* Berry. By this time I'd forgotten Berry's bad points and remembered only that Dianne had married a far-out poet and lived in a cradle of learning. I never asked about her marriage; I made jokes about my own so she would see that I knew as well as she how ludicrous was my life. I told her I was considering going back to school for a degree so I could practice something in the field of psychology; maybe I'd be an assistant to someone who could help people. She thought it was a wonderful idea for me to go back to school although she was still dubious about the whole field of psychology. There wasn't much you could do with just a B.A. anyway. Maybe I should go to graduate school and then teach psychology instead of trying to use it directly. Meanwhile I cooked at Joe's.

It took months for her to tell me her truth and then it was only because one night I did a lengthy drunken monologue whose subjects were my husband and my marriage and whose specific content I can barely remember except that I ended up at four in the morning standing on one of the wooden tables in the empty restaurant, a half-filled stein of beer raised over my head, yelling, "I WILL NOT DIE IN THE SERVICE OF A COMIC STRIP!"

At dawn Dianne and I crept up to the apartment over the restaurant, she to a sleeping bag on the floor of the kids' room, I to my marriage bed. Joe was lying there peacefully, snoring but not in that extraordinary way he sometimes did—unbelievably loud and accompanied by violent thrashings, trying to toss me out of the bed, or so it seemed. The bottle of vodka stood on the table next to his side of the bed, the half-filled glass beside it. The glass had to be half filled or he couldn't sleep.

I leaned over and kissed his forehead, guilty because he looked so sweet and I'd been saying such terrible things about him. He clutched me to his chest, kissed me passionately, rolled me over so that he was on top of me, undressed me, fumbling sleepily in the darkness, sucked my nipples, and so on. Then he began snoring again because the whole routine was in his sleep. If he'd made love to me that night maybe I'd have gotten pregnant and had his baby and stayed married to him and lived happily ever after. Just like other people.

I left my marriage the way I'd left my jobs, like a thief in the middle of the night. I left notes for the kids. I told them I loved them but I just couldn't hack it. Actually in 1959 there wasn't a word for not being able to hack it; everyone was going to hack it for another year or two or five. I told them that someday they were going to have the mother they deserved but I wasn't her. In retrospect those notes seem like the second most disgusting thing I ever did.

For a while Dianne and I were closer than ever, the two of us in a cozy little fourth-floor walk-up on Morton Street, talking about men and marriage and life. Now our defenses against each other were down and our defenses against men were up. We compared notes on men we met and found them all wanting in some crucial quality. We agreed bravely that there was no law that said we had to get married again and indeed we never would unless the perfect men for us came along. I found it difficult to envision such a man in my own life. Surely such a person, if I were to find him, wouldn't like me for long. Anyway, it would be far worse to have a wonderful man and lose him than never to have him at all. As opposed to someone conspicuously mortal and flawed, the loss of whom it might be easy to survive.

Not that I could picture that person, either. In my erotic fantasies I was between two (remarkably flexible) men in a swimming pool that looked like a pond. While in my daily fantasies, the kind I had when I was walking along the street not wanting to feel alone, I was forever running into some man out of my past who'd never before realized how much he loved me—Shlomo, Alex, my old psych teacher, whom I'd heard was now separated and living in New York. But I seemed unable to envision some unknown man out there I might want to meet.

I got accepted at Columbia for the following fall but had no plans to go. On the other hand, I was working as a barmaid at a pub on Sixth Avenue and I couldn't see doing that indefinitely, either. I hadn't seen my parents in a couple of years although I was pretty decent about writing them elaborate lies.

"I have a yen to go back to California for the summer," I told Dianne one evening in May.

She thought that was funny. She didn't know why anyone would ever really want to go to California. She'd already told her folks they'd have to come to New York if they wanted to see her. Anyway, there was a guy in her office she liked. He was married but she didn't think it was going to last long and she didn't want to be away when they broke up.

"My folks can't just pick up the way yours can and come here," I pointed out. "It's different for them. . . . Anyway, there's nothing but you to keep me here. It's not as though I have a job that interests me." Once that first postpartner-depression camaraderie had worn off, feelings of jealousy had begun to invade my simple affection for Dianne, *who had something to do*. Something she wouldn't have to be ashamed of if anyone she knew stumbled across her doing it. "Maybe I'll latch onto something out there."

"What does that mean?"

"I don't know." Grin. "Maybe a couple of Siamese twins."

Her lips curled.

Silence.

"Anyway," I said, "if I had *your* parents I'd really look forward to seeing them." Dianne's mother was interesting. She had things to say that I wanted to hear. Not only that, but I'd always been impressed by the way Dianne's mother treated her (and me)—as though we were adults. When she asked Dianne's opinion it was because she valued it, not because there was a small rubber bath toy in the part of her head where the decision-making apparatus was supposed to be.

"I have nothing to talk to my mother about," said Dianne, whose opinion of her respective parents was the opposite of my own, who thought her mother a superficially charming monster actually avid to dominate everyone she touched. Dianne was convinced that her father's somewhat cool and remote exterior was a result of his having been driven underground by years of life

73

with this monster, a view which left me in a state of confusion. If her picture of her mother was accurate, how could I like and trust the woman so much? For all the jokes I could make about my own mother's passivity and indecisiveness, it was already clear to me that I didn't like women who had qualities opposite to those. Domineering women alarmed me even when it wasn't me they were trying to dominate. Why did I not fear Dianne's mother? Maybe it was just that the surface was tranquil. I liked women who behaved calmly and quietly, like my mother. The way she behaved was the way I thought women were supposed to be—however miserable it made them. The truth was that my failure to possess those qualities, that fear that made me do any crazy thing rather than do nothing, make insane, explosive decisions rather than let life make them at me, also made me less a woman in my own eyes.

Now I thought guiltily of my own mother. If she hadn't been my main reason for wanting to go to L.A., she should have been. It was two years. By the time I'd told them about my marriage I'd been telling them it was over. She'd pleaded with me to come home but I'd been afraid to face her. How could I hold at bay the depression that perpetually threatened me if I had to deal with hers as well?

But the more I thought about it the more certain I was that this summer I should go home.

I was just working myself up to call them for the plane fare when my father's sister called to tell me that my parents had been killed in an accident so bizarre that even all these years later when I try to set it down from the descriptions provided me I find myself shaking my head . . . pausing . . . thinking, no one will believe me, why go through it all? Too ghastly. Too comical. Too Southern California.

They had a party. Once a year on my mother's birthday my father threw a huge party around the swimming pool. There had been some trouble with the heating equipment but it had been taken care of, supposedly, just in time for the party. The guests were already there, my father's sister and her husband who lived

74

in Minnesota among them. One round of drinks had been served but my father, as usual, had a big head start on everyone. He announced that he was going to refresh himself with a little dip before he started the barbecue fire. He left my mother standing at the side of the pool, a corsage pinned to her swimsuit, talking to his sister Marlene. He mounted the board and jackknifed into the water, from which he never came up because he was electrocuted upon touching it. There was a loud crackle. My mother screamed and, reaching out toward him, flat-dived into the water in his direction, as though to save him. As though she herself were immune to the deadly circuit.

Or maybe simply to follow him.

She'd said often enough that she could never bear to be a widow.

I doubt I will ever lose the physical memory of the sick, hollow feeling I had when Marlene told me. It was terrible news she had to call me with, she said . . . my parents . . . was I sitting down? . . . an accident . . . they were both . . .

No! Wait a second! I'm just coming ou—

They were both . . .

HOLD IT! STOP!

dead.

I couldn't see anything. I was falling but not from anything or to something. Everything solid in the world had vanished. That was why I couldn't see, there was nothing there. I fell toward the bed but hit the floor and was still there, my head whirling around in the blackness, when Dianne came in to find out what had made such a thud.

"Nady!" she screamed from the other end of a long tunnel. "Nady! What happened?" She shook my shoulders. "Nadine! Speak to me!"

At some point she seemed to have noticed the phone and picked it up and talked with Marlene. I heard her say, "Oh, my God, oh, my God!"

75

My vision began to clear. I could see the expression on Dianne's face. Anguish and disbelief.

"Oh, my God, no! No! Oh, my God!"

I wasn't alone in the universe.

I could cry.

I began.

Dianne came back to California with me. She took her vacation early. She told her boss she had no choice; her mother was very ill in California. I was cold in the June breeze coming through the windows of the cab that took us to Idlewild; colder in the plane; coldest as we disembarked into the California sunshine. Once at the scene of the crime I tried to stop Marlene from telling me exactly what had happened, but I couldn't. She needed to tell me. And once containing the unwanted knowledge I spent days trying to push it out of myself. Without succeeding, of course. All that happened was that over a long period of time its power over me diminished so that I could live with it. In the daytime, anyway.

Dianne's parents met us at the airport and brought us back to their house. They were wonderful to me, naturally. Even Dr. Mr. Shapiro, usually so cold and reticent, put his arm around me as we walked from the plane and told me that he knew I was going to bear up through all this, even if it didn't seem that way to me now. I moved through the airport like a zombie, nothing real to me except the cold that made me shiver and the sunlight that hurt my eyes and made me close them until I stumbled.

The ride to Beverly Hills. Dianne's house, at once familiar and strange. They brought me a glass of iced tea. Silence. It was hard, sometimes, to remember what I was there for.

"Your father's sister," Dr. Mrs. Shapiro said after a long time, "Mrs. Je— it's hard for me to remember her name."

"Jenczewicz," I said absently, although at other times that week I couldn't remember it myself. "One of those Polish names. Jenczewicz."

"She seems to be coping quite well, under the circumstances."

"They're solid," my mouth said, my mind still someplace else.

It was what my mother had always said about Fred and Marlene, a comment on her idea of herself as much as on them. "They're good, solid people."

"I've only talked to *her*."

"They're very much alike, the two of them," I said. I noticed my speech was lax, as though I'd been drugged. "My mother talks about that a lot. They have the same taste. They play cards and they bowl. They talk about the same things. She's a good cook. My mother—" I stopped, confused and a little embarrassed. As though I'd been caught doing something a little gauche, talking about a dead person as though what she said mattered. Tears came to my eyes, which had been dry since we left New York. On one side of me Dianne held my hand; on the other side Dr. Mrs. Shapiro put an arm around me.

"It's important for you to know," Dr. Mrs. Shapiro repeated her husband's words, "that you're not always going to feel like this."

I stared at her. I couldn't relate to her use of the future tense. The future, if there was such a thing, would begin too long from now to be relevant.

"Do you have a cigarette?"

My request didn't strike me as strange although in point of fact I'd never smoked before, except for an occasional joint. Dr. Mr. Shapiro gave me a cigarette and lighted it for me and I smoked it as though I'd been smoking all my life. After a while Dianne's mother said that if it was all right with me she'd just call the Je— my aunt and uncle—and tell them I'd arrived safely and would be in touch with them when I was ready.

The word made me uneasy. Ready for what? What could I be ready for? For what had happened already? How could I ever be ready for that?

"Ready?"

"I don't mean ready to go to the house," she said quickly, seeing my alarm. "There's no rush at all about that, Nady. They can come here if you like."

Maybe that meant I would never have to go into the house. But then why was I here? Why had I returned to the scene of the crime? Dianne and I had just sort of assumed we were coming back but really, why had we come aside from the fact that I'd been planning to, anyway?

Someone had to Take Care of Things. But what did that mean? Clean the house? The house was empty. Anyway, what difference would it make to anyone? Dr. Mrs. Shapiro called and told Marlene and Fred they would be quite welcome to come over. I stretched out on the sofa, my head propped up on half a dozen pillows so it wouldn't sink below sea level, and went into the kind of fully awake, motionless trance that saved my sanity, such as it was, over the next several weeks when real sleep was out of the question. When I opened my eyes Fred and Marlene were standing over me. They were both crying and after a moment of hating them because I was going to be swept away on a tide of new tears, I let go, too.

I kept thinking I wouldn't cry anymore, that I'd cried as much as I could cry in my lifetime, and then it always turned out I'd been wrong. Some brief vision or combination of words was enough to set me off again. Usually it was Marlene who did it, with her memories of my father's childhood and his early years with my mother. As my mother had yearned for the closeness, the *alikeness* of Marlene and Fred, Marlene had looked at her handsome older brother and the beautiful, artistic, *exotic* stranger he brought to meet his family and seen her own vision of romance brought to life. She talked about them as though they were Cinderella and the Prince, the tall, athletic prince out of Minnesota sweeping off her feet the lovely, slender, ballad-singing Miss California, and settling with her in the land where there was never any winter outside of the soul. Marlene seemed oblivious to everything that had followed. In Marlene's version of my parents' saga the prince and princess had taken an express trip to the end of a rainbow which had turned out to be badly wired, while all I could remember was the time in between. The time they had on their hands. The boredom. The times I'd gone home thinking

78

something *must* have changed by now, only to find that my mother's depression hadn't lifted to a point where she could enjoy life or spread into a real madness that would have constituted some kind of escape. I resented Marlene's tales of how wonderful their lives had once been. How their home, in the early days of their marriage, had been full of my father's bachelor friends, adoring my mother in a respectful way and swapping jokes with my father. More than once Marlene had saved every penny she earned to have travel money so she could vacation with them. In my version theirs were two lives whose abrupt termination was virtually a happy ending—if not for me then for them. Her words pulled off the scab I was trying to form.

Yet I couldn't tell her to stop. It would have been too cruel. She needed to recite her version as badly as I needed to hold on to mine. I was relieved when they prepared to return to Minnesota. Marlene had only one request—she wanted one of my father's swimming trophies. I told her to take all of them. She said she couldn't. I insisted but when the hired help was packing and I saw the trophies, I pulled out the best one of all and kept it for myself. On the pedestal was a beautiful bronze diver who looked just like him. The Shapiros arranged a rental and brought the cartons of personal belongings to their home until such time as I would find it tolerable to go through them. Dianne was wonderful; I don't remember that she talked much but we held hands a lot.

I kept waiting to feel better. Any day now I would lose this dreadful sense that everything was at once entirely unreal and terribly dangerous. I was lonely beyond belief; when people exited from the room I talked to the solid objects they'd left behind.

How could my parents have left such a gaping hole in the existence of which they'd been so small a part for years? What was the use of growing up? Of leaving home? Of putting your childhood behind you? What good did it do if you still had no protection against the kind of feelings I was having now? I could have stayed in Beverly Hills, immersed myself in their needs, lightened my mother's life a bit and eliminated some of my own guilt, for all the sense I had that there was anything left of my life now that they were gone. For years now I'd dismissed them as unreal, made jokes about my California roots and the sandy soil they were sunk in. Why then did their deaths leave me feeling as unreal as I had judged them to be? Had I been selling myself a bill of goods when I pronounced their unreality? Or was it that I'd been all too correct and was only now discovering that unreality was passed down through the genes?

Dianne had to go back to New York but I stayed. I wasn't sure why. It wasn't that the twins were on my mind. They were, in retrospect, conspicuously absent. When I finally thought of them again it was because on one of the aimless drives I was habitually taking I passed within a few blocks of their home. The sages among you may question how aimless that drive really was. But for whatever it's worth, the only question in my mind on that day when I touched my fate . . . or at least my fate as it was to be written for the next thirteen years and ever after in the faces of my children . . . was how to shake the depression that occupied me with a force so great as to displace the weight of my own body.

I slowed down when I realized where I was. A picture of the two men in the pool slid in front of my eyes and I began to cry. I hadn't cried in a week or so and I was surprised and disappointed to discover that there was more left after all this time. I pulled over to the side of the road because the tears were blinding me; almost immediately a cop car materialized behind me and a cop came out to find out where I got off crying in such an expensive part of town.

"Do you need some help?" he asked.

"Yes," I said.

"What's wrong?" he asked.

"I don't know," I said.

He asked to see my license and I showed it to him. It was a New York hack driver's license, acquired in one of my sudden career decisions some months before. I'd driven a cab for three days and not been able to stand having people in back of my head all the time. I kept thinking they were going to clap something over my face and pull out a tooth or a tonsil. He asked if I was lost and I said only metaphorically speaking. He got stiff and suspicious and said that I'd better keep moving, then. I tried driving slowly but he followed me at a distance, obviously wanting to give the car a ticket for loitering.

I gave up and went home to the Shapiros but the twins stuck with me, though in a slightly different way than before. My mind kept coming back to that first idyllic image of them but as it arrived it seemed to literally *collide* with the image of my parents' watery electrocution, and the collision resulted in a monstrous static that left no room for anything but panic. A panic which couldn't be resolved because the image that drew me and the image that terrified me were essentially the same.

It couldn't be resolved in my mind, that is. My body wasn't going to stop trying. Every day I drove past their house, slowed down, looked around and drove on. I got to know the cop, Sharpe. He stopped being hostile when I told him the real reason that I was there; I was dying to meet the famous people in the house. It made me someone he could understand. I was smart enough not to ask him any specific questions about the twins. That would have spooked him, while being after a piece of their celebrity was normal. He tried to interest me in a couple of other nearby celebs and I feigned interest to convince him I wasn't some kind of nut.

We got more and more friendly. The twins' next-door neighbors were in Europe for the year and Sharpe was keeping a little extra eye on the house. We'd crawl over to the bushes and look through to the pool. The twins wouldn't be there so we'd crawl into the neighbors' garage, screw on the back seat of the extra Cadillac, then look again. After three weeks Sharpe confessed that they only swam in the morning and at night. Maybe he was getting tired of me. Or the Cadillac. Or maybe he was just offended that I didn't want to go to the movies or talk to him, I only wanted to screw next door to the Siamese twins. Finally I came on a Thursday, which I knew was Sharpe's day off, and

82

drove right into the twins' driveway. I got out of the car, walked to the front door, was about to let the knocker drop when I changed my mind and walked around to what turned out to be a living-room window. Squinting as my eyes tried to see into the dark room.

In the midst of the room on that beautiful sunny day was a color TV set tuned in to a game show. Facing the game show, the backs of their heads toward me, were the twins. In a nearby armchair sat the housekeeper. Bertha. It was a chilling vision, enough to make anyone half sane run, even if you're willing to grant that someone half sane might have been there in the first place. This was 1960, after all, and not all of America had turned in its sunlight for color TV tubes; it was fair to assume that of the three people sitting in that dark room on that sunny day at least one didn't want to be there.

Why didn't that make me shudder?

Why wasn't I upset—repelled—*horrified* by the sight of two hearts that didn't beat as one and two brains and souls which might function in entirely different manners locked together into what was in effect the same body? Neither ever able to be *I* but only *We?* Neither ever simply to do what he wanted to do, each having to perpetually convince the other to engage in some activity in which the other had little or no interest? I could visualize only the other times. The times when communion made them move together without speaking.

It was because I had experienced my life until then as the opposite of their condition. There I was with an empty space beside me. How could I consider the freedom that empty space gave me when I was perpetually frightened that no one was there to keep me from falling? How could I consider the horror of being Amos, who detested TV, attached to Eddie, who could easily watch it for five or six hours at a stretch, when I was so certain that the only thing that prevented me from being a normal human being who could relax in front of a TV set at night was that restless feeling that stemmed from not having found my soul mate? I saw that the housekeeper would get up every few minutes to get a snack, go to the bathroom, whatever. A single woman, like myself, with vague needs to pull her from room to room and nothing to keep her from floating away entirely. But the twins just sat there in what appeared to be peace.

I half closed my eyes so I wouldn't be blinded by daylight again and groped around to another window from which I could see their faces. One of them was smiling slightly; the other reached for a deck of cards on the table in front of them and began dealing without conversation. I was surprised to see that they barely resembled each other, the smiling one being much the handsomer of the two.

The living room was hideous. They didn't give a damn for their surroundings (The poor things, no one ever made a place beautiful for them! was the way I thought of it then) and the furniture had been chosen from department-store floor models without regard to color or texture, but only to comfort. A chartreuse velvet love seat stood between an orange-canvas, mission-style sofa and two gray-and-pink, striped-damask dining chairs. There were bookcases. More surprisingly, especially for Los Angeles, there were books in the cases. Also stacked on the table and floor near the love seat. Reading was what Amos did when they were sitting in front of the TV, unless they were playing cards or checkers. He read books and subscribed to magazines and newspapers as well.

Eddie's left arm was around Amos. Amos's right leg rested over Eddie's left one. They wore white sport shirts. The joint stretching between their abdomens was covered by fabric that appeared to be part of the shirts. (They had the shirts made, each with half a joint covering and snaps. It was one of my innovations to decree that there was nothing to be hidden and no covering required except in cold weather.) Amos used both of his hands when they played cards but Eddie managed with only one, his other remaining on the rim of the love seat in back of Amos.

The smiling one (Eddie) was really quite handsome.

The window I was looking through was half open. The third time the housekeeper left the room I called to them through the screen.

"Hi. My name is Nadine Tumulty. Can I come in and talk to you?"

They both nodded. I found out later it was because I was the first sightseer who had ever told them her name.

I walked around to the front door, which Bertha opened, scowling.

"You cannot stay for long," she said. "They are busy."

"Roger," I said.

I followed her into the living room, where she sat down again and stared at me with suspicion.

"I'm your neighbor," I said nervously, beginning to speak almost before I really looked at them. "No, that's not true. I mean, I live in Beverly Hills, more or less, but not that close to here, but I wanted to meet you."

"It's nice to meet you," the handsome one, Eddie, said. "Would you like to have a seat?"

"No," I said, feeling Bertha bristling at me. "I mean, yes, I guess so."

I sat uneasily on the edge of one of the hideous damask dining chairs.

"Are you a reporter?" Eddie asked, but he didn't seem to think it important, he was just making conversation.

"No," I said. "Just a person." I laughed nervously. "I always wanted to be a Siamese twin."

Oh, my God! What am I saying? They'll think I'm out of my fucking mind! I am out of my fucking mind!

In point of fact it turned them on. No one had ever suggested that they were less to be pitied than envied. Even the scowling one put down his unplayed hand of cards and regarded me with a little interest for the first time.

He's the one to be courted, I thought to myself as it was borne upon me that I hadn't made a *faux pas*. He's the difficult one.

I smiled winsomely. "I mean, I've tried doing it with mirrors but that's not so good because mirrors break too easily."

By now Bertha was practically beside herself, so to speak, with rage. Maybe her future was passing in front of her eyes, or maybe

85

it was just that I was daring to try to be funny in a serious house. She stood up as though I'd just committed some outrage.

"Would you like a drink?" Eddie asked.

"No, thanks," I said.

"I want a drink," Amos said to Bertha. "Would you get me a Tom Collins?"

Reluctantly she left the room.

"Is she the housekeeper or the gatekeeper?" I asked, then giggled, astounded by my own gall.

"She takes care of us," Eddie said. "The house. The clothes. Celebrity hunters."

"What does she do with celebrity hunters?"

"She just tells them to go away and they go."

I shuddered. She was twice my age but twice my width, too, and she looked as though she could bend horseshoes.

"If *you* tell me to go, I'll go quietly," I said.

"We don't want you to go," he said as Bertha came back with Amos's Tom Collins. "We're glad that you came. We were bored."

Bertha settled her black cloudship back into the chair and stared at me.

"What I was thinking," I said without thinking, "was that maybe you'd like to come to my place for a barbecue."

My place. What the hell is my place?

"Sure," Eddie said promptly.

I began scrabbling around in my mind. Where was I going to make a barbecue? At the Shapiros'? Fat chance. That was just what I needed, to get out from under Bertha's evil eye only to land squarely in the field vision of two shrinks.

"I don't mean a big deal kind of barbecue," I said, more anxious than ever. "Not a lot of people. Just . . . some chow . . . and we can talk."

"That sounds nice," Eddie said.

Especially if I could think of someplace to hold it. Not that there was ever any real doubt.

"When should we come?"

"I guess tonight's as good a time as any," I said. "Unless you have other plans."

He shook his head.

Silence.

I gave him the address of my parents' house.

"Can you drive?"

"Bertha will bring us."

"Okay," I said. "I can get you home." Just to make sure she didn't think of staying.

"Well," I said, standing up, "great. I'll see you in around an hour, okay?"

He nodded. I skipped out the front door, which Bertha nearly slammed on my backside.

Jesus Fucking Christ, what am I doing?

I must be out of my mind. How could I cook for them? The house was all closed up and the new tenants were arriving in three days. I'd given Dr. Mr. Shapiro the extra keys.

On the other hand, I might be able to pull off the whole affair without ever going indoors. Get away with paper plates and stuff like that. I'd tell them the house was being painted. I had no intention of telling the twins about my parents. After all, this was the first fifteen-minute period in months during which I hadn't thought once about them. Why should I spoil all that? Besides, their deaths said something gross about me, although I wasn't sure what it was, only that I didn't want to know it.

I wasn't even sure I could still cook! I hadn't cooked a decent meal since I left the Unoriginal Joe, this being the form of freedom I'd found most readily accessible. Freedom. All it had turned out to be was freedom to stay in the gray areas where you never got high. High the way I was now. Fuck freedom and fuck the gray areas. You could stay in the gray places all your life and your fucking, crazy parents whom you barely knew existed could still fry themselves to death in a swimming pool and turn your insides out forever.

Better to throw your last quarter down the grate than give it to life, that fucking, one-armed bandit, to do with it as it will!

An hour later, still strung as high and tight as the drone string on a banjo, I stood in the middle of the terrace, the brown bags from the supermarket filling my arms.

It was very quiet.

The porch furniture was still there, as was the furniture inside the house, but it didn't look like furniture anyone had ever used. It was a stage set.

The pool had been emptied, the wiring fixed and grounded in the way that it should have been years before only there were no laws in California to force people to do it. The water was trickling back in.

I took the purchased items out of the bags and set them one at a time along the flagstone rim of the barbecue pit. The ghosts of solid objects hovered around the pit: the huge bag of charcoal that was too often left out and got damp in the rain; my father's big white canvas apron with the red stenciling—KISS ME, I'M MEDIUM RARE!—the oversized, mug-shaped salt and pepper shakers that read PEANUTS and POPCORN instead of salt and pepper, your really far-out Los Angeles pool humor; the stand with the barbecue implements, the long fork and the short fork and the spoon for the barbecue sauce. At some point I would have to find those things in the garage. Meanwhile, I should start marinating the meat; even an hour or so might do it some good.

Oh, God, no bowl!

In desperation I ran to the garage to see what I could improvise without finding a way into the house. But the garage door was also locked. Panic. Without thinking twice I heaved a rock through the side window of the garage, stared at the jagged frame of glass that would still make it nearly impossible for me to pull out the wooden frame, and then remembered that we'd always kept a garage key on the ledge of the back window. I found the key and pulled up the heavy door. Someone had been in there, cleaning and packing, and it was immaculate. In the cartons stacked neatly against one side wall were garden tools, rags, stuff for cleaning the pool. Nothing resembling a bowl. Getting more frantic by the second I ran outside, tore the cellophane off the meat and confirmed my suspicion that it was almost as tough as my teeth. Ran back to the garage and found a flat skillet. Put the meat on the skillet, first briefly chewing each piece to tenderize it. Added some oil and oregano and tomato and onions and garlic, each cut up with the manicuring scissors from my purse. All the while getting higher and higher, tighter and tighter, more and more anxious, although the focus of my anxiety shifted from whether they'd come, to whether they'd come too early, to whether they'd come too late, to whether they'd be comfortable, to whether the beer would stay reasonably cold. The beer! I took the cold beer and uneasily climbed down the pool ladder to the bottom, where three or four inches had flowed back in since it was fixed. I deposited the six-packs on the bottom and climbed back up, shivering.

The bottoms of my jeans were soaking wet. I wrung them out as well as I could but I was still cold. In my mind I was arguing with Dianne about the reasonableness of what I was doing. There was no way, Dianne was saying, that she'd voluntarily spend time in a room with a couple of men who were attached to each other. I assured her that when you were talking to them you didn't feel as though you were in the presence of anyone strange or upsetting. They were these two perfectly ordinary-looking men, except maybe they didn't move around as much as some men, they tended to sit quietly because it was difficult to move. Couldn't you see It, though, Dianne asked me? It, I mocked her. It. She was being childish. Like a kid seeing someone's sex organs for the first time. Of course you could see it, it stretched between them, but what was the big deal about that?

Tension mounted. I got colder and colder but didn't want to break into the house to look for clothes. There was no house there, I reminded myself. I was going to use the house like a stage set and could only pray they wouldn't need to take a leak. (Two leaks?) They might think I was crazy, of course, but then maybe they liked crazy people. They were used to them. They'd traveled with the circus for years, after all.

Notice who has already become the freak in this relationship. Notice when I worry at all about who will like whom my concern centers around their liking me, not whether I will like them. I have already determined that I will like them. What are the alternatives, after all? To drift forever like this, nothing to hold me down, to lock me in . . . no ballast? If I hadn't come to understand much more about the limits than I knew when I first left California, I had at least found a couple of bodies that set their own limits and in so doing partly eliminated the need for such understanding.

NO CHARCOAL! There wasn't a piece of charcoal in the whole goddamn garage! What now? I opened cartons and ransacked shelves that were too small to have ever held the huge bags of charcoal. I turned up one half-used can of Sterno and a box of long fireplace matches. Everything was so fucked up it was almost funny. As a matter of fact, the more I thought about it the funnier it seemed, although I wasn't laughing. This meal would be a total disaster. I had blown my big chance to get locked in. Why hadn't I done this in a sane way, like inviting them to dinner the following night when I'd have had a chance to prepare properly? Oh, well, I could relax now since all was lost. Smiling to myself I walked out to the patio with the Sterno can and the matches, discovered the earthly remains of my parents' last barbecue still lying neatly in the pit, clustered them around the Sterno can, thinking once the fire got going I could spread it to the charcoal, and lighted the can. A nice neat little flame. I'd figure out a way to make the charcoal catch, and if I didn't, well that wouldn't matter either, tra-la. From the garage I got some small pieces of leftover construction wood. Nice and dry. And newspapers that were lining the shelves. Eventually I got a nice fire. I put the skillet on the grate and it began to get hot. So everything was going to cook, after all. If only they didn't come too soon . . . except I wanted them to come right away. Where the hell were they? I wanted them to come and get the whole disaster over with.

When they finally arrived I was holding the skillet handle with the end of my T-shirt and with the long-handled barbecue spoon prying loose the gunk from the bottom of the skillet. Hearing the car door slam at the front of the house I made a last effort to shift around the Sterno can to change the area of maximum heat, and as I did so, I pried out the whole thing so that the can came toward me even as the skillet and grate flew in the opposite direction. AAAAAAAAAAAGGGGGGHHHHHHHHHHHH!

"GODDAMNSONOFABITCHMOTHAFUCKAHHHHH!" I screamed in pain as the Sterno can hit my arm as though they were old enemies. Then I stood rooted to the spot in a state of shock until they appeared at the other end of the patio and I heard the car drive off.

They watched me. Eddie's arm was still around Amos, because that was their basic position. He was slightly taller. They moved toward me very slowly with that awkward gait they had that I soon learned to push out of my mind. Eddie's right foot came down then Amos's right foot a few seconds behind it, then Eddie's left foot and Amos's left after another tiny pause. It was a pathetic shuffle, although I didn't let that register for years; I just felt a surge of sympathy and then looked at their heads and their arms.

I said, "I just burned myself and fucked up our whole dinner at the same time."

Eddie smiled his smile that passeth for understanding. Amos looked at me with what I assumed to be curiosity. It was 1960 and he might not have heard a woman say fuck outside of the circus before.

I said, "Maybe I'll go out and get a pizza."

Eddie said he was sure the dinner would be fine. I told them to have a seat and they took the flowered settee, forming into exactly the position they'd been in when I first saw them. My arm was hurting like the devil but I didn't want them to know that. I got some beers from the bottom of the pool and while I was there let my arm rest in the cold water. It didn't do much good; the water wasn't cold enough. When I'd given them the beers to distract them, I kneeled on the patio and very carefully with my T-shirt picked up the Sterno can, which had fallen upside down. I put it aside and picked up the skillet, then began scraping the stew off the flagstone, wiping the pieces of dirt off with the bottom of my shirt, my back turned toward them so they wouldn't see. Huge blisters were already beginning to form on my arm. I put the grate back over what remained of the fire and set the skillet on it. Then I covered the Sterno can and set it near my pocketbook at the end of the terrace. I carried it everyplace with me for the next thirteen years without ever knowing exactly why. It was my Judge, my Sterno Judge. It—he—had a message for me about the times I got really high because I was trying to make a dream real. Someday I'd decipher the message and then I'd get rid of the Judge, but in the meantime he was a reminder to me, his existence a warning. Even if I was going about it in the wrong way, there was little doubt that I needed to be locked up.

They were pretty quiet. While I was preparing the food (I made hero sandwiches so if I'd missed any of the dirt it wouldn't be as noticeable) I wasn't as aware of their silence, but then when I sat down I was acutely uncomfortable. They were capable of sitting for hours without a word between themselves or anyone else, but I didn't know that at the time, I just felt my arm blistering in the dreadful silence.

I began to talk. They seemed to be interested in what I was saying but they seldom made comments so I just kept talking. About my childhood. About my life, up to and including the minute before the phone call about my parents came. Still, I showed them a lot of other vulnerable points. My dumbs and my crazies. I wanted to show them I wasn't condescending to them (something which by its nature you can't show anyone). I wanted to say to them, if there's anyone here I think of as a freak, it's me, although I have to admit to being interested in the particulars of your experience. I talked about my marriage, telling them all the terrible things Joe had done to me and none of the awful things I'd done to him, which I couldn't remember anymore, anyway. I talked a lot about my friend Dianne in New York. How nice she was and how smart. I hoped they might meet her someday. It was amazing, I said, how well Dianne and I got along, with all the differences between us.

We drank both six-packs of beer. It had no effect on them. Neither of them ever got too drunk, Eddie because he didn't drink much, Amos because he apparently had the capacity for two without his drinking affecting Eddie. Anyway, liquor was just another better-tasting juice to them. I got drunker and funnier by the moment, or so I thought, and nothing appeared in their demeanor to challenge my view. I paid more attention to Amos because Eddie was handsome and obviously easier to please. Amos, Amos, let me entertain you. . . . I got higher and higher on the beer and hornier on my own beer-soaked monologue, as though the words were some dildo I was riding for their amusement.

". . . And now we are at the point of my marriage to the Unoriginal Joe . . . mmmmm . . . what *was* the point of my marriage to the Unoriginal Joe? Oh, I remember, he had the same name as my father . . . not the Unoriginal, just the . . . I married Joe because . . . he appreciated me. I didn't know that was the worst possible reason to marry anyone because it's the one that's least likely to hold up in daily intercourse, so to speak. . . . I liked Joe's kids . . . better not think too much of how much I liked them, better to think about Joe, you big sloppy prick, Joe, not about your beautiful kids . . . anyhow he liked that. The way I liked taking care of his kids. He was very nice about it all. He let me cook for his kids, baby-sit for his kids, clean for his kids, he was a prince. An openhanded Prince of Chores. To me. Prince of Booze to himself. He was really unoriginal, Joe. . . ."

I presented them, in short, with the bowdlerized Nadine. Nadine with her shit-flinger removed. Little Nadine, the Victim Supreme, too busy taking abuse to hurt a fly. Nadine V. Dentata lives down the block and Nadine the Shark is vacationing at the Sound. Here with me you are safe! If you get really bad to me I promise to run and not fight back!

93

At about eleven o'clock they yawned. The moment I'd dreaded; they were going to ask to go to the bathroom. But they never did. They had the best two bladders of any two I ever met. They peed twice a day. And crapped in the morning. The second time they yawned they stood up and asked to be driven home. They were also the only two people I ever knew who decided to leave, said good-bye and left, no apologies or explanations, no lingering, not even a husband or wife to do the lingering for them.

I dropped them at their home, promising to come by again.

The next morning I turned in my rental car and bought a three-year-old Ford station wagon. Dianne's parents asked why I didn't buy a new car, since my parents had left me some money, but it didn't seem right to buy anything new or shiny or pleasurable with that money and I stuck with the Ford.

I called Dianne and told her I was beginning to feel a little better. She said she was so glad and asked when I'd be coming back to New York. I said not just yet and asked if she wouldn't consider coming back to California for a while. She said no, she was still pretty involved with that married guy in her office and she didn't want to be away from New York just now. I told her about the twins and there ensued a probably record-breaking time for silence on a West Coast to East Coast pre-six-o'clock-at-night phone call.

I told her I thought they were the reason I was feeling a little better. They were distracting me. They were interesting. (!!! I was still doing all the talking. !!!) She said that anything that made me feel better right now was welcome but she just hoped I wasn't going to take the whole thing seriously because that would be crazy. Disastrous. I lightly scratched the skin around the healing burn on my arm and told her not to be silly. I was telling her it was too late but if she wanted to hear it that way she could think I meant I'd never get serious about a couple of freaks.

She must've not been sure which way to take it. I told her not to tell her parents but a few days later they confessed to me that she'd called them and said they'd like to talk to me. They said they'd tried to avoid interfering in my life although they'd often wanted to help. They had a good friend they thought I should talk to. A shrink. I needed someone like him at a time like this. There were explanations for what I was doing and the explanations would help me. I didn't want to hear the explanations until it stopped working. I told the twins I was going to have to get out of where I was staying and they suggested I move in with them. There was plenty of space.

"What about Bertha?" I asked.

Neither of them thought Bertha mattered.

I laid plans to get rid of fat Bertha and get Dianne there in her place. Not to clean the house. I could do that myself; there was no big deal about cleaning a house. It could be fun if you went about it in the right way. Not if you were married to a Joe Tumulty and felt you'd been tricked into being his housekeeper and you weren't even getting laid. This time I'd be going in with my eyes open. That would make all the difference in the world. (Don't laugh now, there'll be plenty of time later.)

I wrote to Dianne telling her what had happened and giving her my new address and phone number. She'd need a lot of time to get accustomed to the idea of my being with them, even more to start being attracted herself, but sooner or later she'd give in. She would get a job out here and go to work every day, just the way she did now, and when she came home at night I'd have dinner ready for the four of us. After I washed the dishes we'd sit around on the terrace, or in the living room, making a fire on cold nights in the modern, metal-flued fireplace, and we'd talk . . . and we'd snuggle together . . . maybe make love right in front of the fireplace. The very thought, unaccompanied by any detailed image of how this would be accomplished but consisting of soft and dreamlike visions of bodies melting together in technicolor, made me warm all over.

Actually, they hadn't made a move toward me and I occasionally worried about whether they found me undesirable or they were just waiting for me to bring along a friend. Maybe they really didn't want to sleep with me. That they hadn't made a move wasn't necessarily significant because from the beginning I'd made all the moves, been pretty much in control all the way. Did that control extend to sex or did it effectively eliminate the possibility of same? How did they *see* me? Not that I tried to find out. I just kept talking, my sexual torment channeled into a verbal torrent as I tried to relieve myself with words. Roughly comparable to fucking yourself with a feather.

"Know what I mean?" I would ask in the midst of one of my monologues.

Eddie would nod as if he understood.

What he understood was that the nod was what I required to go on. They wanted me to go on. They loved me to talk. I was the first person they'd known in the eleven years since they'd left New Hampshire who wanted to give them more than she took away.

On the other hand, maybe they didn't like girls who wore glasses. I took them off when I went swimming but I hadn't been able to bring myself to the pool and I was inhibited anyway by the thought of skinny-dipping with Bertha around. I finally managed to get her into a screaming, thumping brawl that ended with her threatening to leave if they didn't send me away.

An hour later she was packed and the cab had picked her up.

I said I thought we should have a picnic to celebrate. Maybe down at the pool. It was an extremely hot day in July and external factors were beginning to weigh in against my memories. I made sandwiches and brought down a jug of California red and after lunch we stretched out on the grass that sloped down to the pool. Me on my back. Amos propped on his left elbow, Eddie propped on his right one, never exactly looking at each other.

"Mmmm," I said lazily, "that pool looks good."

"Why don't you take a swim?" Eddie asked.

"I don't have my suit," I said demurely.

"We won't look," he promised.

He was lying, of course. They looked like crazy as I moved away from them, pretending not to know they were looking, and began taking off my clothes. They loved to look as much as they loved to listen. I stretched and yawned in the hot sunshine, not because I was sleepy but because I thought it looked good. Then I ran to the edge of the pool, stopped at the edge, sat down and dunked one toe. If one toe goes in you get a shock, if both feet are in the current runs through your heart and you're dead. I never again went into a body of water without doing it, no matter how many people were in that water already.

Having dunked my toe I stood up, casually made my way toward the deep side of the pool and executed a graceful shallow dive into the water, my heart missing only a beat or two at the moment of entry. They were sitting up now to watch me—it hadn't occurred to them that I was a swimmer since I'd never been near the pool—and I did a few laps of crawl and then, shameless, a languorous backstroke. Look, Eddie, look, Amos, see what happens to the four-eyed daughter of Mrs. America when she jumps into a pool! I'm just like you, air is not my natural element! The air made me crazy and ugly and then I talked all the time so no one would notice but there in the water . . . I had doubts, of course, about which was the real me, but if I could convince them that it was the one in the water then maybe I could convince myself. After an unconscionably long period of time I climbed out of the pool and sauntered over to where they now sat watching me unabashedly, Amos sitting on the grass but his legs thrown over Eddie's so that he was almost in Eddie's lap, twin hard-ons poking up from between his legs.

"Hm," I said gleefully, toweling myself dry two inches from their feet, all pretense of modesty discarded. "There must be less than this to life."

They looked at me expectantly. I dropped to the grass on the other side of Eddie from where Amos's torso was. With each hand I fondled a penis. They stirred, but I didn't know what to do next.

"How do we go about this?" I asked.

"Tell us what you want us to do," Eddie said.

"I want to get in between you," I told him.

Obligingly they went back to their lying-down, facing-each-other position. I climbed over Eddie's legs and inched up on my belly until my nose was touching their joint, which was closer to the ground than I'd hoped. Too close for me to crawl under.

"You're making this very difficult," I told the joint.

"Here," Eddie said. "Lie down over there." He pointed to the grass near their feet. Obediently I lay flat on my back on the grass, sexual desire temporarily smothered by anxiety. But it was too late to turn back. My heart beat wildly. They squirmed onto their knees.

"Now lie on your side," Eddie said. He wasn't at all embarrassed. It was a simple academic matter of finding possible positions.

I turned so that I was facing Amos when they came down on either side of me, the joint now as far as possible from the ground. Still, my bones were too wide and the joint pressed heavily against me until I leaned back against Eddie partway so that my full width wasn't upright. And then the excitement returned.

I couldn't see Eddie. We were all almost the same height and his head was in back of mine. He lifted my wet hair and kissed my neck. I touched Amos's cheek and he leaned forward and we kissed. Eddie's body curved tightly around mine, his left arm around me now, his penis pressing between my buttocks, his body straightening with mine as I stretched out to be up against Amos. Somehow they got off their pants, although they never did make it to their shirts. Somehow Eddie got into me, although for a while it was touch and go whether I was going to be able to tilt my bottom enough for him to reach my vagina. I played with Amos while Eddie was in me and then later somehow turned so that Amos got into me. And somehow with all the fuss and muss and bother a good time was had by all. A wonderful time.

Having a wonderful time, Di. Wish you were here.

I wasn't disconcerted by their lack of passion. The grunts and groans of pleasure and exertion passed well enough with me. If someone had pointed out to me then that they lacked passion I probably would have laughed and said that was fine, I had enough for all of us. If my imaginary interrogator—my Stern Ol' Judge,

98

perhaps—had pointed out that I hadn't learned a thing in the time since I'd let my head do all the work for Alex, I probably would've replied that there was a case to be made for living that way. After all, what you only had in your head you could only lose in your head, so that the loss of Alex had barely been any loss at all.

Afterward, tired and sweaty, we all went back to the pool, where they treaded water facing each other then watched me do my White Rock Girl Unchained act in and around the water. When we'd finished swimming I joined them where they sat in their basic Eddie's left leg entwined with Amos's right one position, holding on to each other's penises until someone (who else?) could do something with the new excitement my performance had evoked. With a suddenness and ease that seem remarkable in retrospect I was mounted on Amos's penis and sucking Eddie's. All of which as I write it now seems quite easy and natural, no more difficult than biting my own toenails, which I was also fond of doing. And no more interesting. Not half so interesting, for example, as the fact that once Dianne entered the sculpture nothing was ever so easy and spontaneous again. Once Dianne was with us there were rules. She didn't impose them but her presence led to them. I had to close my eyes, for example, if she was sucking Eddie. Not that she ordered me to close them, but if he happened to want her to do that and my eyes happened to be in a place where they might fall on her while she was doing it, she wouldn't.

The truth is that with all my uninhibitedness bullshit, I didn't like being observed by *her* at that particular act, either. It was a truth I didn't have to face for a long time, of course, because I was too busy despising her for her hypocrisy. Much later on I tried to figure out why on the Tumulty-Smith Guilt Scale sucking someone off sends the little red ball, so to speak, right off the meter, while fucking barely makes it bounce in the pavilion. Certainly it had nothing to do with strictures laid on me in my childhood, all of which had to do with keeping my legs crossed and not having my fingers smell of having been in the wrong places.

When I remember the sex games of my childhood, as a matter of fact . . . playing chiropractor, and the others . . . the forbidden quality seems to have had to do with the combination of sex and *looking*, nothing at all to do with my mouth. The only thing I wasn't supposed to do with my mouth was scream. Or say dirty words. So what's the big deal? Why does my forbidden uck begin with an S? What wasn't I supposed to—aha! I just thought of something. I wasn't supposed to uck my thumb. But to take it a step further, why not? I mean, what was the big deal about sucking a thumb? A few warts never hurt anyone.

Di got twice as mad now if I begged her to come out and just meet the twins. Maybe it was because somewhere deep down she was just beginning to want to. Sex with Franklin, her married lover, had petered out, so to speak. He and his wife had campaigned for Kennedy in the New Hampshire primaries and fallen in love with a little town named Bootville they'd passed through. They'd spent their vacation there and then Franklin had suggested that Dianne might be interested in renting the house to get away for a while. There'd been a vague understanding that if she were in Bootville Franklin might have a good excuse to spend a weekend or two up there with her, he would claim to be renting the house for the winter, and so on, but now he was saying he didn't want to endanger his marriage by pushing that hard so Dianne was stuck for weekends in this little house in rural New Hampshire in a town with fifty people in it. She was having a series of minor accidents. Cutting off a piece of finger when she meant to slice a pear and falling down small flights of steps that materialized in front of her.

"You really ought to come out for a while," I said to her one weekend when she was up there alone, desolate, having been informed by Franklin for the third time that he just couldn't come with her after all. "If only for the sex. The sex is fantastic."

Silence.

"No kidding, Di. I never had such a fantastic time with *anyone.*"

100

"I hope," she said stiffly, "that I never need sex so badly that I'll travel three thousand miles to get into bed with someone."

"What if you didn't have to travel?" I asked off the top of my head.

"You're welcome to come here," she said. Meaning Bootville, of course, not New York. She'd never have invited us to New York. (Not that I would have gone.)

"Are you serious?" I asked.

The idea seemed reasonable to me right away. The twins had come from New Hampshire and they never talked about the past but maybe they would like to go back.

"Sure," she said. "You can come today, if you want to. I don't mind."

"Dianne is in New Hampshire," I said to the twins. "She's renting a house there."

"Oh, yuh?" Eddie said.

"You grew up in New Hampshire," I pointed out, just in case they didn't remember.

"Uh-yuh," Eddie said. "Dixonville."

"Do you remember your childhood pleasantly?" I asked. They never talked about it but of course they didn't talk much about anything.

"It was okay," Eddie said.

Amos looked at him in such a way as to contradict this assertion.

"What do you remember most clearly?" I asked.

"I remember everything," Eddie said. "He doesn't remember anything."

"There was nothing to remember," Amos said. "We were bored all the time."

"We learned to do a lot of things; we could always keep busy if we wanted to. The thing they didn't like was to see us sitting there fidgeting with our hands."

"There was nothing to do except fix cars."

"Everyone was always nice to us," Eddie pointed out to him.

"Because we behaved," Amos said. "We did what they told us

101

and we didn't run around. If we didn't behave they would've been on us in a minute."

"I think Mrs. Storm really liked us," Eddie said.

"She liked *you*," Amos said.

"Nah, that's silly," Eddie said, smiling. "She treated us the same."

"She had to. But she *liked* you," Amos persisted.

"How could you tell?" I asked.

"I could tell," Amos said.

"Dianne wants us to come and visit her," I said. "She wants to meet you."

I don't know what I'd expected but they were instantly amenable to the idea. It made me wonder if they'd been so contented with our little *ménage à trois* as they'd seemed all along. The following weekend we took a plane to Boston and drove a rental car from Boston to Bootville. I was acutely miserable for the length of the trip, although one of the virtues of the kind of rock-bottom depression I'd been in had been to make acute misery seem bearable by comparison. Anyway, I was plane sick, carsick, sick sick. Sickened by the cabdriver's monologue on celebrities he had known, sickened by the staring creeps at the terminal (I'd never been in public with them before) and the children saying, "Hey, Mom, look at that!" I suppose, I thought forlornly, my cheeks burning, my eyes on the floor as we advanced with agonizing slowness toward the correct gate, I suppose they got used to being stared at a long time ago. The plane ride was interminable and the hike off the plane, through the baggage checkout and to our rental car was worse. We were in the East now, where people could really tell what was crazy and didn't think being famous canceled it out. The twins slept on and off as we drove toward Bootville. We'd lost three hours in transit and it was nearly midnight when we reached the house.

Dianne came out to greet us as though she were Perle Mesta and we were a bunch of World War II basket cases being wheeled in for a reception. She was teddibly gracious and never took her eyes off anyone's face. I wouldn't have been able to stand the whole routine, the time it took to get out of the car, to get into the house, through the kitchen, into the living room and so on, had I not been numb from the whole trip.

I kissed her.

"We're exhausted," I said, gesturing lamely in the direction of the world in such a way to suggest that it and the trip were responsible for the men's condition. They didn't speak at all although Eddie smiled a lot.

Dianne talked about her work. She was having a difficult time at the office these days because most of her colleagues were so involved with John Kennedy's presidential campaign that they weren't doing any of the routine work and it was falling on her shoulders. Since she herself thought there was no hope with Kennedy or anyone else, she ended up feeling excluded from the easy office conviviality (not to speak of being excluded more thoroughly than before from Franklin's marriage). She was doing nervous-talk à la Nadine. The first time I'd ever heard her do it but, after all, she had to do the talking.

"Did you know Amos and Eddie are from New Hampshire?" I asked when she finally ran down.

"No," Dianne said, cool again, and polite. "Really?"

"Even further from Hanover, though," Eddie said cheerfully. "We never even got to Hanover."

"How come?" I prompted.

Eddie didn't answer.

"It's a college town," Amos said. "Towns like Dixonville and Hanover have nothing to do with each other."

"Mm," Dianne said. "Of course." She was appraising him now, surprised that he was reasonably articulate. "How long did you live in New Hampshire?"

"We were born and raised here," Eddie said in a tone that made it clear the words had been recited before in the same order. "We stayed at a home for children until we were sixteen and then—"

"Nobody asked for the whole routine," Amos cut in irritably. "What time is it, anyhow?"

Neither of them had any sense of time but Amos checked it out occasionally—the way you'd ask when it's noon here what time is it in China?

"Past midnight," Dianne said. "Would you like me to show you your room?"

She had set up separate bedrooms for them and for me. (She told me later that she'd been prepared to put sleeping bags in the living room if they couldn't get up the stairs.) She took them up while I waited, drinking coffee so I could stay awake long enough to talk with her for a while. But when she came down there didn't seem to be much to talk about. She was terribly unhappy. She felt lonely and abandoned up here in New Hampshire without so much as even a phone call from Franklin, and she wasn't looking forward to another year at her job. She felt empty and bored and dissatisfied, at a total stalemate in her life, and the only thing she couldn't conceive of doing to help herself feel better was to muck about with a couple of freak men.

I shrugged. "I'm not saying you have to fall in love," I pointed out. "I'm not saying you have to get married. I'm just saying enjoy them with me for a while. The sex is incredible, Di, I'm not kidding." She didn't know which she wanted more, to leave the room or ask for the details.

"You're not even going to be here for a while," she pointed out.

"We can be," I told her.

"I have to go back to New York on Monday," she pointed out.

"We can wait until you come back next weekend. There's no rush."

"It'd really be good," she said wistfully, "to have you waiting for me here when I return."

"Then I'll do it," I said, hugging her. I was sure the men would be willing. "We'll stay and you'll get to know them. Just for fun, Di, honestly. That's all I'm talking about. Fun."

The countryside was lovely. The men were more than contented to stay. There was a pond in back that was theoretically owned by the town but no one else used it because it was stream-fed and always very cold while there was another warmer one not too far away. The twins seldom left the house except by the back door to go to the pond. If the neighbors even knew they were there with us, I couldn't tell they knew, but of course that was typical of New Hampshire. I never did find out what the neighbors knew. I shopped at the general store which was a few hundred yards down the road, swam with them, played cards as we had in California, occasionally took off to go antiquing. I had developed a mild interest in antiques since my return to Los Angeles. We were on the main road but even so the traffic was negligible. The house was set well back from the road and surrounded by trees, so that we had real privacy. The twins began whittling when they found a nicely shaped piece of wood. Together they made a long, smooth miniature canoe. Maybe someday we would have a store with antiques and miniature canoes. We played together at the pond, sometimes making love without leaving the water. There was a beach ball we'd found in the house and I would throw the ball over their heads then race with them to catch it. We'd get into a laughing struggle which I would resolve by ducking under the water and grabbing their penises and trying to get them both into my mouth at once. Or hanging from their joint I would place a sole of each foot against their bellies and push their bodies up and out. We were all less inhibited in the water; on land I was unsure of how far I could go without hurting them, particularly the joint.

During her first weekend back with us Dianne moved in a little but still kept a good distance and never came back to the pond. The next weekend was Labor Day, though, and at noon when the thermometer on the porch hit 102 I told her it was driving me crazy to think of her sitting in the house sweating while we were cooling off in the pond.

"It's pretty hot," she said hesitantly.

"What's the problem, then?" I pressed. "Would it make any difference if we put on bathing suits?"

"I guess so," she finally admitted.

"Okay, then," I said. "If it'll make you feel better we'll all wear bathing suits."

Oh, shit, of all the days to have to put on a fucking bathing suit.
She put on her suit and came down and watched us like a
tourist at an aquatic circus.

But the next time she came down to the pond it was supposedly
an accident that she was there at all. She just sort of stumbled
across us in the woods. We had been talking just before she came
about the possibility of moving here permanently. We were more
comfortable in our isolation than we'd been in Los Angeles and
the men could probably find more to do. Carpentry. Fixing cars.
It would be more like a real life than the one we had in L.A. I
talked, they listened, we fucked. They took a nap. They fell asleep
facing each other on the slope. It would be difficult, I thought,
noticing Dianne coming through the woods, head down, a stick
in her hand weakly poking at twigs and leaves on the path in front
of her, it would be difficult actually to add another ingredient to
this pleasant mixture. What would be in it for me, anyway, sharing these nice men with Dianne? I must have sensed that she was
about—in her own fashion—to give in.

"Hi, Di," I said, full of guilt at my thoughts. "What's doing?"
She tried to act surprised but she was a lousy actress.

"I didn't know you were here, I was just . . . I felt like being
alone, like taking a walk in the woods." Her eyes went to Amos
and Eddie, napping on the grass. (They always napped rather than
sleeping for long blocks of time. And when they passed from sleep
to wakefulness the transition was minor. Calm.)

"See those two paths?" I said to Dianne, who *never* walked in
the woods. "The one on the left has lots of poison ivy, I discovered. Be careful."

She waited indecisively. Her mouth was trembling but I wasn't
about to relent. In our last conversation about the men, that
mouth had looked as though I were trying to feed it bat shit for
dinner. The mouth, not exactly your standard, generous, Medi-
terranean job to begin with, had pulled itself inside out as it
formed the words, "Oh, Nady, I just couldn't ever do it. I don't
see how you can!"

"Maybe I'll just sit with you for a few minutes, if you don't
mind, Nady."

106

I shrugged. "Make yourself at home." And then the incongruity of my saying that to her struck me. "What's happening with old Franklin?"

"I don't think I'm going to see him anymore," she said. "I think we've reached the point of diminishing returns."

"I thought that was where you began." Rebecca of Sunnybrook Farm. "I mean, doesn't he even talk to you anymore?"

She burst into tears. "That's practically it," she said. "I mean it isn't but it might just as well be. I feel as if maybe he just wanted to rent me the house, he never even intended to come up. He said he . . ." She couldn't finish but it didn't matter; the tears had done the job. Made my guilt at wanting to be rid of her outweigh the desire for her to be gone.

"Listen, Di, just as well to be rid of the jerk," I said. "It's too bad you wasted so much of your time on him."

She nodded, still weeping, her knees drawn up, her head down on them.

I thought I saw Amos stirring. I was uneasy. If they woke up and saw Dianne crying maybe they'd think I had caused it. Furthermore, they would feel sorry for her and turn against me.

"Hey, Di, you know what you need?"

She looked up.

"You need to take off your clothes and get in the water with me. It's hot as hell here; you must be uncomfortable."

"I couldn't," she moaned.

"Sure you can. It's easy."

She shook her head.

"Look at me, Di, I'm naked. Did you even notice?" It's the beginning of the nineteen sixties, Di. We have to hurry or everyone'll be all caught up. In another five years the word outrageous'll be out of the dictionary. "Look at the boys. Do they look shocking to you?"

"They look beautiful," she said wistfully. "They look much nicer without clothes on. Natural."

"Everyone does," I said, "it's not just them." Although it was true that clothes made even more of a difference on them because they got twisted and rumpled more easily. "Come on."

"I can't."

"Try."

She stood up and very slowly slipped out of her jeans and her T-shirt. Then she stood in her plain white panties and bra, the stuff most of us wore before all the nylon in the world sprouted flowers.

"I guess I can go in like this."

"Oh, come on, Di."

"I can't."

She couldn't.

"All right, then. Come in. You can go in in your underwear."

We walked down to the pond, Dianne picking her way carefully because her feet weren't as tough as mine. I felt very proprietary. I dived in as though I were back at the pool in California instead of at the shallow edge of a pond with a gravely bottom and immediately scraped my face and still-tender burned arm on rocks I'd watched out for previously. I came up smarting. Dianne was standing at the edge in her underwear, looking forlornly into the water. Eddie and Amos were awake now but her back was to them and she hadn't noticed.

"Just plop down fast," I called, then swam out to the center with my all-American crawl, doing a few dolphinish arabesques in the water. I couldn't resist showing off, I was already so frightened they would like her more than they liked me. Dianne sat down at the edge of the water and swirled it around, patting her face and her chest with her dripping hands. After a while I got out of the water and walked nonchalantly to where the men lay watching us. I stretched out on the grass with my head between their feet as though I had nothing on my mind but to soak up a few more minutes of sun.

Silence.

After a few minutes I edged up so that I was between their legs —one arm over Amos's, the other over Eddie's—and looked down toward the water where Dianne was still noodling around waiting for someone to pour the warm sauce of life over her.

"Hey, Di," I finally called out, impatient to end the charade. "Come on over and meet my friends."

108

"We've met," she called back. Sounding very goddamn soft and demure. I could imagine her face, pained. Her eyes lowered like a nun trapped at a porny. She'd inched farther into the water.

"Come on out, for Christ's sake. Your goose pimples are so big I can see them from here!"

I was going too far. She would cry again. Not that I really cared, but I didn't want them to see me being shitty to her. I scrambled to my feet and brought her a dry towel.

"Here."

She turned to get up and take the towel but was transfixed by some sight in back of me. I turned. The twins were lying in approximately the position that I'd left them, still with erections, and it was those twin towers of flesh standing in the afternoon sun that were hypnotizing Dianne, making anything I might do or say in the ensuing moments irrelevant. I led her back to them now and sat between Amos's legs. She settled near Eddie's feet. Eddie smiled at her winningly. Jealousy messed up my face, rearranging my mouth in a downward position. Dianne smiled at Eddie shyly. As though she hadn't had to cry and connive to get where she was. She was shivering. I wanted to suggest that she go back to the house and put on some dry underwear.

Where would we find room for her, anyway? Even if I had the inclination to suggest that she take off her wet underwear and get into our sculpture, where would she fit? My openings seemed to take care of what they needed one way or another with a minimum, all things considered, of fuss, muss and bother. Mostly I was between the two of them, occasionally on top, as when I sat on the lap of one who was more or less sitting on the other. Or we did virtually the same thing but lying down at a slight slant to the ground. In any event, there was no position I could think of in which we'd be better off with a fourth party present. Why the hell had we come East, anyway?

"You're shivering," Eddie said to her. "Come up here and I'll help you get warm."

Right out of my hands. The whole ball game.

"My clothes are wet," Dianne said timorously.

He didn't say anything. She edged up on the Eddie side of us.

109

He and Amos sat up, their legs as they did so moving up the slope so that I was no longer between them. Symbolically confirming my worst fears.

I turned on my belly to watch them. I remember how hard I'd urged Dianne to share them with me earlier. When it might have been easy. I remembered a repeated dream of my adolescence in which a hideous fortune-teller told me that everything I had wished for would come true in such a way that I'd wish I had never asked. Dianne, blushing, looked at some point below Eddie's eyes. Was she really shy? Is there really such a thing as shyness? I sometimes suffer from a desire to be fair but I know shyness only as a mask for my desires. Are there people for whom shyness represents a specific delicacy? A genuine fear?

He made it easy for her. He twisted around to help her get off her wet underwear and put an arm around her to draw her between them. He didn't mind at all that I was watching from their feet, and Dianne wasn't noticing. Eddie's outside knee was raised so that his arm rested on it as he held her. Amos was stroking her hair, wondering when I would move up to join him. Or I was wondering. Instead I nuzzled up to Eddie's penis, enjoying the fact that Dianne didn't seem to realize it was my hair against her buttocks. Amos by this time was curved so that his member of the wedding was practically in my ear.

"Move over," he said to me.

Dianne froze. Turned to a block of ice right above me in Eddie's arms.

"What's the matter?" Eddie asked her.

"Hello, up there!" I called gaily, and she bolted out of the space and stood above us all, trembling, although no longer with the cold.

"What happened, Di?" I lied.

Did you think I'd disappear just because you finally decided to try it?

But she was shaking. Poised on the brink of flight. I was being a shit. I scrambled to my feet. "I'm sorry, Di. I was horsing around. I didn't realize . . ."

110

She was crying again. Gently I pulled her down to the grass.

"You know I love you, Di." It was true. I felt very tender toward her again; it was just that my tenderness couldn't wipe out my jealousy. "You know better than to take me seriously. My clowning around."

"I don't see anything to clown about," she sobbed.

She wasn't kidding. She really didn't. First it repelled her and then it attracted her but she never saw anything funny about the whole setup.

"You're right," I said.

She more or less stopped crying. She eyed me, trying to decide if I meant it and/or if I would end up fucking it up in some way whether I meant it or not.

"I'll be good," I promised. "I've just been anxious about . . . you know . . . about this for a long time. I promise to be good."

What the hell, I really was glad she was joining us. It would be a relief having someone like Dianne around who had at least a better sense than I did of what wasn't done. With her little interior rule book, that most precious of my missing possessions, she would guide us over the tricky shoals of life. After all, I might know what was funny but she knew right from wrong.

"Let's just sit together for a while," I said tenderly. "It was all so sudden for you, you didn't realize . . . I think maybe you need time to . . ."

So I brought her back on a silver platter instead of just letting Eddie grab for himself. Eventually we all made love. Not all, exactly; from the first time with Dianne there were ground rules. Eddie was hers and Amos was mine. In the normal(!) course of events we were all quite intertwined but for the next thirteen years Amos entered only my vagina or mouth and Eddie entered only Dianne's, the latter only if I feigned sleep or nonattention.

My pleasure in sex with them was never as great from that day on. I don't know whether the sheer mechanical difficulties, so much greater with two female bodies than one, were what put me off, or if the cumbersome quality of our sex was the effect rather

111

than the cause of the way I felt about it now. Maybe I didn't sit around the way Dianne did trying to write some kind of etiquette for the outposts of the ridiculous, but the truth is that I was perpetually aware of Dianne's concern even if I seldom focused on my own, and in effect the two concerns were the same.

The following week, in a burst of enthusiasm, Dianne quit her job and we rented Franklin's house for the winter.

If ecstasy vanished when Dianne came into our scene, it was replaced by a certain kind of comfort. The very awkwardness of sex, the difficulty of arranging practical matters now that there were two strong wills functioning in the group (albeit one of them a seemingly weak and deferential one) gave our lives a humdrum quality that took the edge off what had become a perennial—and increasingly scary—high. If I was no longer coming in colors that hadn't been cataloged yet, I was also not experiencing moments where I suddenly feared that if I couldn't get just a little more oxygen into my lungs I would surely collapse and die. We did more things that you could classify as Things to Do. We went to the movies and ate dinner in a diner where we were never stared at except by kids. When I commented on the comfort of being in a place where adults never stared, Eddie said that was what they had always remembered best about their New Hampshire childhood; the more interested you were in something the further away you had to look. We usually saw Dianne's or my second choice of movie since our first choice was never the same. We were proud of our flexibility—our compatibility, we called it—and never asked ourselves what we were getting that was so marvelous as to justify never doing exactly what either of us wanted to do.

Eddie said it was the best time in their lives. Each had his own woman. They started thinking about selling the house in California and settling here. They suspected there was plenty of work around Bootville of the type they did anyway. They referred to being married and settling down but didn't ask us directly to marry them.

112

THEN Dianne got pregnant.

She missed two periods before she told me and then she made me promise to let another month go by before letting them know. Only someone with my passionate disregard for details could have failed to notice the first misses, of course.

"My God!" I said. "Don't you *use* anything?"

It had never occurred to me to discuss it with her.

"Sometimes," she said.

"Should we try to find that guy in Pennsylvania?" I asked, remembering the famous patron saint of abortions, known in Bard as well as dozens of other liberal arts colleges. But I might have said Transylvania, the way she looked at me.

"Then what are you going to do?" I asked.

"Nothing, for now," she said.

"But later'll be too late," I wailed.

"Too late for what?" she said calmly.

"Too late for an abortion," I said.

"But I don't want an abortion," she told me.

Now it was my turn to stare. She meant it.

"What if . . ." It came out in a whisper. "What if . . . you have . . . you know . . ." I couldn't even say it. I couldn't face how I felt about giving birth to Siamese twins because then I might have had to look at how I felt about living with them.

"While being a twin is genetically coded," Dianne said, still a mass of impenetrable calm, "the physical linkage between them is an extreme freak of fate and there is absolutely no medical evidence to suggest that it could or would ever happen in the next generation."

"So," I said, my head spinning, "you've been doing research."

She nodded.

"You *want* to have a baby."

She nodded again.

"Have you thought about your parents?" I asked, groping around for solid forms for my objections.

"Why should I? They have nothing to do with it. Or with me."

"What about the twins? Is it fair to them?" Meaning, is it fair to *me?* "Shouldn't they have some voice in the decision?"

"What decision?"

"Whether to go ahead with it?"

"They don't have to decide whether to go ahead with it," she said. "It's going ahead with itself."

I'd never seen her so *deeply* certain, so *contentedly* certain, before. She was more like the image I'd once had of her than she'd ever really been. Had Getting with Child done this for her? If so, I'd have to consider doing the same thing sooner or later. Later, I promised myself hastily. Right now I had about as much desire to have a baby as to . . . but comparisons failed me. There was nothing scarier than having a baby, than holding another life in your hands. Not just in your hands, in your *insides*. No one knew the damage you could do to a baby with your own churning insides before it was ever even *born*, although the awful effects you could have on it later were on their way to being

114

overdocumented. It wasn't the Giving Up One's Freedom aspect of motherhood that bothered me . . . at Bard I had read without negative feelings Helene Deutsch's prescription for the Woman Who Would Be Mother . . . no jobs, no outside interests, no anything but the baby . . . the freedom they gave you from freedom seemed to me the greatest attraction of children. The liability was in having the freedom to imprint one's own insanity upon their open minds. If each of them had come born with a rule book around its neck I probably would've wanted one sooner. Instead I had to wait for jealousy of Dianne's precious new possession to hit me. Not to speak of the desire to prove that I could get pregnant just as easily as she.

In the meantime, Dianne's point of view was very simple. It was her baby. True, she'd had a little help in creating it, but basically she didn't require assistance to raise it. Certainly she would consider a nice offer of marriage but this was not a pressing issue.

I thought she might be out of her mind, after all. Remember, this was years before the bullshit about unnecessary fathers had reached epidemic proportions; the vision of raising a child alone took on surrealistic qualities. A huge Dianne Mother and a teensy Dianne Baby alone on a windswept shore with only each other to feed off.

"You won't go back to work, then?" I finally asked. (As we'd settled in she had talked briefly of finding a job in Concord or Hanover.)

"Of course not," she said serenely. "I'm not bringing a whole new person into the world just so I can leave it with a maid."

For the next month I walked a tightrope between nervousness and hysteria. Would they or wouldn't they? Want to marry us, that is. Once or twice I accidentally found myself asking if I wanted to marry *them*, but I pushed that one out of my mind. I had to know what they wanted before I could know what I wanted myself. After all, I wasn't about to walk away and leave Dianne in this lovely conglomerate that was entirely a product of my imagination. If they were getting married, so was I. If they weren't then I could sit down and figure out what I really wanted to do.

I kept my promise not to tell until she'd missed her third period but I was angry with her all the time. I said things I knew would drive her up the wall. Like I suggested that we attach a rope to her chest and mine and try crapping together just to see what it felt like. Other times I bit my tongue to keep from saying something awful to her and then I got twice as mad at her because my tongue hurt.

On the thirty-first day when she hadn't said anything by dinner I announced that Dianne had an announcement to make.

She dropped her fork.

So she hadn't planned to tell them today, the way she promised.

"What's the matter?" I asked innocently. "It's a month isn't it?"

She turned beet-red.

We were sitting at the kitchen table. Eddie and Amos were on the split-level bench they'd built for themselves to duplicate the one they had in California. She turned to me helplessly. Her eyes were brimming with tears and her mouth, old tremblymouth, was going again.

"What is it now?" I moaned. "I thought we had a simple agreement."

"It's not that I don't want to tell," she said tearfully. "I just wanted to do it in a nice way."

"All right," I said. "I'm sorry. Forget the whole thing. I never said a word."

But you could tell from her face that I'd wrecked it. Destroyed her chance to do it the right way. Given her baby a bad start in life. God only knew how the child might be scarred by my disastrous error. It might never get into Radcliffe.

"I had hoped," she said shakily, "well, anyway, something very nice has happened . . . and it may affect you and it may not. . . ." She was looking at Eddie only. "But it's something I want, it doesn't have to have anything to do with you unless . . ." She

116

went on and on until even the twins began to look uncomfortable. "I'm going to have a baby. In the spring." She blushed. Eddie was grinning like an idiot—as if he'd just hit the jackpot—and even Amos looked pleased. In proportion, perhaps, to his share in the conception. "I want you to know that I don't expect anything from anybody," she went on, as though they didn't look the way they looked. "I'm prepared to care for this baby entirely by myself." Eddie's expression changed from joy to bewilderment. "I ask nothing of anybody." She stopped. She waited. But her message had been so mixed that they were confused.

"All she's saying," I interjected, impatient with this silly melodrama in which I had such a peripheral role, "is that you don't have to marry her if you don't want to."

"But we want to," Eddie said quickly.

I looked at Amos. He was looking at me with shy longing. I blushed and looked down at the table. When I looked up Dianne was smiling and Eddie was holding her hand.

"This is too fucking corny for words," I announced. "What are we supposed to do while they get married? Throw rose petals?" A mixture of coyness and irony so sticky as to sicken me as I uttered it.

"We'll get married, too," Amos said. "That's what we want."

"You're sure?"

"Of course."

"Oh, all right, then, by all means let's get married. It's good weather for it."

Very lightly. As though I hadn't just consented to chain myself for a long period of time into an act that would make real life seem reasonable by comparison.

Not that I thought of it that way. I thought that whatever the problems and however much I didn't like the way it had all happened, I'd finally found my niche.

Things We Did Not Discuss Before We Got Married
1. What the form of our lives would be after we were married.
2. What the content of our lives would be after we married.
3. Where we would live other than this temporary rental home.

4. Who would earn our living, and how. Whether, indeed, it would be necessary to earn a living or whether the money already accrued from freak lives and freak deaths would make it unnecessary.

Things We Did Discuss Before We Got Married
1. . . . I can't remember.

I think we all knew each other's favorite color. Amos's was blue. Also which sign each of us was born under. Amos was interested in astrology long before it became a fad. I thought it natural for him to seek a mystical explanation for the accident of their birth. It didn't occur to me for a long time that his own charts couldn't conceivably be valid because the birth date that had been used was made up by the matron at the home.

We talked some about travel. Dianne and I knew they'd been to places we'd barely dreamed of going and seen sights we'd never see. Amos knew a lot of facts about the places they'd been but they'd actually taken in relatively little, although we didn't realize it at the time. When you're on display you don't see. Actually, they loathed travel, but they never told us that until the first time we got restless and wanted to go someplace, and that was years later.

So we married these guys with whom we had in common an interest in travel. And, oh, yes, Amos and I had the same favorite color. Blue. That was it. That was how come I liked Eddie's looks and manner and went first for Amos. He and I had more in common.

There did have to be a reason, didn't there? It wasn't just enough to say that they had penises and we had vaginas and always the twain would meet, no matter what the difficulties and inconveniences attached to such a situation. There had to be a reason.

Still, blue is a pretty color.

The ceremony was performed in the home of the justice of the peace of Bootville, New Hampshire, where we would make our home for at least a few months. (We later bought the house from Franklin and his wife.) There were problems. There was something wrong with the twins' birth certificates, something to do with the fact that they had been made out when the twins were sixteen and they had two different years of birth on them. The civil servants in New York who'd given them passports a while later had never noticed but the justice of the peace in Bootville, one Cuthbert Baddely, pointed out that one was obviously invalid and had to be corrected.

The attractive quality about Bootville and about Cuthbert Baddely was that they couldn't have cared less. Mr. Baddely married us without expressing any more interest in the fact that one of the brides was conspicuously pregnant than he (or any other Bootville native) would ever display over the fact that the two grooms were attached at their abdomens. Elvira Baddely smiled and chain-smoked during the entire ceremony. I felt she was laughing at me, as opposed to at all of us. After all, I was the one who knew she might be laughing at us but I was going through with it anyway. Later I would try to become her friend but she would never stop laughing.

Dianne wore a simple white dress whose style seemed calculated to make her four-month belly as conspicuous as possible. She was calm to the point of being sepulchral, which made me angry and then nervous. I remember at one point having an overwhelming urge to duck around the twins and goose her. Aside from that urge, what I remember most clearly about the ceremony was hearing the words: Until death do us part.

They lodged in my brain to be dealt with at a later time.

Unbelievably much later.

Amos and I had argued about something and I thought to myself, *Drop dead, you prick,* and then suddenly my thoughts went to Eddie, whom I wished no harm.

"Jesus," I said suddenly, "what would happen to one of you if—"

"The doctors say different things, actually," Eddie said cheerfully.

119

"Like what?"

"Cut it out," Amos said. Before I'd been mad at him but now he was the one who was mad.

"I was just asking," I told him. "I never thought about it before."

"They agree," Eddie said, "that something would have to be done."

"Stop this conversation right now," Amos said. "Just stop."

Until death do us part.

We kissed our new husbands, then stood for a second like a snapshot in an album, a moment removed from everything that had gone before and all that would come after. The moment of record. We separated.

Help! Get me out of here!

No. Wait a minute, Nadine. You're being ridiculous. Nothing has changed.

Nothing has changed?

Nothing.

But now that I'm married what'll I do all day?

Same as before.

But what was that? I can't remember.

We all stood there a little embarrassed. Like strangers caught in a steambath during an air-raid drill.

I laughed. "I'm hungry."

Dianne smiled at me from that mountain of the gods where she'd always known she belonged even before she'd done this miraculous thing of growing a baby in her belly.

"We're not even having a wedding breakfast," I complained. "I mean, it's one thing to keep everything casual and another not to have a meal to eat."

I wanted a big bowl of Crunchy Granola but it hadn't been invented yet.

"Isn't anybody else hungry?"

"I could have some bacon and eggs," Eddie admitted.

"Good," I said. "I'm going to make a wedding breakfast." I would fill up myself and the house . . . the whole town . . . with food. "Bacon and eggs and . . . whatever else I can find. I'm going to make a FEAST!"

I invited the Baddelys to join us but they had a subsequent engagement. I took Di and the twins home and drove off to buy more stuff. I had decided that there couldn't possibly be enough food in the cabinets and refrigerator to quiet the ravening beast within me. Back home an hour later I made sourdough biscuits and steak and eggs and a ghastly punch with orange juice and ginger ale and some stale Chianti we had in the refrigerator, and when I was finished devouring the lion's share of that feast, I combined a big can of peanuts and a box of raisins in a bowl and began on that. Then I threw up and started all over again.

"I'm afraid you'll get sick, Nady," Dianne said tranquilly.

"I was sick before," I told her. "I'm fine now."

I ate a banana, an orange and a pear.

"Now what?" I asked. It just slipped out, before I knew what I was saying.

They stared at me. They didn't know what the hell I was making such a fuss about. All that had happened was that Di had closed up her apartment in New York and moved up her stuff. (They'd rented the California house without going back. Their old manager had taken care of sending them their clothes.) Nothing else had happened. NOTHING. I started trying to get them all upstairs to make love so I could get a baby, since it had become obvious to me in the few hours that I'd been a married woman that this was the way I was going to fill up the remainder of the life that yawned before me.

I yawned. "I'm sleepy."

Dianne smiled. "I'll bet you are. You could go into hibernation for the winter now."

Maybe that's what you'd like, I thought resentfully. I go to sleep for twenty years and you have the twins *and* the baby.

"I could dig an hour or two of hibernation," I said. "Especially if someone comes with me."

Dianne smiled. She had that fucking contented expression on her face. What did *she* need to go upstairs for? She was full.

121

The goddamn baby was making love to her, she didn't need any of us. I looked at the twins. They were willing but they were waiting to see how Dianne felt.

Jesus Christ, is this how it's going to be for the rest of my life? I can never do anything I want to do without dragging three other people along, often unwilling?

Not that I needed them to take a nap but taking a nap wasn't what I had in mind . . . except maybe a kid nap. Why couldn't I tell them that? Why couldn't I just say, Let's go upstairs and make me a baby?

Why on earth do you want a baby?

Because SHE has one and it's making her happy.

"You all go up if you want to," Dianne said. "I'm going to clean up the dishes and then maybe I'll come up in a while."

I was disconcerted. Since we'd been together we'd never made love apart. She was busy clearing dishes from the table. If she minded my bedding down with the twins when she wasn't there, it wasn't showing in her face.

"Okay."

Amos finished his coffee. They rose from the bench.

I had never realized how much effort was involved in their just getting up from a bench! Effort. Coordination. A signal had to go from one to the other, then they would get uncrossed from each other's legs, place their inside hands on the bench and push up. Why hadn't I ever noticed the little grunt Amos made from the exertion at that crucial moment when they pushed to rise? And why had I suddenly noticed it now, when I needed them so badly to make me into a mother?

I walked upstairs ahead of them. I took off my Rumanian peasant wedding dress and was about to take off my pants but felt constrained. I remember looking briefly around the room as though someone might be watching me. It was a pleasant room with floral wallpaper and now a huge, foam-rubber slab on a platform several inches off the floor.

"Mmm," I said when the men came up. "I can't believe how tired I am." I stretched out on the bed in what I hoped was a seductive position but I couldn't look at them. I kept wondering if Dianne was wondering what we were doing up here. They struggled out of their clothes, neatly hung up their dark blue shirts and pale blue suits. They couldn't wear ties, which got sidetracked by the joint. They performed each act together. Automatically. Always.

Well, naturally. How come it had never seemed weird to me before? And why was my mind doing this to me now? Maybe once they climbed into the big bed, the two of them with just me once again, all the rest of it would become irrelevant.

Except they didn't exactly climb into the bed, they sort of lowered themselves in a horribly awkward, careful, precoordinated way—like a crippled octogenarian dance team! I couldn't believe I'd never noticed that before! I closed my eyes so they couldn't see what I was thinking. They lay down next to me. I opened my eyes. Eddie was on his back, Amos on his side, propped up on his elbow, tilting somewhat toward me. Amos had a hard-on but Eddie didn't. As though they'd been to obedience school since the last time it was just the three of us in the sack. I felt like fondling Eddie to get him excited; I thought of Dianne and turned my back on both of them.

Someone was touching my hair. A hand was gently running up and down the arm I wasn't lying on. Who was it? Or was it both of them? In the days before Dianne I'd never worried about who was doing what to whom, they were just a mass of lovely spare parts. Dianne's presence had changed that. Now Dianne was even more than usually present because I had to conjure her presence when I was in danger of forgetting her rightful place in the puzzle.

So I turned away from them again, sulking.

"Is anything wrong?" Amos whispered.

"Yes, but don't ask me what because I don't know."

"Why don't you turn around?"

I turned. He smiled at me. I kissed him, feeling Eddie's breath in my ear. I went down on Amos, lying across both of them,

123

superconscious of Eddie as my arm curved around his penis, which was big and hard now. I started to alter my position so he could enter me from behind but then remembered that he wasn't supposed to father my children and turned so that Amos could get into me instead. I rolled over him so that I was again on my side and Amos came over me while Eddie stayed in back, the way it had once been often. I was just beginning to forget Dianne and enjoy myself when I realized that she'd come upstairs after all and was standing there watching us. Watching me with both of them. Holding her husband's penis! *Dianne, I didn't know what I was doing! I didn't mean to*— Maybe she could tell just by looking at me that it was Eddie I'd really liked from the beginning! In a spasm of guilt and confusion I squirmed out from between them just as Amos was coming, the result being that my new husband shot his first married load directly into his brother's belly button.

Oh, Jesus, I'd really done it! Blown the whole marriage. Gotten it off on the wrong . . . whatever.

God only knows how often they'd done it to each other before. It wasn't something they were ever willing to talk about. I think a lot of craziness about child sex had gone down in the state home, although I'm not sure where in the hierarchy of sin as it has been revealed to state home matrons jerking off your Siamese twin fits in.

I burst into tears.

"Nadine, what is it?" Amos asked. "What happened?"

I bawled uncontrollably. Well, maybe I wasn't really trying to control it. Through my heavy tears I watched Dianne watching me. Her expression had changed from disgust to curiosity. I didn't even want her to know that I wanted to get pregnant so how could I tell her that I was weeping my head off because my first few hundred babies lay gasping for air in Eddie's belly button and its environs?

Eddie reached for a tissue from the box on the night table—he could just barely touch it without making Amos move. He wiped off his stomach, then carefully bunched up the tissues and put

124

them under one of the pillows. Something about the gesture repelled me. Why hadn't I ever been repelled before by the way they automatically cleaned up after themselves all the time; the way they pushed the bench back under the dining table as they arose and never left up the toilet seat after they'd peed? They had been trained at an early age not to displease the women they lived with. I cried some more. By this time there was a lot of momentum behind it. Besides, if I stopped crying something worse might happen.

Dianne began to look really worried. Amos and Eddie were hovering as though they wanted to make me feel better but of course they couldn't do that without my cooperation and I wasn't cooperating. It was bad enough I'd married the crazy freak bastards, I wasn't going to cooperate with them, too. Dianne sat down next to me on the bed and held me, murmuring soft comforting words in my ear. I began to relax a little. She was lovely, so loving. I didn't have to understand the words, I was getting the music. I was so grateful to her for loving me in spite of everything, even if it was only my misery that was enabling her to love me. I was so unfair to Dianne most of the time. Why did I do that to her? Why couldn't I accept the fact that she was just another imperfect human?

"I really love you, Dianne," I burbled.

"I know, I know," Dianne said. "Sssssshhhhh."

I stretched back on the bed. I was exhausted. I didn't want to let go of Dianne's hand. With my left arm I reached across the men, my hand touching Amos's thigh. I felt unspeakably tender toward all of them.

"Why don't you lie down next to me?" I asked Dianne.

She took off her clothes and stretched out beside me. We had never all been naked together in the daylight since that first time at the pond. I kissed Eddie because he was closest to me, then I kissed Dianne, who had lain down beside me. How could I keep forgetting how much I loved her? She had changed my life. Opened my mind to places and ideas I hadn't known existed. It was because of Dianne that I was feeling so good now. It was because of all of them. What a beautiful and amazing thing we had done. I was enormously happy and excited. I closed my eyes. We all got tangled up, but in a fluid, easy way, like a kitten with a ball of wool in a slow-motion movie. Most of the time I didn't know who was where. I was so sleepy afterward, so contented. I'd lost all sense of time. My eyes closed.

When I awakened it was dark. The others were still asleep. Someone had covered me. I'd had some sort of pleasant, abstract kind of dream that I couldn't remember. I felt as if I were pregnant. I felt fulfilled. I could envision a pleasant life, here in this little town, in this pretty house, if we succeeded in buying it from Franklin and his wife. With a little effort it could be as lovely as any old Colonial that had ever graced the cover of *House & Garden*. We would have a garden, too, of course. Not just vegetables, like the natives, or flowers, like the summer people, but both. We would have gladiolus because I'd once seen in *National Geographic* photos of lovely little hummingbirds hovering over a row of gladiolus. We would have roses and magnolias and all sorts of West Coast vines that you never saw around here. (It wasn't until that winter that I would read enough to know why you never saw them outside of a tropical or semitropical climate.) I would cook a lot—marvelous lusty stews and crusty breads on checkered tablecloths. We would have wonderful, sturdy, secure boys and girls who, growing up in a warm, closely knit family, would be free of the fears and insecurities that had dogged me. Who would never know what it was to be alone and falling. We would have a collie like Lassie. I would undo my own childhood.

I was hungry. I would make some dinner and surprise the others when they came down. The room was cold. I put on jeans and a sweater and crept downstairs. I turned on the kitchen light. The kitchen looked a little strange and bare. It needed curtains at the window, although I hadn't noticed until now. I opened the refrigerator. In my orgasmic feast of several hours before I'd pretty well cleaned out what I'd bought in the morning but there

126

were a few eggs left, some milk, a hunk of cheddar and a sack of oranges. Amos and Eddie were addicted to oranges, which they'd never seen until they were seventeen years old. (And detested pasta, which they'd seen every day.) Cheese, eggs . . . I would make a soufflé. I'd never made a soufflé but it seemed like a good time to start. I'd never done the kind of cooking you needed recipes for. Time to learn. Also, a soufflé would be an excuse to turn on the oven and warm up the kitchen. By the time the soufflé was ready to be taken out of the oven, the room and I were warm, the table was set and the kitchen clean. The others were still asleep. I would carry the soufflé upstairs and awaken them with its wonderful, warm, cheesy smell. A perfect mountain of delight. But when I took it out of the oven it barely rose halfway up in the pot I'd used for a soufflé dish. It wasn't the kind of thing you woke people up for. Although it tasted good enough. I ate the whole thing, telling myself that I was eating for two. I continued eating for two until a week later when I got my period and began eating for four to ease the feeling of emptiness within me.

OCTOBER, November, December. I still couldn't conceive and Dianne didn't want to learn to drive while she was pregnant, so once a month, then once a week, I drove her up to her obgynoid in Hanover. The rest of the time I spent reading *House Beautiful* and redecorating the house, which we now owned, to have matching flowers on the walls, curtains and anything else I could find. Nothing by halves. The men said they loved it. Amos paid the bills without complaining (the last time). Dianne, the bitch, never said a word until I started talking about the last room, the bedroom adjoining ours. The room would be the Baby's and then the Babies', when there was another one. I'd assumed she was grateful to me for handling everything since she herself seemed inclined to do little but rest with her hands on her belly.

Then, one night as we sat at the dinner table and I began chattering about nursery cutouts, she said in the tiniest voice imaginable, her Please, Sir, Can I Have Some More? voice,

"Please Nady, do you think I could do just that one room? I'd like it to be a sort of retreat."

"Retreat?" I stared at her blankly. "From what?" Her due date was three months away. What was she talking about retreating from now?

"You know, just from all the . . ." She gestured vaguely around her. "You know we don't exactly have the same taste, Nady."

"Don't you like what I've been doing?" I asked incredulously.

"It's not that I don't like it, it's just—" That vague gesture again. The suggestion of having been overwhelmed.

"How come you said Mmm every time I asked whether you liked it?" Even as I asked the question I heard what Mmm sounded like for the first time. It didn't sound like No but it didn't sound like Yes, either.

She shrugged. "I didn't know what to say. You were having such a good time and I didn't want to spoil it."

I stared at her. My mouth was speechless; my eyes spoke tears.

"You see?" she asked softly. "You see how you react when I say anything?"

I looked at the men. They were eating. Neither of them appeared to be getting seasick.

"What do you mean, see how I react?" I had to yell to push sounds past the lump in my throat. "It's not the same as it would have been if you said it earlier."

"Yes, it is," she said philosophically, rubbing her fucking belly in a counterclockwise motion. "It's just the same."

"THAT'S NOT TRUE!" I'd thought for a while that I was standing on the earth just like everyone else and now it was turning out to be just the same as it had been a long time ago. I stood up and prowled around the kitchen like a frightened animal. I was not only barren, I was crazy. And tasteless. Maybe it was because I was crazy that I couldn't get pregnant. Maybe my craziness was the only baby I'd ever have!

"Don't you see, if you'd just let me know," I pleaded, "we could have compromised?"

She shook her head sadly. "I'm sorry, Nady, I don't want to upset you. But there was no way."

"Why not?" How could I not have sensed what was going on? I was so frightened. "Show me why not!" I waved my hands around the kitchen, at the wallpaper with its neatly labeled pictures of herbs and wild flowers, at the hutch full of gay pottery, at the dried Indian corn and flowers hung in various places, at the china canisters with their huge purple flowers preserved under glaze, at the pots and kitchen implements hanging all over the walls on mounts neatly made by Amos and Eddie. "Show me what you would have done differently in this kitchen!"

"Everything," she said softly. "It doesn't matter now, Nady. Please . . . I just would have done things differently, that's all."

I wilted. I sat down. I looked at my food. My appetite was gone for the first time since September. (It was just as well; Dianne had gained eighteen pounds during her pregnancy and I'd gained twenty.)

"Does anyone else have anything to say?" I asked, my voice tremulous now, my spirit broken. "Do *you* like the way the house looks?" I asked the men.

"We think it's beautiful," Amos said.

"How about you, Eddie?" I was down but not out. I wanted him to love it, too, so it would be all of us against her.

"It's okay," he said. He wasn't about to go one way or the other. I thought it was his best quality until that day, when I decided it was his worst.

"I don't understand," said Dianne, the treacherous, hypocritical, pregnant shit, "why it bothers you so much for me to do just one room."

"What bothers me isn't the room." Now I was quiet, too. "Do the room. Do the fucking room any way you want to, I wouldn't touch the room with a ten-foot pole. It's that you've been making a fool of me! Letting me go on and on about this gorgeous wallpaper and that stunning doohickey and thinking they were awful the whole time!"

"I didn't want you to be angry with me." Oliver Twistess again.

"AND TELL ME, DI, DID IT WORK?"

Pause. Then, "It did while you didn't know."

So she was making an airtight case for lying to me. The problem wasn't that she'd been lying to me before but that she was telling me the truth now.

I took the car keys and left the house without a coat on. It was the middle of a New Hampshire December. I didn't know where I was going but it turned out not to matter because a few minutes later I racked up the car on the metal rail bordering the ravine that ran along the ice-covered winding road out of Bootville.

I went to the nearest house, about half a mile down the road, and called the local garage. The guy who ran the garage came down with the sheriff, who was also the justice of the peace, Cuthbert Baddely. They hooked up the car to the tow truck and gave me a lift back to the house. When I walked in the men were watching television. Amos was also reading a book. Dianne wasn't visible. I didn't say a word about the car and nobody noticed that night that it hadn't returned to the driveway. Di turned out to be up in the little room already, arranging stuff, pulling boxes away from the walls for painting and so on. She began painting the next day and insisted upon doing most of the work herself although she had a huge belly by this time and could barely get close enough to the walls to touch them with the brush.

She painted the walls a pristine white. She and Eddie and Amos plastered them first so they were perfectly smooth. After painting the walls they scraped and bleached the floors and applied three coats of Fabulon. They built a crib because we only had a basket and she hadn't been able to find the kind of Scandinavian Modern job she wanted anywhere in New Hampshire. The crib was birch and nestled neatly in one corner of the room. In another was a simple bureau that she painted white. For curtains she used two bright serapes that her mother had given her when she came East; they'd been in a trunk since college and it hadn't occurred to her to suggest using them in connection with the decorating of the house. On the wall opposite the crib was a changing table or work desk or whatever, an unfinished but well-sanded pine board set on two white file cabinets. The chair she bought was a yellowish glove-leather swivel with a light wood back. Her obstetrician's nurse picked it up for her in Boston; there was nothing like it in New Hampshire.

The whole job took about two weeks and didn't really hit me until the day it was finished and I was invited in to see the final result. It was a retreat. A genuine fucking retreat. It worked. Far from the rest of the house, in feeling if not in fact. Far from me. Far from the world. My voice that wasn't ready to cave in so fast said it was pretty cold and bare for a baby's room but it didn't matter, the room wasn't for the baby it was for Dianne. It was a retreat and a reproach. It stood there in the midst of a large home cluttered with dark (sticky) wood, wildly flowering wallpaper, painfully intricate Oriental rugs and mantelpieces full of Christmas cards from freak agents and other people who sent Christmas cards, chastising the house and me for our messy, half-assed, capitalist sexuality. For our very existence.

My depression deepened. The holidays smothered but did not extinguish it. A bunch of Amos's and Eddie's circus friends, on their way down to Florida from Montreal, stayed with us for most of Christmas week. Dianne suffered a lot but I kept thinking the townspeople had to be enjoying it just a little. Serena and Herman, Sal and Evvie. Serena was having a crisis. She'd gone on a diet and lost so much weight she couldn't be the Fat Lady anymore but she still weighed 250 pounds so she wasn't slim, either. She worried about money constantly because Herman's job, cleaning up after the elephants, never seemed secure to her. She wanted either to lose more weight and be beautiful (she had quite a lovely face beneath the fat that was still on her) or gain back enough to be Fat Lady again. But when she tried to lose weight she felt as though she were starving and when she tried to gain weight she lost her appetite or felt sick to her stomach all the time. She thought of herself as being in some sort of limbo between two poles. She was depressed all the time now, she said, except when she had company.

She was a lovely, easy guest, as were all the others. They never assumed as did people of great beauty or charm that you might want to have them around just for the pure pleasure of it. They helped with the cooking, insisted on cleaning up afterward and never demanded special attention of any kind. What they did most of the time was to sit in front of the TV and drink beer. In addition to Serena and Herman there were Sal the Friendly Giant and his manager-girlfriend Evvie. Sal was not only eight feet tall but fairly wide, not fat but solid and bearlike, with a bit of a potbelly and bushy brown hair and a beard. He sat on a big cushion on the floor, his back against the wall, and smiled a lot. I was excited by him. By his size. I wanted to sit in his lap. I found myself thinking that I could get pregnant by a man like that, although I didn't for a minute consider it might be Amos's fault that I couldn't conceive. Evvie was a tiny, chubby, roly-poly, tough little broad who bossed Sal mercilessly, which he loved. He was most gleeful when she was giving him orders but he also took delight in being asked to do chores, particularly when it was a job only he, by virtue of his size and strength, could do. We were using more wood than we'd anticipated, for example. I was always cold and making fires in the woodstove, then Dianne would go away saying she couldn't stand the heat. (She hid most of the time they were there; they thought her very sweet and painfully shy.) Chopping wood wasn't one of the things the twins could do so we'd ordered more, then tried to get it split but couldn't find anyone to do the job. Sal went through the thick logs with one or two swings of the ax and after an hour and a half of his work we had enough to last beyond spring. He was also able to repair and tape for us some pipes that ran along the basement ceiling, a job I'd meant to do myself when I could get help dragging the big ladder down to the basement. Sal did it without a ladder, of course.

When they left I was colder than ever, partly because it was January.

Dianne was huge and hadn't been able to have sex since the end of December, her sixth month. Well, maybe if she'd really cared they could have found a way for a while longer, but she didn't seem to miss it, she was too absorbed in her belly, and she just sort of ceased participation. This put a damper on the rest of us, although I was not about to relinquish sex for the duration when I wanted so desperately to get pregnant. (Especially I wanted to have the seed in me before Dianne gave birth.) Anyway, Amos and I continued intercourse in a sort of dutiful way, seldom passionate enough to inflame Eddie's senses and make him miss what he was missing as he lay patiently waiting for us to finish. Dianne, on the other side of the big foam slab, was asleep or very quiet the whole time. I think she may really have been asleep; during her pregnancy she drifted in and out of sleep very much the way Amos and Eddie did, as though there were no barrier between the sleeping and waking states and no serious pitfalls on either side.

I asked Dianne if she thought she'd ever go back to the practice of law.

"Oh, Nadine," said her serenely pregnant highness, "how can I even think about that now?"

As though it were vulgar of me to have mentioned it.

But there I was without a baby and without anything else much to do, either. For a while I'd made a career out of fixing the house but even if it hadn't been pretty well done by now my pleasure in the job had been effectively destroyed by Dianne's distaste. I had nothing to *do!* Besides, I was *lonely*, a condition I'd never have thought possible in my present circumstances. But I felt isolated from the others. Amos and Eddie had each other and Dianne had her baby. The fact that Amos and Eddie didn't seem to take very much pleasure in having each other was irrelevant; a certain security stemmed from their togetherness. And Dianne's pleasure in her baby was so great as to virtually eliminate any need for other human contact. I'd try to start a conversation with her and she'd put her hands on her belly and say raptly, "Sssh, Nady—it's moving, do you want to feel?"

134

I woke up at three in the morning thinking they'd all vanished and left me in darkness. I was the last person on earth.

The other houses on our road were occupied by (1) the Bells, summer people from New Jersey who were retired, who came in June and left in September and talked to some of the older townspeople but not to us; (2) the Winthrops, a young family with a baby and a slightly older child, the mother of whom walked by our house every day on the way to the general store without ever letting her neck swivel even a fraction of an inch in our direction; (3) the Whites, a couple in their eighties, maybe nineties, who'd been born and raised in Bootville. They had children, grandchildren and great-grandchildren who visited. When I went to the general store I stopped to exchange a few polite words about the weather. She was in a wheelchair and he attended to her. Every morning, no matter what the weather, he came out to the porch to feed the birds, wearing a woolen bathrobe which was open in the front. If the sun was shining, then having put seed in the three birdhouses that were suspended from the porch overhang, he held his genitals up to the sun's warmth for a couple of minutes. Then he went back to the house.

I decided that if I hadn't conceived a baby or made a friend by fall then I would go back to school and get a degree. Then I decided to consult Dianne's obstetrician to find out why the God of Babies was so certain in advance that I'd be an awful mother that he was refusing to even give me a chance.

She seemed to be avoiding having me meet Dr. Miles even casually. At first I thought she was afraid I'd embarrass her by saying something outrageous or asking a dumb question. When we reached the parking lot of the hospital she'd dash out of the car with a few words about meeting me in the lobby in an hour. I wasn't to worry about being late, she didn't mind waiting.

"I think maybe I should make an appointment with Dr. Miles."
"What for?" she asked, looking absolutely alarmed.
"Well, I have to see *someone*," I said. I couldn't let her know

135

how badly I wanted a baby. "I haven't seen a gynecologist since I got my diaphragm."

"Why now?"

"Well," I said carefully, "it seems like a good time since I'm taking you up there every week, anyway. Maybe I'll ask him if he thinks it's okay for me to try to get pregnant."

Silence.

"Perhaps," I said, straight-faced, "you think he's not good enough to handle both of us at the same time."

"He can handle *anything*," she flashed back quickly, as though I'd just suggested that Jesus Christ wasn't such a hot carpenter. "He's *wonderful*. He's the *best*—" She stopped suddenly, confused by her own vehemence. "I just— I just—"

"You just don't want to share him with me."

"You make everything sound so sinister, Nady."

"It is sinister," I said. "If he's the best doctor around why shouldn't I have him, too? You're not his only patient, after all. It's not like sharing a husb—" Now *I* was confused.

She pounced on it in her mousy way.

"You see, Nady? Do you see what it is?"

"Huh? Do I see what *what* is?"

"We're so inbred," she said. "We do everything together. We need to make separate lives for ourselves, to have something to do with different people."

"By the time I'm seeing him regularly," I pointed out, "you won't be seeing him anymore."

Silence. Bitterness. Quivery mouth. "Do whatever you want to do, Nadine. I won't stop you."

I was too much aware of being in competition with her to think of looking for another motive in her anxiety to keep me away from him. But even had my brain been working from a better vantage point I'm not sure it would have occurred to me that any apparently sane woman would've gotten this far into her pregnancy without telling her doctor that she was married to Siamese twins.

Dianne said she didn't want the men to come with us when I took her to Hanover for the delivery. They seldom came with us for any reason and Dianne was concerned that their presence in Hanover would create a commotion that would be bad for the baby.

"Bad for the baby?" I blinked. I could've understood if she said she wouldn't dig a bunch of freak-lovers trying to get into the hospital, but how could it affect the baby?

"Babies," Dianne said, calm and unequivocal, "are very sensitive to everything that goes on around them."

"So'm I," I said. "And so are Amos and Eddie." Maybe. "Maybe they'll be hurt, being treated like some kind of freaks that can't even be around to see their own baby."

"It's not *their* baby," she pointed out patiently. "It's *Eddie's* baby. Besides, I talked it over with them."

"YOU DID? WHEN I WASN'T THERE?"

"It was a coincidence, Nady. It just happened to come up."

"Oh? Who just happened to bring it up?"

"I don't remember."

Hah.

"There's something very weird about this," I said slowly.

"Oh, my God, Nady . . ."

We were both always saying My God. That was the day I decided she thought he was really hers.

"I mean," she said, "it was basically between Eddie and me. Amos wouldn't have been there either, if they hadn't happened to be . . . I mean, he's not someone I talk to, particularly. Not someone I ever would've discussed it with if—"

"What are you saying?" I must have been wild-eyed. "What the hell are you saying?"

She clutched at her belly.

"What is it? Why are you doing that?"

"Nothing." She grimaced. "I felt . . ." Another grimace.

I was seized with dread. Her due date was two weeks away but I'd heard plenty of stories about wrong due dates. My father's sister Marlene had given birth to a ten-pound baby during a snowstorm in Minnesota six weeks before the date her doctor had told her she was due. It was snowing heavily now, in March, but Dr. Miles had told Dianne not to worry. First time mothers, he said, always got to the hospital too early. No amount of my talk was going to convince Dianne that it had ever happened otherwise.

I watched her for more spasms. If I was causing them I wanted to stop. I was frightened to death of having to deliver a baby on the back seat of the car. I had already arranged with the Hanover Inn that we would stay there once the doctor felt Dianne was close.

"Are you all right?" I asked when a couple of minutes passed without another grimace.

She nodded.

"Those weren't labor pains, were they?"

"I think they were false."

"How can you tell the false from the real?"

"I told you to read the book, Nady. I don't understand why you won't read the book."

"Why should I, Dianne? After all, this is between you and Eddie."

Silence. Another spasm. A spasm of silence.

"I'm pretty sure it's what they call false labor."

I smiled sarcastically. "Maybe it's a false pregnancy."

I walked down to the public phone booth in front of the general store and called Dr. Miles. His voice was deep and soothing and when I told him who I was and that I was anxious about Dianne he said that by all means we should have a talk. Perhaps the next day.

"Would you mind if I just called Dr. Miles to ask him a few questions about your delivery? About getting you to Hanover, and so on?"

She lost the little color that was normally in her face.

138

"I won't do it if you don't want me to," I lied quickly.

"I don't." Just as quickly.

I don't know what made me ask next, "Di? Would he know who I was if I called?"

"What do you mean?" She was stalling.

"Just what I asked."

"Of course he knows."

"Knows what?"

"That I have a friend who's going to take care—who's going to drive me to the hospital, and so on."

"A friend."

She nodded.

"What else?"

She couldn't evade it anymore but she couldn't say it, either.

"He knows . . ." Her eyes filled and the tremble came to her voice for the first time in many months. "He knows that you're married to my husband's twin brother."

Fortunately I was so appalled that I couldn't even yell at her. This was the person who was going to provide the sanity in my marriage! The mistress of the ground rules! I turned away from her, a caldron of so many emotions that I couldn't deal with any one of them.

She knew.

"It has no genetic importance," the trembly voice pleaded to my back. "The twins thing does, but not the link."

I couldn't answer.

"I've read every study in existence. When you drop me off in Hanover, half the time that's what I'm doing." Then she recited chapter and verse, her voice getting firmer and clearer as she went deeper into the studies that claimed there were no known instances of successive generations of Siamese twins. But of course she'd told me that a long time ago. I knew she'd checked out the whole number before she got herself knocked up. It wasn't the genes or the studies or the risks that were gnawing at my brain but the fact that she was making a dirty secret out of our lives. I could understand why she'd never told her parents. I wasn't sure

I'd have told my own. There were plenty of things about yourself you weren't exactly ashamed of but you still didn't want your parents to know. But not telling her obstetrician . . . Week after month she'd talked to this man, tiptoeing around the central fact of our lives like a devoted scoutmaster who just happened to have a record for child molesting.

"Why don't we forget it, Dianne?" I finally said, so weary that at that moment I thought I might sleep through the following day and never go to see Dr. Miles. "Why don't we forget I ever asked?"

"I suppose it seems funny to you that I'm here," I said to Dr. Miles, who had white hair and a golfing tan. At the moment it seemed funny to *me*. I couldn't remember why I'd called him originally. "I don't know anything about babies, but I feel responsible . . ." I heard myself and stopped. Dianne had made me anything *but* responsible. "At least I'm responsible for getting her here safely, and so on."

He was polite if not friendly. He gave me the averages on first labor and mentioned having recommended to Dianne that since finances weren't a problem, if she appeared to be very close after an examination she might stay at the inn rather than risk the trip from Bootville, which was over an hour in good weather.

"I guess that's why I'm uneasy," I told him. "She didn't say a word about the inn. I suggested it."

He was silent. Waiting.

"Is there anything else I should know?" I asked. "To help her?" I meant it. The jealous anger and frustration had vanished as I talked to this professional person who seemed to think I wasn't crazy to be there.

"What kind of thing did you have in mind?" he asked.

His tone was utterly neutral, his face expressionless.

He was playing poker.

He knew!

After all, why would he be playing poker if he didn't know?

I felt relieved but then confused. And maybe a little angry. I decided to take a chance.

140

"I guess I'm more concerned about what *you* don't know than what *I* don't know," I said.

He nodded but his expression didn't change.

"But now I realize," I said slowly, "you do know, you've known all along. That's the only reason you're talking to me. Doctors don't usually just let a friend come to talk about their patients . . . right?"

"That is correct."

"How did you find out?"

He shrugged. Amos and Eddie never shrug, I thought to myself, and it had the weight of an important discovery but I forgot about it immediately.

"It wasn't a question of finding out," he said. "You're very well known; I should say *they* are, particularly in the state of their birth. The first time I took a history and gave it to my nurse she recognized the names. And if we hadn't been sure the twin history would have told us. They have extensive medical histories, as you must know, both here and at Boston Children's Hospital."

I felt spooky. All those people who didn't look at us or talk to us knew who we were anyway.

"You never mentioned any of this to Dianne."

He was silent.

"Do you think that was wise?"

I had hit him below the MD. The suggestion of a sneer played at the corners of his mouth.

"Are you asking me, Mrs. uh-Smith, if I believe that I am acting in a manner injurious to my patient?"

"Oh, no," I assured him hastily. "Not at all. I just—" Tears, the kind of tears I'd envied Dianne for producing so easily, came to my eyes. "Please understand . . . , I haven't known what to do about this whole . . . it wasn't my place to interfere or force the issue but . . . but . . ." The tears flowed rapidly now although somewhere in the back of my mind I kept asking myself what the hell I was doing. Wherefrom came the implicit lie that it was Dianne's concealment of the facts that had been troubling me all those months when the truth was that all I wanted was to have my own baby?

"Hysteria won't help us right now, Mrs. Smith," Dr. Miles assured me.

I stared at him. The tears stopped. If he thought this was hysteria what would he think about ten minutes in my house on the right day? I began to dislike him.

"After all," he went on, "the matter of concern is Mrs. Smith's health and welfare, isn't that so?"

I nodded. If it wasn't it should be.

"And the fact is that she is in excellent hands. Receiving the best possible medical care. The entire staff is familiar with the family medical history, to the extent that it's known, at any rate. There is no indication that this pregnancy involves twins; what we seem to have in there is one normal-size fetus with a normal heartbeat, but we are prepared for the possibility that this will not be the case and we are equipped to deal with the entire range of abnormalities."

I stopped crying and stared at him. I didn't like him any more than I had a minute before but I would readily have put my life in his hands. A man who was prepared to deal with any possibility without even knowing what the possibilities were! Who could ask for anything more in a doctor? In a human? A man who had charted the still unknown?

Dr. Miles perceived that his doctor magic had worked and he smiled.

"So," I said, "it doesn't matter that she doesn't know."

"That is correct."

"I wish I didn't know either," I said wistfully.

He wasn't interested. He was ready to terminate the interview. He stood up. I stood up. I thanked him for his time. He said that if I had any questions I shouldn't hesitate to call him.

I drove back to Bootville at about ten miles an hour because it had begun snowing again and my head was considerably more fucked up than it had been an hour before.

BUT when she finally went into labor, Dianne got hysterical and I was calm. We were in Bootville, not Hanover. Dr. Miles had examined her two days before and said she was nowhere near beginning; the baby had dropped but she wasn't even slightly dilated.

Every evening we watched television, Amos and Dianne reading at the same time, Eddie and I glued to whatever crap was on. Dianne frequently looked up as though she were about to ask us to turn off the set but then never did it for fear her application for sainthood would get shuffled to the bottom of the pile.

Her bag of waters burst and she burst into tears simultaneously, crying, "It's happening, Nady, it's happening! Help me!"

It was snowing out but strangely that didn't frighten me. Dr. Miles had said we'd have hours to get to the hospital and the reality of the snow wasn't nearly as upsetting as the fantasy of dense, white, impenetrable places had been. The fact was that the roads were kept in pretty decent condition and I was accustomed to driving them by now.

I picked up the phone and called the hospital. I told the nurse Dianne had gone into labor and I was bringing her up. She said she would call the doctor but just to make sure I called the doctor's house and got him away from his corned beef and cabbage. I told Eddie and Amos I'd call them when there was news and not to worry. I wasn't worried myself, I was utterly calm. Dianne was weeping uncontrollably. I got her overnight bag and our coats. I helped her into her coat then told her to sit in the warm kitchen while I got the car engine warmed up. I made the men sit with her. When the car was ready I came back and led her out to the car, my arm around her. The roads were bad; it had been snowing for less than two hours and the plow hadn't come through yet. I drove slowly and carefully; I had no chains but my snow tires were new and good. Once or twice I asked Dianne if she was having labor pains but the way she responded—"No, no, Nady, I'm not feeling a thing"—was somehow a denial rather than an answer, so I stopped asking. She gave birth to a baby girl twenty minutes after we got to the hospital, having had no anesthetic until the last minute, doubtless because she had no labor pains to speak of. After I heard I went out and had dinner. Two dinners. Then I called Amos and Eddie and told them the news.

"Gee," Eddie said, "that's great. We're a father."

I went to the inn, registered for the night and fell asleep with my clothes on.

I was astonished by the strength of my own instant love for Dianne's child. I was grateful, consciously grateful, that my mixed feelings toward Dianne and her pregnancy hadn't carried over to this tiny creature, bright pink and quite bald with tiny—later large—dark eyes and arms and legs that waved wildly as soon as the blanket that confined them was removed.

Dianne wasn't all that interested in the baby. Childbirth, the doctor told me and I kept reminding myself, was an exhausting experience. She did give her a name, apparently planned long

144

before. Carlotta. "Carlotta, the princess of New Hampshire," I said with a smile, but Dianne accepted my words while sifting out the ironic content.

She talked to the doctor, in front of me and without apparent shame, about her husband, a person I'd never met. She'd asked him not to come since Nadine was there anyway and his work would suffer. He was a wonderful man, wise and strong and loving, who worked as a carpenter rather than earn an enormous amount at other unspecified enterprises because then he could stay home close to his wife . . . and now their first child. The father of them all. The father of the whole fucking country, to hear her talk. I was frightened by the scope of the lie but even more by the fact that her guard was down with me. If she wasn't on guard with me then something she needed to survive wasn't there. I told the doctor that I was really worried about Dianne; something worse than plain exhaustion seemed to be going on. He was irritable and evasive, as though in delivering a normal baby for her he'd done as much as anyone could demand of him in a lifetime. He had to have known what postpartum depression was; it is still totally beyond me to fathom why he didn't mention it to me. Maybe he thought like any ordinary dumb mortal that he could keep her from one by not acknowledging its existence. Maybe he was more scared of the whole subject than I was.

Anyway, I'm not sure that anything could have prepared me for the lengthy pall that settled over our lives.

Dianne couldn't breast-feed the baby. She didn't seem to have enough milk. When I asked if she didn't want to discuss the problem with Dr. Miles she replied in the most listless voice imaginable that it probably didn't pay to bother since if she went back to work the baby would have to be switched to a bottle anyway. I was dumbfounded. Standing there, holding to my fleshy but milkless breasts her one-week-old baby, I stared at this woman who not a month earlier had said that going back to work at any point was the furthest thing from her mind.

"Work?" I echoed.

"Well," she said, still listless but eminently reasonable, "after all, I'll have to go back sooner or later."

I was never angry with her anymore, of course. The smugness, the queenly certainty that had irritated me so were gone. It seemed incredible that I should have ever been awed or angered by this sad and fragile person. I felt guilty. As though the way I'd behaved toward her during her pregnancy had affected what happened later on. I cared for Carlotta as though she were my own and then felt more guilty because in my fantasies she was.

The twins seemed pretty much oblivious to what was going on with Dianne. Through Mrs. Singleton, who ran the general store, they'd landed their first large job—the wiring for a modern home summer people were building a few miles outside of town—and they were putting in six full days a week over there. It was mud season by now. In the morning I would bundle up Carlotta and drive the men over to Sudbury Road, not wanting to leave her "alone" in the house even if Dianne was awake, for Dianne didn't notice when she cried. I'd drop off the men with the lunches I'd prepared in the morning with Carly on my shoulder, then in the evening I'd fetch them. They were good enough about helping with Carly when they were around if I asked for help but if I didn't it seldom occurred to them to do anything. Obviously I was the one who ran to her first when she cried; it was easier for me than for them. On the rare occasion when I was too busy to stop for her bottle I would set her with the men, in one of their arms or between them on a pillow, and they would be quite contented to give her the bottle. I was the only one who ever diapered her. I was also doing the cooking and cleaning for everyone. I didn't mind that, either. I had more energy than ever before. My eyelids snapped open at Carly's first cry in the night. I carried her down with me to the cold kitchen and held her under my robe while I warmed her bottle. Nor did I make her wait in the daytime. It seemed to me now, as I watched Carlotta, who stopped crying at the moment she was picked up, who was responsive to virtually any distraction, who seemed from the first so amenable

146

to reason, so willing to be happy, that had I been treated as a child the way I treated her, I would surely have grown up to be a different and much better person. Sometimes I wished my own mother could be there to see my warmth, my competence, my ease with this baby. I would have dialogues with her in which everything was on my side until she pointed out that it wasn't as if Carlotta were my own. I would get angry with her and then my anger would turn to confusion because she was dead.

The mud season ended and Dianne was still spending most of her time in bed. She didn't want to be anywhere near a doctor; I drove Carlotta to her checkups. The men finished the job on Sudbury Road and painted the outside of our house. It took them six weeks because of the obvious difficulties, some of which they solved by working on heavy aluminum ladders that they'd attached to each other with chains. I began taking Carlotta for walks in a carriage and the other young mother on the road finally spoke to me. (See how easily I still fall into it—the other young mother?) Anyway, her younger child was only a year older than Carlotta and she was willing to be a tiny bit friendly now that we'd done something recognizably of this world like having a child. I felt it necessary to make excuses for Dianne, who wasn't there with her own child, and was astounded to discover that no excuses were necessary; Laureen claimed that she had never noticed that of the four outsiders who'd bought the old Nye house, one of the women had been pregnant while the other one now had a child.

"Are you serious?" I asked. "You didn't realize it was Dianne who was pregnant?" My mind, full of problems like how I could talk Dianne into seeing some kind of shrink because it was three months now that she'd been like this and I was beginning to get scared, could not cope with this one as well.

"We knew it was one of you," she said calmly. She had short brown hair and a pale face, bony but pretty. At least in the city, with makeup and a cleaning lady, she'd have been pretty. In Bootville she looked haggard, older than her twenty-three years.

147

"Didn't you care which it was?" I asked.

She shrugged. "No business of mine."

Each man is an island. But of course I always loved to swim.

"What about the men?"

"What about 'em?"

"When they first came here . . . I mean, I know everyone takes them for granted now, but what did you think when they first came? How did you feel about them?"

"Feel?" she said dubiously. "Well, you don't feel . . . it's not as if they was kin . . . but I remember . . . you could see they were close."

I thought it would be good if I could take a walk with Dianne. Get her out of the house for a while. Share my Laureen conversation with her. We shared very little these days. Not animosity. Or sex. Our sex life was virtually nonexistent. Dianne was too listless and somehow the rest of us . . . Well, for one thing, I didn't care so much. I was too wrapped up in Carlotta to think about having a baby of my own.

Dianne was sitting in the kitchen near the woodstove, as though it were the dead of winter, reading the Keene paper.

"It's warmer outside in the sun than in here," I said. "Maybe we could take a walk together."

"Mm," she said. "That's all right."

"I'd really like to," I said.

"I think I'm too tired."

What she was reading was the employment section.

"Maybe you should go to the doctor," I suggested gently.

"All I really need is to get out of here every day," she said, her forlorn manner suggesting that the powers that had brought her to Bootville and forced her to have a baby would also now keep her from leaving. "To get a job."

"How are you going to get a job if you don't even have enough energy to take a walk?"

"If I could get out of here," she said, "I'd have the energy."

"Then go," I said. "Get a job, if that's what you want."

A flicker of light in her eyes. The first.

"Do you mean it, Nady?"

"Sure." Very casual but my heart was thumping as though something strange or important were happening. "Why not?"

"What about the baby?"

"What about her?"

"You won't mind taking care of her all day?"

Was she serious? What was I doing now?

Of course she was serious. What Dianne was doing was very seriously rewriting history before it happened so it wouldn't be necessary to rewrite it later on. She was planting in the ground the seed that would come to full flower years later when she and Carlotta, joined against me in argument about who did what to whom (guess), will tell me in almost identical words that I know perfectly well that Dianne only went to work when Carlotta was an infant because we needed the money. And I, depending on my mood, would point out either wearily or furiously that money was never a topic in our household until long after Dianne returned to work.

"I'm taking care of her already," I pointed out. Then, afraid of sounding harsh (as in the Truth Is Harsh), I added, "Remember, there'll be three of us here a lot of the time. I'll have as much help as I need."

She burst into tears. "You're being so wonderful, Nady." Actually, burst is too strong a word for anything Dianne did during that year. She spilled. She spilled for so long that I got more frightened than I'd been before. I think I expected to see her cave in with the loss of the liquid. She was terribly thin, anyway, although her waist hadn't gone back to its old tiny size, a fact on which she often commented when she passed a mirror. A sigh. Her waist was gone. *Dianne* was gone, but that she didn't seem to have noticed. It was spooky. I would be *glad* for her to go away every day and leave me with my darling baby. That was the truth of the matter. Having Dianne around was a weight on my heart

149

and mind. When I was taking the greatest pleasure in Carlotta I was most aware of the pathetic figure in bed upstairs who couldn't enjoy Carlotta or anything else.

I thought about calling her parents but feared she would think this the ultimate betrayal; if she got better she would never forgive me. She had written to tell them she was married and was going to have a baby but hadn't told the truth about the twins, and didn't believe that her parents suspected the truth. (She was wrong, of course.) I tried talking to Eddie and Amos about her condition but they didn't seem to think anything was particularly amiss. Nobody actually consulted psychiatrists; they were just these names that were beginning to have columns in the ladies' monthlies. I talked to a local general practitioner who looked at me as though I were crazy when I suggested that there was something abnormal about being permanently depressed. I tried Amos again but he still thought I was making a big fuss over nothing. Just give her some time.

Time.

Time passed.

Now that Dianne was free to look for a job I'd anticipated her attacking the classified ads with new vigor, beginning to write letters. Instead she stopped reading the papers altogether.

Summer. I worked in the garden with Carlotta tied to my back, like an Indian woman. Eddie and Amos did best in the garden in facing, squatting position, working parallel rows. Dianne sat in the sun on a plastic chaise in the front yard where she wouldn't have the effort of seeing us work. She'd become convinced that she had a deathly pallor and needed to collect enough sunshine so she'd have some to store for the winter ahead. She was talking about the winter ahead before the annuals began to flower.

Only in the garden could I forget her. In the garden there was the sun and the dirt and Carlotta and me. When the sun got too hot I put Carlotta on a cotton blanket under an apple tree. We'd set the garden fairly close to the house so the men wouldn't have to walk too far to get to it. By now I was so accustomed to the way they walked that I often forgot why we'd done it and wished we had left more space for lawn.

In general, I took the men for granted. With Carlotta I had the intensity which had once pervaded my vision of them.

When we finished in the garden I would fetch Carlotta from under her tree and bring her down to the pond to wash up. In the hottest weather I'd lay her right down at the edge of the water, which lapped her toes, and she would squiggle around enough to see me—or the three of us, if the men had come down —swim. Once I swam under the water as far as I could go, almost to the edge of the pond, and came up to find her meeting my eyes. Just staring at me, holding her own bottle of apple juice and examining my face as though it were the world. I wondered if she noticed when I wasn't wearing my glasses. I got them from the grass and put them on and she grabbed at them, trying to pull them off, but couldn't quite make it. Another time I came out to find her happily playing with her own shit. Examining it on her fingers, smushing them together so it slid out between them. She was naked. It was an idyllic sight. When the flies started buzzing around I picked her up and brought her into the pond, holding her close and dipping her. I remember making some joke about this shitty baby to Eddie and Amos but the joke stemmed from embarrassment at my own pleasure in the scene, not from anything that was really funny.

It was the middle of winter before Dianne started reading the classifieds again. She celebrated Carlotta's first birthday by walking to the general store to get a loaf of bread and pick up the mail. Carly was fourteen months old and taking her first tentative steps when Dianne began the driving lessons which were the prerequisite for her finding a job.

It wasn't easy.

This was 1962 and the OEO programs hadn't begun yet. Organizations like New Hampshire Legal Assistance, their equivalent of the Legal Aid Society, a natural for Dianne, wouldn't be in existence for another couple of years. When she finally got a job with the Division of Welfare in Concord, helping draft rules and regulations on who would receive AFDC (Aid to Families with

Dependent Children), it was through acquaintances of friends of friends of her parents. (She was ashamed to tell me this and I only learned much later that she'd been in touch with them. I doubt that anything but getting a job would have been important enough to make her ask for their help.) Anyway, the job was in Concord—a grueling trip of about an hour and a half each way —but by this time she was glad to get anything and she minimized the difficulties, claiming that the trip helped her think about what she needed to do each day.

The next year or two were fairly smooth. Fifty weeks of the year Dianne went off to work. Occasionally during the winter, when the side roads were bad, she stayed over in Concord at the home of one of the secretaries in her office.

The twins sold the house in Beverly Hills, which had become more and more of a problem, but by the time they'd paid off the huge mortgage and the lawyer's fees, they realized something like $20,000 from the sale. We thought of that money as a buffer (I could never think easily about using the money from my parents) and most of the time lived on what Dianne made and what the twins earned, the latter amounts being erratic. In addition to carpentry they did seasonal work like picking apples. They did some plumbing. Gradually they acquired a reputation in the towns around Bootville because they were the only ones who would come quickly when someone called with, say, a plumbing emergency. Or who'd fix a sick car by noon if it was dropped off in the morning. (Our garage was practically buried by this time in a pile of old sinks and car parts.) They didn't mind working day and night as long as they could rest frequently between jobs. If they happened to be going in Dianne's direction she might drop them off on her way to Concord in the morning, but that was seldom. The rest of the time I drove them, strapping Carlotta into the car seat in the back. They would call to let me know when they were ready to come home. Dianne had a Volkswagen Beetle; the rest of us used a van.

We talked about the weather and about where and when the men would be working. Dianne never mentioned the office. It seemed to be a condition of her functioning that she keep her two lives separate. Or maybe I should say her life and a half, since she came home at seven or later in a state of exhaustion and seldom did more than eat dinner, read for a while and go to bed. We had a sex life again although it was somewhat lackadaisical.

As Carlotta grew further away from her first year the urge to have my own baby—another baby, I almost said—reasserted itself, and I was pretty turned on during those times of the month when I thought I could get pregnant. But I wasn't nearly as anxious as I'd once been and it's a funny truth that when I finally did get pregnant I was more than a week late for my period before I noticed the date.

Anyway, between Dianne's noncommunication and the men's lack of imagination and the fact that there was nothing in my own life to talk about, our conversation seemed to be competing with my womb for some kind of sterility award. I tried to get the men to talk about the people they worked for but they never had anything to say except that so-and-so couldn't be relied on to get materials or someone else paid his bills faster than most. If I asked whether they liked one of those people Eddie generally said, "Sure, why not?" while Amos said, "No, why should we?" or failed to reply at all. Once, desperate for some fleshy chunk of conversation to bite into, I asked about their dreams. But their dreams, when they weren't simply of colors and shapes, tended to be series of pictures or events out of real life, devoid of meaning or affect. Like pot pictures. They woke up in the same mood as they went to bed. I talked to Carlotta all the time and pretended to myself that she understood me.

Her first words were Mama and Dada. Dianne noticed that Mama was me and Dada was her and got upset. I understood how she felt so I made it a point, when Dianne was arriving home at night and even at other times, to say, "Look, Carly, here's your mama." Dianne became Awmama and I remained Mama. Dianne experimented with small doses of affection to cure her child of this misconception. She took Carlotta on her lap for a few minutes before bedtime and then sometimes read her a story. If I came into the room she would frequently say, "Look, Carlotta, here's Nadine." Carlotta continued to call me Mama. For a long time she hadn't had a name for Eddie or Amos. If she wanted them to give her something she said, "Me-me." Now they became Deedee or Damo but she never attempted to differentiate between them. Her wisdom being greater than ours.

It would be difficult to exaggerate the closeness of Carlotta and me until the time that she was about two and a half years old. People in town—Laureen and Mrs. Singleton and so on—said she even looked more like me than like Dianne, and I was never loath to believe them. She spoke beautifully, in an accent closest to my own Western one but here and there with some verbal twist out of Dianne's Manhattan youth or an uh-yuh from her New Hampshire fathers. Dianne grew attached to Carlotta in direct proportion to Carly's age and ability to speak. By the time her daughter was two and a half years old Dianne was quite genuinely fond of her. At that time I became pregnant.

It's only by an extreme effort of will, by reminding myself that lies will make it worse, that I can force myself to tell you what happened next.

WHAT did she do? you ask yourself. Pain is leaping from the page; what the fuck did the crazy broad do?

What she did, this woman whom I have briefly pushed into the third person so that I can bear to talk about her, was to gradually turn off, and eventually turn against, this child whose existence for more than two years had been the center of her own.

At first even the Stern Old Judge couldn't have proved anything. He might not even have thought to try. He'd just have noticed this woman whose face had once lit up at the sight of "her" baby . . . child . . . this same woman becoming more and more self-absorbed. Staring endlessly at her face in the mirror. And at her stomach. The Judge might've said it was the natural thing for her to do, become absorbed in her own pregnancy. He might also have pointed out that the child's own mother was becoming more and more affectionate to her so that the child's need of her surrogate mother was diminishing.

155

Would the Judge have raised an eyebrow upon observing that the woman who had once carefully set aside choice morsels and desserts for that little girl now gobbled them up before they got to the table? After all, pregnant women get hungrier, don't they? Unless they're Dianne? He might even have stretched a point, if he weren't feeling too stern after the baby's birth, and claimed that the mother's extreme caution in the presence of the older child, her tendency to watch Carlotta as though Carlotta might do irreparable damage to her precious baby, had a certain reality basis. Children have been known, after all, to do funny-horrible things to siblings. A little anxiety is permitted. But there's no way the Judge, if he had two eyes and a brain, could have failed to be dismayed by the way the woman looked at Carlotta when the once-loved child entered the room—as though she were watching the first large insect walking on the moon.

The woman's arms tighten around the baby who nurses at her bosom. The three-year-old Carlotta climbs up on the bed, stares intently at the nursing baby.

"Can I do that when he's finished?" asks the big-eyed dark-haired, dimple-chinned little girl.

"No," says the woman, looking at the baby. "That's just for babies."

"Can I have a taste on my finger?" presses the child, who has been allowed to sample beer and wine in that fashion.

"Don't be silly," says the woman, whose Mother Earthiness had once come so effortlessly as to let her believe that she had been the earth's model instead of vice versa.

"Why not?" asks the child, who has not resigned herself to this new, unpleasant state of affairs and in point of fact never will.

"Where's your mother?" asks the charming woman. "Isn't she home yet?"

. . . I was scared. I was afraid to give Carly a little because she would want more and if I gave her more, if I gave her what I had given her before, I could have little left for this child that was growing first inside me, then outside me. I felt wonderful during

156

my entire pregnancy but after all, so had Dianne. Not to speak of my mother. My mother had been physically destroyed, or so it was writ in the family mythology, by childbirth and motherhood, while Dianne had given in to forces in her mind that might or might not be natural and for a solid year had seemed unlikely ever to rise to the surface of life again. Dianne had regained her equanimity only by running daily from the demands of her child which I'd happily met. But now there was a new child with new demands and Carly was still totally dependent on me. Not to speak of my other obligations. Not to speak of feeding four adults and taking care of a home and providing transportation for the male occupants. I needed Carly to grow up fast to help me and instead my very pregnancy seemed to make her go backward in time.

When I felt the first labor pains I brought Carly out to the men, who were working in the shop in the garage, and drove myself to the hospital in Hanover instead of calling Dianne home or asking one of the neighbors to take me. (I had a different doctor, a handsome young snot who was totally indifferent until he knew who I was, and then became solicitous in a way I found intolerable.) My childbirth was lengthy and difficult. Philip lay sideways and it was hell getting him straightened out, the pain was endless and the drugs only put my surface to sleep; underneath I was feeling it the whole time. I never told all this to Dianne. I was annoyed at the facts of my delivery, embarrassed by my body's refusal to cooperate with the Mother Earth myth. Who the fuck was Dianne to give birth to a baby as though she were dropping a pear from a tree?

The week that I was in the hospital with Philip, Dianne took Carly to New York to meet her grandparents for the first time. The meeting was a success. Her parents obviously marveled, she said, that she and this strange man she had married had managed to produce such a beautiful, brilliant child. Her parents hadn't suggested coming to New Hampshire to meet Edward or asked why he hadn't accompanied her and Carly to New York.

Dianne was particularly loving to Carlotta now but Carlotta was more interested in being with me and the constantly nursing baby than in hearing Dianne read Little Bear stories or receiving other forms of endearment from this relative stranger in her life.

"The one thing that has to happen," I told the men, "is that you have to keep her away from me more of the time." If Carly was present when I was nursing, her face face full of need, I got tense and Philip ended up being colicky. Still, there was a limited amount the men could do. They ended up hanging around when I was feeding Philip because that way it was a little easier for me to tolerate Carly and it was nearly impossible to keep her in the shop against her will.

Anyway, Amos also liked to be present when I was nursing Philip, although Eddie was indifferent and sometimes a little impatient during our milk marathons. When I had my six-week checkup and we were cleared for lovemaking again, Amos displayed a new and strong interest in my breasts and made it necessary for us to invent whole new ways of doing things to accommodate this interest. It was as though Philip had awakened a thirst that slumbered within him. He felt no embarrassment at all about sucking from my breasts what was left at night of the milk my body was producing for his son. Sometimes I nearly went crazy with excitement as I waited for him to finish sucking and get into me. Not that he didn't want to; he just couldn't do both at the same time.

I weaned them both when Philip was six months old and then our sex life got back to normal.

But the situation with Carlotta became increasingly difficult.

I was very absorbed in my beautiful boy baby and didn't want to be bothered by her. On the other hand, what were the alternatives? I couldn't ask Dianne to stay home. By this time there were six mouths in the house to be fed and we needed the money she earned if we weren't going to eat up our savings. Besides, Dianne was in good shape but that shape was obviously contingent upon being allowed to continue work, which was central to her life now. If I'd developed considerable resentment over her ability to drive away five mornings a week from Real Life and Its Problems, I had no illusion that matters would be better if she stayed home. As a matter of fact, Saturdays and Sundays were often the worst part of the week, with Carly bouncing back and forth from Dianne to me, asking her for what I'd denied, doing in front of me some little number which Dianne had proclaimed to be acceptable when Carly was with her. Needless to say, Dianne's ideas on child raising—my raising, that is, of her child—turned out to be substantially different from mine. Dianne thought Carly should be allowed to do anything that wasn't distinctly harmful to herself or others. While there was a vast category of actions Carly might engage in . . . like coming into the room where I lay on the bed with Philip on my belly, googling at him, and sitting down on the rocker, rocking violently and clapping her hands and rhythmically kicking the leg of the rocker with her two little work-shoed feet . . . actions, that is, which didn't fall into the category of being harmful to self or others but just happened to be a ROYAL PAIN IN THE ASS . . . I didn't see why, with all my other cares and responsibilities, I should have to put up with them.

By Sunday evenings the tension between us was thicker than the twins' joint. And just as controlling. We moved around uneasily within the limits it imposed on us. Rigid necks got kinks if the heads on top of them moved too quickly. Emotions tiptoed where their normal tread might break through the shaky floor of our lives.

During the week it was better and worse. Better because I didn't have to deal with Dianne every time I told Carlotta to do something. Worse because without Dianne to divert her she hung around me constantly, arguing, asking questions, doing sly, hostile things to Philip when I wasn't looking. I worried constantly that she would hurt him. (It never struck me that for years I'd worried about the harm I myself might do to a child while now I worried only about what Carly might do.)

One day when Philip was about ten months old she decided it was time for him to walk although he wasn't yet standing without support. She took him for a walk across the kitchen floor while I was in the bathroom and halfway across got bored with the enter-

159

prise and let him fall backward on his head. I heard him howl and ran out of the bathroom, barely stopping to pull up my jeans, scooping him up from the floor and yelling at Carlotta, who stood stock-still two feet away from him, her eyes full of guilt, her mouth full of thumb: "What did you do to him, Carlotta? Damn it, can't I even go to the bathroom for a minute? What did you do?" Carlotta, the four-year-old mass murderer, evil incarnate, danger to all smaller than she! I couldn't live with this. It was too much. It was March and the snow was still covering the windows of the living room. The men were in the shop. I put Philip in his crib, still crying, bundled up Carly and putting on nothing but my workboots, took her out to the shop, tugging her along the path I'd shoveled for the men. She didn't cry. She wanted to be punished when she did something like that, in spite of any of Dianne's ideas to the contrary.

"Here!" I shouted, startling the two of them so that Amos dropped a hammer on Eddie's toes. "I brought you a present. It's called Carlotta and it's a pain in the ass and it's just as much yours as mine! Take it, I've had it!"

From then on, every morning no matter what the weather, if the men were working in the barn I brought out Carly to stay with them for a couple of hours, and in that time had the solitude with Philip that I felt I needed so badly. (Solitude without another breathing, thumping object nearby was not an idea that would enter my emotional vocabulary until a few more years had passed.) When they came in for lunch she came with them and then early in the afternoon she took a nap. That left a couple of hours from the time she woke up until Dianne came home, during which time I did the cooking and baking and any other household chores that I could manage with two young children bugging me in the kitchen. She trailed me around the whole time. Talking. She was the only kid in the whole fucking town who talked. Laureen's kids were both older than she but when they came to visit Carly did all the talking. All the other kids who were stuck in that town knew there was nothing to talk about but she never stopped.

160

For a while we were doing pretty well on the new regime.

The men gave her some tools of her own to work with and she got quite adept with a hammer and nails, pliers, etc. Sometimes she was even helpful to them in picking up and finding small objects. Then one fateful day in the late spring the men put on the first shirts they'd ever worn without cloth covering the joint itself. We'd been having their shirts made in Beverly Hills according to the old pattern but they'd needed new ones and it had occurred to me that we could buy store shirts if I just made an opening in each and the joint was uncovered.

They came down to breakfast. Philip was stacking some plastic doughnuts in one corner of the floor, Carly was eating in the high chair she still used. They—IT—must've been just about at see level.

"What's that?" she asked.

She must've seen it hundreds of times in the first year or two of her life but now a fall and a winter and part of a spring had passed, eight months, perhaps, and she was seeing it with fresh eyes. Taking it in for the first time.

They didn't know what she meant. Eddie looked down quizzically. Amos thought she meant the new denim shirts. I was uneasy.

"What's what?"

"That." She pointed to it with her toast.

"For heaven's sake, Carly," I said, embarrassed, not wanting to look at the men. "You've seen it a million times."

"What is it?"

"It's their—" *You know perfectly well what it is, damn it, it's their . . . their—no, not their joint, sounds weird to a kid, their . . .*

"It's their attachment."

" 'Tachment?"

I felt my face burning. I was furious with her for my idiocy.

"It's where Eddie and Amos are attached. You know they're attached." *Did you think it was all done with magnets, you creepy kid?*

161

She was staring at it intently. The men sat down on their bench. She climbed down from her high chair and walked around to the back of the bench. The twins watched me for a cue. They were uncomfortable and probably couldn't tell that I was a hundred times more uncomfortable than they were. If she asks Why, I thought, I'm going to scream. She'd been through a lengthy Why stage and I'd tried to be good about providing answers but if she asked me why they were attached I was going to scream.

Why wasn't what was on her mind, though. Squeezing between the men and the table she touched the joint, running her little fingers back and forth over it. Then she climbed up on Eddie's lap and grabbed the damn thing and squeezed it.

"Does it hurt?" she asked.

"No," Eddie said, smiling. "It doesn't hurt."

Pause.

"Can I have one?"

I exploded into relieved—and premature—laughter. Who can I tell this story to? is what I remember thinking. Dianne was in Concord and maybe she'd dig it but I couldn't be sure; we really didn't share humor. In this period I missed enormously having someone to tell stories to, someone who'd laugh at the right places instead of saying Mmmm. Not that this was the right place as far as Carly was concerned. She was in dead earnest.

"No," Eddie said.

"Why not?" she asked.

"You have to be born with it," Eddie said.

"Maybe Dianne can get one in Concord," she suggested.

"No," Eddie said. "They don't have any in Concord." Neither of the twins was particularly perturbed by this conversation.

"Or *anyplace,*" I pointed out, irritation replacing amusement. I felt he was dodging the issue. What *was* the issue, anyway? Carly had that talent so widespread among firstborn children for picking the scabs off sores one hadn't even known were there.

"You can't buy it," I said. "You're born with it or you're not born with it."

She quite deliberately ignored me. Standing up on Eddie's leg, she put an arm around his neck and whispered in a voice loud enough to be heard ten miles away, "Will you make me one?"

"Dianne," she said that night, "could I get a 'tachment?"

I gazed at Dianne, waiting for her to question which of her daughter's natural human demands I was denying now.

"A what, love?"

"A 'tachment."

Dianne looked at me quizzically.

"It's very simple," I said, smiling. "She wants an attachment. Like the men's."

Dianne laughed and moaned at the same moment. "Oh, my poor sweetheart," she said, hugging Carlotta to her bosom, "oh, you are darling. I love you so much."

"Can I have one?"

"For heaven's sake, Nady," Dianne said softly, "why didn't you just explain to her?"

"Explain what?" I asked innocently.

"About Amos and Eddie, of course."

"Oh, that. I did. I explained they were born that way and if you weren't born that way that was it."

"That's not much of an explanation," she said after a moment. "Wait a minute."

She got a piece of paper and a pencil. She drew a circle with a baby inside it, explaining that this was the mommy's "belly" and the unborn baby, then drew another "belly" with two babies, then a third with two babies who were joined at the abdomen. Accompanying her drawing was a running commentary about the seed growing in the mommy's belly and the double seed and how they usually separate fully, etc., but once in a very great while, etc. and when that happens, etc. and so on and so on, *ad infinitum*. I enjoyed the whole routine enormously, maybe because I anticipated what was coming. Or maybe because I was remembering myself, age fifteen, listening to Di explain why the world was the way it was, the bosses and the workers and controlling the means of production, and so on, all that wonderful Marxist poetry that had turned out to have less relevance to our reality than the rhymes of Matthew Arnold. . . . Ah, Di, let us be true to one another, for the world . . . bad things will happen . . . the children will grow up and leave us and the men . . . who knows what will happen to the men? . . . and you and I will be left together on the darkling plain and if things get too horrible now, how will we be able to return to each other then?

(I was wrong. Given the motivation we turned out to have mind-numbing capacities for denying the past.)

Anyway, here I was age twenty-nine being amused instead of impressed by Dianne's attempts to impose an orderly blueprint on the chaos of reality.

"I know," exclaimed Carlotta, who had been thoughtfully examining the diagrams. "You could get another baby with a 'tachment and we could share it."

I chortled.

Dianne was upset. A little too upset, I suddenly feared. I tried to reassure her.

"She's pretty young for that stuff. I've been trying to tell you that, one way or another. She's not—I mean kids, Di, they're just not that much in touch with reality."

I never had less trouble with reality than when I was pushing it to Dianne or Carlotta.

Dianne took Carly to bed, then, which postponed but did not terminate Carly's attempts to deal with reality by extinguishing it. At various times during the next couple of weeks she suggested that:

1. She reenter Dianne's belly to find her twin and her 'tachment.
2. Eddie and Amos could make her one if they really wanted to.
3. If she would grow breasts when she got older, as Dianne had promised during one of these discussions, then there was no reason she couldn't grow a 'tachment as well.

She cut the leg off a big cloth Raggedy Ann Di's parents had bought her at F. A. O. Schwarz when they were all in New York, and tried to tape it to her own chest and the doll's. The tape

164

wouldn't hold, of course. I ended up helping her because at the moment it was the path of least resistance. I tied a cord around her chest, attached it to the cloth leg, tied a knot around the cloth leg at one end, running it to the other end of the leg, made another knot, then tied the cord around the chest of Raggedy Ann.

I defy you to name ten human activities that are more sensible than this.

It got to be a way of life. She slept with the damn contraption and if it had become disengaged in the morning when she got up she'd have one of us fix it at the first possible moment. At meal-times she clambered up onto her chair with the doll and made a big stir about feeding them both. I had to sew up the stump where the leg had been attached to the doll because the stuffing was leaking out.

I guess we all assumed she'd get tired of it.

The first week it rained every day, anyway, and it was mud season and no one was particularly anxious to go out-of-doors. It crossed my mind briefly that if Carly didn't give up her 'tachment soon, the group of us, Philip in the carriage, me, Carly, Raggedy Ann and the 'tachment would make quite a sight, walking down to the store for a carton of milk. But I wasn't really concerned. I was delighted that she had something to occupy her. Gone now were the times when I had to keep a close eye on her for fear that she would hurt Philip during one of those wonderfully imaginative games in which she stuffed him into various roles the way you plug up a hole with an inanimate object. Now she had Raggedy Ann and Tachment to keep her company.

"Now, Tachment," she would say, "you go with Raggedy for a few minutes while I take my bath." (I'd managed to convince her that neither of her friends would survive the water.)

Or she would make three cups of tea in the toy dishes her grandparents had recently sent, and feed Raggedy and Tachment by turns, murmuring instructions and endearments to them.

165

Unlike the games that had once been postponed when the men came in from work, this one got more elaborate (and loud) when they were around. At first, because they didn't complain, it was possible for me not to notice that what she was doing was upsetting them, or at least upsetting Amos. He would stare at his niece intently, his eyes narrowed, and then some change would occur within and his expression would alter from hostility to pain. Once or twice I thought his eyes grew moist.

"I think the Tachment thing is bugging the men," I said to Dianne that night.

"Oh? Why should it?"

"I dunno. But Amos looked all upset."

"Oh. Amos."

"Eddie never shows it," I pointed out.

"I doubt he feels it," she said, leaving me upset because she'd managed to put the whole debate on the level of her amiable husband and my difficult one. I didn't get into an argument with her because Philip had awakened and was crying from his crib. Dianne never noticed when he cried, needless to say. I had to remind myself that when Carly was little Dianne hadn't heard *her*, either.

"Does it bug you, what Carly's doing with the doll?" I asked the next morning.

"It's ridiculous," Amos said. "You know what Dianne's parents must've paid for that doll?"

I stared at him. He was serious. He thought that was what was bothering him. Not that I should have been totally surprised. He'd been complaining about money constantly in recent weeks. I didn't know what had brought on this sudden concern. Since Philip's infancy he had been the money worrier in the house but now he was constantly warning us that our expenses were close to outstripping our income.

"Dianne's parents have plenty of money," I pointed out.

"That's not the idea," Amos said. "It's the waste."

"I wish she'd waste it away to nothing," I said. "It's an absolute pain. The whole business of tying her up all the time, watching

166

her drag around that damn—" Whoops. I backed off nervously. "It's so artificial," I added, a transparent attempt to correct what I'd said. But it wasn't necessary. If my mind had been all too quick to link my complaints about the Tachment with feelings about the men's joint that I hadn't known I had before, Amos's head was in an entirely different place. A ledger, to be exact. He sat there complaining that we weren't taking in enough to care for six people properly without even knowing that in recent days I'd begun to suspect that I was pregnant again. My period was quite late and the funny truth was that again I hadn't really kept track so at first I hadn't been sure of the date.

"I'd love," I said, "to find some way to get rid of the fucking doll."

Amos allowed as to how that might be the easiest thing for all concerned, obviously unconcerned himself with the logical flaw in his fiscal position.

"But how?" I asked. "No, never mind. I'll figure it out."

More easily said than done. For the next few days I watched and waited, hoping she'd magically forget the whole game before I had to do anything. (Then running to the bathroom to see if I'd gotten my period yet. But I was pregnant.) No such luck, of course. Then the weather cleared and we were going to walk to the store and I told her she couldn't take Raggedy and Tachment with her.

"Yes, I can," she said. "I can just leave my coat open."

"It's not that," I said. "I don't want you to take them out of the house." *It*, I corrected myself mentally.

"Why?"

"I just don't. It's . . . it's a very expensive doll and I don't want anything to happen to it." *Thanks a lot, Amos, I don't have enough bullshit of my own, I have to use yours, too.*

"I'll get another one."

"No," I said, "you won't. They won't send any more."

"I'll take them anyway," she said. "I don't care if something happens."

"Yes you do."

"No I don't."

"You can't take it and that's all there is to it."

"Then I won't go."

Silence.

I am holding Philip, who's already bundled up for the brisk spring air. I am wearing my heavy sweater and my rubber boots. Carly is in her boots but hasn't gotten on her jacket yet. The men are off at some job in the next town. I can't leave her in the house alone and I CANNOT TAKE HER TO THE FUCKING STORE WITH THE FUCKING ATTACHMENT!

"Carlotta . . ." I try to sound calm but I am filled with the rage of helplessness and my voice trembles. "Carly, please leave it here for now and we'll talk about it later." *I'll take the fucking thing to the garbage dump after she goes to sleep, that's how I'll talk about it.*

"I want to stay here with them."

"I can't leave you in the house alone."

"I'm not alone. *They're* with me."

I smack my forehead. "I mean you have to be here with a grown-up."

"Is my mommy coming home soon?"

All of a sudden Dianne was her mommy. She'd *never* called Dianne her mommy before.

"You know it's just morning; you didn't even have your nap yet."

Silence. Philip squirms in my arms while my mind squirms in my body.

"Why can't you leave it just this once?" I finally ask.

"I'll take them just this once," she says.

I got Philip out of his sweaters, took off my own and stayed in the house for the rest of the day.

Dianne didn't see what the problem was. A four-year-old girl wanted to take to the store a rag doll with another piece of stuffed cloth attached to it and tied to her waist. Dianne really would like to help but she couldn't understand why I was getting so upset over such a little thing. A little thing like being asked to walk into the general store in this tiny town in New Hampshire where we could live in peace because *anyone* could . . . the neighbors had never developed all those strange suburban notions about being able to pick who lived nearby . . . but that didn't mean they took you into their fold, which was frozen hard anyway from eight-month winters . . . that didn't mean they weren't always making sly jokes behind your back. That didn't mean that since we'd moved there we hadn't provided the punch line for three out of every four jokes told around the woodburning stove in the back of the store by the stolid-faced group with their hands permanently curved around beer cans. . . . Dianne just couldn't see what was the big deal about walking into that store with a miniature, mock Siamese twin in tow.

"NO? FINE! THEN YOU CAN STAY HOME AND DO IT AND I'LL GO TO WORK EVERY DAY!"

She sighed. "Oh, Nady, you're not being reasonable. What would you *do?*"

"Never mind that! What would *you* do? Stay home and take care of Philip and Carly? That would be wonderful; I'm sure you'd be crazy about it. Anyway, I think I'm pregnant again!"

She stared at me. I stared back. I hadn't planned to tell her so soon but I needed the ammunition too badly to hold off.

A long silence. I'd won. Relief mixed with guilt.

Dianne—beaten, wasted. "What do you want me to do?"

I got scared because she looked so awful. "You don't have to do it," I promised. "I'll do it. And I'll take the rap."

That night while Carlotta was sleeping I cut the string from around her waist, took the whole contraption and drove with it to the dump, slogging through the mud to bury it in a far place, then dumping the rest of our garbage on top of it.

Then I waited for the shit to hit the fan.

Carly slept a little later than usual, not waking up until well after the time when Dianne had left for Hanover. I waited for a howl from her room but it never came. She appeared in the

169

kitchen, rubbing her eyes and asking for her cereal, shortly after the men had gone out to the shop. I didn't take her out there after breakfast, thinking that the sight of them might set her off. She was subdued, easier than usual to handle, not questioning anything and everything I asked her to do. She played briefly with Philip, putting his plastic doughnuts on the stack and nesting spoons and cups, but then she lost interest and went into the living room, where I found her poring over the Sears catalog. After lunch she went back to the catalog and fell asleep with it on the rug. In the afternoon we did the first spring work in the garden, preparing rows for the spinach, lettuce and early peas. Then I bathed Philip in the big kitchen sink while Carly took a long bath in the tub. I gave her soap detergent bubbles for a special treat.

Dianne arrived home while Carly was eating dinner. She opened the kitchen door with a look that suggested there was no way she was going to find us all alive and well behind it. Carly scrambled down to run and hug her. Except that halfway across the kitchen floor she stopped dead in her tracks, the expression on her face turned from pleasure to shock and pain, and she let out a wail of indescribable horror:

"MY TTAAAAAAAAAAAAAAAAAAAACCHMENT!!!"

A moment of silence, with everyone frozen in position. Then Carlotta began to sob.

"All day she didn't notice," I said to Dianne. "This is the first time she's even noticed."

Dianne knew I had to be lying. She kneeled on the floor and threw her arms around her daughter. The men, having heard the scream, lumbered into the kitchen. They watched without asking what had happened and nobody told them.

I'd expected Carly to search but she never did. She knew it wasn't there. She never asked for another one. She didn't ask for *anything* for several days. She was full of mistrust. She'd been robbed. A few times I was tempted to try to jolly her out of it but I stopped myself because I knew it would be pointless. If I made any effort to please her we would end up with her wanting a replacement for Raggedy Ann and the Tachment and then we

170

would in turn be back with the question of where she could take them and where she couldn't. And there was no way I could ever live with having anyone see our little girl Carlotta walk down the center of Bootville with a fake Siamese twin attached to her.

No way.

And so you see, gentle reader, if Nadine has still not learned what the limits should be or how she can impose them upon herself, she has learned the next best, far worse thing—how to impose them upon that child who is as a daughter and a *doppel-gänger* to her, the little Carlotta. If she has not yet considered the dangers in attaching oneself to others out of sheer terror of the alternative, she has at least absorbed the reality principle insofar as Carlotta must live with it.

Carlotta, interestingly, seemed to bear me no grudge. Could she really not know? Maybe she suspected the men because she seemed to avoid looking at them for a long time and once or twice she rallied to my assistance when I was arguing with Amos about something we needed that he claimed we couldn't afford. She looked forward to having the new baby, who was due in January. She fervently prayed for a girl. She began playing house with her normal dolls, an activity she hadn't engaged in before. If Philip interrupted her play she would incorporate him into the action with some line like, "Oh, dear, dolly, Daddy's home early from the garage."

It was 1966. Carly was six years old now and Philip was three. The men were thirty-three and Dianne and I were both close to turning thirty-one. I had warded off any consideration of what it meant to be thirty years old by getting pregnant again. Dianne did the same job by wearing her hair in two ponytails that streamed off each side of her head and made her look about fourteen years old if you didn't pay attention to the lines in her face.

THE Office of Economic Opportunity had initiated, among its other programs, Legal Assistance of New Hampshire. In Concord, Dianne met a nice young lawyer who was going to be in charge of the Keene office and offered her the second job there. She liked the idea because she was bored with the work she was doing, which had become increasingly dull and routine in the years she'd been there, and because she was tired of making the long trip to Concord every day. On the other hand, she was afraid of losing what seniority she'd built up in four years in Concord, and she wasn't sure the OEO funding would last. She was more in touch than I with the winds of change that were rippling the surface of our culture and creating the appearance of an alternative to it. She thought these winds were less likely to end in change than in total repression. In such an event programs like those instituted by OEO would be the first to go.

I myself had gotten no closer to the counterculture than to listen to the Beatles when the reception from Boston was adequate.

As usual, everything Dianne said about politics sounded reasonable, but none of it seemed to have any relevance to my life. For me the realities were: First, if Dianne worked in Keene instead of Concord she could be home by five thirty or six instead of six thirty or considerably later. Since four in the afternoon until seven at night were the witching hours, this would be most helpful, particularly when I had the new baby. Second, I had on my hands an active six-year-old girl and an active three-year-old boy. Carly had missed kindergarten because of her birthday but there was a half-day nursery group beginning not far away and if Dianne left the house a little later in the morning than she did now she could drop Carly off in the morning. I was angry with Dianne for hesitating but tried not to show it because I didn't want to be the villain who'd made her switch to a job she didn't like. I was also afraid I would have more than I could handle with this new baby in my life. For the first time I found myself regarding the men's joint with conscious discontent. Wishing they could do some of the jobs that I had to do now. Wishing they could drive. Wishing it didn't take them so long to get places. Wishing they could be close fathers to their children in a way that their closeness to each other seemed to prevent. Not that they were unkind, although Amos was occasionally short-tempered. It was just that neither could ever be purely and simply there with his child. Someone else, closer and intrinsically more important, was always there with them.

In other words, I was beginning to feel frustrated by that very feature which had drawn me to them.

I finally told Dianne I didn't think I could manage to get Carly to and from the play group (which she was anxious that Carly attend) but if she'd take her in the morning, I'd pick her up at midday. With all my shrieking and moaning, I think it was the first time I'd ever made a simple demand on her. She gave notice before her summer vacation and then announced that she was going to take Carly to visit her parents in Beverly Hills for those two weeks.

173

That was what I really needed, I thought jealously. Grandparents for my children. Two little old white-haired people down the road whom Carly could run to when I was being unjust and who would take Philip overnight when the weight of Carly was too much for him.

"Who's going to pay for all this?" Amos asked.

"It won't cost you a penny," Dianne said smugly. "My parents are sending the tickets." Her manner reminded all of us that she had the only steady income in the family. Dianne as martyr trudging off to the office every day to earn a living.

In the guise of supporting Dianne I competed with her. "I still have plenty of money in the Fund, anyway," I pointed out.

"How much is plane fare these days, anyway?" Amos asked.

"I really don't know," Dianne said coolly.

"He's just curious about the numbers, Di," I said. "No one's being critical."

Now they were both annoyed with me for interfering.

But all I'd been trying to do was create a pleasanter atmosphere. I was sometimes troubled by the suspicion that Amos and Dianne didn't really like each other, and in this period when I was pregnant with my last child and anxious about the burdens it would impose on me and the others, I was eager for the feeling of warmth and support that would come from a loving family. Love would overcome all difficulties! If I wasn't too familiar with the facts of the counterculture, I had long since immersed myself in its fictions, which weren't counter to any of the pap on which I'd been raised.

"How would you feel about me having another baby?" I asked Amos.

"We can't afford it," he told me.

"I'm pregnant," I said.

He stared at me.

If he were a regular person, I thought, he'd just get up and storm out of the house.

I threw him two decks of cards so they could play double solitaire and I stormed out myself.

We didn't discuss the matter again except to come to the understanding that the delivery money would have to come out of my Parents' Electrocution Fund, as I'd called it until Dianne begged me to stop.

If dissatisfaction was knocking at the door of my head I wasn't about to let it in until I'd finished with the business of having children.

The placidity which had been the mark of Philip's temperament vanished upon my return from the hospital with Daisy in my arms. He got manicky and wild, running around the room screaming as though someone had sent a few thousand volts through his body. Screaming became his normal conversational tone, although I was much better at handling his jealously than I'd been with Carly's.

He put the cat, a huge mouser named Otto, into Daisy's crib, and when I explained why the cat couldn't lie right across Daisy's chest, he found a chipmunk Otto had killed and brought it into the house. When he lost interest in the dead chipmunk he put that in Daisy's crib instead. He said he thought I wouldn't mind because it was much smaller than Otto and couldn't hurt Daisy. Upon being discovered at any of his tricks he laughed—a real glass-shatterer. When I left Daisy naked in the middle of our bed to get a diaper, he stuck his fingers in her vagina to see what was there and, when that failed to make her scream, he pulled at the lips until she did. He told me he was seeing if she had diaper rash. He was scared to death that I wouldn't love him anymore now that I had a younger baby to love (he'd seen it happen once, after all) and the only thing he would not do to make me love him was behave in a halfway reasonable manner for even a small portion of any day. He wanted to nurse when Daisy did and had fits when I calmly refused him. Carly, not very surprisingly, really got off on this whole scene. She seemed, more surprisingly, to do about five years' worth of growing up in the first few months of Daisy's life, and turned out to be so helpful in caring for Daisy (not to speak of in protecting her from Philip) that I missed her instead of

175

being relieved when she went off to her play group. The pleasure she derived from playing Little Mother with Daisy was of course intensified by the correct sense that Philip took her bond with the baby as a conspiracy against him.

Dianne wasn't crazy about her new job. Her boss had turned out not to be the way she'd thought he was when she knew him in Concord—dynamic, radical, eager to break new ground—but just a rather gentle soul who was eager to find a meeting ground with the Establishment. Dianne looked at Daisy wistfully as I nursed her and talked about having another child. Her words and manner suggesting that only our need for her income prevented her. That if only I would take care of a second child of hers, too, there'd be no problem at all. When she talked about the period of Carly's infancy, when she was home with her baby all the time, the implied description of our lives then was unrecognizable.

The arguments with Philip about not sucking my milk made me self-conscious about letting Amos's mouth anywhere near my breasts when we were making love, which loused up further our already mundane sex life. I wanted to ask him why the hell he didn't just bring another drink up to bed, he drank so much anyway he'd barely know the difference. I realized now that Amos had gradually, since Philip's infancy, become a bigger and bigger drinker; my trips to the package store had become more and more frequent without my thinking much about them. When I said something to this effect Amos dropped casually the fact that since money was so tight he and Eddie had been thinking of going back on the road.

"You're not going on the road and leaving me alone all day with three kids," I exclaimed.

"Nobody asked you to have them," he replied.

I stared at him. "What does that mean?"

"Just what I said," he replied.

I glanced at Eddie, who was smiling.

"Didn't you want to have children?"

"We wanted to get married."

176

"Why get married if not to have children?"

"For steady sex," my husband said.

I felt betrayed, although sex and not children had been on my mind when I got hooked into them.

"So what were the children?" I asked, tears in my eyes. "Just a bunch of accidents?"

"The first one was."

"What about *ours*?"

"They were no accident, that's for sure. You practically drove us all out of our fucking minds until you got pregnant the first time."

Rage. Pain. *Confusion*. What was I doing here? Who was this nasty man I had married six and a half years earlier? And why had I thought it didn't matter who he was when he was going to be the father of my children? Maybe I'd thought I was the Virgin Mary and he was just a cover for God? No wonder Philip showed little interest in his father and increasingly spent his time around other men in town.

"You're making her feel bad," Eddie said to Amos.

Through my tears I smiled at Eddie, who had some of Amos's drawbacks but at least was a good person.

"Oh, shut up," Amos said. "Don't be such a—"

"A human," I filled in. "That's the trouble. He's too human."

But I stopped talking about Amos's boozing and he stopped talking about going on the road.

My feelings about Amos got worse and worse but fortunately for the running of our busy household they were contained in a small hard lump whose locus might shift from my head to my throat to the back of my neck but whose size didn't change. Until one day I made the mistake of exposing it to the fresh air.

"Sometimes Amos is impossible," I sighed to Dianne, following a lengthy argument about money. I'd left them in the living room and come upstairs to where she lay reading in bed.

"Mmm."

I looked at her. I wanted to know what Mmm meant this time.

177

"Do you think he's impossible?" I asked, then quickly added, "Most of the time I think it's me."

"He's awful," Dianne said mildly, not even looking up from her book. "I don't know how you can stand him."

I stared at her. I might have been bargaining for a small dose of the truth as she perceived it but this was rather more than—

"How I can stand him?" The lump had burst into my brain and was spreading around, assaulting all the soft spots. "I don't under— I mean, we all live together, Di, I'm not the only one who has to stand him."

"It's different for me," she said complacently. "I'm away most of the time. Besides, he's not my husband."

Was she crazy or was I? Or both? The last seemed most likely but I couldn't get a handle on the various types of craziness or decide which was serious.

"How long is it that you've . . . not liked Amos?"

She shrugged.

"I don't mean some exact date," I said. "I just, I'm curious as to when . . . I mean, when we got hitched you must've liked him."

She was silent. Her lips were set, as though she were expecting me to do something crazy or violent but was prepared to stand her ground.

"Di?" It came out in a whisper. "Please tell me . . . are you telling me you never liked Amos?"

She nodded. Gentle but stubborn.

"How could you?" I whispered. "How could you do it, not liking Amos?"

"How could you?" she replied.

"But I did like him," I said, trying frantically to clear my head so I could be reasonable. "I'm talking about now. It's only recently that I've come to . . . to . . ." I fumpfered around, not willing to say it outright.

"Well, you're still managing to live with him."

"You don't just get up and walk out on a marriage when you've got a bunch of kids. . . ." I paused, waiting for the significance of the "bunch" to sink in, waiting for her to understand what she

178

was talking about when she referred to my leaving so casually. "Just because you find at some point that you are . . . that there are . . . that you . . ." . . . *that you can't stand your husband.*

"Well," Dianne said calmly, "I felt the same way. You don't not marry a man you've fallen in love with, just because . . . there are some difficulties attached."

Again I was reduced to just staring at her.

She meant it.

She was quite mad.

This person whom I still in spite of everything thought of as a more trustworthy (less dangerous) person than I . . . this person who, however often she might let life knock her about, knew how far you could go in getting back . . . whom I'd thought, in short, knew the limits . . . Was it possible that no one really knew? Was it possible that everyone's book of rules stemmed from an ignorance as deep as my own? From an impossibility of knowing? That was a terrifying idea because if it was true my confusion might never end. Worse, there might be no one I could safely turn to in that confusion!

The room was too close. I turned and ran downstairs then out to the porch. The back lawn was still two feet deep in snow but the moon was out and everything was quite beautiful. I ran down the back steps and into the snow. Dianne followed and stood watching me from the porch. She was calm; my outbursts always had that effect on her. She walked down to calm me. She waited.

Should I explain to her that she too was in snow past her ankles?

No, I decided. That wouldn't be nice. The only person who needed more than I to believe that she was the same one was Dianne. Dianne was a fragile person, really—and often a dear one. Sometimes when I was angry with her it wasn't because of anything she'd done but only because I expected more of her than I did of myself and got angry when she didn't fulfill my expectations. This conversation tonight was a perfect instance. We had committed the identical insane act of marrying men who were

179

permanently joined at the abdomen and for almost seven years, largely on the excuse that it had originally been my idea, I had chosen to believe that her motives were somehow saner than my own. Poor Dianne. I often got angry with her for believing the same thing.

What would happen to us now?

I became aware of my feet again, stuck in the snow like a couple of bottles of champagne in an ice bucket. A little sheepishly I pulled out one, then the other. We walked back up to the porch and into the kitchen together.

"Are you okay, Nady?" she asked, uncertain now that I was calm.

"Yes," I said, "I'm okay. But I better change my shoes."

"What were you thinking just now?"

I'd often asked her that question but I think it was the first time she'd ever asked it of me.

"I don't know."

I was thinking about you, I was thinking about me, I was thinking about this crazy marriage which cannot last forever.

"I guess," I said, sitting down and taking off my soaking wet slippers, "I guess I was thinking of how cold and wet my feet were. And that soon it'll be mud season."

A short while later Dianne got a job she liked more. It was with a private law firm in Hanover, not at all the kind of place you'd have thought she would go for (or vice versa) but they had university clients and were beginning to get what we would call Sixties Cases, involving the children of some of these people . . . dope, radical politics and so on. She was as close to being bubbly and optimistic as I'd ever seen her. She enjoyed being in Hanover, a university town. She liked being near a good library. She loved the cases she was handling. And the people she worked with, if not fascinating, were easy to take. I felt happy for her, particularly since I'd been feeling affectionate anyway. Also, it was spring. In the daytime I felt good, too.

Daisy was fifteen months old. She'd been walking for almost three months and verbally she was at that wonderful stage where each new word is a precious breakthrough. Philip's placid way of being in the world seemed to have passed on to her when he lost it. She was easier to have around than either of the others had ever been. When she used some new word it wasn't because she was frantic to communicate with me but generally because she was sitting on the floor absorbed in a pile of pots and utensils and the word just slid out of her mouth. When Carly and Philip were home she tagged around after them, falling constantly, getting yelled at by Philip for being in the way, but always scrambling to her feet undaunted and starting all over again. I was jealous because she invariably chose to be with them when they were there and often I would have preferred that she stay with me. She was the greatest pleasure in my life, although I enjoyed the other two as well. Carly was eight, an age where it's possible for parents to believe for another year or two that we're not going to pay for our worst sins. My only real problems with Philip, who was almost six, occurred when he was stuck in the house in bad weather. Now in the spring when he could ride his bike and play ball and so on, he was fine.

My second greatest pleasure came from gardening. The early vegetables were all in and that spring I started an asparagus bed on the far side of the strawberries and rhubarb. Asparagus, of course, puts down deeper roots and requires more time to produce good cuttings than any other vegetable. If there'd been something that went deeper and took longer I'd have put that in. I could feel my own roots half willingly working their way out and most of me was still fighting to keep them down.

By the time I'd finished cleaning up after dinner and the children were in bed my body was too exhausted for further activity. If I didn't go to bed very early I sat in the living room and stared speculatively at the men's joint.

It had become the enemy.

It made Dianne dislike Amos and it made Amos furious with Eddie most of the time. It constricted our lives. Who could know what our lives might be without that piece of flesh that bound them and in so doing imprisoned all of us?

I had an unpleasant fantasy in which I yanked at it furiously

181

and it came off at both ends and I stood there holding this warm bloody thing which began screaming at me. (The men were in the background bleeding to death but that didn't seem very important.)

My other fantasies were more realistic. In a sense. The joint had been surgically removed (or maybe it had never been there in the first place) and the four of us lived together in peace and harmony relieved only by an occasional sex orgy. Or we moved to New York, two couples and their children, close friends all. Maybe we had adjoining apartments in the same big building. Daisy began kindergarten and I went back to school to develop my mind. I was beginning to think I might have a mind, after all, because what else could be causing me all this trouble? Physically I was in perfect health with a supply of energy any normal person might envy. But something was at me all the time except when physical labor could fend it off, something that made good enterprises turn bad, simple projects metamorphose into horribly complicated affairs, good intentions seem evil or ignorant or both in retrospect. Something that wouldn't let me do nothing just because there was nothing to be done. If all that mental energy could just be turned toward something useful. If I could get the few credits I needed for a degree then go to graduate school maybe I could learn what I needed to do something real, to help people. Back in full force was my old daydream of being a sort of Goddess of Psychology, dispensing magic words that would help mortals change their lives.

But the joint always pulled me back to reality. In one fantasy a patient who with my magic encouragement was about to change his life left my office and ran into that monster one-half of which I called my husband and then knew that nothing I said could be of value to him.

How could I briefly fantasize about living in a civilized place like New York? The center of learning? Of sophistication? Of *humor?* With two men who were joined by an obscene joke of flesh at their abdomens?

Yes, it was obscene and I hated it. That was what I kept coming back to. I endowed it with the slowness of Eddie and the irritability and stinginess of Amos and having done so I was able to avoid questioning how I would feel about living alone with Amos, a man with whom I had virtually nothing in common; who talked too little and drank too much; who gave little to me and less to his children; whom in some very crucial way I didn't know and who might in fact be unknowable; a man I didn't like and couldn't respect.

I hated that fucking joint.

DR. Miles would see me right away, which gave me pause because there were four other people waiting, all of whom probably had appointments. He looked exactly the same.

"Are you still keeping track of us?" I asked with a nervous smile.

He smiled back. "We have the children's medical records."

"So you know I've been here."

"For the children."

"The rest of us don't go to doctors."

Silence.

"I guess we're pretty healthy."

"Is there anything we can help you with now?"

"It's about the sep—" I stopped. I'd been about to say I'd come to discuss the separation but it sounded as if I were talking to a lawyer, not a doctor. "It's about . . . it's not about me. It's about Eddie and Amos." Two lies in a row. I'm worried about myself. I want them to be fixed up so I won't have to hate them anymore. "You told me once that they had extensive medical histories here. And in Boston."

He nodded.

I took a deep breath.

"I know from a discussion . . . an argument . . . they once had, a long time ago, that at some point there was talk about trying to . . . separate them."

"Yes. Of course."

Of course.

"Could you tell me something about that?"

"I wasn't directly involved in the discussions," he pointed out. "It's not my province. But I was a sort of sidelines participant, you might say, and of course I did tell the other Mrs. Smith when we talked about it a long time ago—"

"Dianne?"

"I believe that's her name."

"She never talked about it at home . . . much."

Dianne!

"Maybe she was trying to avoid unnecessary stress."

Here would be no ally for me, no knight in a white smock defending my right to participate in those decisions that had a crucial effect on my life. He'd seen Dianne and he'd seen me and he knew which one of us was sane.

"Well," I said, "it's come up, now. Someone has to talk to me now."

He picked up his phone and dialed. "Len? Do you think you could drop by my office for a moment?"

Was there an undercurrent of excitement to his voice or was that my imagination?

"Yes, well . . . yes, Mrs. Nadine Smith is in my office and would like to . . . fine." Dr. Miles hung up and looked at me. "Dr. Thom will be here in a moment. He's the surgeon who was most involved with your . . . the men."

A moment of paranoia. How could he be trusted, how could I trust any of these men who forgot all their other patients in the

185

interest of transacting a little freak business? I had an urge to flee; the office briefly took on the atmosphere of a submarine. I gripped the arms of my chair for the descent.

Leonard Thom was thin and intense with straight brown hair, big, farsighted eyes behind thick glasses, and a body that looked permanently stopped between the moment of shock and the moment of response. He chain-smoked Pall Malls, held in his right hand, while the fingers of his left hand combed his hair to get in better touch with what was inside his head.

"Mrs. Smith," Dr. Miles told him, "is interested in the possibility of surgical separation of the twins."

"What would you like to know?" Dr. Thom asked abruptly.

"Should they be separated?" I asked almost as abruptly—although I hadn't meant to, he'd just confused me with his directness.

"Of course."

I stared at him. Did he mean of course I'd like to know or of course they should be separated? I couldn't believe it was the latter. It couldn't be that simple.

"They should be?"

"Of course."

"Why?"

He sighed—or he did what for some people would have been a sigh; with him it was a short, forceful expulsion of breath.

"Mrs. Smith, the condition is enough reason to attempt the cure."

I was speechless. I looked at Dr. Miles, who was fiddling with some paper clips on his desk. No help there. I'd been waiting for suspicious queries about my sudden interest in this surgery, for condescending explanations of the medical complexities and of the threat to one if the other felt ill, for revelations of dangers I hadn't imagined. Instead here was this very straight, intense man telling me that the surgery I'd agonizingly begun to consider was the only sane course. The condition that had drawn me to my husband was an operable one.

186

My lips were dry. "I know you have people waiting."

He shrugged. "It'll be worth it if we can get some kind of understanding here."

"You've wanted them to do this for a long time."

He nodded.

"Does everybody? I mean, is there unanimity on that point? That it should be done?"

"There is unanimity in the feeling that the benefits would outweigh the risks. But of the specialists who saw them a few felt that the risks were somewhat greater than the others estimated them to be, and for that reason didn't feel it was correct to pressure them into surgery."

"What are the risks?"

"I think they can best be summed up simply as the risk of the unknown and the risks inherent in any major surgery. This particular surgery, obviously, is very rare. It's only been done a few times—properly recorded times, at any rate—and in only one case where there was what you might call a bridge of liver. In earlier cases there were deaths, one or both of the twins, but they were many years ago. Surgical procedures, as you probably realize, have advanced hugely in recent years. Not to speak of our ability to make certain advance determinations before surgery."

I paused to digest what he was saying. I was so numb that I was amazed to find myself coherent.

"A long time ago," I said, "the subject came up, and Amos, my husband, he was the one who was more against it, he—"

"I know, I know," Dr. Thom interrupted. "He had a sort of idée fixe, it had no basis in reality, this notion that if we had to save one of them we'd save his brother."

So that was it.

"With newborns, if one has to make a choice, one might give the larger the chance because with newborns the larger is more likely to survive by virtue of its weight alone. Even then there are other factors, who has which organ, and so on. But weight simply isn't a factor with adults."

187

"Then how would you choose if you had to?" I asked, thinking it wasn't what had been on my mind at all.

"I don't foresee that this would be an issue," Dr. Thom said, lighting his umpteenth cigarette of our short interview. "A large surgical team would devote all its best efforts to the care of both patients. Two coordinated teams, actually. The men would be put in separate rooms as soon as possible after surgery to minimize the likelihood of cross-infection, and so on. If any complication should arise during surgery we'd examine the exact problem, but we have absolutely no reason to believe there would be any complication that would involve the sacrifice of either twin. They seem to have equally well-developed livers and they're both in good health, or at least they were in their young manhood when we last saw them. To assume that we'd abandon Amos because he's a little shorter and weighs a few pounds less than his brother doesn't make any sense. Any more than it makes sense for us to save Amos because his intellectual capacities are greater."

"Is that why he's harder to get along with?" I asked. "I should have known. No, that doesn't hold because Dianne's smarter than I am but she's easier to get along with, not harder."

"Is she?"

"Well, smarter definitely. Easier, I don't know. Maybe she's just quieter. Definitely quieter." I laughed, a little nervously, because I sort of knew what I was doing. "She's so quiet she never even told me she talked to you. I never knew any of what went on here."

"Is that true?" he asked sharply.

I nodded.

"Why did you never ask?"

He'd found my Achilles' heel. My ignorance was a conspiracy but I was a leading conspirator. "I didn't think of it as a genuine possibility," I told him, which was also the truth. "I guess I assumed if it were reasonable it would've been done a long time ago. I knew they'd been to all kinds of doctors and specialists when they were first discovered. But the joint was—it's the way they *are*, do you know what I mean? It doesn't even seem fair, the times when I don't want them to be that way. It was what attracted me to them; it doesn't seem fair to dislike it now. I used to think it was cozy."

Now you know the worst, gentlemen.

"Cozy." Dr. Thom's lips curled down around the word but Dr. Miles looked as though he didn't know whether to laugh or cry.

"Cozy," I said defiantly. "I can hear how that sounds to you but I don't care. It's the truth."

I stood up. I couldn't stand what they must be thinking. It was a long time since I'd worried about what someone else was thinking. In our early times with the twins I'd sometimes worried about what *they* were thinking but then it always turned out that Eddie was warm and wishing the window were open wider and Amos was cold and wishing it were shut, so I'd been driven back into myself.

"I've taken enough of your time," I said.

"Not at all," Dr. Thom said quickly. "This is well worth it."

"If I go it's not because I don't care," I blurted out suddenly, "it's because I care too much and I don't think I can do anything."

"Why don't you have a seat?" asked Dr. Thom, his manner softer now. Cold, abrupt Dr. Thom had decided that it might be worthwhile to manipulate me. "You must have other questions."

Uneasily I sat on the edge of my chair.

Silence.

I fidgeted.

I thought of Amos and Eddie, of how the children would be bugging them by now because I'd been away for so long.

"What about money? This must be very expensive."

"Funding is not a problem."

Funding is not a problem. Somewhere there were people eager to pay to see this operation performed.

"How come? Why is everyone so anxious to see this surgery done?"

"It's not a question of our being anxious," he lied. "It's a question of their condition. Of the way they have to live."

"Of the way they have to live," I said slowly. Not to speak of the way *we* have to live.

"Not to speak of the way they'll die," he said.

"You mean . . . together," I said.

"That is a rosy estimate," he said.

I looked at Dr. Miles. He was uneasy, too, with what Thom was doing to me but of course doctors are duty bound to let anyone else do anything as long as he has an MD.

I cast around in my mind for something I could talk about that was related to the subject but not, so to speak, at the dead center of it.

"I guess we all worry about having a lot to do with doctors," I said. "My mother spent half her life in doctors' offices and I don't . . ." I trailed off, not knowing why I'd begun this way and not knowing how to finish. I don't *trust* doctors, Doctor. At this moment he had become the surgery salesman, eager to sell me a product that he claimed was better than the one I had. "I guess Dianne has a doctor."

He nodded.

"Is it you?" I asked suddenly.

He shook his head. "A close colleague."

I laughed nervously. "She never mentions him by name."

"You said before that you never discussed this matter of the separation," Dr. Thom said. "Yet Mrs. Smith, the other Mrs. Smith, apparently felt that you had strong feelings against such surgery."

I shook my head. "We never talked about it. You can believe me or not believe me. She never told me she was here."

I promised him I wouldn't just disappear back into Bootville, that I would think about our conversation, perhaps even broach the subject at home. But their obvious eagerness to perform the surgery made me unsure that I could trust them or myself. I kept thinking of the awesome responsibility involved in initiating such a step, even aside from the problems of convincing the twins. If I succeeded I would be responsible for anything bad that happened. And if I failed to convince them . . . The truth was, and I could see it right then at the beginning, that I was unwilling to gear up for this battle and lose. I knew that once I started trying to make them do it I would want it more than ever, that the longer and harder I fought the more I would want it, and that if I couldn't win I probably wouldn't be able to retreat, either.

And then what would happen?

I nearly went off the road on that one, after which I pushed the whole business out of my mind and concentrated on what I had to pick up at the store in Pomstead since I'd forgotten to go to the Hanover market after leaving the doctor's office.

It stayed out of my mind until the children were asleep, the men were in front of the TV playing checkers, and Di and I were in the kitchen having tea together, a pleasant little ritual we'd fallen into during these months when the ties between us had become somehow easier.

"Why didn't you tell me when you talked to the doctors about the twins' getting separated?" I asked her. "Were you afraid I'd get hysterical?"

Pause. A lawyerish pause.

"I won't get hysterical," I continued after a bit, "but I talked to Miles and Thom today and I think it would be a good idea for us to talk."

She got hysterical, at least in her fashion. She stood up so suddenly that her chair fell over backward and she began pacing around the room.

"What's the matter?" I asked her.

"You just sprung it," she said, "out of the blue."

"I'm sorry, Di," I said. "It may have sounded that way but I didn't really know an easy way to bring it up."

191

Silence. I'm calm, not engaging her womb to womb.

"I feel as though you're issuing an ultimatum."

"What kind of ultimatum?" Naturally I was getting even calmer on the other side of our emotional seesaw.

She stopped pacing. Her eyes narrowed and her face took on a meanly speculative expression I'm certain she'd never displayed before.

"I was afraid to mention it to you," she said. "I knew you'd be ready to push them into it no matter what the risks were."

She got you on your most vulnerable point, Nadine. If you can stay calm through this one you'll be all right.

"Which risks?"

"Nobody even knows. They could die."

"There's no reason to believe that would happen."

"The last time twins like them were operated on they died."

"That was fifty or a hundred years ago." (I'd made up the numbers.) "Surgical techniques have improved."

"There's no way to be sure that would make the difference."

"They're going to die anyway, eventually," I said. "Maybe sooner than if they were separated. From the extra strain on their hearts of dragging each other around." I thought it was an inspired point. Surely one of the doctors might have made it if our conversation had continued. "Don't you realize," I pressed softly, "what a burden it is on them, having to go around the way they do?"

"They don't think it's a burden," she said, tears in her eyes because I'd managed to turn myself from the woman who was willing for them to die into the woman who cared more about their feelings.

"That's only because they never had it any other way."

Silence.

"The thing I don't understand, Di, is you don't even like Amos. It seems to me you'd be the one to be pushing for the surgery."

"Naturally, I've thought about that." She sat down. She was a little calmer.

"Then why are you so against it? I mean, aside from the other reasons."

"I don't know." She was groping around now for reasons. She really didn't know why. "There's something . . . it would change our whole way of life."

"You mean if it worked."

She nodded.

"Only to make it better. We could live as close to the way we do now as we want to only we'd have more choices. You could still go off to—" A light dawned. "You couldn't be worried about Carly. That I wouldn't take care of her anymore." I only begin to believe, because of her startled, embarrassed reaction, that this indeed was on her mind. "You can't really think I wouldn't take care of Carly anymore. And even if I wouldn't, which is ridiculous, how could that matter compared to everything else that's involved? Can't you see this can't hinge on something like baby-sitting?"

"Then what should it hinge on, Nadine?" she asked, a bitter note suddenly in her voice. "Your sudden whim that you happen to feel the operation should be performed?"

It wasn't fair but there was enough truth in it so it had to be answered. "All right. It's true I want my life to be better, but I think it'll make theirs better, too. And yours. And the children's. I'd love to see Philip with a real father he could trail after instead of a freak."

"What makes you think the kids view them as freaks?"

"If they don't yet they will. Maybe here in Bootville they can manage not to think about it, but when they start busing to school in Pomstead there's no way they're not going to catch a lot of shit about it. Carly first."

"Since when are you so concerned about Carly?"

In her quiet way she was pulling out all the stops.

"Come on, Di. You raised the question so I answered it."

"What if one of them dies? Or both? How will *that* be for the children?"

"The doctors say it won't happen."

193

"They say they *think* it won't happen. . . . Nady, I'm not saying we should never consider it, but why now? Things are all right now. When the kids get a little older, then maybe . . . Why upset the balance now? Why turn our lives inside out?"

I smiled. "My insides have always been out. I suppose I have the least to lose."

She pounced on it. "And they have the most."

I was silent.

"So in the long run," she said, "they're the ones who'll have to decide whether to take the risk."

"You're absolutely right," I said quietly. "They're the ones who'll have to decide."

I was careful. Patient. I waited. I was amazed at my own patience. What was happening to me? If it was true that I'd calmed down considerably over the years, that I'd mired myself in the men, the children, the routine of a rural housewife's life to a point where they'd formed a genuine protective wall against the insanity both within me and in the outside world, it was also true that I was now dealing with the possibility of breaking down a portion of that wall and I was staying reasonably calm. The kamikaze who usually took over my head when the going got rough seemed to have been replaced by some terribly efficient automatic pilot.

Not that it mattered, in the long run.

I could feel Dianne watching me wait, not believing how patient I was being.

They had a fight. Amos had a cold and was horribly congested. Eddie wanted to take a lying-down nap, he was so sleepy he couldn't stay awake. But Amos's decongestant pills hadn't worked and he was thoroughly miserable and absolutely wouldn't lie down for even fifteen or twenty minutes to accommodate Eddie.

"You know," I said, "at times like this I always wonder . . ."

"Wonder what?" Amos asked irritably.

"Wonder if it wouldn't be an enormous relief to the two of

194

you to get . . . Maybe you should just *think* about getting separated."

Amos looked at me as though one of the snakes that I grew out of my head had just bitten him.

Eddie said, "Mmmm, uh-yuh," in a kind of rueful way; I was talking about a far-off place he could never visit because his partner didn't want to go.

"I mean," I said, "doesn't the thought of just being able to lie down when you feel like it, without—"

"Maybe you mean lie down and die," Amos growled.

"No," I said. "That's not what I mean at all."

Eddie yawned. Amos glared at him as though it were an editorial comment.

"I'm tired," Eddie said.

"You can take a nap sitting up."

"It's not the same thing."

"Tough."

I was about to ask him if he didn't realize how much better he would feel when I remembered my own perception that he could not. I waited until the next time they had a similar argument on another subject and then I told them that I'd talked to Dr. Thom just to get some sense of the possibilities in case they should ever feel impelled to . . .

Amos picked up a bread knife and said that if there was any cutting to be done, he was the one who was going to do it.

"Don't be silly," I said, secure in the knowledge that if he actually came after me I could get away without difficulty. "That's no solution to the problem."

"You're the problem," Amos said. "There's no problem except you."

I glanced at Eddie but he wasn't about to say a word while Amos was holding the knife.

"Listen to me," I said, "please. Can't we have a reasonable discussion? I know what it seems like to you; maybe you think I'm being very casual about this whole thing. I know you're the ones who'd be taking the risks. But you don't know the benefits. You

195

don't know what it's like to wake up in the morning and just think about what *you* want to do. Or even just wake up and get out of bed without having to worry about whether someone you're attached to wants to do the same thing. You don't know . . ." He slowly put down the knife. I thought I was making headway. I proceeded with my catalog of the joys of being a single person . . . of bending over to pick a flower when you felt like it . . . of walking the streets of a new city when nobody knew you were there . . . of hiding in the bathroom for an hour at a time with a book and maybe something to eat because you had a delicious desire to be absolutely alone with your digestive system. I thought I was being at once sane and eloquent, humorous and comfortably bizarre.

"Why don't you shut the fuck up?" Amos suggested.

Stalemate.

Once in a while when Amos had dozed off Eddie would ask me some question like, "Remember when you were talking about what it's like to pick a flower?" He wanted to hear about being single although he thought he'd never get to go there.

While Amos thought he already knew: discomfort, pain and probably death. I would check out his objections with furtive (later open) calls to Dr. Thom but when I got the answers they never, in Amos's mind, applied to the questions.

I thought about the surgery all the time now. I didn't know what would happen if it took place but I was certain nothing good could happen if it didn't.

KEN McDougall and his girlfriend and sometime co-worker Michelle Sapirstein came to Bootville directly from the '68 Democratic Convention in Chicago, where they'd been through the mob scene and Ken's cameras and other equipment had been stolen. Supposedly they'd come for a rest. They had the use of a log cabin on a huge piece of land that had been bought by some friend who'd meant to build a home on it and bring his family away from the pressures and terrors of middle-class life in Brookline, Massachusetts, but meanwhile the friend's wife had left him and the land and cabin were unused.

I met Michelle first—with her four-year-old son, Jason—in the store, and asked her if she wanted to come back for coffee although I was anxious about whether she knew about us and if so what she thought. But I needn't have worried; Michelle was more tolerant than I. Michelle had already visited places in her mind where everyone was connected to everything.

"Did you know that our husbands were Siamese twins?" I asked her on the way back to the house.

"Far out," she said calmly.

Over coffee I told her that I was bored, that there were times I wasn't sure I could face another winter in this house, in this town, alone with three kids for much of the day.

"Yeah," Michelle said, "well ..." My boredom made her more uncomfortable than my Siamese twins. "You gotta ... you know ..." She was pretty in a quiet blonde way, very skinny, with John Lennon glasses and wispy chiffon blouses over her jeans.... "You trip?"

I shook my head. She had to be talking about LSD, which I'd read of in the Sunday paper from Boston. "I don't have anything against it," I assured her. "I, I just...no one's ever offered me any."

She sipped her coffee. She wasn't a proselytizer.

"I smoked a lot of grass in school, of course. Years ago." I felt very old as I said it, although Michelle must be close to my age, she was too calm and wise to be much younger. "Grass was pretty far out in those days."

She nodded. And yawned. She was twenty-two years old, this emissary from a world where people didn't have the same old dumb problems. I couldn't come to terms with her age. It was the first time I experienced that sense of obsolescence that gripped so many people during the sixties, as the Beatles and heart transplants conspired to prove there was no longer any sufficient reason for growing old.

Ken was a small, quiet, handsome man, older than any of us, actually, but with that hairy, blue-denim, counterculture ambience that made you think indiscriminately of people as being young. He'd been doing commercial films until a few years earlier, when he'd become a radical political "activist" and started making documentaries. Now he'd used up his grubstake from the commercial days and had been just about wiped out by the loss of his equipment. He said he didn't know yet what he wanted to do but he couldn't go back to making commercials. He knew what he wanted to do, of course. He wanted to do a documentary about a Siamese twin marriage, although I was never certain whether he'd heard about us before coming to Bootville or had come because somehow he'd heard about us. I didn't worry about it much one way or the other; I was too busy developing a crush on him.

At first he dropped by with Michelle and Jason in the afternoon or evening; later he came alone, often in the morning. Michelle had gone to Boston for a while; whether she needed to or was just giving him room to play with us I also never found out.

I thought he was dropping in because he liked my cooking. Michelle was a noncook. I'd make him bacon and eggs or even pancakes, or some wonderful biscuits. I was showing off. He was very appreciative. We talked a lot.

He never pried into our lives in a way that would have made me anxious. He didn't have to. He just let me talk and God knows I was eager to do that. I talked about the surgery because it was on my mind, expressing my doubts about whether I was fair in wanting them to be separated now, telling him how angry I got with Amos for wanting to hold on to that joint which had drawn me to them. I talked about my childhood and about how I'd come East to college to be near Dianne and find wisdom, and about Dr. Story, whom I hadn't mentioned to anyone ever since the Shlomo days. I told him about my parents' deaths and about how wonderful Dianne and her parents had been to me, how intricately my life was wrapped up with Dianne's, partly because she was the only person I really knew now who had known my parents. I told him how I'd pushed mindlessly for the union with the twins and I thought I might be crazy. I even told him how when I did something good—like taking care of Dianne's baby so she could go back to work—I never felt as though I'd done it for the right reasons.

"You're so hard on yourself," he kept saying.

"I know," I replied, "but I feel I have to be. I keep thinking if I let up on myself the rest of them will come down on me for something I don't even know I'm doing." I laughed nervously. "Except that they're just as crazy as I am, in different ways." In a burst of total confidence I told him of my discovery that Dianne didn't even like Amos. "It really blew my mind. It made me think about a lot of things I should have been thinking about all along. I'm not trying to put down Dianne," I said quickly, although this wasn't exactly true. Once or twice now he'd come by in the evening when Dianne was home and they'd ended up talking about her work to the exclusion of everything else. I was jealous. "I love Dianne," I said, "but always . . . I think maybe I've learned more than she has over the years." I smiled sadly. "Housewives learn more than anybody and have less use for what they learn. By the time I know how to raise kids they'll be gone."

Philip came home from kindergarten.

He would be six in another few months. He was big for his age, with huge, serious dark eyes and thick, shiny, nearly black hair like the twins'. A charmer. He charmed Ken and he charmed me —practically out of my pants. Being in a room with him and Ken was . . . the way it should have been with the twins.

"Who'll be gone?" Philip asked.

"You will," I said. "Someday you'll grow up and . . . you'll want to go places and do things. You'll have a job that you like to do."

"What are you going to do when you grow up, Phil?" Ken asked him.

"What do *you* do?" Philip asked.

"I make films," Ken said. "I'm a filmmaker."

"I'm going to be a filmmaker," Philip said.

I was embarrassed. Everyone knew who little boys were supposed to want to be like when they grew up.

Daisy wandered down from the bedroom, where she'd been all by herself cutting up magazines for well over an hour. A girl version of Philip, with lighter hair like mine, she was the first of the three children who could be in the house for long periods of time and be invisible. Quietly she watched everything that was going on and then floated away. While when Philip wandered he was always looking for something. Someone. Often someone else's father to hang out with. From the time he'd been allowed to traverse the road by himself he'd often wandered up to the general store to be with the teenaged boy who helped Mrs. Singleton there, and he was always attaching himself to men who chopped wood and drove snowmobiles. He seemed to particularly like Ken, maybe because he saw that I liked him. Or maybe Ken was just one of those men little boys were always wanting to be like when they grew up . . . and housewives were always thinking might ease their loneliness.

"Would you show me how?" Philip asked Ken as Daisy climbed onto my lap.

"How what?" Ken asked.

"To be a filmmaker," Philip said.

"Oh," Ken said. "Sure." He considered for a moment. "I'll tell you what. I'm going to Boston next week to get a new camera; I'll pick up some film and we'll make a little movie."

"I want to make a big one," Philip said.

Ken laughed. "Well," he said, "we'll start with a little one."

It was ready a month later. All sixty seconds of it. Ken brought it over the evening he returned with it from Boston. (He'd hoped to bring back Michelle as well but Michelle hadn't quite gotten it together to return to Bootville, although she let Jason come with Ken. Jason was quiet and easy and I never minded having him around.) Anyway, Carly had made up the story and she and Daisy starred. Carly was the mommy and Daisy was the daughter and Philip the father, although this was purely understood since he didn't appear in the movie but was behind the camera with Ken the whole time.

The name of the movie is *Dangerous Things*.

Carly is doing mommy activities at the stove and Daisy, sitting on the floor with her back to the camera, is in danger from some object she finds on the floor. The object (Carly explains to us after the movie) is something the daddy has left around that babies aren't supposed to have.

Carly, turning from the stove, perceives Daisy's clear and present danger from the object, dashes over and scoops her up, throwing away the dangerous (invisible) object. Daisy, frightened by the sudden gesture, bursts into tears. As the minute-long movie ends, Carly is cradling Daisy in her arms, singing a silent lullaby.

Dianne and I clapped enthusiastically, then Eddie picked up our enthusiasm and clapped, too. Philip was in a state of near hysteria, so excited that we had to play the movie five more times before we could get him up to his room. Carly was acting quite sophisticated about her part in the enterprise and claimed not to understand for the life of her why Philip was running around like a maniac.

"What's doing at the office?" Ken asked Dianne when we'd finally gotten the kids up to bed.
"We have a terrific possession case," Dianne said happily. Ken brought her out in a way I never could. Besides, more and more was happening at her office. Not just possession cases. The children of some of their middle-aged, prosperous faculty clients had gone through Berkeley or to Chicago and returned to raise hell; tenure problems were beginning to ripple through the university. People were acting crazy. A whole generation was skipping blithely over the limits. "Friends of mine in Lebanon," she went on. "A commune. It's one of those obvious cases where the town is out to get them in any way it can." She wasn't even sure the charge would hold up in court. In a raid on the commune the sheriff had found a lot of grass and some mescaline but there was no warrant and the raid seemed to be the result of some insane impulse that . . .
I was too jealous to concentrate for long on her words. When Ken and I were alone I felt that he was interested in me but when Dianne was with us I was sure that only she interested him, although I couldn't point to any specific difference in the way he treated me. I got angry at her. If these were her friends, how come I didn't know them? Anyway, we were thirty-three years old. Wasn't she aware of insurmountable differences between herself and a bunch of teenagers who were somewhat more dependent on Mother Dope than on Mother Food and who lived with each

other in what seemed to be nearly interchangeable skins? I was aware of the similarities between them and us; how could she be unaware of the differences? Did she think she was young because she was radical?

Then I got confused because I remembered that Ken had that same radical youth mentality as Dianne and he was older but it didn't bother me in him. If I could buy his act and not hers it was probably sheer jealousy. His interest in her work had once again kindled my feelings of boredom and loneliness.

Why had I ever wanted to be a housewife anyway? How could I have longed to be a housewife and mother when I grew up—when I'd grown up knowing that my housewife-mother was the loneliest of women? Society hadn't had to thrust the role upon me, I'd run around begging for it, like so many of the other women I'd later meet in New York, raging at the discovery that salvation had only been masquerading in Mommy's apron and high heels; its reality was somewhere else!

(But where? We might find out if only we had the time, the money, the youth. That's what we need—to be young and firm and beautiful again. If only we could be like our daughters when we grew up!)

"Why is he here all the time?" Amos asked one evening when Kenneth had left. His manner wasn't nasty because he'd already put away about half a bottle of whiskey and that always quieted him down.

"It's not all the time," Dianne said.

"Every night, nearly."

"He's interested in us," I said. "He likes to talk to us."

"What for?"

It wasn't that he disliked Ken more than other men he'd known; he just didn't know why anyone should bother to make friends.

How nice for Amos, not to know what loneliness was.

I wondered now if the twins' comfort in each other hadn't added to my terrible sense of isolation instead of curing it; if their togetherness had made me measure my loneliness and find it less tolerable. For the first time in a long time I thought of the childhood night or many nights when awakening in the darkness I looked down to the courtyard and saw my parents swimming together in the pool, their strokes so gentle that they barely splashed the water, doing the sidestroke, facing each other, looking at each other, never speaking. Eventually I would move away from the window and lie down again but the bed that had been my cozy shelter was now a cold and lonely place.

Dianne was explaining to the men that Kenneth probably just needed to communicate with some other intelligent adults.

"Actually," I broke in without prior thought, "he probably just wants to make us into a movie."

Then I stared at them and they stared at me.

"What are you talking about?" Amos demanded.

"Movie!" Dianne exclaimed in horror.

"Sure," I said with false nonchalance, "it makes sense, doesn't it?"

"Why does it make sense?" she asked.

"Because we're here," I said patiently. "And he's here. And that's what he does."

Silence.

"I'm sure you're wrong, Nady. He doesn't even seem interested in—" she waved an arm around the living room, "in everything here. He never asks *me* about anything but my work."

In other words, he wasn't interested in anyone but her.

"That's because he gets the rest from me." I was beginning to enjoy myself a little. "After all, it's fine to assume he just happened to stumble on us and we're so fascinating that he happens to keep coming back for more . . . but the fact is, he's this unattached man with an occupation but no job . . . hanging around this little town in New Hampshire his girlfriend won't stay in for more than a few weeks at a time."

He doesn't have to escape from the real world; he's not a bunch of freaks.

"He doesn't seem like a bad guy," Eddie said.

"I don't care what kind of guy he is," Amos growled. "I don't see why he has to be around here so much."

And the subject wasn't raised again until the day weeks later when Dianne told me, in a manner suggesting it hadn't come up before and was of no major importance, that she and Ken had been discussing the possibility of his making a documentary about our lives.

"Oh? What a fascinating possibility. I wonder how come no one ever thought of it before."

She had the good grace to blush.

"I haven't forgotten what you said, Nady. And you were partly right. I should have understood that, but you somehow presented it in such a sinister way . . . as though he were sort of sneaking up on our lives. I couldn't accept that version of Kenneth so I couldn't believe what you were saying."

She sounded unbelievably proprietary. He'd gone from being everybody's Ken to being her Kenneth.

"And how," I asked, very slowly and deliberately, "did you resolve this intellectual dilemma?"

"We talked about it."

We. They. She was sleeping with him, I was sure of it.

"How did it come up?"

She hesitated.

"Here," I said, "I'll start you off to make it easier. You were lying in bed . . . no, on the couch in your office, late at night . . . last Tuesday when you called and asked if I could take the kids to the movie in Keene because you were supposed to but something important came up. . . . You did tell me you have a couch up there, didn't you?" I'd never seen the inside of her office. On the rare occasion when I was supposed to meet her in Hanover she always found a reason to meet elsewhere. "Okay, so you're there on the couch. You've been fucking and now you're all happy and relaxed and you start chatting." The further I went, of course, the more certain I became that it was true. Dianne's expressions were priceless, going from startled . . . to furtively proud (she'd not only bagged the bird but another envious hunter was present to make her triumph visible and complete) . . . to impassive. The next ice age had arrived and left a cold white mass where her face had once been.

The glacier cracked in one spot just enough for a few words to come out.

"I'm sorry. I can't deal with you when you're this way."

"All right. I'm sorry. Just tell me."

"We were talking." She paused, still trying to see how much bullshit she could slide past my shit detector without making the siren go off. "I asked him what his next project was going to be. He told me that the problem was that he didn't even have the equipment that he needed to do a real film now, that without financing he'd never be able to get the equipment. And without a good solid project, script, whatever, he'd never be able to get financing."

I nodded.

"What he really wants to do is a sort of personal film, a *cinéma vérité* kind of thing, and it occurred to me as he was talking that he could use us as a kind of, whatever you'd call it, collateral, maybe. He'd use the *idea* of doing a film about us to get money for new equipment and to live on for a while."

So he hadn't just screwed her into complicity, she'd come running to make the sacrifice of our lives.

"But then there'd be the film."

She shrugged. "As long as we get final approval before distribution."

"Final approval."

"According to the terms of the deal he makes with the company that finances him, we'd have final say over whether the film actually ever came out."

"But we don't want a film, do we?" I asked.

"Of course not," she said.

"Then why are we . . . why will we . . . you mean we'd know all along that we weren't going to approve?"

She nodded complacently.

206

"But . . . but . . . just . . . leaving aside the question of honesty, why would *they* go for it? The companies? They'd have to be too dumb not to protect themselves in some way."

She shook her head. "The initial investment is too small for them to worry about in terms of what they could get later."

"What makes you think they'll see it that way?"

"In the past ten years," she said, "the twins have had dozens of offers."

"You're exaggerating. I remember years ago they'd get an inquiry here or there. Or their manager would call to ask what they were doing because so-and-so wanted . . . but—"

"There've been a lot more," she said, very quiet and nononsense, now. "I was looking for something in . . . I was looking through Amos's files. I mean we think of them as his files but most of the stuff is about all of us. I thought we had a right to know a little more than he tells us about financial matters. He's the only one who knows what's—"

"Okay, okay, go on."

"There are more letters than you'd believe. And the interesting thing is that he answered them all very carefully. Politely. Sort of keeping the doors open. As though someday we'd definitely let someone do it."

Sure. Why not? They had no sense of privacy.

"That makes sense," I said. "He's always worried that we're going to run out of money. But I don't understand how all those letters could have come without my noticing. I'm the one who usually gets the mail."

"They have a separate box number," she said quietly. "They pick up there once a week or so."

"No." Just as quietly. I was mortally wounded. By a symbol. "For how long?"

"The whole time. Ever since they came to Bootville."

"All through? They never dropped it even for a while?"

She shook her head.

I was limp. She could have done anything with me at that moment. She was smart enough not to press her advantage.

207

"Sometimes I'm certain," I said wearily, "that this marriage can't go on forever."

"Don't overreact, Nady," she pleaded. "We just have to be very adaptable."

"What does that mean?"

"I mean we have to grab new opportunities when they come along."

"Do you mean opportunities, or do you mean men?"

"No, that's not what I mean. Or maybe it is, in a way. But you shouldn't overestimate the importance of . . . Ken is just a nice, intelligent man, passing through. This is not a serious thing for me."

Just a frivolous little affair she was willing to turn our lives inside out for. Of course she managed not to think of it that way because she wanted to help him, but I knew better. I knew something would come out of the movie whether it was good or bad. Which was why I was finally willing to do it. Something will happen. Amos and Eddie will look at these two awkward, semihuman creeps shuffling around the screen and will suddenly be willing to risk the surgery, was the way my reasoning went. Amos and Eddie will—anyway, something will happen. Anything.

"I just hope he's a good lay," I muttered.

"Why do you have to reduce everything to obscenities?" she asked.

"You're the one who's doing it," I pointed out. "I'm just talking about it."

Which struck me as a model of my life.

The men—Amos, I should say—turned out to be remarkably easy to convince. Amos wanted to know what was in it for us and Ken told him we'd have a percentage of the film if it was distributed. He haggled over our percentage, ending up with a full half of Ken's share. His only other condition was that he didn't have to do anything special, just let Ken be around. He didn't have to talk or be agreeable. Dianne drew up an agreement among the five of us and Ken went to New York and a few weeks later came back with Michelle and his new equipment.

208

AN AMERICAN MARRIAGE

A FILM BY KENNETH MCDOUGALL

The setting is primarily a farmhouse in New Hampshire, a state with no growing season to speak of. It is spring of 1969. The mud season has just ended. Two children are running and playing in the backyard. Suddenly what has been an idyllic scene dissolves into tragedy as the children get into a fight and the older one, a girl, starts hammering at the head of the younger one, a boy.

PHILIP (*screaming*): Mommy! Mommy! Carly mashed my head.

He runs toward the house, crying hysterically. His "sister" stands in the yard, waiting to see what will happen next.

NADINE SMITH *comes out of the house trailed by* DAISY, *a child of two.*

NADINE: What happened?

CARLY: He got mud on my shirt.

NADINE: Why didn't you change after school?

CARLY: You didn't make me.

PHILIP (*sobbing steadily*): It hurts. My head hurts. I think she broke it.

DAISY, *watching* PHILIP, *begins to cry.*

NADINE: Oh, shit. (*She picks up* DAISY, *seems about to go back into the house but changes her mind, turns back to* CARLY.) YOU KNOW YOU'RE NOT SUPPOSED TO HIT ON THE HEAD!

CARLY (*beginning to cry now, too*): I didn't mean to. He was too low.

PHILIP: I was not, I was standing up.

CARLY: You're still too low.

NADINE: Carly, go to the shop and stay with the daddies for a while.

CARLY: I don't feel like it.

NADINE: Go anyway.

PHILIP: What'll I do?

209

NADINE: Come on in the house with me. We'll bake some brownies. As a matter of fact, you take Daisy in and I'll be right there. But keep your hands off her.

PHILIP *and* DAISY *go up the back steps onto the porch and into the house.* NADINE *grabs the hand of the still crying* CARLY *and heads toward the garage.*

Close-up: Two sets of legs coming out from beneath a car whose end is jacked up. The legs are intertwined but only visible from the knees down, somehow conveying the impression that parts of the car's engine have dropped out and are having an orgy.

NADINE: Hello? Anyone home? (*A low grunt is heard from under the car.*) Carly's here. She's going to stay with you for a while. I mean, she has to stay with you for a while because I've had it. CAN YOU HEAR ME, GODDAMN IT?

Laboriously the two sets of legs inch out from under the car, followed by two sets of arms and two attached torsos, then two heads.

CARLY (*sinks to her knees on her father's side, her tears renewed*): Philip got mud all over my new shirt!

EDDIE *twists to embrace his daughter, leaving huge grease stains on her face and her blouse, which neither appears to notice.* NADINE *turns around and walks out of the garage. Camera dissolves to* NADINE, *putting tin of brownie batter into the oven, slamming the door and plopping down on a chair.*

NADINE (*laughing nervously*): It's funny, instead of making me act better than I usually am, the camera seems to be making me worse. I guess I have the feeling that I have to show you the true me. The worst me. (*She looks away thoughtfully, takes off her glasses and rubs her eyes, then puts on the glasses again.*) I don't know what the best me is.

Camera dissolves to garage, where EDDIE *sits on* AMOS's *lap and* CARLY *sits on* EDDIE's. CARLY's *crying subsides. After a bit she gets up and begins to put in order a small tray of nuts and bolts lying on the floor.* NADINE's *voice is heard over this vignette.*

NADINE: We work, we play, we do the things other people do. Of course it's difficult sometimes. The men can't drive, to take one of the obvious examples. So if they have a job away from home I have to take them.

Dissolve to men getting into car, NADINE's *anxious face seen dimly through the windshield as she brushes away the steam that has accumulated on the glass.*

NADINE: Since I'm a lousy driver *(nervous laugh)* this isn't such a hot arrangement. On the other hand, nobody's been killed . . . yet . . . ha-ha . . . Di's a very cautious driver but by the time she's finished driving back and forth from Hanover every day she naturally doesn't feel like doing any extra driving, even if they have to go someplace on a Saturday.

The camera, having shown Nadine getting the microbus started, shows DIANNE *getting out of the other car, a Volkswagen Beetle, in Hanover.* DIANNE *walks along the street, checking out a couple of store windows before going upstairs to her office in a neat little two-story building over a bookstore. She looks pretty and very ladylike, in her fur-trimmed storm coat and high-heeled boots. She nods to the receptionist and a partner in the firm, who's giving some papers to his secretary, and goes to the back room, which is her office. Clearly this is a woman's office, differing from the others in mood and substance, with a flower-fabric-covered sofa on one wall and matching curtains at the window. Clearly this is a woman who has more of the maternal juices running in her than have outlet in her home, for she has turned her office into a little home away from home. The sills are lush with plants and photos of her daughter cover*

211

the desk. She is obviously very attached to her daughter, particularly in effigy.

NADINE'S *voice is now heard over the sounds of* DIANNE'S *office—the phone ringing,* DIANNE *speaking on the phone, the rustle of papers as she opens and scans her mail, low conversation with a secretary.*

NADINE: I have to admit that sometimes I'm very jealous of Dianne. It's not that I want to do what she's doing, at least not a poor imitation. I'd rather be taking care of kids than pushing papers around some desk all day. Kids are very interesting, even if they're difficult, and they give you more love and warmth, along with all the crap, than you'll ever get in a court of law. But . . . anyway, even if I wanted to do what she's doing I couldn't. I don't have the academic background. Not even a B.A. I was a dropout. (*Again she takes off her glasses, rubs her eyes, replaces them.*) Sometimes I think I'll go back to school when Daisy does. (*laughs*) It sounds as though I mean to go off to kindergarten.

Dissolve to DIANNE *in her office. Talking to the camera. A much less painful experience for the viewer because the surface of her face is much clearer than that of the other woman, whose face irony and doubt have contorted to the point where it sometimes looks like a side of Francis Bacon.*

DIANNE: I suppose what I'm most involved in right now is Harold's case.

Camera pans briefly to HAROLD CRAMPTON, *a handsome but somewhat pallid young man, bearded without exactly being hairy. A sort of Clark Kent for the sixties—an aristocratic head, so to speak, in a costume by L. L. Bean. While* DIANNE *talks there is a moving montage of headlines from local newspapers:* CRAMPTON FIRED, CRAMPTON APPEALS, CRAMPTON WILL SPEAK ON CHICAGO, *etc.*

DIANNE: Harold, as you know, was an instructor in the Chemistry Department who was fired for reasons relating to his political

212

activities, not to his competence as a teacher of chemistry, which was never questioned. When asked why he should be so concerned about Harold's political activities when they didn't in any way impinge on his effectiveness in the classroom, the chairman of his department initially replied that it was the very fact that politics had nothing to do with Harold's work that made all his headline-creating radical politics so distressing and inappropriate. It was only when the obvious First Amendment implications of this position were called to his attention that Dr. Lederer began searching for a work-related reason to retroactively justify having fired Harold. Naturally this is totally unacceptable to us, as his lawyers . . . and the lawyers for the estate of his father, Dean Owsley Crampton.

One cannot help but like this person who has all the right ideas and manages to package them in a hesitant, ladylike manner that makes them acceptable not only to you and me but to a third-generation law firm in Hanover, the blue-haired lady of New Hampshire towns.

DIANNE: We'll go as far with this case as we have to, unless the school comes to its senses. (*Smiles. Looks over at* HAROLD.) Or Harold decides he can't go on. This has been quite an ordeal for him.

HAROLD: I can go on as long as I have to, as long as I have Dianne. I don't know what I would do without Dianne.

Dissolve to Smith house, where DIANNE *is being greeted at the end of a hard day by* CARLY, *who's hugging and kissing her and trying to tell her a story before she gets off her wet raincoat and muddy boots.*

DIANNE (*laughing*): Hold it a minute, Carly, hold it. You can't imagine how hard the rain was on the highway, Nady.

CARLY: Nady's going to take Philip and me to Brattleboro tomorrow.

DIANNE: That's wonderful, Nady.

Camera pans to DIANNE *at her office desk.*

DIANNE: I don't know what I'd do without Nadine. I never particularly intended to get married or have children, and although I'm delighted now that I had Carly I also know it's terribly important to me to be able to work. Nady's been wonderful, she's really a second mother to Carly, and of course closer to her than any houskeeper would ever be. (*She smiles at some question, not audible to the viewer, from the off-camera interviewer.*) Would I have gotten married if we hadn't all happened to come together? Oh, I doubt it. I suspect I would have made myself a little book-lined studio nest in New York and led a rather scholarly, spinsterish life when I wasn't working.

Camera returns to Smith kitchen, where NADINE *is kneading bread.*

NADINE: Would I have gotten married if the twins hadn't been around? Oh, I guess, I guess we both would've. We were both married before, I guess Di told you that, so you couldn't really say this was a total fr— whatever, that we were meant for each other and if they hadn't come along we'd have entered a nunnery or something. We were both always looking to nail down some guy for life. (*laughs*) I think I mean that literally.

Camera moves slowly into living room, where EDDIE *and* AMOS *sit with the TV set on, knitting Irish fisherman sweaters. On the floor nearby* DAISY *is putting together a wooden jigsaw puzzle which the men have made for her. As the camera moves toward the twins they look up, the expressions on their faces so different as to blot out the physical resemblance between them.* EDDIE *smiles at the camera as though it were a friend while* AMOS *glowers as though it were the enemy.*

EDDIE: We started this knitting thing after we read an article this past winter about the real Irish fishermen doing it in their off-season. It made real sense, you know, because one of us can do it, or both of us . . . and if I'm watching TV, I like to watch a lot of TV and Amos don't . . . he used to be more bugged because even with earphones just the flickering lights bothered him and all. But when he's knitting he doesn't mind as much. Or sometimes we do little woodwork jobs. Like we're trying out these puzzles, like Daisy's. We'll sell them through the crafts fair next summer. We do some of the small sanding stuff and so on when we're sitting around. Or we just sit. We play a lot of checkers. And double solitaire.

His speech, which is identical to that of his brother, who will seldom speak during this film, has a strange, thick-tongued quality.

NADINE: It's funny, when you live with someone you're used to the way they talk but I really *hear* Eddie in a different way, now, just because I know we're in a movie.

AMOS *glares at her.*

NADINE: What's the matter, Amos? I'm just telling the truth.
AMOS (*growls*): You're always just telling the truth.
NADINE (*obviously torn between a desire to avoid an unpleasant moment and the need to justify herself before the camera tribunal*): What does that mean?
AMOS: It means I'm not jumping through any hoops for this joker.
NADINE: Nobody asked you to jump through any hoops, Amos. Anyway, this whole thing was hardly my idea so don't put me in the position of . . . (*turns to camera*) Do you think maybe it would be a good idea to turn off the camera so we can settle this and go on with the real thing?
VOICE: Doesn't matter. We can just cut it later on if it doesn't work.
NADINE (*blinking*): Doesn't work?
AMOS: Oh, shit.
EDDIE (*smiling at camera*): The thing about these long winters up here, by the time spring comes tempers ain't too good.

AMOS *gives him a disgusted look but says nothing.*

215

NADINE: Mmmm. The winters. That's when the natives turn to drink.

VOICE: How about you folks? Do you put it away in the winter?

NADINE: Oh, sure. Or at least . . . more than in the summer. . . . Amos is what you might call a real drinker. I get smashed now and then but I'm not really . . . the rest of us aren't what you'd call real drinkers.

VOICE: How does that affect you, Eddie? Amos's drinking, I mean.

EDDIE: That's the funny thing. No matter how loaded Amos gets I hardly feel it. It's funny because we do share a liver, or at least our livers, they're connected, there's a bridge of liver. (*His tone has taken on the quality of a guide at a tourist attraction— at once perky and informal, rote and remote.* AMOS *is knitting again.*)

NADINE: That's the main reason they think surgery to separate them would be successful (AMOS's *head snaps up but she appears not to notice*); their circulatory systems don't communicate that closely.

EDDIE: Right.

AMOS *starts to rise from the love seat without signaling* EDDIE, *who unwittingly pulls* AMOS *back down by remaining stationary.* NADINE's *voice is heard at this moment.*

NADINE: It's the first time I ever saw that happen. They always just get up or sit down.

AMOS: Stop the camera. Stop right there. Stop the whole thing.

EDDIE: Come on, it ain't going to happen just because we talk about it.

NADINE's VOICE: I never heard how awful Eddie's speech was until now. His grammar.

EDDIE (*to camera*): As you can see, my brother doesn't exactly like to discuss this subject.

AMOS: Shut up. Stop the camera. I'm not making any fucking movie. (*Again he tries to rise but* EDDIE *doesn't move with him.*) Come on, God damn it, I wanna get out of here!

216

EDDIE (*softly*): Be reasonable. We're just talking. I just wanted to expl—

> AMOS *smacks* EDDIE's *face. Tears spring to* EDDIE's *eyes but he doesn't speak.*

NADINE: Oh, my God, I can't believe what's happening. Stop for a while, Ken, please! Don't you see what's happening?

VOICE (*inaudible*):

NADINE (*frantic*): He's terrified by the whole subject. He thinks they'd sacrifice him. Please, Ken, we can talk about it some other time. I *want* to talk about it. But he's terrified because no one can tell for sure what'd happen, he just—

AMOS (*his whole body shaking with rage, his wrath now entirely on* NADINE): YOU STAY THE FUCK OUT OUT OF THIS! DON'T YOU DARE STICK YOUR FUCKING NOSE INTO THIS, IT HAS NOTHING TO DO WITH YOU!

> *Camera pans to* NADINE *sitting on the porch steps the following morning.*

NADINE (*rueful*): It sort of blew my mind, his saying it had nothing to do with me. It made me face . . . maybe I'm only just beginning to face . . . what strangers we are to each other. Not that it's always such a bad idea, being a stranger to someone you have to live with. (*laughs softly*) It can be harder to live with someone you know too well. Like Dianne and me. Sometimes it would be better if I didn't know . . . she's there in my head. I don't have to do something to know how she's going to feel about it. Before I do it I have an argument in my head, her side and my side . . . as though we were the ones who were attached. Only in the head. (*She shudders.*) Maybe that's worse. There's no surgery for it. (*She takes off her glasses and rubs her eyes in the gesture that has become familiar to the viewer. But when she puts back her glasses there's no feeling that the gesture has accomplished whatever it usually does for her. She stands up and looks restlessly out toward the garden.*) Dianne could be on the other side of the earth . . . she could be *dead*, for that matter . . . and her voice

217

would still be there in my head. (*She kicks some junk lying on the porch in a sudden decisive gesture.*)

Camera pans to the interior of small office in Boston General Hospital.

DR. RHODES: Of course there are perils involved in any such operation. I can't go into the specific possibilities with you, waiver or no waiver. It does seem fair to state, though, that the perils involved in their staying together would have to be given a very strong weight on the other side of the scale.

VOICE (*inaudible*):

DR. RHODES (*flatly*): No. It's not possible. There's no way in the world that it's possible they could be comfortable the way they are.

Pan to another office in Boston General, this one with a couch in it in addition to the normal office furniture.

DR. FERAUC (*smiling slightly*): No way it's possible, hmm? (*shrugs*) Well, he must be very comfortable, being so certain. My own guess . . . but I'd like to emphasize that it's strictly a guess and I'm not acquainted with the gentlemen . . . is that in some sense comfortable would be the best word to define what they *are* right now. And what they might *not* be for a long while after such an operation. Twins, you know, have a sort of cushion against the world, and that kind of cushion is what many people spend their lives trying to find. And in the case of Siamese twins, of course, the cushion is so much more extraordinary. They never wake up . . . or sleep for that matter . . . without another heartbeat accompanying their own. Think about that for a while.

VOICE: Would it be fair to say, then, that in your opinion the twins are better off staying as they are?

DR. FERAUC: No, I wouldn't say that.

VOICE: You're not against the surgery?

DR. FERAUC: Not at all. What I'm against is the idea of people's going into such a proceeding without any realistic sense of the difficulties that are likely to ensue.

218

VOICE: But you wouldn't care to predict whether the difficulties are likely to outweigh the advantages.

DR. FERAUC (*impatient*): I wouldn't. I'm not in the prediction business. Furthermore, I don't even *know* the men you're talking about. . . . Look, I have another appointment now so I've got to interrupt you.

VOICE (*inaudible*):

DR. FERAUC: How can you get to know them by talking to me? Why don't you . . . if you haven't done it already, why don't you talk to the people who knew them when they were young? Get a stronger sense of who they were . . . who they are. You're trying to make a movie about people you don't know at all.

Exterior of the State Home for Retarded Children in Dixonville, New Hampshire, a shabby, decrepit building in beautiful country surroundings, with a beautiful lake visible around the back. In front of the building, on an ordinary kitchen chair which looks almost surrealistic in the middle of the overgrown lawn, sits a little white-haired lady who appears to be almost as old as the building itself. She's wearing blue jeans and a red and black checked lumberjack shirt and sneakers. She seldom smiles and when she does there's a furtive quality to her amusement—as though God would prefer that she be otherwise occupied.

MRS. STORM: Course I remember 'em.

VOICE: What do you remember best?

MRS. STORM: I just remember 'em.

VOICE: Were they good boys?

MRS. STORM: Uh-yuh.

VOICE: How were they different from the others?

MRS. STORM: Smarter.

VOICE: Anything else?

MRS. STORM: Not so's you'd notice. Better behaved.

VOICE: Would you say you treated them the same as the others?

MRS. STORM: No different. Except, course, they needed special clothes. To keep their, y'know . . . covered.

219

MONTAGE: Clippings, first the original story from Life, then the Time article and various newspaper headlines: SIAMESE TWINS DISCOVERED IN NEW HAMPSHIRE, etc.

Then, exterior of a neat white-frame home somewhere in New England. BRIAN TULLY, the Time-Life stringer who was vacationing in New Hampshire twenty years earlier when he discovered the twins, leans on the handle of his power mower as he talks to the camera.

TULLY: Do I remember the first moment I saw them? If I live to be a hundred I'm not likely to forget it. I was a kid, twenty-three years old, just married. Mary and I were vacation honey-mooning, tooling around New Hampshire and Massachusetts. I'd been working for the Pittsfield paper for a couple of years and just landed the stringer assignment. It was a Sunday night and I was supposed to be back in Pittsfield early Monday morning, and outside Dixonville, maybe a few hundred yards past the home, the engine just died. Totally. Mary said we might as well try that big, ugly building we'd just passed, since there were still some lights on. When we rang the bell two women appeared. We told them our problem and one of them turned to the other and said, "Emma, get the boys." She asked if we wanted to come in. We did but the place was very cr— It was a sad place, if you get my meaning. A couple of the older kids were still around. Mongoloids or worse. It still bothers me after all these years when I think of them. Anyhow, it took so long for them to come downstairs I was thinking maybe they weren't around after all, whoever they were. I was about to ask if I could just use the phone to call a service station when I hear there're some people coming toward the room, or something . . . there're these sort of dragging noises across the floor. Then in come these two boys with their arms around each other, pretty normal looking, at least not like the others, except I can't figure out why they're holding on to each other that way and moving so slowly and awkwardly. . . . Then the little lady that fetched them, I think it was the younger sister of Mrs. Storm actually, anyway, she moved away and I can see they're really attached in some way. There's this thing be-

220

tween them. I can't really see it because it's covered, same fabric as their clothes're made of, and I swear to you that at first I didn't even realize it was part of them, I just thought to myself, they're doing something funny, here. Then Mary grabbed my hand and squeezed it as though her life depended on it. She knew right away but she was scared to death. I never could figure out the reason but she was always bothered by them, just the idea of them, d'y'know what I mean? She didn't sleep well for weeks after that and sometimes she'd gag on her food. She'd say she knew she was wrong to feel it but she felt as though there was something disgusting about them.

Anyhow, the twins had made themselves this sort of dolly for going distances, and they rode it down the road to where the car was, taking a box full of tools with them. We followed on foot. When we reached the car they'd gotten up the hood and set out a couple of lanterns so they could see what they were doing. The whole thing was so weird. I'm not sure I believed it all until I got back to Pittsfield and wrote it down. Amos never talked to me. Eddie was polite. Smiled. When they wanted me to do something, like turn the key and try to start the engine, Eddie would direct me. But the wildest thing was it hardly took them any time to find the broken wire that'd caused all the trouble. It was tiny and very unusual. My mechanic in Pittsfield told me it would've taken him hours to find but the boys went right to it, like a doctor who puts his stethoscope to the heart and instantly has a feel for what's wrong. The whole thing that went on was between them and the engine, they had this enormous feel for engines, especially car engines. What they did had nothing to do with a favor for us, or showing off what they could do, or any of the usual motives folks might have in doing something for strangers who seemed decent. Do you know what I'm trying to tell you? They didn't talk to each other and they didn't talk to us. It was like one person with two heads and four hands working on the engine in an otherwise vacant space.

Camera pans to a circus arena. No audience. Rehearsals are going on in the various rings. A young man with semi-

221

long hair and an Edwardian suit speaks to the camera. He represents the publicity office of the circus troupe. In the ring in back of him, TRESSALINA *practices.* TRESSALINA *is an acrobat the highlight of whose act is to hang by her beautiful thick brown hair, which goes down to her buttocks under normal circumstances, from a ring suspended high over the nets. As seen from the audience, where the camera is, she has a gorgeous, shapely body and a beautiful, vivid face.*

TRESSALINA *unties her hair and bounces gracefully into the net. She makes her way toward the seats, vaults easily over the gate and runs gracefully up the steps toward the camera. Seen from close up her vivid features are so powerful as to be hideous; lines of age and strain are deeply etched between her nostrils and cheeks and along her forehead; her gorgeous, shapely body is so muscular as to be fearsome— even her breasts seem rocklike; and her hair is as coarse and lifeless as that in a horse's tail. When she speaks her voice is tiny and breathless, her manner extremely shy and demure.*

TRESSALINA: Oh, yes, you could say we were very close. (*She giggles nervously.*) I'd say closer than they were to any of the others. They liked women better than men, anyway . . . but the three of us were a regular . . . threesome. I think they would have liked to make it permanent but I couldn't . . . Georgie had already come into the circus anyway.

Camera pans to GEORGIE, *a fierce-looking little bald man, the smithy for the circus horses, working at the forge and giving orders to two assistants.*

TRESSALINA: . . . with Georgie and me it was like fire and water right from the start. He had fits if he ever saw me near anyone else . . . especially them. They spooked him. Some of the other freaks didn't bother him but they did. When I tried to ask why, he got mad at me so I stopped. Anyhow, it was mixed up with the other thing, you know, the jealousy. Georgie is always jealous of anyone who, you know, really cares about me.

222

Camera pans to farmhouse, EDDIE *and* AMOS *at the TV. A bottle of Jack Daniels on the table in front of them and a glass next to it.* AMOS *is visibly drunk.* KEN *has worked his way back into* AMOS's *half-acceptance by bringing him a case of Jack Daniels, a fact which is not clear to the casual viewer.*

EDDIE *(puzzled)*: Tressalina?

AMOS *(speech more slurred than usual)*: The one with the hair.

EDDIE: Everyone has hair.

AMOS: What's wrong with you? You're the one with the memory. In the *circus*, stupid. She hung by her hair.

EDDIE: Oh, yeah, Tressalina. I remember her. She was a nice girl.

AMOS: She was ugly as sin.

EDDIE: Yeah. But nice.

AMOS: She had to be nice. She was so ugly nobody would've talked to her if she wasn't nice.

Camera returns to circus. TRESSALINA, *in an otherwise empty arena, swinging by her hair, then untying it again and bouncing gracefully into the net, where she lies, breathing hard, looking up at the camera above her on a high platform. Meanwhile we hear her voice.*

TRESSALINA: They had a thing about my hair. Not like what other people have, you know, this curiosity. My hair's so strong, how much do I weigh, like that. They used to play with it, you know, wind it around their *(she giggles nervously again)* . . . Oh, my Lord, I just thought to myself, what are you going to do with this picture? If Georgie ever sees it he'll kill me!

The Smith living room a little later the same night. The bottle is now about two-thirds empty. EDDIE *is joining* AMOS *for one drink;* AMOS *is close to conviviality.*

VOICE *(inaudible)*:

EDDIE: Not too bad. It was different from year to year, depending on how many families there were, and how many single girls. There was a lot of segregation.

223

AMOS (*This memory would infuriate him if he weren't drunk and happy.*): The families treated the unmarried ones like lepers. They'd have some big, fucking Rumanian feast and they'd only invite the other *families*, never anyone who wasn't at least living with someone for a long time.

EDDIE: Once in a while we got invited because there were two of us.

AMOS: But then there were never girls for us.

VOICE: Did you have a lot of girls over the years?

EDDIE (*grins*): A few.

VOICE: Who were some of them?

EDDIE (*trying to remember*): It's hard to remember one from the other.

AMOS (*pouring another drink*): There was a troupe of Danish acrobats. That was the best. Six sisters.

VOICE: Why the best?

AMOS: Just easy. One or two of them were always around. Or all. They didn't like to go out touring the cities we were in because they had hardly any English. They had some in school but they were dumb.

EDDIE: They'd just take over and do everything. You didn't have to . . . you could just relax and they took over.

VOICE: Were they good-looking?

EDDIE: Uh-yuh.

AMOS: Two of them were. Three were just all right and one of them was ugly. (*His speech is nearly unintelligible by now and his head drops occasionally.*)

VOICE: You seem to have a real eye, Amos. Are looks more important to you than to Eddie?

AMOS (*his eyes half shut*): Important? Not important. I just see what's in front of my eyes, 's all.

Terrace of a two-story, white-stucco apartment residence of the sort that abounds in Los Angeles. SALLY DEMAREST *sits on a vinyl-webbed chaise, chain-smoking as she talks. She's forty-five years old but looks twenty years younger. Her body*

224

is that of a young girl although in the case of her body nothing artificial has been done to maintain that look. She is extraordinarily beautiful. She has smooth, olivey skin, large gray-green eyes and hair which is naturally a deep, near-brown blond but which she bleaches to a chorus-girl yellow. She never touches her hair or straightens her halter or makes any of those other gestures which convey insecurity while at the same time calling the observer's attention to the speaker's body. There is a remote-control device for a stereo next to her chaise. The music from Shane is playing in the background and will play repeatedly during the interview.

SALLY: Of course I remember them. Nobody's very likely to forget fucking a pair of Siamese twins.

VOICE: You wouldn't say that you were in love with them, then?

SALLY: Love? Is that a serious question?

VOICE: However you want to take it.

SALLY: What's your name again?

VOICE: Ken.

SALLY: Ken. Love is for T-shirts and tattoo artists, Ken.

As DEMAREST speaks we become aware that she has an extraordinary facility for making raging bitter comments like this in a manner so quiet and appealing that they don't make us squirm or turn off as we might if they were uttered by someone else.

KEN: Okay. How did you feel about the twins?

SALLY: They were two more pieces of meat. That is not to be considered in any sense a criticism of the twins. It's about me and about Los Angeles. All I can tell you about is me.

KEN: All right, what about you?

SALLY (*sighs*): All right. I asked for it. It's true that I agreed to talk about the twins.

KEN: Why did you agree?

SALLY (*shrugs*): Part of the daily struggle against anonymity we all wage out here.

225

Silence as the camera eats up SALLY's *large eyes, her ripe perfectly shaped mouth, her tanned slender legs.*

KEN: Tell me about yourself. Enough so I'll know what you were coming out of when you met them.

SALLY (*closes her eyes for a moment, then begins*): I was brought to Hollywood when I was fourteen years old by a middle-aged businessman named Victor Ginsberg who became a producer named Eduardo Mincieli. He was my mother's lover. He had an electronics business in Chicago, where I lived, at a time when private enterprise was just beginning to enter electronics. He'd also just begun to get involved in certain areas touching on the motion-picture business. He was divorced. He was also remarried, but that wasn't something that ever came up until after we'd run off to Hollywood. He set me up in a place I can see from this terrace, which is probably a perfect commentary on how far I've come in these thirty-one years. Yes (*obviously responding to an expression on* KEN's *face*), that's how long ago we're talking about. Funny, isn't it? I want approval on this interview, by the way.

Anyhow, Victor eventually convinced my mother to sign the necessary papers so I could go to school here. When he wasn't around I lived on my own. Came home from school, studied, maybe took a swim in the house pool, read hugely, everything from *Madame Bovary* to Victor's electronics magazines—and went to bed. He was around maybe ten days each month and then we'd eat out, make love and go to sleep. He was a lousy lay, like most middle-aged men who specialize in teenyboppers, but of course I didn't know that yet. When I was sixteen Victor came in one night with a very complicated problem on his mind. It's probably more than enough for your purposes to know that it had to do with a sophisticated relay system his company had been developing. He talked for an hour or so about the problem. He'd always talked about his work without realizing how much of his talk I absorbed. Anyway, I asked a question which crystallized the whole problem in his mind so he was able to solve it in ten

226

minutes. Then he whirled me around a couple of times, took me out for a celebration dinner, and never fucked me again.

All right. (*no break in narrative*) It is now eleven years later. I had graduated first in my high-school class but failed to take advantage of the scholarships that were offered to me because the man who was supporting me at the time promised me the lead in a movie he was raising the money to make. All I had to do was take acting lessons. I took the lessons but he never raised the money. I had small parts in a couple of other movies but I'm no actress. By the time I was twenty-five I'd been doing the same basic routine for eleven years. My current pillow of support was a baby-faced, apple-cheeked hustler named Selwyn Stern-heim, who was a theatrical agent for, among other brighter lights, Eddie and Amos. They'd just become his clients because there was considerable interest in making a movie about their lives and their old manager simply wasn't up to such negotiations

KEN: Do you know who'd decided that?

SALLY: Amos, of course.

KEN: Whatever happened to the movie?

SALLY: It was dropped, the way most things are. There was no way to make a movie of their lives. They had no lives to speak of. No events. No plot. There wasn't even any way to handle the sex because it was still the fifties. (*She stands up and looks out over the terrace wall as though she wants to take wing, fiddles with the stereo, which returns to* Shane, *sits down again.*)

KEN: How did you meet them?

SALLY: Sel threw a party for them. Very depressing. They all are. This one was particularly bad because the weather had turned awful so we couldn't use the terrace. In New York or Chicago a crowded party's sometimes great because you end up rubbing up against some interesting people. Being in a crowd at a Holly-wood party is like being in a window full of Easter eggs. They all look so perfectly beautiful you don't even notice the small hole where their insides were sucked out. But you also don't press too hard because if you ever faced the emptiness behind those shells . . . your own shell—

227

KEN: You're no empty shell.

SALLY: (*ignores him*): Anyway, this one was particularly awful because the guests of honor sat in one spot and didn't circulate. There was a receiving line, like Buckingham Palace. Only it was no king and queen at the end of this line, only these two attached country boys who had speech that was a little difficult to understand.

Sel disappeared. I think he already sensed from the evening that the big movie deal wasn't going to happen and he'd turned off them. There I was, saying good-bye to the last guests except for the twins. I didn't even know if they were supposed to be staying over, nor did the help. I went to the john to think for a few minutes and decided to play it straight. When I came out I found them poring over my magazines. In the first throes of his infatuation with me Sel had bought me lifetime subscriptions to all the magazines I loved. *Popular Mechanics, Scientific American,* a couple of hot rod books, and all the electronics trade magazines that were in existence by this time. The boys and I got into a marvelous conversation about electric engines, computer-run engines, and so on. It was the best conversation I'd had in years outside of a service station.

Sel went off to New York and the twins and I talked through the next day. Once in a while one would nap for a few minutes but then get right back into the conversation. I went back to their hotel, talked for a while longer, said I'd come back the next morning. And it never occurred to me until I was back at the house that I'd been with them for twenty-four hours and it hadn't once crossed my mind that all they really wanted was to fuck me. I knew they were straight. Sel had checked them out before he'd consented to take them on; he was terrified of homosexuals. They were straight but they hadn't made a pass at me or ogled me or done that devouring thing men do with their eyes. They'd just talked to me as though we were all people. Naturally I got into bed with them to show my gratitude.

During the last part of SALLY's *monologue we have been see-ing her on a screen within a screen. We're back in the Smith living room and the four Smith adults are viewing the inter-view.* NADINE's *voice is heard over* SALLY's *last lines as the film freezes.*

NADINE: Wait a minute. Stop everything. Please hold it a minute.

VOICE: What's doing?

NADINE: I'm beginning to feel very funny, sitting here watch-ing this stuff.

VOICE: All of it or just this one?

NADINE (*frowns*): Well, it's worse with this one, because of the jealousy and so on, but that's not the whole thing.

DIANNE (*amused*): What are you jealous of?

NADINE: Are you kidding? To look like that and know how to fix a car, too?

DIANNE: Look like what?

NADINE: My God, Di, she's gorgeous!

DIANNE: I don't think so. Her nose is too long and her hair is hideous.

NADINE: I don't think I believe this conversation.

Silence. NADINE *looks at the twins, who are looking at the screen as though the film hadn't been interrupted, although what was on it was of only minimal interest.*

NADINE: Were you both in love with her?

EDDIE: She was pretty nice.

NADINE: Were you heartbroken when she— (*breaks off, con-fused by her own assumption*) —how did you break up?

EDDIE: I dunno, I guess she found somebody else.

NADINE: You must have felt awful.

EDDIE (*smiles his shrug smile*): I don't remember too well but I think someone else came right along. (*Turns to* AMOS.) Remem-ber?

AMOS: What difference does it make?

NADINE: It would've made a difference in how you felt about her leaving.

AMOS: Why?

NADINE: Having someone else would've comforted you.

AMOS: What makes you think we needed someone to comfort us?

NADINE (*floundering around, unable to stop asking the questions even though she's beginning to suspect she doesn't want to hear the answers*): But it's sad when someone leaves you, isn't it? I mean, don't you care when someone leaves? . . . Well, what if I left you? Or Dianne? Or both of us?

AMOS: If you left you'd be gone.

Silence. NADINE *stares at them.*

DIANNE: This is very unproductive, really. Why don't we let Ken finish showing us this portion so he can get home and get some sleep?

NADINE: I don't want to see it.

DIANNE: Why not? Because you're jealous?

NADINE: No, because things are happening from seeing it. Don't you see that it's supposed to be a picture of our lives, but it's a part of our lives, instead. You're a part of our lives, Ken, and you're making things happen just by being here and making a movie.

DIANNE: Please don't get hysterical, Nady.

NADINE: I'm not hysterical.

KEN: What have I made happen?

NADINE (*thinking*): I don't know. It's not exactly that we're doing things we wouldn't have done . . . but it's as though we're going to. You're making things happen. I mean, why are you showing us these clips?

KEN: I thought you'd be interested in them.

NADINE: If it were just for us you wouldn't have brought Michelle over to run the camera at the same time.

KEN: Okay. I thought your reactions would be interesting.

NADINE: Are they?

230

KEN (*soft laugh*): I don't know. You haven't told me what they are. Not your reactions to the interviews themselves.

NADINE: All right. I'll tell you my reactions. My reaction to that old lady and the home was pity for the twins. My reaction to Tressalina was pity for Tressalina. And my reaction to Sally was pity for myself.

KEN: Why did you pity Tressalina?

NADINE: Because she was so gross! And she thought she was so important to them (*increasingly upset*) and really she was just a hole for them to come in! (*She bursts into tears but continues speaking as she cries.*) Because nothing's important to them except each other; they hardly know the rest of the world exists. Because if she ever really knew what they were thinking while she was jerking them off she'd probably have killed herself. Amos probably thinks—was thinking—about the balance in his checking account and Eddie was wondering if Amos was going to wake up mad at him in the morning. (*She breaks down into helpless sobs and can't speak anymore.*)

Camera closes in on the twins. AMOS *is scowling at* NADINE. EDDIE *smiles apologetically at the camera.*

EDDIE: Nadine is very dramatic.

AMOS: Nadine is a pain in the ass.

DIANNE: You have to understand, Ken. I love Nadine but off the wall isn't just someplace she comes from occasionally. It's her favorite position.

NADINE *stares at* DIANNE, *says nothing.*

KEN: What she was saying, is it true?

EDDIE: What?

KEN: That you two are more important to each other than anyone else could ever be? That you don't care that much about anyone else?

AMOS: Sure. Why should we?

EDDIE (*reasonably*): After all, in a way we're all we have. We have to take care of each other.

231

KEN: Have you ever been in love?

AMOS: Tell us what it is and we'll tell you if we did it.

Camera returns to SALLY DEMAREST *but she's still on the Smith's wall and in one corner of the picture we see* NADINE *sitting on a chair. Her body faces the screen but her head is buried in her lap and her arms are around her legs.*

KEN: What did you mean when you said the twins were just fresh cuts of meat, or however you put it?

SALLY: Oh, that wasn't fair. I was just being a wise ass, reacting to your asking me about love. In a sense it was less that way than usual.

KEN: Less a matter of meat.

SALLY (*nodding wearily*): After all, we actually started out with a conversation about the real world. We were *friendly*.

KEN: Did that change later on?

SALLY: No, as a matter of fact. Things changed less than they usually do after sex. We'd talk a little and screw a little.

KEN: You wouldn't care to go into what the latter was like, would you?

SALLY (*laughs*): Please, that's the one thing that might finish a kid in this town, grading lays in public.

KEN: You did it before.

SALLY: Cut it.

KEN: So, you'd do a little of everything and you just sort of passed the time pleasantly with them.

Sally nods.

KEN: How did Selwyn react?

SALLY (*shrugs*): It was the end. But it would've been the end soon anyway.

KEN: Was he threatened by your brains, too?

SALLY: Oh, no, with Sel it was an entirely different matter. His whole life was auditions of one kind or another and something new and better was always turning up.

KEN: Your friendship with the twins continued for how long?

SALLY: Most of the time they were in California. For a while I had a boyfriend who was an amateur pilot and I really got into planes. I got my next guy, a Texas oilman, to buy me a plane, and it was a passion with me for a long time. The twins got to know something about planes. I brought them books, magazines and so on. Once in a while I took them up. They were fascinated by small planes, never got sick in the roughest weather and weren't at all nervous about flying with me, which pleased me, of course. Amos started toying with plans for an interior where they could run the engine together, one facing the controls and one with his back to them. For some reason that turned them on more than the thought of driving a car ever had.

NADINE's *voice is now heard over the L.A. sounds and the camera stays on* SALLY.

NADINE (*voice monotone*): You never told us about any of this. You never told us you were interested in planes. You never told us anything about yourselves.

KEN: So you'd just see them occasionally and talk about cars and planes.

SALLY: I'd also bring them girls. Hollywood had females who'd fuck anything with a recognizable name long before it was a nationwide phenomenon, you know. Hollywood and Washington. And the twins never went out hunting because of the obvious difficulties.

VOICE OF NADINE: Anyway, they didn't care enough.

KEN: Would you say then that basically they led fairly lonely lives out here?

SALLY: Lonely? No, you couldn't really say they seemed lonely. Loneliness . . . You know, there's something you have to realize. Amos and Eddie are really not qu— they're really not like other people.

Bootville. Late spring. EDDIE *and* AMOS, *seen from a distance, leave the house by the side door, wearing bathing suits, and make their way down the path toward the pond. We see only their backs and we feel they are unaware of the camera. At*

233

*the pond they drop their towels and walk slowly into the
water without checking for temperature and without hesitation. At some point they're swimming instead of walking.
They turn to face each other and tread water. The camera
pans to* NADINE, *on her knees in the garden, wiping sweat
off her forehead.*

NADINE: On a day like this it's hard to believe there's disaster in
the air.

VOICE (*inaudible*):

NADINE: It just is. I feel it. I feel as though I'm losing something
I don't want but there's nothing to replace it. I thought maybe
the film would have an effect on the twins but it's having the
effect on me, instead. I feel as though things have to change here
but I don't know how. I don't know which is harder, trying to
change yourself or trying to change other people. I only know
if we don't get better we'll get worse. I saw that with my parents,
especially my mother. She was always trying to find out what
bothered her but looking in the wrong place. She never faced it
head-on and it just got worse and worse. My tendency is the opposite, to do things head-on rather than do nothing. I'm trying
to get more careful. Everything you do changes you. Has conse-
quences. I know that's hardly an original insight but I've felt it
more since we started this movie than ever before. This movie has
changed my life. No, my insides. The trouble is, the outsides of
my life are so well set right now, with young kids, and so on, that
what it's done is to change the insides and make the outside
harder than ever to live with.

VOICE (*inaudible*):

NADINE: I don't know. I don't know about any of them. I don't
know if they saw what I saw on the screen, or heard what everyone was saying. I don't know if they saw a bunch of people who
hardly know each other.

The pond. AMOS *and* EDDIE *are doing a graceful backstroke,*
EDDIE's *right arm moving in counterpoint to* AMOS's *left one,
the top of their joint arching just over the surface of the*

234

water, their feet occasionally breaking the surface as they kick. The camera remains on them as NADINE *continues.*

NADINE: I have no power now to make anything happen by myself. Sometimes I feel as though everyone but me has some outside source of light, of power, and they can all go on the way they are forever. I'm the only one who'll stay at home getting old. Then I'll die and they'll replace me with someone new who doesn't make as much noise.

Nothing will ever happen to the men unless they do the surgery and it seems they'll never do it. They'll just go on living the way they are . . . if you can call it living . . . and eventually they'll die. Together. Maybe if I knew I could die together with someone I wouldn't bother to change, either. . . . I don't understand how Dianne can go through this whole thing so calmly. I never thought I really understood Dianne but I used to think she understood me, and that was reassuring. She had a sense of who I was. A sense of which things in life were important. Now I often wonder. She seems not to have realized what she was doing when she got us into doing this movie. How important it was. Now we'll have to see. Things will happen but there's no way yet to know what they'll be.

NADINE *picks up spade and starts working the earth again. The camera leaves the garden, returns to the children on the road and then slowly makes its way down the path to the pond. The men are still swimming.*

T HE most important thing that happened, although I didn't find out about it until much later, was that while Ken was putting together his movie, Sally Demarest ran into Selwyn Sternheim at a party and mentioned the young guy who was doing a documentary on the twins. Ken had screened some of the footage for her and she mentioned, among other scenes, those with the doctors who thought they should get separated and the two wives, of whom one was also certain they should. By a couple of weeks later Sternheim had bought out Ken McDougall with some money, the promise of representation in the big time and the assurance that he would use his best efforts to see that Ken was considered for the job of directing a movie about the twins' lives if such a major movie were to be made. By a few weeks after that Sternheim controlled the rights to the twins' lives. He got this control by promising them a very large amount of money ($25,000 for starters, just for signing the agreement) with all kinds of percentages and royalties.

The most significant part of the agreement, though, was the clause under which these rights acquired geometrically greater value if Amos and Eddie should happen to elect, within a year of the contract's date, to have surgery for the purpose of becoming two single human beings.

All I knew was that Amos, once Ken had showed us the movie in its nearly final form, became obsessed with the question of money. He wouldn't admit to being upset by some of the scenes although once or twice I'd stolen a glance at him and he'd looked as though lightning had just struck him. He would admit to no problems in life that having some money couldn't solve. No expense incurred by any member of the household escaped his disgruntled attention with the exception of the fifteen or so dollars a week that his booze cost us. That was a necessity; he wanted us to cut down on fringe items like shoes for the kids. When I finally challenged his overwhelming concern with finances at a time when we did in point of fact have enough income to support the way we lived, he asked in a tone at once angry, condescending and matter-of-fact, how come it had never entered my thick skull that it might be nice to get away from Bootville once in a while? Change the way we lived? Take a Caribbean vacation in the winter? Just plain *get away?*

I stared at him. I was at a loss for words. He glowered back. I looked at Eddie.

"Do you feel the same way?" I asked.

"Sure," Eddie said. "A little vacation would be nice."

Dianne allowed as how it might be pleasant to take a little vacation sometime but said it would be hard for her to get away just then. What she really meant was that she didn't want to be away from the telephone. She was upset because Ken McDougall had disappeared. Her first question when she came home in the evening was whether there'd been any calls for her; she claimed to be having trouble with the long-distance wires at work.

Ken had apparently made another conquest, as well. Carly talked about him constantly and planned for the day he'd spoken of with her, when they would make a movie together. She was high all the time on her expectations. She wanted to know whether she could take a couple of friends from school when we went to see the final version of the film. Her hopes were more visible than Dianne's (although slightly more difficult to pin down, since she was nine years old that year) and died harder. She badgered Dianne to know when Ken would come back and at first, before Dianne's hopes had died, Dianne was patient with her queries, but later on she would run from the room when Carly started.

When Amos told us about Sternheim it was because Sternheim wanted our signatures on the contract in addition to the men's. (Amos had protested but Sternheim's lawyers insisted it would be cleaner.) And when they told us they were "probably going ahead with the surgery" it was because they needed me to drive them to Boston. Why would they have told us otherwise? It wasn't as though it had anything to do with us. It never occurred to me that they were going for surgical examinations when they said they wanted to go to Boston, but it occurred to Dianne.

"Maybe they're going to have the surgery," she said.

"Don't be silly," I told her. "You know how Amos feels about the surgery."

"He'd probably do it for the money," she said contemptuously.

I was annoyed with her, of course.

For being right.

"Are you considering having the surgery?" I asked lightly.

Eddie was grinning.

"Why is he grinning like that?" I asked Amos.

"Because he's an asshole," Amos said.

"Are you having the surgery?" I asked.

"Of course we're having the surgery, idiot," said my loving husband.

Of course.

"I'm so confused," I said. "After all the talking and the pleading and the coaxing . . . how come you arranged it all without telling us? Something that's going to change our whole lives?"

238

"The only thing that's going to change our whole lives," he replied, "is that we're going to get some freedom because we're going to be rich."

"But the money isn't the only thing," I said slowly. "It'll change our lives."

"That's why we didn't tell you," Amos said. "We knew you'd make a big deal out of it."

"I'm sorry," I said, catching a note of fear in his voice. "I didn't mean to make you uneasy, it's just that I think we should know what's involved so we can—"

"You didn't make me uneasy," he said irritably. "There's nothing involved."

I stared at him.

"It's basically very simple surgery," he said. "We'll be in the hospital for a couple of weeks and then we'll come home and take it easy for a few more weeks. After that we're going to take off for a vacation in the Caribbean. One more winter in this place just might drive me nuts. Anyhow, you can come if you feel like it or stay here if you don't. When we get back we're going to put up a new building on the back lands. We'll have a real shop, and an apartment over it for rental that'll cover the mortgage if we need one, and maybe an indoor swimming pool. . . ." He went on and on, detailing their plans for the building, the rote quality of his voice finally sinking in, making me realize how hard he was sitting on his fear.

Dianne was silent.

It was going to happen, then. Someone was going to put them on a table (two tables?) and cut the tie that bound them.

I shivered. Felt a little nauseated.

What if it didn't work? What if something went wrong? If they cut too far?

Or if it did work, what then? I hadn't actually posed that question to myself before. Amos was making up some fairy tale about life as usual except better because of the money, but the truth was that nobody had any way of foreseeing what was going to happen.

In the past I'd thought longingly of two complete men who

239

could drive themselves to work and take us to bed separately. In theory we could even live in separate houses, Eddie and Dianne with Carly, Amos and I with our kids. Now as I looked at Dianne sitting there, pale and silent, she seemed too precious to let out of my sight for five minutes, much less to live in a separate house.

Then there were the children.

In the past I'd invoked them as reasons for getting the operation (to have normal fathers) and Dianne had invoked them as reasons for delaying (children's dislike of change). Again, nobody could really predict what this separation would mean to them.

A separation. From Eddie, too. I loved Eddie at least as much as I loved Amos, or at least I found him more sympathetic. If I needed a sympathetic ear it was Eddie's I was really talking into when I approached the twins. With his sympathy I could reach solutions that didn't occur to me when I was alone.

Alone.

By next year Daisy would be in nursery school.

I felt a surge of panic.

But wait a minute, Nadine, you'll still have Amos.

Amos.

I looked at him.

He drank too much and had a foul temper.

But of course both of those qualities stemmed from his difficult life. If Eddie managed to be so much more amiable about that difficulty, maybe the reason was that he wasn't as smart as Amos and didn't perceive how bad things were. Of course it was Eddie who'd always been ready to endure the difficulties of surgical separation. But maybe that was for the same reason; he couldn't envision how scary it really was. After all, I hadn't even been willing to consider that until now. I felt a surge of pride in Amos, who'd known all along. Maybe I'd shortchanged Amos. Maybe he was the one of the four of us who really knew what was important.

Dianne looked so frightened. I pulled my chair close to hers and hugged her reassuringly. I felt guilty because I had an advantage over her in having the more intelligent husband but I also felt very loving because I was the life manager of the two of

240

us and she needed me and maybe she was worried about losing me now.

"Don't worry," I whispered. "It's going to be worth all the trouble."

"What about the children?" she whispered back. "They're going to be scared to death."

"What are you two whispering about?" Amos growled.

"We have to figure out the best way to tell the kids," I said.

"Maybe we should wait until afterward," Dianne said.

"No," I told her. "They'll sense we're hiding something and they'll be more scared."

The twins said nothing.

"What do you think?" I asked Amos.

"What difference does it make?" he asked.

He was too frightened for himself to worry about the children. I had to be patient and understand that.

"Is there anything you need us to do?" I asked.

"Just leave us alone," he said. "We need you to leave us alone."

We told the kids a couple of days before I took the men to Boston for the actual surgery. I wanted to tell them all at once so they could reassure each other but Dianne wanted to tell Carly alone, "without an observer."

I was hurt. In another time I might have been angry but Dianne and I had drawn too close for anger. Besides, how could I be angry when I was the one who had needed to get distance from Carly—and had succeeded? If she'd never forgiven me for abandoning her when Philip was born, she got along well enough with her parents and with kids in school, particularly when she could control them. She was a leader who dropped out when she wasn't elected leader but that was seldom enough. At home Daisy accepted her authority and Philip rebelled against it, but they all got by. If either Philip or Daisy got opposing answers to a question from Carly and me, they knew without difficulty that Carly was the one to believe. I knew nothing of Carly's day-to-day problems and feelings, which she concealed from me as though they were undeclared revenue and I were a tax inspector. I only knew she was upset that Ken hadn't returned to make a movie with her because Dianne kept telling me so.

"How did she react?" I asked Dianne when she came out of their heart-to-heart.

Dianne smiled. "She's very happy about it. I haven't seen her so happy since she and Ken talked about making a movie. She thinks it's going to be marvelous having a regular daddy. The only thing she's mad about is that she can't go to Boston and see the surgery."

"Philip," I said, "have you ever thought about the daddies? About the way they're linked together and can never do anything separately?"

"No," Philip said. His dark handsome face was impassive.

"Really?"

"No."

"Haven't you ever wished they were more like other daddies?" I asked, thinking of how in his entire school career he'd never invited another kid to come home and visit.

"No."

"Well, I have."

He was silent and in his silence I heard an accusation.

"Because I've wanted them to be happier," I said. "More comfortable. Wanted them to be able to get away from each other so they could like each other more."

Silence.

"Anyway, they want it. They want to get rid of the joint that binds them together."

"Get rid of it?" he asked with sudden interest. "How?"

"Well," I fumbled, "I don't exactly mean get rid of it. I mean . . ." He'd turned away as soon as I said I hadn't meant it. "I mean . . . they're going to have it cut in half so they'll be separate."

For the first time I wondered exactly what would happen to those two halves. Would they be cut off or tucked in or would

242

the two men be walking around with a ten-inch piece of flesh sticking out of each of their chests? I shuddered and hoped Philip didn't see me. Maybe it wouldn't occur to him to ask what would be done with the remaining pieces. Maybe I'd have a chance to check it out before he asked. What was he thinking, anyway? He still hadn't said a word.

"Philip?"

"What?"

"What are you thinking?"

"Nothing."

It was clear that he was lying and just as clear that I had to leave him alone.

An hour or so later I tiptoed up the stairs and listened at the door of the children's room.

Philip and Carly murmuring in low voices.

Then silence.

Then Daisy's uncontrolled three-year-old soprano, loud and clear through the door: "Now you two be the daddies and I'll be the doctor and cut."

We didn't make love—by common consent. We were all too anxious. There was a nearly visible shell around the men. The shell had graffiti all over it which said things like, "Don't rock the boat," and "Don't talk or we'll scream." The children seemed to understand without being told and carried on as usual when we were all around, never asking questions. They spent much more time than usual together in their room.

The men got closer to each other.

The children got closer to each other.

Dianne and I got closer to each other.

The children ended up in the same bed every morning no matter how they went to sleep and Dianne and I woke up with our fingertips touching. We never talked about what our lives might be like later on. We were afraid to jinx the operation by taking it for granted that everything would be fine, and we didn't know

243

how to consider the possibility that it might not be. Amos drank much more than usual. Two weeks before they were scheduled to leave for Boston he was starting to drink before breakfast. He drank so much that the doctors got worried and they decided to have the men in Boston ten days before the surgery instead of a week, as planned, to give him plenty of time to dry out.

The men were quite clear on not wanting us at the hospital until after the surgery. Anyway, it would obviously be best for the children if we were home. We agreed not to tell the children the exact day of the surgery unless they asked.

They'd cut too close to my side and I was dying. The part of me they'd taken was the part I needed to live. For a long time after I'd awakened I didn't know it had been a dream and I lay there trying to figure out in precisely what manner death would touch me. It was there in the room. I began shivering wildly, and crying. I woke up Dianne with my crying.

"Nady! What is it?" She hugged me.

"A dream," I cried. "I think it was a dream. . . . Of course it was a dream." The operation would be that day. I couldn't stop crying. My brain knew the dream wasn't true but my feelings didn't know yet. "No wonder Amos was furious with me," I said after a while. "I had no idea . . . I didn't really think of what it would be like to go through that. That's what the dream was about. In the dream I was the one who was getting, you know . . . separated."

"Try to forget it."

"I can't. They cut too close."

"What happened?"

"I don't know. It hurt terribly. I was going to die, unless I found what they'd taken."

"Yiiiccch."

We huddled closer together under the quilts.

Why should I feel guilty? Amos and Eddie could still huddle together for comfort if they wanted to. Besides, I hadn't made the decision.

244

"Don't laugh," I said, "but I've been thinking lately . . . about what I'll do when the kids are all in school. I mean, next year Daisy'll be gone, too."

"Maybe you can get a job in Hanover and we can have lunch together sometimes."

We giggled because we both knew there was something silly about this discussion.

"Now my lunches are taken care of," I laughed, "and all I have to figure out is what I'm going to do with the rest of my life."

She was silent.

"Now you're really going to laugh, because I think I know . . . well, I don't exactly know what I want to do with it, but I've been thinking I ought to at least go back to school and finish up my psych courses. And then maybe do something in psych."

She didn't laugh but she didn't say anything, either. We were both remembering that time when I was as high on Freud as she was on Marx and the feelings between us had gotten very strained.

"I think I could handle it better than I did then," I said defensively. "I remember how fanatical I was. I had an explanation for EVERYTHING."

She didn't say she remembered the way *she* was, too. Maybe because she didn't.

"I was always looking for the One True Answer," I said, "and getting hysterical every time I thought I found it."

"You really did get hysterical," Dianne said, but there was such affection in her voice that it didn't bother me.

"I've calmed down a lot, haven't I?" I stroked her hair as I asked.

"You really have."

"I think that's one of the reasons I wanted to get married," I said. "To get calmed down. I was afraid to just be on the loose."

"Where would you take your psych courses?" she asked, changing the subject so quietly that I just went along without realizing there was more I wanted to say about life, marriage and other connected matters.

"I don't know," I told her. "Maybe Goddard or someplace like that. I haven't really investigated, but I've been playing with it in a dim sort of way for a while." I was getting sleepy again but I was afraid if I fell asleep the nightmare would come back.

"Dianne? All this money we're getting, what do you think they're really going to want for it?"

"The rights to our lives."

I giggled. "How can anyone else have the right to our lives? What do we do? Say to them, here you are folks, this was my life, now it's your life?"

"We don't talk to anyone but Sternheim and his people and we don't authorize anyone else to write about us. They're going to film the surgery but not necessarily all of us. At home, I mean. And if there's a movie it'll be done by professional actors. We're not actually obliged to do anything but if we want to cooperate, you and I, we can talk to Sternheim's people. We're not selling ourselves, only the story. It's an important difference."

"I hope you're right," I said. "I hope everyone can keep the difference straight."

Night passed into morning without either of us going back to sleep. By the time dawn broke exhaustion lent the day an air of unreality—as though the actual surgery were the dream, rather than what had happened the night before. Dianne didn't go to work, although she'd meant to. The kids didn't ask any questions about her staying home, a sure sign they knew although Dianne didn't think so. She never wanted to believe they knew things we didn't tell them.

Dianne and I followed each other around the house, everyplace except the bathroom. Morning coffee went on forever. Daisy kept herself occupied with some wood blocks Dianne's parents had once sent Carly, and left us alone to drink coffee, talk and rearrange things in kitchen cupboards. The more coffee we drank the more inert we became. Our hearts raced wildly each time the phone ran although we knew it was much too early for word from Boston. At three o'clock we called the hospital and were

246

told they were on their way into the recovery room. There was no word yet but someone would call us soon. At three thirty Philip and Carly got off the school bus and came into the house, appearing subdued.

"Is it over with?" Carly asked.

"We think so," I said. "We haven't heard yet."

Dianne asked how she knew this was the day.

Carly shrugged. "We could tell."

She and Philip went upstairs and Daisy followed. I looked at the clock. Three thirty-five.

"This is crazy," I said. "We should go down there."

"Amos didn't want us to."

"Not for them. For us. We'll go crazy if we stay here. He doesn't even have to know we're there. Unless . . . if they need us, if something goes wrong we'll need to be there. Let's just go."

We got a sitter, a high-school girl we'd used once in a while, and hit the road at four. We were in Boston a little after six.

They were still in the recovery room. All their doctors were in attendance except one who'd taken a break to phone us and couldn't be found. Dianne sat on one of the plastic lounge chairs and went into an open-eyed coma. I paced like a madwoman and consumed candy bars and cups of coffee until Dr. Rhodes finally told us that the twins seemed to be absolutely fine.

"Fine?"

He beamed at us. "The surgery is completed. Your husbands are now two separate human beings. Their life signs are good and we are most optimistic that they will have a full and rapid recovery."

Dianne and I both burst into tears. I sat down and we held each other.

"It's natural for you to cry," Dr. Rhodes assured us. "You should be able to see them in the morning, if all goes well."

"If—"

"It's not common surgery. We don't know the possibilities but we have no reason to think anything will go wrong. We're putting them into separate recovery rooms to minimize the danger of infection. Each will have an RN in twenty-four-hour attendance for the next few days, and a doctor for much of that time as well."

"Are they asleep?" Dianne asked.

He nodded. "They've been under heavy anesthesia. It's doubtful they'll wake up before tomorrow."

But Amos woke up and called for Eddie repeatedly in the night. They didn't want to give him any more real anesthesia and he wouldn't take a pill. Nor would he stop calling for Eddie. Finally they woke up the Attendings to get permission to put the men in the same room because they were afraid Amos was going to damage himself and wake up others screaming for Eddie. They rolled his bed just close enough to Eddie's so they could touch fingers if each half-extended an arm.

Dianne and I slept almost the same way on two fake-leather lounge couches that we pulled together. Or at least I rested; she slept. The weight of my exhaustion wasn't enough to balance the weight of my fear about seeing them, which was so great and so incomprehensible to me that I couldn't even mention it to Dianne.

"Well, ladies," Dr. Rhodes asked, "are you ready to see your husbands?"

"Yes, of course," we both said, but I wasn't really ready. My stomach was churning with fear. I was afraid they would look different. I knew their wounds would be bandaged but the fear of seeing them was not allayed by that knowledge. I wanted to ask what the wound itself would look like but I was ashamed.

Even more than I feared seeing them, though, I feared their seeing me. Amos's seeing me. I felt responsible for the surgery even if in the long run I hadn't made the decision. Whether or not I was responsible, I had been the one ready to expose them to this ordeal, to risk their lives, and they—he—*had* to hold this against me. In one of my brief fantasies he screamed that he never wanted to lay eyes on me again and only Dianne was to be admitted to the room.

248

"You mustn't be put off by the tubes and all the equipment," a young doctor warned as we walked down the hall. Hospital staff parted to let us go by and whispered to each other who we were. The first reporters stood at the admission desk, a special guard there to stop them from breaking in or sneaking to the room. "They're really in remarkably good condition," the doctor continued as we pushed our way past everyone. "Strong as oxen, both of them."

"Are they lying on their backs?" I asked, trying to prepare myself for what I would see.

"Yes, except that they're propped up in various places with pads. For comfort. Their knees are propped up, for example, to minimize the strain."

I was barely conscious of the people who were beginning to crowd the corridor because the word was out. The sounds were muted. In my mind was a room as white and silent as snow, with two pale, silent men lying on adjacent beds, their fingers just touching.

The reality being a huge bright room, intended for six but occupied only by two beds and huge quantities of equipment and doctors and nurses and a camera grinding away in a remote corner and a young woman with a notebook.

We couldn't see the men's faces at first, there was so much stuff around them. Then I saw Eddie. Looking very groggy. I'd never seen either of them looking sleepy before; their eyes were open or their eyes were shut. I let my own eyes move across the rumpled white sheets that covered the space between them, until my eyes met Amos's. He was looking at me. He seemed limp with exhaustion but he was wide awake.

"Nady," he murmured, "I'm so glad you're here. I couldn't wait for them to let you in."

I began to cry. With pleasure, with relief, with *everything*. Was it true or was I making it up that until then he had never called me by my name?

"Oh, Jesus," I said, laughing and crying at the same time, "I

249

want to kiss you but I can't get anywhere near you." He was surrounded by equipment.

"Where's Rhodes?" he asked. "Or Thom?"

"Right here," Thom said from somewhere behind the apparatus.

"Can somebody move some of this stuff so I can kiss my wife?"

"Well," Thom said, "we'll see what we can do."

I glanced at Dianne to see if she'd noticed that Amos was being not quite his usual self but of course she was absorbed in Eddie, who was also smiling only at her. They got some of the apparatus moved slightly away from the bed on the side that didn't border Eddie's bed. I slid between the bed and the apparatus and sat down near Amos. He winced.

"Did I hurt you?" I asked anxiously.

"No," he said, "it's all right. I wanted you here."

I scanned his face for some trace of sarcasm but there was none.

"I'm so glad you're all right," I said, carefully bending over and kissing his forehead. I noted that on the other side equipment was being moved so Dianne could sit with Eddie. The woman with the notebook was still writing and the camera was still grinding away.

They can't even tell the difference. They don't even know, any of them, what it was like before.

He cupped his left hand over mine, alternately stroking and clutching. He was staring at me in a way that made me feel funny. Self-conscious.

"Did you do something to your hair?" he asked.

I laughed. "What could I do?" It hung down my back, thick and wavy, as it always had all year round except the summer, when I braided it.

"I don't know," he said. "You look different. You look beautiful."

I blushed furiously. I couldn't think of anything to say but I got a little warm and excited. I looked at Amos's form under the bedsheet and my mind leaped ahead to the day when he'd be all healed and we would be able to make love again. You could

250

hardly say again because you could hardly say we'd made love before, or at any rate we hadn't made love just the two of us alone in a room. We weren't alone now and yet in a sense we were more alone than we'd ever been. I felt like creeping right under the covers with him. Too many people around. I could feel the people but I didn't look at them because I couldn't bear not to look at Amos.

Can you see what's happening, people? Camera? Lady with the notebook? Nadine had feared that matters would be worse and instead, from the evidence of these first moments, it seems they might be immeasurably better. See Nadine being happy. See Nadine getting high. Watch Nadine over the next weeks getting higher and higher and telling her anxious self that her highness is happiness.

"Have you met Robyn Wycliffe?"

"No."

She nodded coolly, a good-looking blonde in a T-shirt and jeans. Later on I might joke about her shirts with the nipples painted in or claim that she'd gotten her secretarial training in a window in Amsterdam, but just then I was too happy to be jealous.

"Do you work for Dr. Rhodes?" I asked politely.

"I work for Sel and Biff," she said.

"Sel," I said. "Oh, yes. Selwyn Sternheim."

Dr. Rhodes introduced her to Dianne and Eddie, who were holding hands but not speaking.

"Is she here all the time?" I whispered to Amos.

"On and off." He winced.

"What's the matter?"

"It hurts."

"Why don't you ask them for something?" I glanced at Dr. Thom, who made a wry face.

"I don't want anything," Amos said balefully. "That stuff messed up my mind."

"That was general anesthesia," Dr. Thom said patiently in a voice that made it clear they'd had this discussion before. "Now

251

we're talking about a simple painkiller, not a central nervous system depressant."

"Without making me sleepy?"

"Wouldn't you rather be a little sleepy than be in pain?"

"No."

End of subject. Dr. Thom looked at me as though appealing for help but I wasn't about to risk these good feelings by interfering. I smiled at Amos instead.

"You don't know how glad I am to have you here," he said.

They wanted us to take a hotel room and stay in Boston but we couldn't. Dianne had to get back to her job and I had to be with the children. I'd talked to the kids the evening before to tell them everything was fine, but now they needed me to be with them. In the next week I shuttled back and forth to Boston every other day. I didn't mind. I was relieved to be able to siphon off some of my energy. I was as crazy and horny as I'd been from the junior-high-school day I'd discovered that by taking off my shoe and sitting on my wiggly right heel I could come in Spanish and various other courses. After which the course of learning, needless to say, had never run smooth.

At first the children bombarded us with questions but the one question we couldn't answer—because neither of us had been able to bear to ask the doctors—was what had happened to the joint itself—and how much of it. Not only did the question sound foolish, but it would be one thing to hear the extra piece had been cut off or neatly tucked in, quite another to hear that my lovely new husband would be walking around with a penis-like object sticking out of his chest for the remainder of his natural life. Some vacation in the Caribbean that would be. I'd go to the Hilton Jambalaya with Siamese twins before I'd be seen with a man who looked like that! Maybe it wouldn't even tan, like the Stern Old Judge scar. (The Caribbean turned out to be irrelevant; the men forgot about a vacation after they came home.)

Daisy kept asking where the daddies were and not wanting to

believe they were in a hospital because they weren't in Hanover. She was also not interested in hearing that they were any different from the way they'd been when they left. I tried drawing stick figures, before and after, to show her what had happened. In the second one a man lay straight on his back in each of two separate beds with nothing but space between them. She got furious when she saw it.

"No!" she shouted at me. "That's not the way the daddies are!"

By the next time I saw them the chest bandage was no longer there. On Amos's abdomen was a small, neat, slightly diagonal scar about three inches long.

"It's beautiful," I said, beaming.

We kissed fondly, lovingly, wetly. Long. Longingly. It had been two days since I'd left with Dianne, three days since the surgery. Eddie watched TV but Amos talked to me. He wanted me to know how incompetent the staff was, how dumb the doctors were and how the food was the worst he'd eaten since the home.

"The children miss you like crazy," I said. "I told them maybe you'd be able to call."

"Tomorrow," he said.

The next morning Eddie walked for the first time. Then he walked again when I arrived. Holding on to the doctor's arm. It was weird to watch him; his feet moved in the same awkward deliberate way they'd moved when he was attached, his left leg halting as his hip bumped around another hip that was no longer there.

Amos refused to watch him or to try himself for a week after the surgery, insisting upon using a bedpan during that time. After a week he tried it with me on one side and a doctor on the other, but he only got as far as standing at the side of the bed, then was overwhelmed by dizziness. The doctor promised the dizziness would go away but Amos was convinced that it wouldn't and forced us to let him sink back onto the bed. A couple of days

253

later, a young resident he'd decided he trusted persuaded him to try it with me on the other side when Eddie had dozed off and none of the other doctors was around. His body was stiff with tension and his face beaded with sweat as we walked to the bathroom, a total of eight or nine steps, in what seemed like hours. At the toilet Amos let go and sank down, crapping into his hospital pajamas in relief. He told me after he'd been cleaned up that he hadn't expected to make it. He'd thought he would collapse, probably die. He was horribly dizzy and sick to his stomach the whole time and only the thought that I was there holding him had kept him going.

"You were wonderful," I said. "You were very brave to do it, feeling as scared as you were."

He smiled wryly. "Braver than Eddie, right? Because he wasn't as scared so he didn't have to be as brave to do it."

I smiled back. I thought him not only braver but more charming. And he loved me so much!

By my next visit we were walking down the corridor together, just the two of us. He wasn't getting nearly as dizzy except in the first moment or two that he was standing. The doctors were hoping I'd stay in Boston because Amos made better progress while I was there, unlike Eddie who seemed to progress slowly but steadily between TV programs whether Dianne was around or not. But there was no way I could stay; the children were getting more hopped up with each day and the baby-sitter was finding it increasingly difficult to handle them, particularly Philip.

"Let's call Philip now," I said brightly. I'd had no luck with urging him to call and thought Amos might respond if it were a sort of joint project. "He's dying to talk to you."

"Tomorrow."

"Please, Amos. They need you, they need to hear your voice. I'll dial."

"Oh, all right," he said, grumbling but not unloving. "For you."

Philip picked up, sounding as though he'd had to outrun a gazelle to get there first.

254

" 'Lo?"

"Hi, Phil," I said. "It's Mommy. I'm just leaving the hospital in a few minutes to come home."

Silence.

"Your daddy's right here with me. Would you like to talk to him?"

His yes came so quickly as to make it clear he'd not asked only because he was afraid of hearing no. I handed Amos the phone.

"Hi," Amos said. ". . . Uh-yuh. Sometimes it does. . . . Nope. Nope. Nope. He's right here. He's okay. Be a good boy, now." He handed the phone back to me.

"Phil? Are Daisy and Carly there?"

"No," he said, and hung up before I could challenge his exclusive right to talk to his father.

I laughed. "The little bastard, he wanted to be the only one who talked to you."

(Dianne let Carly and Daisy call a while later when I was gone.)

Amos smiled. "Do you really have to leave already?"

I kissed him. "I've been here for two days."

"I'm not going to do anything while you're gone."

"Then it'll take longer for you to get home."

As soon as he'd walked he'd begun bugging the doctors about going home. The doctors wanted them there at least through a second (postoperative) week, maybe more. All kinds of tests were being done and there were a lot of observers, visiting doctors and so on. Amos grumbled about the tourists but Eddie only minded if they interrupted one of his favorite shows. To my astonishment Amos was a great deal more amiable than his brother about granting newspaper interviews; I could only assume they helped pass the time. I myself found it very difficult to answer such questions as, "What do you think your life will be like now, Mrs. Smith?" with a straight face, but while the men were still in the hospital the reporters didn't bother me too much.

They were coming home on a Tuesday. Dianne spent the last weekend there with them. I remained in Bootville with the chil-

255

dren, who drove me crazy. All my nerve endings were dangling on the outside of my body and it took very little to rub them the wrong way. The doctor had suggested that I not tell the children Tuesday because it was possible Wednesday or Thursday would be the date. So every time Philip asked when they were coming I was conflicted as to how to answer and I finally assured him, at the top of my lungs, that I really knew the exact day and minute and was only refusing to tell him because I was mean. Philip, at the age of seven, was hardly equipped to deal with this sort of irony, even if it had been delivered as a calm jest. Within one minute of my having screamed at him he had caught his fingers in the hinge space of the kitchen door as though to prove that he could be meaner to him than I could be. Before I could reach him Carly, thinking she could help, closed the door further on his fingers instead of opening it and his howl of pain brought Daisy running from the living room. I led him over to the sink where I held his fingers under the cold water as he cried hysterically.

"You did it on purpose!" he screamed at her through his sobs and his hiccups. "I saw you, you did it on purpose!"

"I did not, you little creep!" shouted the furious Carly. "I was trying to help you!"

"I saw you!" Philip went on. "You slammed the door on me. I'm going to have a scaaaaaaarrrrrrrrrr!" The last wail so long and agonizing that finally Daisy caught it and began crying.

The on-off switch snapped in my head. I got calm. Very suddenly. I stopped worrying about Philip or about any of them. I saw all, felt nothing. I left Philip at the sink and walked over to a chair, where I sat down.

"It's hurting me!" Philip wailed.

"Leave it under the cold water," I said calmly. "It hurts a little more now but it'll hurt less later."

"Is he going to have a 'car?" Daisy asked, coming over to me, weeping.

"No," I said. "No scar."

"How can you tell?" Philip bawled. "How can you—"

"I hope you do, you little creep!" screamed Carly, who'd worked herself into a real rage by this time. "I hope you have a scar across your whole face!"

He clutched his face and went into paroxysms of grief as though her wish had accomplished the deed. Daisy began crying louder and climbed onto my lap. Calmly I stroked her hair.

Daisy is nearly four years old, I thought calmly. *Philip is seven and Carly is ten. Together that makes twenty years.*

Philip brought me his thumb on the air. "I think it's broken."

"Move it a little."

He moved it.

"It's not broken."

"It feels broken."

"If it were broken you couldn't move it."

"How do you know?" he asked angrily.

"I know three or four facts," I said calmly. "That's one of them."

"It hurts."

"I'm sorry. I really am."

"How come *I* got hurt and you're holding *Daisy?*"

I moved Daisy to one knee and helped him up to the other. "Soon," I said, "the daddies will be able to pick you up again. Separately." It even sounded strange to say the daddies, now. We would have to find new ways to refer to them.

"When are they coming home?" asked Carly.

"Not sure," I said. "Maybe this week. Maybe Dianne will know when she comes home." Still very calm. They could have asked me a hundred more times without getting to me, so they didn't.

"I forgot to tell you," I said to Philip that night as I sat on the edge of his bed. "This time I saw the place where the joint was. It looks fine. Very flat and neat."

He looked startled.

"What do you mean?" he asked.

"Just what I said. The part in it that was important, the liver, they tucked into the daddies. Each daddy. Then they got rid of the rest."

"What did they do with it?"

I laughed, a trifle uneasy for the first time since our blowup. "Threw it away," I said.

"Where?"

"I don't know. In a garbage can, I guess."

"Can I see it?"

"Come on, Philip. That was nearly two weeks ago. It's gone."

"Where did it go?"

"PHILIP! STOP!"

My cover was blown.

"Anything else you want to know, you can ask your father when he comes home. I'm tired. I'm going downstairs."

An hour later when Carly went up to bed he was still wide awake. I heard them talking. Much later, when I was ready for sleep myself, I peeked into their room. Daisy and Carly were fast asleep but Philip lay on his foam slab reading a baseball book I'd picked up for him in Boston. Amos read sports books the way some people read science fiction but Phil was an athlete. As I stood at the door I had a vision of Amos and Philip throwing a baseball in slow motion between them. So beautiful. Philip would have a proper father, now.

I tiptoed away from the open door to my own room. Our own room. Amos's and mine. Since Daisy the upstairs had been simply two large rooms; now we had put up a partition in ours so that when the men came home we would have two narrow but reasonable bedrooms, each with a window, each with half of the old foam slab on a new platform.

I lay down on our bed with the current *Ladies' Home Journal*. As baseball was to Amos and science fiction was to Philip, so was the *Journal* to their wife and mother. Together Amos and I would carefully decorate this room. Together, using the marvelous article on How to Create 10,000 New Kinds of Swinging Storage Space for Under $12 Each, we would design a wall to house the belongings that would be just ours, as opposed to all of ours.

We would enjoy all the work because we would be doing it together.

Not only that, but we've turned the bend into the seventies, folks, so the package not only includes the right storage walls and recipes but also sex and a good job, if you happen to have leanings in either or both directions. It's nearly scary, if you let your mind dwell on it for too long, what a good life an ordinary magazine subscriber is allowed to have!

AMOS's dizziness returned in full force as we made our way down the corridor into the elevator, where he threw up his breakfast. Downstairs we were met by attendants with two wheelchairs but Eddie refused to use his, making his way past the reporters and photographers who crowded every exit, snapping flashbulbs in our faces and calling out questions which we ignored. After a while Eddie took over from the attendant who was pushing Amos's wheelchair so he could help keep back the reporters. (WHICH TWIN HAS THE DIZZIES? a New York paper would ask the next day.) Eddie climbed without aid into the back of the car while the attendant helped Amos into the front. The nightmare didn't end as we drove away from the hospital. Amos was carsick for the entire two and a half hours and spoke only once—to protest Eddie's suggestion that we stop to get something to eat. Eddie didn't actually talk, either, except to ask if Carly would be there when we got home. If he was negotiating the obstacles of his new unsupported life more successfully than his brother, the price of that success seemed to have been his sunny disposition, his eagerness to communicate with the world outside his (and Amos's) skin.

We ended up making the drive in one stretch, with Amos hanging his head out of the window for the last twenty minutes or so as we wound through Pomstead then into Bootville on the narrow bumpy road.

"We're almost there, love," I kept saying. "A few more minutes and we'll be home in peace and quiet." He didn't raise his head. "All this will pass."

My head was full of plans and fantasies, not to speak of the doctors' instructions: No sex for the first couple of weeks; no heavy lifting for at least a month (they were supposed to go back to Boston then but Amos had already announced that he wasn't going *anywhere*); any food they normally ate but they should eat a lot of roughage since they were both still constipated; and the doctors hoped Amos would stay off booze, a stricture which Amos had told them was unnecessary since alcohol had entered the category of substances that "messed up my mind" and he had no intention of ever touching it again.

Bootville. A short-lived moment of relief as I reached the crest of the hill that turned into our road and coasted past the general store. Only to find that fifteen or twenty cars, unfamiliar cars, were parked along the road near our house. Strange men stood chatting on the porch of the store and here or there leaned against the cars. Some held cameras.

I panicked.

The car swerved so that Amos looked up to see what was happening.

"It's the fucking reporters," I groaned.

He was too miserable to care. Eddie was silent, too. But I could feel him stirring to life as we pulled into the driveway.

Don't you understand? We need peace and quiet to put together the ingredients of the good life! There's no way we'll be

261

able to do it with bulbs popping in our faces and notebooks waiting to record every dumb thing we say and a fucking TV camera on our porch!

They were going to make it impossible. They were going to be the extra ingredient that turned out to be part of a life that would have been fine without it. They were . . . The Volks was in the garage but an unfamiliar car was parked in back of it. I pulled in behind it and shifted into neutral. A man with a camera stood on the back of the car in front of us and began taking pictures through the windshield.

I blinked back tears. I couldn't see any way to get rid of them. Dianne was at work since we'd decided she shouldn't use up any more of her precious time off. Carly and Philip were in school and Daisy was at Laureen's house. We'd have no help getting into the house. Amos would have had no trouble being nasty to them if he'd been feeling all right but now he was much too sick to do anything. I turned to look at Eddie; he was waiting for someone to do something, too. I turned the engine back on, switched on the windshield wipers and glowered at the photographer through the moving wipers. A flashbulb went off through the windshield and I exploded. I charged out of the car screaming at them.

"Why don't you get the fuck out of here?" I raised my fist threateningly. "How do you expect us to live? Get the fuck out of here or I'll throw a rock through your fucking camera!" By now others had gathered around and flashes were going off like crazy, but I could no more have stopped than a volcano can stop itself from erupting. "GO AWAY! WE'RE NOT FREAKS! WE'RE ORDINARY PEOPLE AND WE WANT TO LEAD ORDINARY LIVES!"

The flashbulbs stopped. I thought it was my fury that had stopped them but it was only that they'd had enough of me in a rage number and were waiting for something new. For a moment everything was suspended. I looked around me. Not a sound, not a movement. Stillness. I returned to the van, moving in a rather gingerly way, as though I'd cast a spell I was afraid of breaking. I turned off the engine, took out the keys and closed

262

my door. I wanted to open the house door before helping Amos out of the car but I was afraid They might sneak into the house before I could stop them. It wasn't locked, of course, we didn't even own a key, but they wouldn't know that. I walked around to Amos's side and motioned to him to unlock his door.

"We'll just have to ignore the bastards," I told him. "Are you ready?"

"Uh-yuh," he said.

He was looking a little better. He wasn't green anymore. He leaned on me heavily as he climbed down from the bus, his right arm around my shoulders. The flashbulbs began popping again and questions were shouted at us but now my rage, as we made our way up the porch steps toward the door, was converted to helpless despair. Amos was holding on to me for dear life and I couldn't fight them. With great difficulty I got open the storm door, then the wooden door. Feeling someone in back of me I kicked without looking to see who it was. The moment we were inside I reached in back of me and kicked shut the door, then staggered to the kitchen table, twice nearly collapsing under Amos's weight. Only when he was sitting safely in his usual spot on the bench did I realize I'd left Eddie outside, surrounded by the vultures.

I took a deep breath, walked across the kitchen, opened the door and was greeted by the sight of Eddie walking slowly but surely toward the house, ignoring the lights and the questions. He never spoke and he never smiled. He just walked slowly and deliberately, with that slight halt in his left leg as it came forward, up the steps, onto the porch and toward me. I opened the door and he came into the kitchen. I closed the door as the reporters crowded up to it, then grabbed a kitchen chair and put it against the door, hanging the top slat over the knob, wishing we'd had the foresight to get a lock. Then I smiled bravely.

"Who wants a cup of coffee?"

Eddie said, "I could go for a drink."

Amos said, "A cup of tea, please. I don't think my stomach'll hold coffee yet."

Bemused I put up water for Amos's tea and got out the bourbon for Eddie. Out of the corner of my eye I could see someone negotiating for a position on the huge natural gas tank that nested in the bushes outside the kitchen window. There were no shades. Other men were doubtless posted in places where I couldn't see them. I put up coffee for myself and called Sheriff Baddely. I told him the men had been in the hospital and had gotten cut apart, which he doubtless knew though he didn't say so. I told him we'd just come home and reporters were all over the house, hounding us. I asked if he could help us and he said he'd see what he could do. Within half an hour he had them cleared away from the house and land, and the car that didn't belong to us was out of the driveway.

Peace and quiet.

They were there but not as close. They moved from my head to my stomach.

Dianne called. I told her we were fine but she should be careful when she came home because the town was mined with reporters. I told her I'd had to call Baddely to handle them.

"The sheriff!" she exclaimed, as though I'd called out the SS.

"I needed to get us some privacy," I told her.

"I know," she sighed. "But the cops."

Harold or one of her other L. L. Bean radicals must be right there listening. I knew Harold had been around again lately, although they didn't have any court cases going. The cops. As though I'd gotten Baddely to turn hoses on children.

"Oh, shit," I said. "Listen, Di, any time you're not happy with the way I'm doing things down here you can come and take care of them yourself." And then I felt awful because we'd been back for such a short time and Di and I were at each other already.

"I really thought you'd approve," I added. "I thought it should be peaceful when the kids came home. It was like a circus and I thought you wouldn't want Carly to come home to that."

"Maybe you're right."

Hallelujah.

Laureen got Daisy through the men on the road by carrying her so it didn't occur to them that she wasn't Laureen's own. At

264

the door I thanked Laureen and suggested she put Daisy down but Daisy wanted to come directly into my arms. I freed one arm long enough to hitch up the kitchen chair again.

"Hello, sweetheart," I said, kissing her. "Here are the daddies." She didn't look at them. She put her head down on my shoulder and clutched me more tightly. I smiled apologetically but they weren't concerned. They were much too tired, I reminded myself, to be concerned. They'd just been talking about a nap.

"The daddies are going upstairs to take a nap," I said.

She put her thumb in her mouth.

"Would you like to say hello, or give them a kiss, before they take their nap?"

The thumb came out only so that she could throw both arms around me again and clutch me for dear life.

"Hey, Daise! Sweetheart, listen to me—" Clutch clutch, harder and harder, "Nobody's making you do anything. You don't have to even look up if you don't want to." Slight loosening of the clutch. "I just thought you'd *want* to—" Tighter again. "They're exactly the same only they're not attached to each other anymore."

Silence. My arms are beginning to hurt.

"Daisy, you're hurting me. I know you're feeling funny but you're grabbing me too hard and you're hurting."

"Why don't you just put her down?" Amos asks, and at the sound of his voice she clutches more tightly again although I wouldn't have believed that possible.

"She won't let me. I'm sorry. I'm sorry I can't help you."

His chair scrapes back. "Never mind," he says irritably. "I can do it."

Eddie is standing already. Now he moves slowly toward the back stairs. Slowly Amos stands, reels slightly, steadies himself, then follows. I feel Daisy peeking.

"Isn't it nice," I whispered, "seeing Daddy move around by himself?"

She buries her face again.

"Call me if you need help," I say to Amos's back.

He doesn't reply. At the moment I am not irritated by his

failure to be interested in Daisy. It seems that it is as much as he can do to take care of himself.

The men were still upstairs when Philip and Carly walked in, threw down their knapsacks and asked what there was to eat.

"Did the reporters bother you?" I asked cautiously.

Carly shrugged. "They just took some pictures and asked a few questions."

"Like what?"

"I don't remember," she said.

"Don't you want to know where the—where your fathers are?"

"Sure."

"Upstairs. Taking a nap."

"Oh. What's there to eat?"

Each of them had two glasses of milk and three brownies. Watching them I got hungry and ate a couple of brownies myself, as did Daisy, who hadn't moved from her chair since the men had gone upstairs more than an hour earlier.

Nothing has happened, was the message the older kids were sending me. A few pieces of flesh are missing from the household. Big deal. If you don't point it out we won't even notice. Just don't go making one of your old mountains out of the molehill of our lives.

Of course I grew up in the West. To me the absence of mountains isn't just the presence of plains, it's an *absence*. Besides, something's *always* happening, if you're really paying attention.

"Did Daisy see them?" Philip asked suddenly, at which point Daisy scrambled off her chair and onto Carly's lap.

"Sure," I said. "She saw them in the kitchen, then she saw them go up to take a nap."

"You're hurting me, Daisy," Carly said. "Don't hold me so tight."

"She's scared," I said. "She was afraid to look at them. Not that they look any different."

"What's the big deal?" Carly asked.

"Well, *I* think it's a big deal," I said. Thinking, some mother

266

I am, trying to get my kids excited when they're calm. "Daisy and I seem to be the only ones who think so."

The three of them went up to their room and stayed there until dinner, although they must have been aware that at some point the men had come downstairs.

I kissed Amos lovingly as though we'd been apart for a long time. I sat down facing them and rested my arms on the table. I'd rolled up my sweater sleeves while I was doing the dishes and they were still up so my arms were exposed on the table. Amos was looking at my arm. At the spot where the Stern Old Judge had put it to me.

"Poor baby," he said, reaching out and touching the burn, which he had never commented on from the time I got it in their presence, through the next times that I saw them, through all the next times through the years until now

I stared at him.

"You should've been more careful," he said tenderly.

Tears welled in my eyes, perhaps for all the years he hadn't seen the burn. He slowly leaned over the table and kissed my arm.

"It doesn't hurt," I said.

Dianne came home with a bottle of champagne, which we opened. Amos wouldn't touch it, he was ready for coffee, he said, but the three of us had some right away.

"The big kids," I said to Dianne, "are pretending life is exactly the same as usual."

"Well," Dianne said, "it really is, in a sense. I mean, if you want to look at it that way."

I didn't want to look at it that way.

"That's just plain stupid," Amos said to her, with such intensity that I was frightened. "Everything's different. Nothing feels the same."

"I understand that," Dianne said, "but actually the outline of our lives is—"

267

"The outline of our lives," he mimicked her furiously. "What the hell does *that* mean, the outli—"

"Actually," I interrupted, "I know what she means." His sudden rage seemed like my own doubts and reservations gone wild. I smiled lovingly. "You do, too."

He nodded, looked down at the table, took my hands in his. He wanted to argue with her but not with me.

Suddenly Eddie was beaming at some spot in back of me. I hadn't seen him smile since the surgery. I turned. Carly and Philip stood in the doorway.

"Hi, Daddy," Carly said nonchalantly.

Eddie held out his arms to her and shyly, *demurely*, she walked into them. He closed his eyes and hugged her.

"Carly, baby," he murmured, kissing her cheek. "It's good to have you back."

"It's good to have *you* back, Daddy," she said happily.

There were tears in Eddie's eyes. And mine. I looked at Dianne; she was toying with her fork. I looked at Philip, standing in the doorway, bursting with eagerness, then at Amos, who didn't seem to have any sense that another scene was waiting to be played out. Philip came toward Amos except that at the last moment anxiety made him lunge toward his father, and Amos, frightened and angry, drew into himself, his arms crossing in front of his chest, and said, "Hey! Cut that out!" Upon which Philip burst into tears and came running to me.

"Philly, Philly," I said, holding him as he sobbed. "You have to take it easy, Daddy just came home."

"I only wanted to kiss him," Philip sobbed.

"I know, but you were so rough, you scared him."

"I didn't mean to be rough."

I looked at Amos, silently appealing for a little sympathy for his anxious seven-year-old son, but Amos wasn't having any. Meanwhile Eddie had helped Carly onto his lap where she sat in bliss, her head against his chest to the side of the spot where the scar was and above it slightly. Philip scrambled onto my lap.

"What time is it?" Amos asked.

268

"Six thirty," I said, trying not to show my surprise. Neither of them had ever had any sense of time or any interest in it. "Why?"

"I'm hungry."

"It's all ready." With some difficulty I disengaged myself from Philip. "I just have to heat it up."

Philip disappeared. He was waking up his sister, who'd apparently fallen asleep upstairs. He wanted to see how Daisy would be treated by their new father, but Daisy, once dragged sleepily to the kitchen threshold, made a beeline for me and let herself be set down in her chair with reluctance, then refused to look at her father for the remainder of the dinner. Her very fear, of course, making her less frightening to Amos, who spoke to her in a normal pleasant way although he made no particular overtures.

I kept staring at the men over dinner. I couldn't take my eyes off them. It was as though I were trying to read their faces to find my future, yet ironically there was less to be found in them than before because they looked more alike than they ever had. Where Amos's ambience had once been Scowl and Eddie's had been all Smile, each looked more neutral now. Strangers would have noticed immediately that they were identical twins. The smile Eddie had bestowed upon Carly was identical in its combination of pleasure and relief to Amos's smile when I first walked into his hospital room.

"Di, don't you think the men look much more like each other than they did before?"

"Mmm," she said.

"Do _you_ see it?" I asked the men.

Amos shrugged and Eddie shook his head but neither looked at the other. It struck me suddenly that they never did. _Never._

So what?

I got frightened. I was observing and I had no way to use what I saw. Observation was what made you feel smart without actually helping you to act. Knowledge, true knowledge, might have helped me to proceed with my new life. Knowledge was facts acquired with a meaning that made the facts move you. But I had no way to turn my observations into knowledge.

I stood up. "I feel like taking a walk." Away from the past, and forgetting about the future. Just using up some of the energy I felt inside me that there was no way to use yet. I was afraid of that energy. Afraid I'd be too needy when we got into bed and I would scare off Amos, who had a wound that needed to heal further and wasn't allowed to make love to me for a couple of weeks. Afraid I'd see too much and want too much and be destroyed by the conflict between what I saw and what I wanted.

"A walk?" Amos repeated.

The children had gone in to watch television by now, Carly having had to be pried from Eddie's lap because his legs were getting numb.

I smiled. "I won't be long."

"I'll come," he said with a grin.

Surprised and delighted I got our ski jackets. Now Amos would be able to close all the buttons in the front. He stood up carefully. I'd assumed he would want help from me but he came toward me, rather proudly, on his own, stopping a couple of times to lean on the stove, then the counter. His final step was more a victorious lunge, combined with a hug. I hugged him back.

"I'll take care of the dishes later," I said to Dianne.

Slowly we went out to the porch, down the steps, along the length of the driveway and onto the road, along which several cars were still parked. I'd forgotten the reporters completely; their car doors flew open when they saw us.

"Oh, shit," I said.

"It doesn't matter," Amos told me.

I looked frantically back toward the house. "We can never get back inside before they reach us."

"It doesn't matter," he repeated.

Lights went on. Flashbulbs popped, though not so many as before. A man with a small hand-held movie camera came toward us, followed by someone with lights.

270

Goddamn-son-of-a-bitch-motherfuckers, I didn't even comb my hair!

"Mr. Smith," one of the men said, "mind if we walk along with you here for a minute and ask a couple of questions?"

"No," Amos said, smiling in an artificial way. "We're just taking a little walk. As you can see, walking is still a little difficult for me."

"How do you feel, Eddie—or is it Amos?" the man asked with a grin, totally ignoring Amos's previous answer.

"Amos."

"Amos, tell us how you feel about your cure."

"Cure?" Amos repeated. I think that for a moment he was genuinely baffled.

"You know, your cure. This wonderful new freedom you have."

"Freedom." He understood now.

"Tell our viewers how you feel about the marvels of modern surgery."

"Just fine," Amos said. "I'm sure as soon as we're feeling a little better . . . we'll feel just fine."

I steered him around so we were heading back to the house. They followed—or rather they walked backward in front of us.

"Please," I said, "you've had your interview. He's tired. Let him rest."

"Just one more question, sir . . . Amos . . . if I may? Your brother? How's he doing? Is he inside? How does he feel?"

"That's five," I said.

"Please don't mind my wife," Amos said. "She's a wonderful woman but she's been under a lot of stress these past few weeks. You've got to understand . . . this has all been very difficult for her."

His arm was around my neck and I had to squirm around to stare at him. I was gripped by a strong sense of unreality. Not only couldn't I believe the message, I couldn't believe it was Amos and not Eddie who was sending it.

"Eddie is fine," Amos told the reporter. "He's in the house with the little woman."

271

"I can't believe my own ears," I muttered under my breath.

"He's had one too many," Amos went on, "and didn't feel like taking a walk. I imagine you fellows have had that experience yourself, some of you."

"You're not talking to four people," I muttered. "You're talking to four million."

"We're all just people," he said to me, except this time he didn't mutter, so that his words on the six o'clock news the following night would appear to be a message from his heart to the hearts of four million people sucking the tube boob. "Every one of us here is just another person."

By the time we got back to the kitchen he was thoroughly exhausted. A reporter asked if they could just get one shot in the kitchen.

"NO!" I said. "NO, NO, NO, NO, NO!"

Amos smiled. "You heard what the boss said."

Oh, Jesus. Having survived a Beverly Hills childhood, an East Coast transplant of dubious success, a Maggie and Jiggs first marriage and a ten-year circus act, was I now to sink beneath the waves playing Blondie to Amos's Dagwood Bumstead? I glared at the reporters with hatred—as though they'd fed Amos the lines.

"D'you think, Ed, uh, Amos, do you think maybe your brother and his wife could be persuaded to come out for a minute? Just to let our viewers see the four of you?"

"I'll check, but he was pretty far gone when we left."

We went into the kitchen. I stayed at the door to make sure they didn't follow us in.

"They're asleep already," Amos called. "Maybe tomorrow, fellas."

I slammed the door.

He sank into a chair. He smiled at me.

"Whew," he said. "I'm exhausted."

"Mmm. I can imagine." Putting on a whole new personality must be very exhausting.

"The fucking vultures," he said suddenly.

Old Amos. He was full of surprises.

"Then why did you do it?"

"It's good publicity. Sternheim wants a lot of publicity."

"Sternheim! We can't live our lives for Sternheim! They haven't even started the movie yet!"

"Sure they have. They're doing the research. They're going full steam ahead. They're looking for actors to play us. We're going to make a fortune. I'll buy you a mink coat."

I laughed. "Just what I always needed for walking to the store."

"Come on, sweetheart," he said, "let's go to bed. I'm really exhausted."

In bed we fondled each other lovingly. We faced each other and kissed noses, cheeks, lips. I wanted him to put his arm around me and realized at the moment I thought of it that it was something we hadn't been able to do.

"Put your arm across my pillow."

He did so.

Gently I rested my head on it.

"That hurts."

I raised my head and he withdrew his arm.

"All right," I said. "I'll do it and you put your head on *my* arm."

He did so. Of course it hurt me, too, but I was more civilized than he was and put up with it.

"Better?" I asked.

"Uh-yuh," he said.

But he still wasn't all that comfortable. He moved down so that his head was in the crook of my arm instead. Our bodies were against each other side to side, his hip touching my hip, his left leg along my right one. I fell asleep in a short while, quietly excited by fantasies of the following week, or two weeks, when we would get the signal from the doctors and life would become one long round of lovemaking, interrupted only by brief interludes of baking whole wheat bread and getting the children off to school.

We were under siege for five days but the number of reporters diminished and their ferocity subsided somewhat. Dianne and Eddie allowed themselves to be engaged in brief conversations but it was beyond me to do the same. Eddie didn't give a fuck one way or the other. He was watching TV day and night now, and drinking most of that time—wine during the afternoon, bourbon at night.

Amos, on the other hand, continued to refuse even a beer with his dinner. He was still experiencing dizziness and nausea when he lay down or stood up and claimed that these feelings had been caused by the anesthesia. I called the doctors to check; they were certain the drug effects couldn't have lasted this long but said if the symptoms persisted they'd run tests during the checkup. I explained that Amos was refusing to return to Boston and eventually it was arranged that we would all go to Hanover, but Amos delayed even then. The thought that making love wouldn't be "safe" until we were cleared didn't seem to bother him, although he remained very loving to me. He was sleeping very badly and needless to say wasn't interested in pills. He had terrible nightmares and gnashed his teeth in his sleep. He clutched me as he fought off sleep at night, fearing the bad dreams that came over him. When he finally fell into fitful sleep, he often awakened me with a moan or a scream or sometimes by grabbing me as though to break a fall. As the days passed by without his ever getting a placid night's sleep, he got increasingly grouchy, I being the one person who was never the object of his temper, Philip invariably creating situations in which he became his father's prime victim.

Carly spent a good portion of her time in the house on Eddie's lap, squiggling and giggling, posing riddles, asking questions about the hospital and the movie, telling Eddie how good it was to have him home.

Amos was cautious, even with Daisy. They had to negotiate at great length her first climb onto his lap, which was finally accomplished only with my assistance. He was gingerly in handling her and frequently would move her head or her shoulders if they seemed too close to The Place on his abdomen. But they managed.

With Philip matters were considerably worse. The first couple of times Philip allowed Daisy half a minute on The Lap and then started pushing for his turn. When she said she'd just gotten on he tried to push her off, thus angering her and infuriating Amos.

274

Philip was then expressly forbidden from coming anywhere near them while Daisy was with Amos. He took to playing with apparent concentration at the other end of the room until the moment when Daisy, convinced that Philip was totally occupied and she wouldn't be giving up her space to him, climbed down. At which point Philip scrambled to his feet, turned himself into a human cannonball and came crashing toward Amos from the other end of the room shouting, "Daddy, Daddy, can I sit on you now?" If only Amos had been able to remain calm and suggest to Philip that he go about it differently! But he reacted as though it were a fully trained Green Beret trying to castrate him instead of a very anxious seven-year-old boy, and matters continued to deteriorate.

"He just wants some of the love he sees the girls getting," I said to Amos.

"Then he should ask the same way."

"He's different. He's a boy."

"Then let him stay away from me."

"You're his father. Be patient with him. He loves you."

"If he loves me let him stop trying to punch holes in me."

It was the only subject on which he was less concerned with pleasing me than with protecting himself. In all other matters his first concern was with my welfare. He became increasingly antagonistic to Dianne. He said he didn't know how it could have failed to strike him how unfair was the distribution of labor in our house. As his bearing got steadier he became increasingly helpful to me and grumbled that he didn't know why Dianne never did kitchen chores like dishes. I said she was tired from working in the office all day, but he pointed out that I'd been working at least as hard at home. I said that was true but there was a rhythm to each of our days. Her rhythm involved steady work all day then relaxation at home, while I worked on and off, relaxing frequently between chores. I felt sympathetic to Dianne although we didn't communicate much these days. Not only were we both busy but I think we each felt unsure of where we were and of what was going to happen as a result of the two movies and the surgery. I kept remembering the doctor in Ken's movie who'd said we shouldn't go into the surgery without knowing what was going to happen and then thinking to myself, but there's no way to know because none of it has ever happened before. Anyway, my relations with Dianne were pleasant, however limited, and I was fearful lest Amos upset the balance with his eagerness to protect my interests. He was giving me all the help I needed, anyway, though he and Eddie showed no interest at all in getting back to their normal work.

"Why is Daddy mad at me?" Philip asked.

"He's not mad at you, love," I lied. "He just doesn't like— He's afraid you'll hurt him when you come at him the way you do."

"The thing you could hurt is gone."

I smiled. "The thing wasn't particularly sensitive," I said. "You didn't have to watch out for it."

"How come your face is all red?"

"What's that got to do with what we're talking about?" Life was turning me into a parliamentarian. "Anyway, no one ever asked you to watch out for it."

"They didn't have to. It was in between where nothing could happen."

"But why did you think it was fragile?"

Now it was his turn to be uncomfortable. Or maybe he just didn't know what fragile meant.

"Listen, sweetheart, there's something I want you to know." What did I want him to know? A lot of things, most of which I didn't know myself. "There was nothing wrong with the daddies' . . . with their attachment. It just made life too difficult. You remember. Remember what it was like just a little while back when they were tied together all the time? They could never do *anything* separately?"

He nodded wistfully. "It was nice."

"They were miserable all the time!" I cried out. "At least *your* daddy was. They had to go everyplace together, one couldn't move without the other. They were miserable!"

276

He didn't even bother to argue. He didn't care what was good, he knew what he liked.

"Listen, Phil, they've only been home for a few weeks. That's not a very long time. Things are going to get better and better."

I finally got them to Hanover because the stitches were itching like crazy and had to be taken out. Rhodes came from Boston for the event. The doctors were pleased with the men's progress. They could participate in all normal activities (wink, smile). Rhodes and I grinned at each other a lot. He was giving me a present and we both knew it. Reporters had followed us to Hanover and would have barged into the doctor's office if he'd allowed it. They were kept at bay with a promise of a medical report after we left.

ALL SYSTEMS GO, the New York *Daily News* reported the next morning. Subhead: LEAD NORMAL LIFE, DOC TELLS AMOS & EDDIE.

I yawned ostentatiously. It was ten o'clock. Eddie and Dianne had gone upstairs. Amos was reading mail.

"Mmm, I'm tired. I think I'll go up and take a bath."

"This pile of stuff is unbelievable."

"Can't you do it tomorrow?"

"Letter from Sternheim. His goons are coming back East to talk to us."

"Oh, shit. To here? To Bootville?"

"Uh-yuh. In October."

I was silent.

"Wycliffe and her husband. They're doing the script together."

"How cozy. . . . She was the gorgeous one."

"Uh-yuh."

He only saw what was in front of his eyes.

"But dumb," he added reassuringly.

"They're not planning to stay here, are they?"

278

"They rented a house up on Stormytown Road. Davis. The big red brick one."

Stormytown Road was where the few really elegant summer homes were. It wound along a high ridge that overlooked the ravine which ran for several miles outside town; the back view was of mountains. Now my alarm turned to resentment; not only weren't we good enough for them but they'd known it without even seeing the house.

"Very fancy," I said.

He grinned. "They need space. They want to be able to tape us for hours. Besides, they're coming with a houseboy and a cook."

"What are we supposed to do?"

"Nothing. Just talk. Mostly Eddie and me; maybe they'll ask you a few questions. You don't have to tell them anything you don't want to."

"No, I don't have to tell them. I can let them make it all up." Make up my life. Make up a better one . . . or even worse. I wanted to get into bed with him fast. I wanted to lose myself in his body. I wanted to quickly acquire a life so rich and wonderful as to make irrelevant a couple of Hollywood hipsters' view of me.

"Let's take a bath," I said. He and Eddie had fit easily together into the big, claw-footed tub. Why shouldn't the two of us fit in there now? An appropriate beginning to our new and wonderful sex life. "And go to bed. I'm tired."

"You take a bath," Amos said. "I'll be up in a little while."

He wasn't there yet when I came out of the bath, all warm and clean and wonderful smelling, but he came up a few minutes later. I pretended to be half asleep, thinking I needed some kind of cover, however transparent, for my eagerness. It seemed to take an interminable time for him to get undressed and washed but then finally he came into the bed and embraced me. We kissed. Mmmm. Lovely. My juices were running like crazy. He fondled my breasts, sucked my nipples. FUCK YOU, HOLLYWOOD, THIS IS WHAT LIFE IS ALL ABOUT! I reached for his penis but he gently pushed my hand aside.

"What's the matter?" I whispered.

"Nothing," he said.

I ran my hand gently over his chest, began kissing it. Slowly I began kissing further down. He didn't stop me although his body tensed a little. I reached his pubic hair and then his penis. At first he let me suck it but when he began to get an erection he stopped me.

"What is it?" I asked.

"It makes me nervous," he said.

"Why?" I asked.

"I don't know," he said. "I feel as if something's gonna bust open."

"The stitches aren't even there anymore, Amos."

"I know," he said. "But I feel as if they are."

Silence.

Tears welled, replacing the juices that had been running before. He reached out and embraced me.

"I love you, Nady," he said.

"I love you, too, Amos," I said.

Don't panic, Nadine. It's just one night. The first. Give him a chance.

But the sounds from the next room didn't help any. The grunts and groans and the murmuring voices.

It wasn't fair.

Everyone knew alcohol impeded men's ability to perform sexually and it was Eddie, not Amos, who'd been doing all the drinking. Was Dianne to be the one who had both an interesting job and a sex life? Definitely not fair!

As the days went on I grew more and more hostile toward Dianne.

How could I get mad at Amos when he was ten times as sweet and loving to me as he'd ever been before the operation? When I walked out of a room he followed me, talking. He made me a beautiful wooden brooch with a heart and a bird and a couple

280

of leaves that were carved out of darker wood than the rest. (Aside from this he showed absolutely no inclination to get back to work. Nor did Eddie.) We never argued. Philip wanted real carpentry tools which Amos thought he didn't need. Amos and I compromised by agreeing Philip would get the tools on his next birthday. We always found a reasonable compromise between our positions. Amos loved me too much to argue and I was afraid that if I showed him how angry I was he'd never want to show his love in some more tangible form.

When summer came Eddie and Amos spent more time than they ever had swimming. They would walk down to the pond together, the contrasting halts in their gaits slightly less obvious as they negotiated the difficulties of the narrow dirt path. At the water they would wade directly in to their waists then fall naturally into their old dreamy position, facing each other. After a few days they began experimenting, swimming separately. The strong outside arm of each remained stronger than the weak arm, while the halt in each inside arm remained constant, but always they first fell into their old position. Never speaking. They didn't speak much at home, either, but in the water it seemed natural.

They began talking when swimming weather ended. What they talked about was how badly they were going to miss swimming during the winter. This led to their talking once again about the building they'd discussed before the surgery, the building that had been shelved, I thought, along with the Caribbean vacation and any other amenities that might have stemmed from the operation money. It sounded so crazy that at first I didn't even bother to butt in and argue. As the days went on the building—buildings— sounded more and more like a monstrosity. The shop would be three times the size of their current one, with a rental apartment upstairs to work off the cost of the building—or the mortgage, if they needed to get one. These would be housed in a two-story, white-stucco cube which would be attached by a covered passageway to a gigantic, glass-domed swimming pool. In the cold weather they could go directly from one building to the other. After the third or fourth discussion I commented on the probable cost of such an enterprise and they stopped talking about it in front of me.

Time dragged on, as it tends to when no one is putting anything interesting into any of your openings. I read a lot, observed a lot, decided I'd definitely go back to school the following year. When the garden was finished I started listening to music all the time. At first I played mostly folk music but gradually I got into rock, which hopped me up and made the time move even more slowly around me. The constant loud rock music was upsetting to Dianne and became a point of contention between us.

"Could you turn it down just a little tiny bit, Nady?" she'd ask me in this high, skinny voice that was a cross between the meanest teacher in the third grade and her most timid student.

"May I ask exactly what you have against music?" *My one pleasure in life? A pleasure that you who are getting fucked royally almost every night of the week—you think I can't hear you right through those walls?—would gladly take away from me?*

The third or fourth or hundredth time it struck me that if I wanted music and she didn't there was no need for us to be in the same place.

"Why don't you go upstairs if you don't like it?" I asked.

"I'm only here for a few hours a day," she said, her voice quivering. "I can't just come home and get into bed."

"Would you suggest that we move the huge, fucking stereo system upstairs so I can listen there?"

I'd meant to drip sarcasm but she took it seriously. In my mind the place that had once been her refuge became a prison for me and my loud dirty music.

"Maybe that wouldn't be such a bad idea," she said.

"Oh, great," I said bitterly. "Then I can play upstairs until you and Eddie feel like making love, then I come downstairs and stay up until morning." Unexpectedly my pathetic vision made me burst into tears. "Don't you realize that music is the only thing I have? You have all the rest, I have the kids and the music!"

She was staring at me.

282

"What do I have?" she asked.

"I can't believe you're asking me that question."

"I'm serious," she persisted quietly. "What do I have?"

"A career. A *life*. A husband who makes love to you."

"Eddie doesn't make love to me."

Now I stared at *her*. Was I crazy or was she lying?

"Eddie fucks me. It's not the same thing."

I was astounded. Dianne never used words like fuck. Besides, the deprivation that concerned me seemed to be encompassed by either word.

"He barely touches me and he doesn't want to be touched," she said. "They're downstairs talking. Then he comes to bed and he gets an erection and he . . . uses me for a while . . . then he comes. Aside from that he doesn't touch me or kiss me. I never enjoy it at all. I've only been able to bear it by telling myself to be patient. It'll change. What happened to them was enormous."

"I've been so jealous of you," I said. I wasn't sure the jealousy was entirely gone because I wasn't sure I'd mind some good, hard fucking right now, loveless or not, but I could confess to her now that I knew things weren't the way I'd pictured them. Dianne, too, was still a ticket holder in the misery sweepstakes. "What about your job, Di? At least if *you're* unhappy at home you can go off to a job you love."

"I don't love my job anymore."

Now I was speechless.

"The pleasure's gone out of it."

"But what about—" I cast around for some case she'd talked about and realized the last name I remembered was Harold because she had stopped talking about her work at home as soon as Ken McDougall disappeared and took with him the part of her heart that made her need to communicate. "What about Harold?"

She shrugged. "Nothing happening right now. Anyway, he went out to Berkeley with his crazy wife."

"I never knew he had a wife."

"He did and he didn't. She was crazy. *Is* crazy. In and out of mental hospitals. He leaves her, then he runs back to save her."

So every time she thought he would leave his crazy wife because

283

Dianne had saved him, he went back to his wife to save her instead and then the fun went out of Dianne's *work*.

"What about all your other cases?"

She shrugged again. "We won them."

"Didn't that make you feel good?"

"No," she said, "because it really hasn't made any difference in anything."

"I don't understand." I could see now that she was listless and had been for a while; I'd just been too absorbed in my own misery to notice. "Why doesn't it make a difference?"

What she said, essentially, was what I and others would hear more and more often in the next few years. It was only the fall of 1970 but Dianne was very smart and she already understood that the sixties had gone bad. Dope would be legalized soon, she said, but aside from that the dreams were dead. Even that dream was dead in the sense that when it was legalized it wouldn't mean that society had changed at all, much less been revolutionized. She'd come to understand that our Mother Culture was so consuming that it could absorb the style of the counterculture without ever learning its meaning. Nothing was going to revolutionize our society; all was futile. She had a recurring dream in which a voice she couldn't identify, except that it was someone in authority, whispered, "Ladybug, ladybug, fly away home; your house is on fire and your children are gone." When she woke up she always thought at first that she was in her office and the children the voice was warning about were Harold and her other cases, but her panic was as great as though it had been Carly who was in danger.

I felt full of love and admiration for Dianne. Admiration for the way her mind worked to grasp the larger issues and understand how they related to her own life. It seemed to me now that one of the saddest facts of our marriage was that her intelligence had become irrelevant or unavailable to me in our everyday lives. I'd been too tied in to her, pitted against her, in competitive knots with her, to be able to relax and enjoy what she had to offer me even if she had offered it more fully. Our friendship had gotten lost in our marriage!

284

I wanted to change that now.

"It's just my mood," she said after a while. "Maybe things aren't really that bad. Obviously the thing we have to do is wait and see what happens with the men."

I nodded. "I've pretended to be patient with Amos," I said, "but the truth is I've been crazy to get laid since the moment I saw him after the surgery. I probably scared him half to death."

Dianne nodded. She knew what I was talking about. I was always scaring her half to death. (Or half to life.)

"A few months seems like such a long time," I said, "but it's not really very long when you think about what's happened to them. I guess I've been pretty selfish. Self-centered. Just worrying about . . . probably whatever's really good about the surgery they're not in touch with yet. Neither one of them has ever even been *alone* with a woman. Just alone in the dark, feeling everything." I wasn't sure what I meant but it sounded right. "It never occurred to me because I thought you and Eddie were having a high old time in there. But now it seems so—do you realize one of them can *feel* love and the other can *make* it? Somehow it all comes together."

Silence. It all came together but what difference did it make?

"Are you thinking what I'm thinking?" I asked.

"What?"

"That we should try sleeping together again."

"No," she said. "I wasn't thinking that at all."

I laughed nervously. "From the way you're looking at me no one would ever believe we'd done it before."

"They'd never do it," she said quickly.

"Would *you?*"

"I don't know," she said. "I don't know what difference it would make."

"I don't know either, but maybe it's worth a try." I wasn't willing to take the responsibility for pushing this time. If we tried it, then it would be because we all wanted to.

"Maybe."

But she refused to be present when I brought it up with them. Nor was I to present the idea in a way that suggested she was sure it was a good one. I wasn't sure I should "present" the idea at all. I hoped it could happen "naturally." For several days I tried subtlety. If we were sitting around the Franklin stove at night I got snuggly. Amos shrugged me off in a friendly way while Dianne eyed me and Eddie concentrated on the TV. Another time Dianne and I came upstairs when the men had spread out on the bed (Dianne's and Eddie's bed) the blueprints they'd ordered for the new shop building before they had the surgery. I called Dianne over to look and then I started hugging Amos playfully but he barely noticed.

In bed, on the other hand, he was more affectionate than ever. If it occasionally occurred to me, as I listened to the screwing sounds in the next room and my brain sent ulcer juice into every corner of my knotted body, to suggest a swap, Amos's visible affection for me and his clear dislike of Dianne seemed to make that idea totally impractical.

What's the big deal, anyway, Nadine? For ten years you had sex without foreplay and for the next ten you'll have foreplay without sex. It sort of comes out even, if you care to look at it that way.

I began nagging at him over a variety of matters ranging from the fact that he wasn't going back to work although jobs were being offered them, to the way he was favoring Daisy over Philip, to the weather, but never specified outright that I urgently desired to get laid. I was too mad and I needed it too much. More than anything what bothered me was that he didn't seem at all disturbed by our situation. I thought often about the shrink in Ken's movie who said we should be prepared for the difficulties. Several times I almost called to talk to him in Boston but I kept remembering that Amos was the one who was having the difficulties and *he* thought our lives were just fine.

286

I~N the next phase of the torture that I had so cunningly designed to look like a life, Robyn Wycliffe and her husband came
to Bootville and settled with their staff into the mansion on
Stormytown Road. It was November, not October as they'd
planned. A miserable gray November when we'd already had several inches of snow.

The first week or so I didn't even see them. At one o'clock
each afternoon they sent their chauffeur down for Amos and
Eddie. The men stopped eating at home because when they got
to Stormytown Road there was always a spectacular brunch set
out—smoked fish flown in from L.A., including something called
sable which I pictured swimming through the water weighed
down by wet fur—a variety of cheeses and breads, fruit and salad.
The Wycliffes themselves apparently ate almost nothing. Robyn
would have a slice of lox with an olive—a sort of solid martini—
washed down with a little champagne, while Lance would have

someone peel an apple. In the evening, still working, the men might be served steak and salad. They would return home some time after eight or nine at night, sometimes later.

Not only had I become superfluous as a cook, what was happening when they did come home was even more disconcerting. They came into the house looking exhausted and slumped down at the kitchen table, facing each other. If I asked how the session had gone they were too tired to answer but as they perked up over tea (Amos) and bourbon (Eddie) they would recover and begin talking to each other. Taping their memories was tripping them off in some way; after a day of talking into the Wycliffes' tape recorder they needed to come home and talk to each other, look at each other, fuck each other with their eyes. That was what they were doing, as a matter of fact. If I ever saw two people fucking each other with their eyes it was Amos and Eddie.

"Remember—what's her name?" Amos might begin. "The one with the curly hair?"

"Marie, sure," Eddie said. "She was the one who came around nights to check when Mrs. Awful was sick."

"There was something funny about her," Amos said. "But I can't remember what it was."

"She was blind in one eye," Eddie told him. "Her good eye was brown and her bad eye was blue. She never yelled or got mad at you but if you were bad, say, she came into the room after the lights were out and you were talking, she'd turn on the light and sit down on the edge of your bed, if it was you that was bad, and she'd close her good eye and fix on you with the bad one and you knew she couldn't see out of it and—"

"Jesus Christ," Amos said, shivering visibly, "it gives me the spooks when you say it but I don't remember."

"She only did it to us once," Eddie said. "We snitched some extra candy from the weekly dole. . . . Remember when she lined us up once a week and you picked your candy?"

Amos shook his head.

"Anyhow, we were talking about how we could get the extra

stuff we snitched from under the mattress and suddenly the light went on and there she was, standing over the bed. She—"

"Don't talk about it. It really gets to me."

"It wasn't so bad. You got used to it."

Silence.

I coughed.

They looked over to see what had made that noise, then looked back at their precious each other.

"Anybody want a cup of tea?" I asked uncomfortably.

They shook their heads without looking at me again. Amos was smoking some imported cigarillos Robyn had gotten him started on; he'd never smoked until now. You could only get these cigarillos at one store in Beverly Hills. I'd cracked that they were giving him cancer so they'd have a good sad ending for the movie but Amos hadn't been amused.

"Can I sit with you and listen?" I asked.

Amos shrugged.

I went up to bed and read some crappy magazines. I was too far gone for books by this time, only the lightest, fastest crap could hold me and that for only a little while.

If I was upset by this excluding closeness between Amos and Eddie, Carly was in a perpetual rage at having her father stolen out from under her nose. The second time they were very late getting home she appeared at the door in her flannel nightgown, arms crossed in front of her, eyes blazing, the perfect picture of the outraged wife finding lipstick on her husband's collar when he stumbles in from a "business" meeting at one in the morning.

"WHERE WERE YOU, DADDY?"

Eddie held out his arms to her but she wasn't about to run into them.

"Up on the hill, Carly," he said. "You know that."

"Why were you there so late?"

"They asked us a lot of questions. Now come here and give me a kiss good night."

She came to him but she wasn't ready to give up. She kissed him, climbed on his lap.

"I want to go there with you, Daddy."

"Okay."

I stared at them. There was a lesson for me in this scene. Amos just waited impatiently for the two of them to finish negotiating the matter of when and how Carly would come with them to Stormytown Road, but I was fascinated by her simple assertions and unembarrassed demands.

"Amos," I said when he came to bed that night. "You know what I would like to do?"

"What?"

"Get into bed with Dianne and Eddie. Like in the old days."

"What for?"

My resolve was in danger of crumbling. "Well . . . I . . ." *Come on, Nadine, there's nothing criminal in wanting a sex life.* "I thought it might be . . . I want to have sex, all of us together."

In one motion he'd pushed me away, turned on his side and sat up in bed.

"You crazy?" he asked. He was furious, the first time he'd been even a little angry with me in all the months since the surgery.

I was mortified.

"No, I'm not crazy. We used to do it all the time. Remember?"

"That was because we *had* to."

"So what? You and Eddie are closer now than you were before."

"What the fuck are you talking about?"

It had made him even angrier, if that was possible.

"I don't know why you're so angry," I said tearfully. "All I meant is you're better friends than you were before."

"You're out of your mind. He was always my only friend!"

"But you used to be mad at him most of the time."

"Don't be ridiculous."

"Well, not most of the time, maybe, but often. He irritated you. You never talked with him the way you do now. Looked at him."

"We didn't *have* to talk."

290

"You don't like Eddie more than you used to?"

"Of course not," he said emphatically.

So there it was. I could believe him or I could believe myself, two people each of whom I had ample reason to mistrust.

"I didn't want to argue with you, Amos. All I wanted was . . . It used to be so cozy, all of us together in the same bed."

And who's tampering with history now, Mrs. Smith?

"It was a pain in the ass."

"You never used to think so."

"That was because I didn't know any better."

"Well it would be different now."

"Then why do you want to do it?"

"Because I want you . . ." I groped around for words in the thorny thicket of my needs. "Because I love you." *Or at least I want to love you.* "Because we seem to be having these problems. And we're not the only ones, Amos; *they're* having problems, too. We were talking about— "

"Who was talking?" he demanded.

"Dianne and me." *Who else?*

"You mean to tell me you and Dianne sit around and talk about that stuff?"

"No," I said automatically. "I mean, not usually, but we—"

"Does she know?"

"Know what?" I was stalling because I was frightened. But I was also getting angry. He and Eddie could sit and talk about the past all night but Dianne and I weren't allowed to talk about the present.

"Does she know about our sex life?"

"Our sex life? Do you mean our lack of it?"

"We don't lack it," he said, "we just don't . . ."

That's what she knows, buddy.

"Look Amos, we've all had some problems since the surgery."

"She knows." Rage and disdain played across the top half of his face while his mouth moved with controlled tears.

"*I* know," I said. "I'm the one you're married to and *I'm* the one who's not getting laid and *I* know. How come that doesn't bother you?"

But it didn't. He had never been a fraction so concerned with not being able to make love to me as he was at this moment with Dianne's knowing he couldn't.

He turned on the light and got into his clothes. I'd never seen him move so fast.

"Please, Amos, running away isn't going to help. Can't we just talk?"

No. We couldn't talk. He didn't answer me. He just went downstairs and slammed out of the house. I heard the car engine trying to start but at first it didn't occur to me that Amos was going to drive it. He hadn't had his first lesson, yet, after all. Still, it was late at night and the engine that was being gunned was very close to our house. I looked out of the window and saw the van backing out of the driveway. I ran into Dianne's and Eddie's room, wrapping my robe around me.

"That was the van you heard starting," I said.

Dianne said, "I don't understand."

Eddie sat up. "Where's Amos?"

"Presumably," I said, "he's at the wheel of the van. Since the engine started a minute after he slammed out of the house."

Eddie leaped out of bed and began putting on his clothes. Dianne sat up and rubbed her eyes. I sat down on the edge of the bed. Eddie sat down on the other side and pulled on his boots without bothering to put on socks first.

"Where are you going?" Dianne asked.

"To find him."

"You're not going to drive, too!" Dianne exclaimed.

"Nope."

He was halfway out of the room by this time.

"How will you catch up with him?" she called out as he clattered down the stairs.

"I'll catch up with him," Eddie called back. "I don't need a car."

Eddie will catch up with Amos because Eddie instantly understands what it will take Nadine a while to figure out, that his brother has driven to the one place which, by the very act of his

292

being there, will constitute a revenge upon his demanding wife, as well as a retreat. Amos, in short, has fled to the mansion of Robyn and Lance Wycliffe, the latter of whom is in Los Angeles, taking a brief respite from the New Hampshire calm.

So the real moral of this tale is that there's nothing like telling your husband he doesn't give you what you need to send him hunting for another woman to give it to.

"How can you sit down with people you hate," I asked Dianne when we heard that their majesties of Stormytown Road were finally ready to see us, "and tell them your life story?"

"I don't think we have to," Dianne said. "My impression is they don't want that much from us. We can stick to the barest facts."

"That's easier for you than it is for me," I pointed out. "I always think I have to explain everything, then I have to explain the explanation, and then by the time I finish . . . That's what I'm afraid of. I'll spill my guts and everything'll come out all wrong. What I can't do to myself they'll do to me."

"Well if you know that's your tendency," Dianne said patiently, "can't you try to check it? Hold back? Maybe you could take a tranquilizer."

"Or put it in writing," I said, almost absently. Then I heard what I'd said. "Hey, that's not such a bad idea! I can put it in writing!" I would prepare a detailed chronology of my life and I would lean on the facts to disguise who I really was. If I gave them enough facts they would never be able to see me. I would create, in short, a *curriculum* to conceal my *vitae*:

Nadine Tumulty Smith
BORN: March 1935
EDUCATION: Academic Diploma, Beverly Hills High School
                June 1952
                Bard College, 3½ years—1952–1955
MARRIED: Twice
Etc.

I put down the pencil.

"Oh, Christ, this thing raises more questions than it answers."

"Why don't you just forget about it?" she suggested. "We'll be together. We can help each other out."

"I keep thinking I have to be prepared. Armed."

"You may be giving them too much credit," she said. "I don't think they're deep enough to ask us upsetting questions. I don't think they care who we really are."

She was absolutely right, of course. As it turned out the Swinging Wycliffe Writing Act gave us about an hour and a half of its valuable time before they took off for Hollywood where they would be free to make us all up better than our parents ever had, of that time about one hour and twenty-five minutes being devoted to our names, rank, serial numbers and major dates, the remaining five minutes encompassing a profound discussion of our views on life and art.

Then they were gone.

Zip.

Off to the airport.

My mind blinked.

I kept thinking more was going to happen but nothing did.

I took a deep breath and went back to my life, but now that I wasn't tense anymore I could feel the depression that had been there all along. I clung to my housewife's routine like a shipwrecked sailor hanging on to the skeleton of his vessel.

Dianne threw herself into work again. I think she'd found some new orphan of the sixties storm to save, although she never really talked about him at home.

The men settled in for the rest of the winter, doing nothing but talk to each other, mostly about their fucking building. The more I heard them talk the more repelled I felt, but they didn't make any move to begin the building, they were just talking, so I stayed out of it. They got a few job offers which they didn't take. When I asked why, Amos said the shop was too cold; in the new building they'd have proper heating instead of the wood-stove they'd always found adequate. I asked if they felt the cold more than they had before; Amos said he'd always felt it but he hadn't minded before. Eddie never talked except to Amos. And Carly. Carly was the only one who ever made him smile.

I thought more and more often about going back to school. It was the excuse I needed to be away from the house for a certain amount of time each week. In the present. And without a degree and a decent job, how could I even think of the future?

In March they got the second installment of the money from Sternheim (no other word from Los Angeles). In April they started actually drawing plans for the building . . . and at the beginning of May they went back to the garage shop for the first time since the surgery more than a year before.

Curiosity moved me to spy on them. I walked around to the side window and stood on a big rock to peer in. The van and the Beetle were both out in the driveway, so I could easily see them working on the far side of the garage.

They stood close together with their backs to me, facing the work counter that ran the length of the wall. Above them on racks and pegboard mounts were their various tools, jars of screws, nails and other small objects, boxes and bins with their more sophisticated equipment, wires and so on. They'd always kept the shop neat, but it was dirty now and as they worked they wiped off the objects they touched. Two of each basic tool (hammer, pliers, various screwdrivers, etc.) hung side by side on the mounts. When they were hammering, for example, they'd always alternated—a blow by Eddie's right hand followed by one from Amos's left—in cases where one of them didn't have to hold the object.

Now they seemed to be rearranging the tools to reflect their separated condition. Except they couldn't decide precisely what that reflection should be. They moved the tools and mounts so the sets were about a foot from each other, stepped back to survey the results, took everything down and rearranged the sets to be at opposite ends of the wall, decided this was too far and settled on a position somewhere between but much closer to the first. They went through similar procedures with the soldering gun and other equipment of which there was only one set, placing them first on Eddie's side, or Amos's, then eventually in between.

For some reason—I thought maybe it was just that I'd been perched on a rock spying—the whole process exhausted me. I went to the house to take a nap. A short while later the men returned. Half asleep I was aware of Amos coming into the room and taking off his clothes. He lay down beside me. I thought he must be exhausted too. He slept badly at night now and felt he needed to be utterly worn out to sleep at all, so he normally refused to rest during the day. When I rolled over now and looked at him I saw that he was asleep, but now his very presence kept me awake by arousing my desire—or it might be more accurate to say, by this point, my desire to desire, since I'd given up hope that I was ever going to get laid by my husband and I had virtually no physical responses to him anymore.

What was my surprise, then, when as I lay on my back in that state of near sleep which is often more restful than sleep itself, Amos, without seeming to awaken, rolled over on top of me with a hard-on and made love to me.

Maybe he thought I was the swimming pool they were talking about putting into the new building.

From that day on we had garden-variety intercourse a couple of times a week. If my desires weren't assuaged, my sense of justice was appeased. Amos was pleasant if not particularly communicative. Life was tolerable—thus enabling me to ripen for rebellion.

Now the men talked about nothing but the new building. I could no more have argued that they shouldn't build it than I could have argued against their taking a new lease on life. It was the only thing that interested them. Maybe it would be a beginning of meaningful activity.

I tried to get in on their conversations. I wanted to relate to Amos in some closer way than low-key sex a couple of times a week. (Note the change in perspective; what was crucial in its absence was only mildly reassuring in its presence.) Anyway, I tried to talk with them. They weren't rude but they were talking oranges and I was always breaking in with apples. They invariably sat facing each other now, looking into each other's eyes, reinforcing my sense of intrusion even before I opened my mouth to make the wrong comment.

EDDIE Winthrop?
AMOS He did a job just like it up the hill.

297

EDDIE   I guess he could do it.

AMOS   If we want him we'd better tell him now. He books in advance a lot of the time.

NADINE   Do you like him? I always thought he was a little strange and hostile.

AMOS   Who?

NADINE   Winthrop. Ty Winthrop. Isn't that who you're talking about?

AMOS   Uh-yuh. We're thinking of getting him to do the plumbing.

NADINE   Well . . . I was just curious to know if you like him.

AMOS   If he does it right we'll like him.

Carly was eleven now. She didn't have a close friend her own age in town for the simple reason that there was no girl in town anywhere near her age. Dianne occasionally urged her now to bring home a school friend to sleep over but for one reason or another Carly never did so. Dianne wanted to know if in some way I'd made Carly feel her friends wouldn't be welcome, but the truth was that it was no longer possible to trace a clear line to read between my (or anyone else's) actions and Carly's reactions. She was becoming moody almost beyond belief. She went through the days seeming like a fairly normal human being except that the tiniest reminder about a job she'd forgotten to do or the most innocent query about school or the most ludicrous challenge from Philip would bring forth a response so furious or a geyser of tears so voluminous as to make it apparent that the tears or the fury had been there all along, only waiting for a trigger to set them free. Anything and everything offended her; her feelings were permanently hurt. Every once in a while Dianne or I tried to isolate some cause; Dianne asked how she was getting along with Philip and/or me, while I couldn't help wondering if she'd been upset about Ken's disappearance, or perturbed by the first movie, or anxious about the next one. On the rare occasion when she wasn't further infuriated by my "nosiness," it was only because I was beneath notice.

Philip and Daisy were growing up (note the optimism), too.

298

Philip was eight years old and might have been difficult at home if he'd spent more time there, but he had a best friend now, one of Laureen's sons who was just a year younger than he, and he was always over at the Winthrops' except on the rare occasion when they were both at our house. Between his age and his assertiveness, he easily dominated Mike Winthrop, who followed him around slavishly and listened to his every command. If I was sometimes embarrassed by his bullying I was aware that I much preferred this situation to the reverse, and this would not have been true if I were thinking about Carly.

Of the lot of us Daisy fit most easily into the life of the town. She had two friends who attended kindergarten with her in the two-room schoolhouse up the hill. She spent time with them but could also be contented by herself for long periods. Sometimes I forgot she was around and left the house without remembering to tell her; she seldom even noticed but wasn't perturbed if she did. I loved Daisy passionately but never felt I knew her in the way I somehow knew both Philip and Carly. The ties that bound her to me were slippery velvet, not particularly susceptible to knots. She was my last child. There were moments when I sorely wanted to have another baby, but I understood that to do so would only be to put off the problem that confronted me now.

"I have to find something to do," I said to Dianne.

She thought for a minute. "If the men really have a lot more business when the new shop gets going, they're going to need help with schedules and billing and so on."

"Thanks a lot," I said sarcastically, but then realized from the expression on her face that she hadn't actually meant to destroy me. "You used to think I was so intelligent. Do you think my brain's entirely rotted away from not being used?"

"Of course not," she said quickly. "I didn't mean—"

"Anyway," I said, "I want something of my own. I'm the only one who doesn't have something of her own."

"You're raising the children," she pointed out, the first time she'd ever really given me credit for the whole job.

"But now," I said, smiling sadly, "I watch the school bus pulling away and I want to run and pull Daisy off it and I can't do that."

Silence.

"I was thinking maybe I'd go back to school. Get a degree."

She looked frightened.

"What's the matter, Di?"

"Nothing."

"That'd be maybe a year if I just took one or two courses at a time. Maybe then, being back in school I'd get a sense of what I'm interested in. If I'm still into psychology, or what. I need something to do when the kids are grown up, can't you see that?" *Why the fuck was I pleading with her? How could she be making me feel guilty?* "I'll still do my full share around here," I reminded her.

"Where will you go?"

"I don't know. Windham, I guess. That's the closest one and I think I can get in."

"What if they don't have a course you really want during the time when the kids are in school?"

"Then I'll take a different course. I'm not going to go upsetting our whole routine." *Your precious routine. Your job. Harold.* "This is just for the degree. Later on . . . later on I'll worry about what's in the courses."

The next day I drove to Putney, Vermont, home of Windham College, and got the catalog. I also wrote to Bard requesting that my transcript be sent to Windham and ascertaining the conditions under which Bard would grant me my degree with my last three courses from Windham. The conditions were not stringent; almost any three courses would do. There were no good psych courses given at an appropriate time and I finally decided to take the lit class I'd gravitated toward since opening the catalog—Twentieth Century Women Writers. These women had something to tell me. I was ready to find out how I was ordinary and how I was extraordinary. I would no longer read about the world outside Bootville as though I were reading science fiction.

300

After all those sealed-off years I was beginning to think about finding my place in that world.

Meanwhile the men were digging deeper into Bootville, a reality which for now I had no choice but to ignore. They were determined to get the twin foundations in before the ground froze, and if possible get up the outside frames as well before cold and snow made further work impossible.

In October a reporter called from New York to ask how our movie was coming along. He took me completely off guard as I'd vowed I would not be taken if I had to deal with those people again.

"It's not our movie," I shouted into the telephone. "It's Sternheim's movie and if you want to know how it's going you can call California and find out."

"It's hard to believe," the voice said smoothly, "that you don't know anything about it."

"I don't give a fuck what it's hard for you to believe!" I was trembling by now, in a raging pain over the fact that it was possible for them to do this to me when I'd been thinking I was on an even keel. "We have our own lives, we're not involved with all that shit. We've got our own lives here. The men are putting up a new building and I go to school and Dianne has a job. We don't give a fuck about the movie!"

By three hours later the back lands were swarming with reporters, and Amos and Eddie had to stop working with the other men who were pouring the concrete and talk to them for a while.

"I'm sorry," I said to Amos. "I didn't mean to draw them here, I just got so angry when—"

"Don't worry about it," he said. "It's good publicity."

"For what?" I asked.

"For the rental apartment," he said after a moment.

"Publicity? What is it supposed to be? An apartment or a museum?"

Suddenly my vague discomfort about the project crystallized. A

301

museum. A freak show. A freakoseum. That was what had been bothering me all along. Here we were slowly but painfully turning ourselves into normal human beings, and now there was this god-damn freak building to institutionalize—to memorialize—our old freakishness.

"Don't you have any homework?" Amos said. "This has nothing to do with you."

All right, I decided after my first incredulity. That was just fine. School was mine and the building was theirs. That was the way it would be. I stayed away from the back lands. Winter came. When they weren't at the building they were in the house with plans and blueprints and the *Pennysaver*. I threw myself into my course.

Happily I dug into Martha Quest. Pure pleasure. For a few weeks it was almost possible to believe reading had been the missing ingredient in my recent life. I particularly loved A *Proper Marriage*. It seemed to me as I read that the differences between Martha and me were superficial, although I would have been afraid to say that in class. I was afraid, as a matter of fact, to say anything in class, and never volunteered. I was eager to communicate with the teacher, who was younger than I but bright and sure and charming, as well as with some of the very young girls in class. I was so eager to make friends that it *hurt*, but I didn't know how friendly I could be without revealing my freak background, and I thought anyone knowing that background couldn't be interested in me *except* as a freak. (No one, so far as I could tell, had connected me to any of the newspaper stories.) Sometimes, when the young girls in class made comments whose underlying assumption was that they were a revolutionary race in a brave new world, I wanted to tell them they weren't so different from us as they thought. But how could I do that when, if it came to reciting chapter and verse, I would have to set myself further apart from them than they'd even dreamed?

The more I liked the people I met, the more I had to lose by letting down my guard.

302

CARLY wanted a horse. A girl from Pomstead who was in her class had allowed Carly to ride her horse and Carly had developed a passion for riding.

"No," I said instantly when Dianne approached me. "I cannot take one additional responsibility around this goddamn house."

"It wouldn't be your responsibility," she said. "Carly's prepared to take care of it by herself."

"What if she sleeps over with her friend in Pomstead? What if she's sick? What if she's— It never works that way; there has to be a responsible adult."

"I'll be responsible."

"What about when you stay in Hanover?"

"It's not likely to happen the same night as—"

"I'm not willing to take a chance. I'm not willing to do anything more than I'm doing."

"Don't. No matter what happens, leave the horse alone. How's that? It has nothing to do with you."

Nothing had anything to do with me. People were always granting me theoretical freedom.

"I can't stop you from buying a horse, Dianne," I said. "And I can't stop you from putting it out in the field." I was shaking. "But if it comes down to the line I'll let it die before I'll give it one meal or get it into the shed."

Dianne told Carly she was willing to get the horse but I was dead set against it. Carly stopped speaking to me.

At first I barely noticed. When I finally became aware of what she was doing, it was because she'd not only stopped being helpful to me in the smallest way but was being horrible to Daisy, whose ally and protector she'd always been.

"You're mad at me but you're hurting her," I pointed out.

"I'm hurting you, too," Carly said coolly.

I told Dianne I thought maybe we needed to have a conference about responsibility because I had more work and less help than ever. Dianne's response was to tell me that at least she and her daughter would be "out of my hair" for a while because her parents had been urging them for some time to come back out to Beverly Hills for a visit and now she'd decided to let them send the tickets. She would take part of her vacation early and they'd go during Carly's Easter break.

I was furious. Not only had she robbed me of my issue without helping to solve it, but I was consumingly jealous that she had parents. It seemed to me that a couple of kindly white-haired folk to whom my children could be dispatched when I was busy and the men were at the freakoseum (as winter lifted they spent more and more of each day there), the knowledge of whose presence would in itself be a comfort to me, was just what I needed. The fact that my own parents had never had any such soothing effect on me was irrelevant; after all, it was Dianne's parents I was wanting, not my own.

While Dianne and Carly were in California I did a lot of walking and a lot of thinking. My thoughts made me need to walk

304

more and my walks gave me increasing food for thought because almost every time I took a walk I went up the road in the direction of the store and every time I did that I passed the Bell house, which had a sign hanging in the window, as it did every spring and summer, saying, FOR SALE.

It seemed to me that it was time to split our families into two houses.

Dianne would be upset. She would assume I was angry about Carly's behavior and there was some truth to that, but beyond that was my anger at still being stuffed into a role I'd partly outgrown. If there was a time when I'd wanted to play the mother of them all and had been unable to conceive any other functional role for myself, I was stepping back from the former now and needed more than ever to believe in the latter. Dianne was not only failing to help me, she was fighting me at every turn. Once . . . and for a long time after . . . I'd given her the space she needed to live. And whatever my own reasons had been it had worked. Now she needed me less and I needed to move away, yet she reacted to my gentle attempts as though they were direct threats. If only she'd understood the crushing burden I sometimes felt or supported me in my desire to eventually find a place in the outside world to relieve and balance that burden, I might have been able to continue as we were. As it was her disapproval became an additional burden.

If we moved to the Bell house I would continue to help Dianne, but my help would be clearly a voluntary act. If I made dinner for the Other Smiths, as I now found myself thinking of them, it would be because I felt like entertaining them, not because I was there to do it. If Carly wanted something Dianne would take the responsibility for giving or denying Carly what she wanted. I was the female person who'd allowed Dianne and her daughter to be friends; now Dianne would find out what it meant to be a mother.

I had no idea of how Amos would react; I only knew that if he didn't want to buy the Bell house with me I would buy it for cash with the money I still had from my parents.

"Amos," I said cunningly that night as we stretched out in bed, "remember how when you first came back from the hospital you realized for the first time that I was doing all the work around the house and Dianne wasn't doing any?"

"Uh-yuh," he said.

"Well, it's gotten worse somehow," I said. "Carly's mad at me over the horse and she's being bad with Daisy and I'm just sort of . . . I think that's the real reason they went to California . . . I'm sort of at my wit's end."

He rolled over on his side and fondled my hair, prepared to give me a little physical comfort. But physical comfort wasn't what I needed just now.

"Just tell 'em they have to do their share." He kissed me.

"It's not that simple," I pointed out. "The fact is, Di's in Hanover all day and I'm here."

"What do you want to do?" he asked.

"Well," I said, very slowly and cautiously, afraid he was going to explode before I even finished the sentence, "the Bell house is for sale again. I saw the sign up and suddenly it struck me . . . if we lived in separate houses, some of these problems wouldn't even arise."

"You and Dianne."

"Well, yes. . . . But I mean . . . what I really want is for you and me to buy the Bell house and live there with Daisy and Philip, and Dianne and Eddie and Carly would stay here. That way there'd be a more natural division of labor and we'd still be close and we'd have all the advantages of . . ." I went on and on, unable to stop now that I'd started, cataloging the advantages of the life lived close to Eddie and Dianne but not practically on top of each other. Then I waited. Thinking he was thinking heavy thoughts. Thinking he was trying to decide whether to tell me to drop dead or simply implement the wish. Thinking he'd tell me if Dianne and I wanted to move across the road we could but there was no way he and Eddie . . . Thinking . . .

"How much are they asking for it?"

I blinked. "For what?"

"For the Bell house."

"I don't know," I said unbelievingly. "I heard they were ready to really negotiate this time."

"Last year I heard Bell wanted some crazy price like thirty thousand. He paid six thousand for it in the fifties."

"Mmm."

Silence.

"What about . . ." I groped around for tactful words. "What about, uh, other factors? I mean, how do you feel about the idea of breaking up the families? The children? About you and Eddie?"

"I thought you wanted to do it."

"I do, Amos. I just think we have to do it in a realistic way. Understand there may be difficulties attached. Remember how you—we—uh—thought it was going to be easy when you and Eddie got separated—and how difficult it turned out to be?"

"Of course it was difficult," he said. "They doped me up so I could hardly walk."

Oh, Jesus. I'd been prepared for anger but not for stupidity. Did he really believe that was all that had been involved? Didn't he remember how miserable he'd felt? Didn't he remember that he'd been impotent for more than a year? Or had he forgotten that because it hadn't really mattered to him?

Actually, the biggest question of all was how I was managing to be so surprised when I was talking to a man who'd made the major decision of his life—which he'd assumed involved the risk of that life—on the basis of cash.

"You don't have any fears?" I asked cautiously. "I mean, about living in a separate house from Eddie for the first time?"

"What difference does it make?" he asked. "We'll just be across the road. Anyway, I have you."

That was true. He had me. For now. This wasn't the time to point out to him that it might not always be true. I had been able to fit my life, my class, my first feeble attempts at self-definition into the life of our family. Someday there might be a class . . . a job . . . whatever that would take me away enough so that he'd notice I was gone. For now he could have mental communion with Eddie and physical communion with me and ignore the small time and small space between Eddie and me. It would be foolish for me to goad him into acknowledging those spaces. For now.

Dianne came home from California in a spectacular mood. I met her and Carly at the Keene airport with the van on Sunday night. They were hungry because the airplane food had been inedible and there hadn't been time to grab a bite between planes. We decided to have a bite to eat in Keene. She and Carly giggled together like two schoolgirls.

Over dinner in the Keene Pub, Dianne told me she'd never had such a good time with her parents. Her mother in particular had been wonderful with Carly. So understanding, so wise. She'd never realized it before, Dianne said without a trace of irony, but her mother was simply one of those women who wasn't comfortable with the needs of young children but got better and better as the children grew up. She said the more she came to understand her mother, the more she liked her. Her father, on the other hand, wasn't aging very well. He was becoming just another hidebound, Beverly Hills Jewish Reactionary. (In all the time I'd known her Dianne had never used the word Jewish as though it applied to herself or anyone in her immediate family.) Anyway, she babbled on and on—I'd never heard her talk so much—and I sat there, eating my veal Parmigiana, rendered speechless by her babble.

She'd called Sternheim. She'd been anxious to know the state of the movie and she hadn't wanted to talk to the Wycliffes. She was as frightened of them as I was, particularly of Robyn, whom she suspected would stop at nothing, while it seemed to her that Sternheim was essentially a very decent character. I thought that was funny, although I didn't say so. How on earth had Dianne, even with her monumental powers of self-deception, managed to persuade herself that Sternheim knew the limits? Sternheim was a chartered prince of Hollywood, a place where the green light stood for yes and the red light for maybe.

Sternheim had taken her to lunch in a very "un-Hollywood" Chinese restaurant called Mr. Chow. He'd convinced her that not only would the movie be a project that wouldn't shame her, but that even if she didn't feel the way he expected her to, which was that she'd love it, it wouldn't matter because in the eyes of the public the actor and actresses playing us would become the characters. It was they, not we, who'd be deluged with TV invitations and letters asking why they'd done such and such. Dianne had to admit she found that whole idea reassuring—and amusing, as well. Not only that but she'd met the actor who was going to play both twins. Bo Sandoval was utterly charming and un-Hollywood, like everything else Di had seen in Hollywood this time around. Like the writers who'd been hired to replace the Wycliffes because their script hadn't been satisfactory to Sternheim, a perfectionist if Dianne had ever known one.

Carly appeared to be hanging on to her mother's every word and when I failed to nod or smile at some appropriate point, she filled the gap. Neither of them had asked about home or the twins, but after all they'd only been away for a little over a week; it probably seemed like a short time to them.

Carly went to the ladies' room.

"She was wonderful," Dianne said, gazing after her fondly. "She's really growing up, Nady."

"Mmm."

"My mother and I talked about her a lot."

I was silent. If I was going to get another pitch for the horse with Grandma's word thrown in for ammunition, I'd tell her about the Bell house then and there. If she had her own house she could get an elephant, for all I'd care.

"She's almost a teenager," Dianne said. "She could really use her own room."

I stared at her.

"My mother had an idea," she went on slowly, "and it's something I want to discuss with you. I mean, before it comes up with the twins, or even Carly."

"I had the same idea." Why was I upset when it was what I'd

309

wanted all along? What difference did it make whose idea it was as long as we did it?

Now Dianne was startled.

"I've been thinking about it for a long time," I said. A lie. It was only since Dianne had gone to California.

"About what?"

"About the Bell house. I looked at it while you were away. I even talked to Amos," Thank God. I had a witness that I'd thought of it first. I wasn't being kicked out.

Now it was her turn to be upset. She'd had to put the idea into her mother's brain to broach it, but if it had to come from one of us, she didn't want it to be from me.

"Amos says he's willing as long as the price is right."

"What about Eddie?"

"I don't know. We didn't talk to him. At least I didn't."

"I wish you had. I don't know how to talk to him anymore."

"He's your husband," I pointed out. Not vindictively. It hadn't occurred to me to talk to him.

Carly returned to the table, but Dianne wanted to keep talking so she abandoned the fiction that Carly didn't know.

"What if the price isn't right?" she asked suddenly. "Or they decide they don't want to do it for some other reason?"

I shrugged. "We'll have to fight it out with them. ·It's not as though we can't afford it." We'd used up a portion of the original $25,000 from Sternheim since the men's incomes had been reduced to nothing, but we still had the big lump remaining after taxes from the installment of $100,000 that they'd gotten for the surgery.

"We should be able to think of some reason they'd want it," Dianne said. "It's good for them, too."

I laughed. "Why? They have us and each other and the children and their work, which takes them away from us exactly as much as they decide that it should." Funny, this whole business had begun as a rebellion against Dianne and now I was sounding —half believing—that it was the men I was against. "They have sex with us and companionship with each other and when they

310

finish the building they'll have a swimming pool they can use all the time instead of just a few months a year." That building was already using up more money than they'd anticipated. If we wanted to split houses this was probably the best time to try. Before they faced the full reality of the expenses for the freakoseum, the only project ever whose cost Amos hadn't worried about in advance. "If we insist on it we can get it. I'd even use my own money."

Dianne looked despondent. "I'd rather convince them than fight with them."

"The truth is," I said, "that we don't know what they want or what they will want. We don't understand them at all. They're strangers to us. Maybe that's why we have to make love to even live together comfortably—otherwise we don't know each other at all."

Why was I in pain? Everything I was saying was true.

That must be the reason.

"Amos won't talk about anything but money," I went on. "And Eddie . . ." Eddie didn't really care about anything except Carly and his bottle. "We can't tell them what they really want. We'll just have to put it on the basis of what *we* want."

She stared at me as though I'd casually spread out blueprints for a mass murder.

I smiled. "We both do want it. Don't we?"

She nodded but she was torn, as was I. I put my hands over hers. She looked very beautiful to me at that moment, so extraordinarily beautiful that I felt crazy and wanted to cry. My eyes were riveted to her face. Which had not a single exceptional feature. A frame of straight, fine, brown hair. Clear hazel eyes. A small almost pudgy nose and no cheekbones to speak of. Her skin was finer than mine and aging earlier. Her full lips showed more than any other feature the disappointments of her life, pulling down gently at each side, sometimes making her look as though she were about to cry when crying was the furthest thing from her mind.

"Do you think it'll happen, Nady?" she asked in a whisper.

"Any time one of us has been hell-bent on something, it's happened," I said. "If we really want it to happen, it will."

The negotiations for the Bell house began in a desultory way. The Bells weren't in a hurry to sell with summer coming but the men weren't in a hurry either because they were totally absorbed in their building and didn't care whether we got the other house or when. I finished my course, in which I got an A, and thought about the decoration of the Bell house. Dianne and I never discussed our plans. We were both afraid of jinxing the deal. Besides, the feelings between us were good in this period, but she was spending longer hours than ever in Hanover and at home she and Carly spent most of the time closeted together giggling, making plans for the time when Carly would be Dianne's "assistant housewife." Carly was learning to cook. My own kids had gotten an inkling of the possible move and were very excited, but I couldn't tell whether they really liked the idea; it was just exciting.

The men were working twelve to eighteen hours a day at the freakoseum, which had become the activity of choice for everyone in Bootville under eighteen or without work once school was out. They just watched in that way rural kids and adults had. No need to speak. When they went home in the evening the humor of the freakoseum might overtake them, but during the day they just watched.

"I wish they'd close the deal on the house," I said to Dianne. "And finish up the fucking freakoseum."

"THE WHAT?" It was the closest sound to a shriek I'd heard from Dianne.

"The building. The dome. The freakoseum."

"Why are you calling it that?"

"I don't know. The whole thing gives me the creeps. Doesn't it bother you?"

"No. They need something to keep them busy."

Their big educational toy. Their Siamese twin doll building.

312

"All right. I'm sorry. I guess I'm just dying to make the move and get the house set up."

She looked at me strangely. "What do you mean, Nady? You won't have to do any of it. We'll manage."

"Why should you?"

"It's our house," she said. "I don't expect you to—"

"Oh, my God," I said. "I've been assuming . . . Amos and I are the ones who're going to move."

"Oh, no, Nady," she cried out, "I assumed . . . I mean . . . this house is so much you."

"No." I didn't know what I was denying.

"I don't mean it as a criticism," she said. "I love this house just because it *is* you, all warm and cheerful and full of crazy funny little things you've picked up. I love them. But I want my own house that's *me*."

Everyone would see Dianne moving across the road and think, The crazy one finally drove the sane one out of the house. I hated myself for the thought but there it was.

"This is silly," I said after a while. "Because we can both fix up the houses."

Silence.

"Let's toss a coin," I suggested.

"No," she said after a minute, "that's all right. You can have the Bell house."

"You mean it?"

"Yes. It's bigger and you need more space with two kids. Anyway . . ." A note of triumph crept into her voice. "The most important thing is that Carly will have a room of her own. And I'll have some privacy. Harold's been living in a house full of people in Lebanon, and we've been having difficulty just, you know, finding a private place to be together."

I closed my eyes.

"Nady," she said, seeing that I was tired and disgusted, "this has been a very difficult time for me."

"It's been a piece of cake for the rest of us," I assured her.

"At least you came out of it with something better than you had before."

I was silent.

"You know Amos is nicer than he was before," she said. "And Eddie's much worse."

"You mean because he drinks?" I couldn't deal with the other issue, Amos's niceness. I suspected he wasn't nicer, he just put on more of a front now that Eddie put on none at all.

"Not just the drinking. He used to be very loving. I could talk to him. Sometimes when you weren't there and Amos dozed off or seemed occupied with a book, I'd just talk to him about what was on my mind. He was so sympathetic."

"What kind of thing did he say?" I was being cautious again.

"It wasn't so much what he said as the way he *was*. I know it sounds, well, corny, but I looked into his eyes and I saw understanding."

I'd seen it, too. Naturally. We were seeing our own reflection.

"Sometimes I think we both just saw what we wanted to see all along."

"Don't say that."

"I'm sorry. I was thinking out loud. I was thinking . . . they were barely human. Almost unborn, in some way. But we never even noticed because we were needing to get married and have babies and do the whole number."

"That's not fair," she said vehemently. "They weren't even alike, so I don't see how you can talk as though we were both doing exactly the same thing. The two of them were totally different."

"Heads and tails," I said almost absently. Then I collected myself. "That's all bullshit, anyway, Di, and you know it. We both married both of them." *Not to speak of each other.*

"I'm sorry," she said stiffly. "I don't agree at all. Each of them always had a very distinct personality in my mind."

In our minds. Precisely my point, of course, although I managed not to say it. Already The Truth, or that week's faction of it, was settling into my head, moving me away from Dianne, who was unwilling to examine it with me.

"You can have the Bell house," I said. I had the sudden sensation that I had too much to do, to think about, to learn, for me to bother spending months decorating a new house.

"We don't even know if they'll end up buying it."

"If they do you can have it."

"No," she said, "I've already gotten used to the idea of this one. I'm thinking about what I'll do here. You can have the Bell house."

They finished the dome and closed the deal on the Bell house in the same week; I managed not to think about one by concentrating on the other. They got the Bells down to Amos's top price ($18,000) by waiting until the end of the summer, when the Bells knew that if they didn't sell it they'd be stuck for another year. It was September already. We painted the kitchen yellow and decided to paint the rest a room at a time later on.

The closer we got to moving day the more Dianne and I were like two boxers sparring in a ring where punching has been declared illegal but neither thinks her opponent will follow the rules. Carly, on the other hand, was fairly pleasant with me (and Daisy) now that my domination of her life was ending. Sometimes the three kids played Monopoly after dinner and Carly helped Daisy enough so Daisy wouldn't quickly throw away the game to her brother, who played to kill. I felt prematurely nostalgic for the children, who would be living apart for the first time in their lives.

At Windham I signed up for two snap courses that would get me through my last six credits with a minimum of fuss and bother. I felt I had to conserve my energy, although I wasn't sure for what. Except maybe fixing up the house. I was having trouble, actually, deciding what I wanted to do with it. Furniture and patterns that had been attractive to me before the closing no longer had any appeal.

THE move itself was simple except that the kids were so excited they couldn't be relied upon to take the simplest object across the road without dropping it. We put the beds and two chests of drawers on a dolly and took them over ourselves—Eddie, Amos and I. Dianne went off to shop; she said she'd better start shopping for herself but I thought she just didn't want to be around for the move. The men were terribly businesslike, and ten minutes after the furniture was in place they were on their way back to the freakoseum. They were beginning to fill the pool. It would take close to two weeks for the water to reach the right level but the Bootville kids, including our kids, Amos told me when he came home for dinner, sat there all afternoon watching the water pour in as though it were some new spectator sport.

"We'll have to be careful," I said. "We'll have to keep it locked so kids can't get in."

"We keep the whole thing locked already," Amos said. "We had some tools robbed the other night."

"Oh Jesus." In its small way it seemed to confirm my premonitions about the enterprise. Nothing had ever been stolen from our home, which didn't even have a lock on the door. "Why didn't you tell me?"

He shrugged. "Didn't think of it. It's all taken care of."

He was very matter-of-fact. Very businesslike. It wasn't his fault. He was a matter-of-fact person relating to me a matter of fact. He could have been the bread man telling me what he had left on the truck or the repairman from Sears telling me what the washing machine needed to work. It wasn't his fault that the quality of our lives was strained. It wasn't his fault that the magic was gone.

The kids ran back and forth between the two houses.

"Carly is baking a cake," Philip said. "Will you bake a cake?"

I laughed. "No, it's too hot." Actually I felt chilly and had all day, even when the September sun was out.

"Why is Carly baking one?"

"Maybe she has something to celebrate."

He looked at me blankly.

"Why don't you ask her if she'll save you a piece?"

He grabbed Daisy's hand and they ran off to Our House (the one we had moved to was the Bells' house, not ours, yet).

When they went to bed it was close to ten o'clock. They moved their beds into the facing doors of their new single bedrooms so they could talk to each other until they finally dropped off to sleep.

I brought a kitchen chair into the living room and stared out of the window at the other house, wondering how Dianne was feeling because I couldn't figure out how I felt myself.

"How do you feel?" I asked Amos, who had doubled over an old braided rug and was stretched out watching the ten o'clock news. The TV was the only piece of furniture in the room aside

317

from the chair I'd lugged in. At the last minute Dianne had stopped insisting we move out most of the furniture.

"Fine," he said. "Why don't you lie down here with me? It's more comfortable."

Listlessly I came down beside him and we watched the news for a while. In Concord an eighty-six-year-old woman had been found dead in her apartment, the furnishings of which consisted entirely of tied-up stacks of the *Manchester Guardian*. I sat Indian fashion; Amos moved so that his head was in my lap. He held my hands as they rested on his chest, under his. I bent over and he kissed me, fondling my breasts. He wanted to make love there on the rug but all I really wanted was to get drunk and there was no booze at all in this house.

"Amos," I said, "I bet you could drink a little without getting dizzy."

"So what?" He wasn't unpleasant because he wanted to get laid.

"I feel like a drink."

"We don't have any."

"We could get some from Eddie."

"If you want it I'll get it for you. I don't want any."

"I don't want to drink alone." On the other hand I wouldn't want a drink if I didn't feel as if I were alone.

"Lie down."

"No. Talk to me. Tell me what it was like when you and Eddie were attached."

"You know what it was like."

"Not from the inside."

Pause.

"I never had bad dreams."

"What kind of dreams do you have now?"

"Different ones." He's fondling me. He is patient.

"Good ones?"

"The good one's always the same. Eddie and me . . . we're attached again. We're swimming or playing double solitaire."

"But do you remember it that way? That it was always good when you were attached?"

"I never had bad dreams."

"What kind of bad dreams?"

"Come on upstairs and I'll tell you."

"Tell me first."

"I'm out in space and it's dark and I'm cold and I'm dying."

"That's really weird, Amos. I've been cold all night and it must still be seventy-five degrees."

"Let's go upstairs. I'll warm you up."

I let him persuade me to go upstairs but then I lock myself in the bathroom and run water for a hot bath. I stay in the bath for a long time, hoping he'll fall asleep. Or get so angry that he doesn't want to screw me.

It doesn't work. He's too anxious to get laid to let himself be angry at me, the only repository for his affections.

I put on a flannel nightgown because the temperature's gone down to about seventy-four degrees. I get into bed armed with three furniture magazines. Desire makes Amos canny; I may be reading oranges but he can always get to me with apples.

"There's something else I didn't tell you because it's not a dream. It's a picture."

What the hell. I drop the magazines on the floor and turn to him.

"Of what?"

"A woman. I think it's my mother."

"Oh, wow!" I sit up in bed. "That's fantastic, Ame. What does she look like? When did you start seeing her?"

"A few months ago, I guess. She's beautiful. Dark hair, long like yours but maybe just a little darker. She's lying down in bed."

"And?"

"That's all."

I am frustrated by the impossibility of seeing with his eyes, of carrying on his dream, but I'm turned on by the idea of trying.

"See if you can remember more," I urge. What I'm turned on by is the feeling that I am knowing him a little for the first time. If there's nothing very interesting in the present to talk about, maybe we can spend our remaining eons together talking about the past. I kiss his cheek, settle down against him, run a finger down the thin line of hair on his chest that runs for an inch or two above and below his belly button. He stirs, holds me more tightly. "Close your eyes," I say. "See if she gets off the bed."

"No," he says after a moment. "She never gets off the bed. But I can see a man coming into the room. Very tall. In one of those red and black lumberjack shirts. He's carrying a bowl of something."

"Oh, my God, I can't believe this is happening!" I'm almost beside myself with excitement which is easily translated into sexual excitement because it's a horny Amos who's actually beside me. "More, Amos, more." I'm all over him, whispering in his ear, kissing his neck, playing with his nipples.

"We're sitting on a blanket," he says, tugging at my nightgown, getting it over my head with my now willing assistance. "Looking up. It's a shabby blanket, khaki, like army blankets. The floor around the blanket is dark rough wood." By now his head is buried in my bush and it's hard to hear him and I'm torn between a desire to have him in me and a desire to hear the rest of this precious memory. "He brings . . . bowl . . . mmmmmphhhh . . . edge of bed . . . dribbles . . ." The words are hopelessly muffled by now but I no longer care. ". . . mmmmfffps it off . . ." His fingers are in me. He begins sucking my clitoris and can no longer speak at all.

"Yes, Amos, yes."

The next morning he confesses that he made up the whole story about his father and the soup because he saw it turned me on.

I was dumbfounded. He confessed slyly—I didn't even ask. I think he wanted me to admire his cleverness in devising the one strategy that would have worked.

"You're not serious," I said. I felt a dead weight inside me. My hopes had died. Not with a bang, as they say.

He nodded, still looking rather pleased with himself. Waiting for me to see the joke and share it with him. And indeed I could see, though I was far from feeling, the humor of the situation.

I kept staring at him because I couldn't pull together the

various thoughts and feelings I was experiencing well enough to know which was most important or how I should be responding now. I was far away from Amos. Probably I had to be because if I were close I would kill him. He was an insect under glass. Unfortunately I was also an insect and I was trapped in the same glass. It was a trap of my own devising but that didn't mean I should never try to get out of it. It was said you had to pay for your own mistakes, but no one had ever been able to specify the currency or tell you how long you were supposed to keep paying. On the other hand, I was just in the process of working my way out of the Dianne trap; it was too soon to be thinking of the Amos trap as well. I had to finish school, equip myself for a job. I had to bring my children as far toward being grown-ups as I could before I let the internal pressure I was feeling explode over the placid surface of their lives. I had to stay under the glass with Amos for a while, and to do this I had to be politic.

"Don't you see it isn't fair to me to do that?" I asked quietly. "It makes a fool of me."

"I wasn't making a fool of you," he protested. Somewhat panicky. He may already sense that the price he will pay for his ability to live apart from his brother comfortably is a slavish dependence on making love to me every night. He won't be able to sleep if he doesn't touch base with my insides. "I only meant— the part about my mother was real, and then you were so excited about it and you were pushing me for more." His voice was plaintive now. "I only wanted to please you, Nady."

I resisted my lips' desire to curl in the wrong direction, forcing them into a smile.

"What will please me is if you're straight with me." Maybe. "If you're just you." Probably not. There is a tone to his voice that will jangle my nerves if I allow this conversation to continue. A humility. An *obsequiousness*. As though I were one of the reporters who'd held his public life in their hands. "Don't try to please me." An activity which by definition can never be successful in a spouse. "Just be Amos." And I stood up and kissed him and locked myself in the bathroom with a book for my course

321

lest I let myself think on whether I can live with the person who is just Amos.

Dianne called from her office at ten o'clock in the morning. "How'd you sleep?" I asked curiously.

"Fine," she said. "Listen, Nady . . ." Her voice lowered to a confidential near whisper. "I'm staying late tonight. . . . I mean, you know, I'm seeing Harold. Carly's all set to make dinner for Eddie, she's really looking forward to the whole routine . . . but I wondered if you'd just sort of be aware that she's alone in the house. Cooking."

She just sort of wanted me to be aware that she didn't need me, she had Harold. Carly needed me.

"Do you want me to go over there and check on her?" Would she have the gall to ask me to do that?

"I don't want to bother you," she said smoothly. "But if you should happen to be taking a walk . . . or looking for something to do."

"What is that supposed to mean?"

"Whoops, have to go, long-distance call on my other wire."

And before I could ask her if she thought I'd needed to be in a separate house so I could use up my spare time taking care of her daughter . . . or maybe just tell her to go fuck herself up, down and sideways, there was a click and she was gone.

Carly's career as Dianne's little housewife lasted about two weeks, not bad for a twelve-year-old. At the end of that time she failed to come home from school for five days in a row. Dianne would return in the evening and find the house empty if Eddie was still back at the freakoseum. At some point Carly would amble in and Dianne would ask where she'd been and Carly would say with friends. Dianne asked what had happened to their dinner arrangement and Carly told her, with a perfectly straight face, "Oh, yuh, I forgot. I'll try to remember tomorrow." Over the weekend Dianne tried having a heart-to-heart with Carly, but there was only one heart in it. No one knew just where Carly's

322

heart was these days. She wasn't showing her usual affection for her father, either. Something had turned her off both of them at the same time. Dianne talked to her mother in California. At her mother's suggestion Dianne told Carly they should forget about the other plan (the dinner plan Carly had already "forgotten") but that it would be nice if Carly brought her friends to the house sometimes instead of always going to their homes. Carly started bringing home her friends but they were always gone by the time Dianne returned and Eddie never had anything to say about them except that they were just a bunch of kids.

I only found out about all this when Dianne got depressed and came over one night to talk. The men had returned to the shop to do some work. They did that often, now, partially to compensate, no doubt, for the sexual indifference of their wives. For me the path of least resistance lay, so to speak, in letting Amos get off in me every night, but I was about as warm and wet as a piece of paper most of the time and he never came up with any new lies to turn me on. Getting into me was such hard work he must've figured he might as well be earning some money. They got a phone for the shop and were thinking about putting out a flier advertising their services in some of the wealthier summer communities. Eddie would drink before and during dinner, then take a nap from which Amos awakened him when he'd finished dinner at our house and was ready to escape from the children's needs.

"What's going on over there?" I asked Dianne.

"Nothing," she said. "Except I'm a little worried about Carly." Then she told me. I asked if Eddie couldn't help; Eddie, after all, actually liked his own kid, while if Amos had been reasonable with his kids it was because that would please his wife, not because he had anything to give—or to get from—the children. Dianne said Eddie was drunk most of the time. She couldn't understand how Amos was even able to work with him. She wasn't sleeping with Eddie, now, which wouldn't have been so bad if Harold's wife weren't on her way back from India.

323

I'd seldom seen Dianne looking so thoroughly miserable. It was hard to understand how I'd experienced her as beautiful a couple of months before. Her skin lacked color, her hair was limp and greasy, she wore a drab gray dress. She was pathetic. I felt awful for her. If I was jealous when Dianne was much happier than I, it bothered me when she was much more miserable, too.

I was in reasonably decent shape, myself. I didn't think a lot about Amos or my marriage. I concentrated on school. I'd really gotten into my courses and not only did I like the teacher but I was beginning to get accustomed to sitting around with a bunch of kids who were half my age. I'd learned how to apply myself to the subject at hand without dragging the specifics of my own life into it and discovered to my surprise that my perceptions were at least as sharp as any of the others: often sharper. My own kids seemed to have weathered the move with remarkable ease, maybe because I was still there with them, maybe because they had each other. They fought as much as always but they played together as well when there was no one else around. Philip had learned to keep his distance from Amos, and if it pained me that this should be necessary, it seemed to be the only practical solution to Amos's absolute inability to give him even the simplest affection. The only good side effect of his nonfatherliness was that it spared me additional anxiety over what I would be doing to my children when the day came for me to take them away from him.

"I guess," I said to Dianne, "I can sort of keep an eye on Carly. Maybe she minds coming home to an empty house, even if she thought she wouldn't."

"You're very sweet," Dianne said.

I shrugged.

"You *are*," she said. "It was silly of me to think she wouldn't miss you. You've been a very important person in her life."

"Tell her she can come over here after school if she wants to," I said. "Have a snack here. Whatever."

324

"Isn't there something I can do for you, Nady?"

I would have told her if I could have thought of something but my mind was a blank. Certainly she couldn't help with my kids; I didn't really need help now and besides, she'd always treated them like distant cousins, not unpleasant, but there was no real connection. Anyway, I wasn't doing this for Dianne so much as for Carly. Once a long time ago I hadn't been there when Carly needed me. My failure had put a permanent warp into the love between us but the love hadn't really dissolved. Maybe now I could undo some of that old damage.

The next afternoon I walked over to Dianne's house. I hadn't been in there since the move and it looked strange to me—small, a little dreary. Heavy rock music pounded through the walls from the children's bedroom—now Carly's room, I corrected myself. I started to push open the kitchen door; thought, I mustn't do that, now, rang the bell. But the bell couldn't be heard over the music so I walked in.

The kitchen was filthy. The sink was full of dishes and the water was dripping. The floor looked as if it hadn't been swept for a week. I turned off the water and wandered into the living room, which was unchanged. With all our plans, neither of us had done a thing with her home. I started up the stairs. Carly appeared at the top.

"Hi," I said.

She had a pale, frightened look.

"I wanted to see how you were doing. Can I come up?"

"I'll come down."

I returned to the kitchen and she followed me. I sat down at the table but she remained standing. In the bright light I could see that she had rings under her eyes. I tried to figure out if she could really look so much older and more tired than she'd looked a couple of months before, or if it was my imagination. After all, I'd thought the house looked different, too. Her beautiful thick hair looked uncombed. Her body was filling out; she had the beginnings of breasts already. Maybe she was scared of what was happening to her.

"I've missed you," I said, feeling as I said it that it was true. Carly had been my first baby. "I guess I thought you'd be over at my place some after we moved."

She shrugged.

"Do you feel like coming back with me now and talking for a while?"

"My friends are upstairs."

"Oh, I'm sorry. I didn't know."

Silence.

I got up to go.

Her manner was neutral.

"Do you know," I asked, "that you can come over any time you want to? That I didn't stop loving you, or being your friend, or whatever, just because we moved across the road?"

She shrugged. "Sure."

She might believe me but it didn't matter to her. She was way out of reach. Sadly I said good-bye and left, fighting off the vague fears that were crowding in on me.

She didn't come over. I had a paper to turn in for one of my courses and I sort of pushed her out of my mind but when I'd finished the paper I decided to try again. I had in mind to approach her more directly than I had before. To tell her that even if we couldn't—and probably shouldn't—be quite as close as we'd once been, it should be easier now for us to be friends. I even thought of proposing to her in a humorous way that where once I'd been her bad mother and Dianne her pal, now that Dianne was her mother it was only fair for me to be her pal. The problem, of course, was that she hadn't seemed to want any pals other than the ones who'd waited upstairs in her room in the midst of the mysterious, eardrum-battering rock ritual.

It was a cold gray day in November. Thanksgiving was only a week away and we were planning to have a big dinner for both families. I would do the cooking but the dinner itself would be at Dianne's house and they'd do most of the cleanup. Dianne and I were looking forward to it; it would be the first time we were all together since the move.

The music was playing—as though it hadn't been off since the last time I was there. I rang the bell, waited, walked in. Nothing. Started up the stairs. This time she didn't come out to head me off. I hesitated. Maybe I should come back another time. But when? This was the way she spent her time when Dianne wasn't home and a time when Dianne wasn't home was obviously the best time for me to talk to her. I walked up to the landing.

The door to Carly's room, the room where all our children had slept from the time they were born and played together for countless hours, was open. Lying sprawled around the room were several youths—three girls and two boys, it would seem at first glance, although there was doubt in the case of one of the "girls." Another girl, of course, was Carly. The others were unfamiliar to me. The kids were all dressed in sweaters and tattered, hyper-patched jeans but their positions were so casually intimate as to suggest that in other circumstances—had the house been warmer, say—they might not have been.

Oh, no! It was my whole body crying out. Aching. *She's only twelve years old!*

One of the boys, the one I later heard called Tex, was stretched out on his back on the rug, an arm lying across Carly's chest, his other hand resting on the head of another girl, who lay between his open legs. Carly's feet were against the chest of the seated youth, whose back was to me, while her head rested on the lap of the last one, who sat yogi style. He passed Carly a joint, which she dragged on and passed to the one next to her. None of them seemed particularly disturbed to have me come upon them this way. Carly never moved.

"Hi," I said.

"Hi," she said lazily, waving away smoke with one limp arm.

I was frightened. I wanted to beg her not to do this but I didn't know exactly what this was, aside from smoking pot when you were twelve years old.

"I wanted to see your room," I said, my voice unsteady. "I haven't seen it since everyone . . . since we moved."

She giggled. "Well, here it is." There was a hostile edge to her

327

giggle and to her ease but it was blunted by the grass and by the wall her friends formed around her.

Don't do it, Carly! Don't lie there making believe you've never been born. Making believe there are no spaces between people. Don't turn yourself into a zombie, smoking dope to avoid finding out what you can do and what you can't do.

I wanted to beg her to come out of that room with me. I wanted to teach her all the things I'd learned that hadn't done me any good. I wanted to teach her and I wanted what she learned from me to filter down to Philip and Daisy so I'd never have to teach it again. It was such a painful lesson—and furthermore, I didn't even know what it was. Unless it was just that the things you did in order to not be alone didn't work.

You're nuts, she would say to me. *If you have people around all the time then you're not alone.*

Only while they're there and sometimes not even then, I would answer. *But even when it works the price is often too high.*

I shuddered.

"Whatsa' matter, Nady?" Carly asked, aggressively lazy. "You look scared to death."

"I am."

"Want a drag?"

I shook my head.

"Why not?" A mild challenge. She'd seen us smoking when Ken and Michelle were around and she was ready to accuse me of hypocrisy.

"Has your mother seen you smoking?" I asked. I had to ask.

"If she looks . . . she'll see." Sleepy. Indifferent. A hundred years old.

"It's not easy, you know. Being a mother."

I couldn't believe I'd said it. The boredom and disgust on their faces were as nothing compared to the physical recoil of my own body.

It's not easy being a mother.

It's not easy being a human.

Oh, shit.

I turned away and walked down the stairs. When I was at the bottom I heard a soft padding on the landing above and Carly's voice called my name. I looked up. She came down a few steps. Her expression was different now. She was a child, after all.

"Are you going to tell my mother?"

"I have to."

"What if I stop?"

"I don't know."

"I've only done it once or twice. Honest. It's not a big thing with me. I'll stop if you promise not to tell her."

"I'll think about it. I'll let you know." She was making me responsible. If she did it again it would be because I'd told.

"It's the only thing I want from you," she said, half pleading, half defiant. "I'm not asking you for anything else."

She didn't want my love or my friendship, and she wasn't interested in having me tell her everything I'd learned about life in twenty-five words or less. She only wanted my silence.

"I promise not to tell her," I said, "without talking to you first."

I decided not to tell Dianne for now. It was possible Carly would keep her promise. It was even possible that the situation in that room had looked worse than it was. There was no question that I'd have to keep a close eye on Carly if I didn't tell, but it wasn't as though Di could keep a closer eye if she *did* know. All she could do from Hanover was worry. And then of course if Carly found out that I'd told . . . So her threat had worked.

Carly asked Dianne if her friends could come for Thanksgiving dinner. Di said it was okay with her if I didn't mind preparing the extra food. I said I didn't, which was a lie, but I thought maybe it would be a good idea for Dianne to get a look at Carly friends.

It didn't work, though. She didn't let herself get worried. She just asked me, as they filed casually into the house, if the other kids didn't look "a bit" older than Carly.

"Mmmm," I said.

"What grade are you in?" she asked Tex as we sat around the

329

table, to which we'd drawn up one of the twins' worktables to get the space we needed.

"Uh . . . tenth," he said. Which made him a high-school sophomore.

"Oh," Dianne said brightly, "you must be a little older than Carly."

"Yeah," Tex said.

"He's fourteen," Carly said. (He was sixteen.)

"Oh," Dianne said. "That's nice."

Silence.

They all ate turkey as though they hadn't seen a complete protein in months. (They hadn't.) I'd bought two, about fourteen pounds each, and had assumed there'd be plenty of leftovers, but at the end of the meal there wasn't an ounce of meat left on the bones. When the last piece of pumpkin pie was gone they disappeared upstairs and the music went back on.

"We could ask them to help with the dishes," I pointed out.

"Oh," Dianne said nervously, "let's just do them ourselves. We can talk."

In the next few weeks I made it a habit to drop around their house after school. Carly and her friends knew exactly what I was doing there, or were convinced they did. There was no sign of dope. Sometimes I wanted to tell her the dope wasn't the issue, that dope or no dope I wanted her to be all right, but she never gave me the opportunity and even if she had, I doubt I could have made her believe it. She was twelve years old. Too young to understand.

Dianne said she was beginning to think these were really decent, gentle kids, quite fine. A new and better generation. Since Carly seemed to be keeping her word about smoking, I kept mine about talking.

My courses had just a few weeks to run.

I bought a more comfortable rug for the living room since there was still no furniture to sit on when we were watching TV.

Christmas came and went. We'd invited a few of the men's old circus pals because Amos and Eddie were feeling nostalgic, but none of them wanted to come. They were stiff over the phone. They assumed that since the men hadn't wanted to be freaks anymore they couldn't genuinely want their friends to be, either. Amos apparently made overtures to Winthrop and a couple of the other men who'd worked with them, but the men were always busy with family or other obligations. The other men didn't like Amos, although I didn't realize this until later. Eddie, who never asked nor gave them much, who wasn't condescending like his brother but also wasn't hostile, who could sit around with them and drink beer for hours without talking except in occasional monosyllables, fell in with them much more easily.

In January I completed my courses and in February I was notified by Bard College that I had received my B.A. In February, also, Carly celebrated George Washington's birthday by disappearing from home.

Dianne called me at half-past ten at night, waking me up.

"I'm sorry," she said, "I just— Nady, do you happen to remember the last name of any of Carly's friends in Pomstead?"

"Uh-uh," I said. "Why?"

"I don't know which one it was whose number Carly gave me . . . but I can't seem to find it."

I rubbed my eyes and looked at the clock.

"Is anything wrong?"

"No, not really," she said. "But Carly isn't home yet and I haven't heard from her."

"Oh, Jesus."

"I don't think it's necessarily anything to worry about," she said quickly. "I imagine she's just sleeping over at one of her friends and she forgot to call."

"Didn't you put the number in the little blue book?"

331

"No." She sighed. "I put it on that board on the wall near the phone, the one that just wipes off . . . and it just . . . wiped off."

"Hold on. Let me think for a minute. . . . We'll have to call some of the kids she used to be friendly with last year and see if they know the names of these kids."

"It's a little late to call people," she said doubtfully.

"It classifies as an emergency," I said.

"Oh, Nady, I don't really think it's an emergency. I think—"

"Look," I said. "Hang up and I'll get dressed and come over. Give me five minutes. Start trying to remember—" I suddenly remembered the one kid in Bootville who was near Carly's age. "As a matter of fact, try Joey Martin. He'll probably know. And you'll be able to explain to his mother. At least she knows us and she'll understand right away we wouldn't be calling if we didn't have to."

"She knows *you*," Dianne said softly. "I don't think I've talked to her three times in the whole time we've lived here."

I sighed. "All right. I'll call Alice. And then I'll be over."

Amos stirred in his sleep.

"It's nearly eleven," I said, "and Carly hasn't come home yet. Di's worried sick."

He muttered something in his sleep.

I dialed the Martins'. The Martins were more comfortable than most of the natives because he had a steady job in a farm-equipment dealer's about fifteen miles away. Alice had five kids and was the perfect suburban housewife, refusing to do a garden or any of the other activities that might remind her of farms or New Hampshire, but using every new wax and cleanser she saw on television and going regularly to PTA meetings. Where many of the natives seemed to have grown even more remote since the surgery, frightened like the circus freaks by our having opted to change our fates, the Martins as represented by Alice had grown just a trifle more friendly. They lived in a slightly different world and knew better the virtues of conformity. Where once I'd gotten no more than a nod at the general store, we were now expanding to brief discussions of the weather.

"Alice," I said, "I hope I'm not waking you up."

"No," she said.

"It's an emergency or I wouldn't have called you."

Silence.

"Joey isn't still up by any chance, is he?"

"Yuh, he's at the TV."

"Could I please talk to him for a minute?"

The phone clattered down and a minute later Joey came on.

"Joey, this is Carly Smith's m— This is Nadine Smith."

Silence.

How in all fucking hell have I managed to live in this town for thirteen years?

"Carly hasn't come home and we're worried about her but wc don't know who to call. I thought maybe you could help us out by telling us the last names of those kids she's hanging out with now."

"Don't know 'em."

"Is there anyone at the school who might know?"

"They don't go to the school."

Of course, how dumb of me. They were all older, they'd be in the high school.

"Well do you know someone at the high school who might know?"

"Nope."

"How come?" He must know someone in the high school, damn it.

"They don't go to the high school."

"*What?*" It exploded out of me without warning. "What are you saying?"

"They don't none of 'em go to the high school."

I tried to absorb just enough of what he was saying to ask some more questions.

"You seem to know who they are," I finally said, afraid if I didn't keep talking he'd hang up and go back to the TV.

"Seen 'em."

"Do you know where they come from?"

333

"Uh-yuh."

I bit my knuckles to keep from screaming at him.

"Where?"

"The farm."

"The farm? Which farm?" Then it struck me; it wasn't the farm but The Farm. I'd never been there but it was famous in the area. It had been bought and settled during the latter part of the freak wave of the sixties, twenty or thirty acres with a couple of ramshackle buildings. There was a permanent resident guru-father named Baxter with a wife who stayed on, then a succession of kids, females, mostly. I'd heard that Michelle had moved in there for a while after she left Bootville. In the first couple of years the local and state police had tried to get Baxter either on dope or on harboring minors, but he'd always outwitted them, delivering long speeches on the damage dope could do to a young mind while the cops searched frantically for his cache. As far as the runaways went, he always had a carbon of a letter to their parents which he'd written immediately upon their arrival saying that your runaway daughter has landed on my doorstep and is in need of parental guidance and please come and get her. In the case of the two or three letters they checked out, the originals had been received by the parents and ignored.

"Joe," I said, "was Carly in school today?"

"Uh-nuh."

"When did you last see her in school?"

"Dunno," he said. "Been awhile."

"Thanks," I said. And hung up.

A dreadful panic welled within me. I didn't know what to do first. Anxiety about Carly mixed with anger at her for doing this just because she hadn't promised not to. Anxiety over Dianne's reactions mixed with resentment that I should feel responsible for her daughter. Many possible conversations went through my mind simultaneously, including one in which Dianne tearfully reproached me for not having warned her that her daughter was smoking dope. But these conversations flashed through on some minor track while the greater part of me was fighting to keep

334

from being engulfed by panic. I struggled out of my flannel nightgown into my clothes as if I were doing some kind of weird reverse-lifeguard test: See if you can get dressed while drowning.

"Amos, listen to me. Can you hear me? Amos? I'm going over to Dianne's. Carly didn't come home and it may be bad. She may be over with the crazies at that Farm commune. AMOS! GOD-DAMN IT!"

"Uh? Whuh?"

He was finally half awake. I fleetingly wished for the days when he'd never been fully asleep.

"Forget it," I said. "Just . . . I'm going out. Pick up the phone if it rings. It'll be me."

I told Dianne as gently as I could that Carly's friends apparently lived at The Farm.

"The Farm," she repeated. "Oh, well, maybe some of those kids are . . . If they're going to school they can't be totally hopeless cases."

"I'm not so sure they're going to school."

She looked at me uneasily. She didn't want to ask any more questions but she had to.

"Who did you talk to?" she asked.

"Joey Martin," I said.

"What did he say?"

"He said she wasn't in school."

"Oh, my God! Something must've happened to her on the way to school!"

I shook my head. "No, Di. She hasn't been there for a while, he said."

She wanted to accuse me of lying but she knew I wasn't. She began to cry. I put my arms around her.

"We'll drive over to The Farm right now," I said. "Where's Eddie?"

"In a drunken stupor," she said bitterly. "I tried talking to him before I called you but it was absolutely no use."

We checked out Carly's room. Her knapsack wasn't there and one or two sweaters and some underwear seemed to be missing. We drove over the icy roads to The Farm. Everyone there seemed to be awake. Or half awake. Neither Carly nor the others had been seen all day. Baxter offered to let us search all the buildings and Dianne said no, it was all right, she believed him. You could tell they weren't there, not any of them. Baxter asked for our phone number so he could call if he heard any word of Carly. He promised without being asked to bring her straight home if she appeared at his door. He was polite to the point of mockery and managed, without ever dropping his front, to make it quite clear that we were beneath competition and/or contempt.

We drove home slowly, Dianne, beside me, weeping softly.

"I think maybe we'd better tell Baddely," I said. "And the state police."

"I'm afraid that if it's not really serious, just calling them will make it serious."

I thought of the dope and wondered if that were a reason to not tell the police but to go out looking ourselves. Then I thought the dope was more than Dianne would be able to handle at the moment.

"I know what you mean," I said, "but I think we have to call them anyway." With a sixteen-year-old it might have been a little different. "She's just too young," I said, and then I was crying, too, and I had to pull over to the side of the road for a while so we could weep in each other's arms.

"We'll wake up the men," I said when I could finally stop crying. "She's not just ours, she's theirs, too." Carly needed four parents right now. "Maybe we'll all look for her. Or they'll help us decide whether to call the cops. Help with *something*." We needed help.

We got Amos first so he could help us with Eddie. I shook him awake and told him what was happening.

"What do you want to do?" he asked, rubbing his eyes. It was almost one in the morning.

"I don't know," I said. "We think we should call the cops but we're not sure."

Silence.

"We need you to help us with Eddie."

He got dressed and we went over to the other house. Eddie was still asleep on the sofa in front of the TV but his heaviest sleep had passed and we awakened him without too much trouble. Dianne tried to tell him but she started crying and couldn't talk. I expected Amos to fill in for her but he sort of stood there.

"Eddie," I said, "we think Carly's run away."

"What? Run away? Where?" He was immediately extremely upset and I found myself caring for him for the first time in a long time.

"We don't know. She didn't come home tonight and she hasn't been going to school this week."

"Why didn't you tell me?" he demanded of Dianne. Then, seeing the expression on her face, he flushed. Another milestone.

Quickly I told him what we knew. I said we weren't sure if we should call the cops or first look for her ourselves.

"Both," he said instantly. "Let them put out an arm for her but we'll look in the close places where she might be."

I was astonished by his forcefulness. Astonished and relieved, because I wasn't going to bear the main burden of the search. Glancing uneasily at Dianne I told him about finding Carly smoking and how she'd extracted my promise to not tell. He said I'd done the right thing and he wasn't sure it was such a big deal. Dianne kept weeping. I was further relieved although I still wasn't sure I'd been right. He called Baddely and he called the state police. He described Carly to the police and also, with a little help from Dianne and me, described the other kids. Then he got road maps from the car and told us each to make lists of the places where Carly might be so we could divide up the territory. Half an hour later we'd staked out, within a radius of about fifty miles of Bootville, various places where they might have gone if they weren't just trying to get far away as quickly as possible. Eddie drank hot coffee Dianne made for him the whole time.

He'd had about four cups by the time we finished and the rest of us were just a couple of cups behind him. He was agitated yet in firm control.

Because of the way Eddie was being I felt a little hopeful about Carly for the first time. If he remained this way—sober, clearheaded and decisive—then maybe we would not only find Carly but we'd be able to manage her better when she returned. And if that could happen, then maybe, although I didn't see how or why, we could make decent lives for ourselves, as well.

But as the hours, then the days, went by, it didn't appear that we would ever find Carly, much less that other good events would ensue.

The state police were polite but they had a list of runaways "that long" and few were ever found unless they chose to be. Sheriff Baddely said he'd do what he could but nothing happened.

From those first moments Eddie was in command of the search. He decided he didn't want to wait until daybreak to start looking. He wanted to drive around on the back roads and see if he couldn't get some feeling about where Carly might be. Amos was the only one of us who could even consider going back to sleep so he was sent back to stay with the children. I held it against him that he could think of sleeping now. I reminded myself that Carlotta was not, after all, *his* daughter, but in the basic human sense that didn't seem important. Besides, I kept feeling as though he'd be the one who could sleep no matter whose kids were involved. Even Eddie, I think, was put off by his brother's equanimity.

Dianne was assigned the Hanover area because she knew it best. She wanted to call in sick but Eddie said she should tell people at her office the truth so they'd be alert for signs of Carly. I had the area immediately around Bootville (a commentary on my life) and Amos was given the area east of us, hundreds of acres of undeveloped land crisscrossed by streams and small ponds, one big lake, a few small farms and a couple of communes. Eddie took the road to and beyond Keene.

338

Amos was always home first. When Eddie commented on this fact Amos said that once he'd covered the communes his territory was the easiest, but it never occurred to him, until Eddie suggested it, to increase the scope of his territory.

Eddie hadn't taken a drink except coffee from the moment he found out about Carly. The three of us were very tense and very close. On the second day, when I got concerned about their hearing it elsewhere, I told Daisy and Philip in the lightest possible way about Carly's leaving. They got a little crazy-high-anxious. We were all spending the time when we weren't searching at Dianne's house but when the kids got too crazy for the rest of us, Amos would take them home. Nobody was doing any work anymore except looking for Carly.

For two nights the three of us didn't sleep. By the third night we were dropping off for brief periods of time. My dreams were all about Carly and she was always lost and crying. Dianne said she wasn't having any dreams. Eddie wasn't interested in discussing anything so irrelevant. By the fourth day I was fairly certain we weren't going to find Carly, but Eddie was still in a round of constant, frantic activity, consulting the police, making phone calls, writing letters, driving around. Amos said they should get back to work or they'd go crazy but Eddie had no interest in the shop and said he didn't see how Amos could, either. Amos was now staying at our house most of the time with Daisy and Philip while I stayed with Dianne and Eddie.

Dianne told her office that she'd be back the following week but she told me that if (she corrected it to *when*) Carly was found she was going to take a leave of absence for at least the remainder of the school year, possibly longer.

A way of life which, when it had begun, seemed by nature to be short-lived and still nearly unbearable, now seemed to have become permanent. Depression hovered at anxiety's edge. I wondered why I'd bothered to get my degree. It wasn't as though there were anything I'd ever be able to do with it. I had before me the lesson of what happened when you weren't there with your children. I'd better figure on staying home for a few more years. Not that it mattered right now. Nothing mattered except that Carly was out there someplace.

By the end of the week Amos began trying to cheer me up. He told me I couldn't go on like this forever even if Carly stayed away. I looked at him with disdain; he was talking about apples and oranges and I was thinking about death. About having a child you'd felt was part of you, whom you'd later abused but had never stopped loving, who'd now disappeared and taken the part of her that was you with her.

I started knitting a sweater. It was for Amos's next birthday but I had to keep reminding myself that it wasn't for Eddie because it was Eddie I felt like making a sweater for now. It had to be for Amos because he was my husband. I couldn't like Amos or respect him and knitting a sweater seemed like the next best thing. I dreamed I was knitting a sweater for Carly but she was lost and couldn't try it on.

On the ninth night, a Friday, Amos took Daisy and Philip to a movie in Keene. About an hour and a half after they'd left a long-distance call came for him. We all jumped, as we always jumped up these days when the phone rang, but then when the call was for Amos we assumed it must be Sternheim or one of the California people. We asked the operator if the party wanted to speak to someone else or leave a message and she asked when Mr. Amos Smith could be reached directly. We told her in about an hour and a half at the other house, and gave her the number. Then we sat around the TV, which Eddie still invariably turned on when he entered the living room.

"I haven't thought about Sternheim or all that," I said glumly, "in I don't know how long." I tried to assess whether the fact of the movie might have any relevance to Carly's flight and decided it was too farfetched. Colors and shapes without meaning passed across the screen for another hour or two and then suddenly Amos burst into the living room, still with the hesitation in his left step but *rushing*.

"It's Carly," he said breathlessly. "Carly just called me."

We rose as one and repeated her name. "Carly?"

340

"Amos! Tell us, tell us!"

"She's all right," he said. "She's fine. She wouldn't tell me where she was but she said she was fine."

"Oh, my God! Oh, my God!" Dianne and I were laughing and crying and hugging each other.

Eddie was staring at Amos. "Wait a minute," he said. "Are you sure it was Carly you were talking to?"

Amos nodded.

"What did she say that made you so sure?"

"It was just her. Everything she said. I asked her how come she called person to person to *me*."

"What'd she say?" Eddie asked quickly. In the midst of his relief he was puzzled and upset.

Amos shrugged. "She said I was the only one she could trust."

"*What?*" Now Eddie was angry as well as incredulous.

"I know it sounds crazy, Ed. All I can tell you is—"

Eddie began pacing around the room, stopping every few steps to stare suspiciously at his brother.

"Maybe you'd better tell us the whole conversation," I said.

"When they asked for me I figured it was Sternheim," he told us, sitting down. Eddie remained standing, staring at him intently. "I said it was me and then this little voice, I couldn't tell where she was but she sounded muffled . . . far away . . . anyhow, she said, 'Uncle Amos? It took me a minute to realize, not just because the voice was so . . . small . . . but—"

"Did you ever find out where she was?" Dianne interrupted.

He shook his head.

"Let him finish," Eddie commanded.

"Anyway, I couldn't hear well. And *Uncle* Amos. She never called me Uncle. But then after a couple of seconds I realized and I said, 'Carly, where are you?' She wouldn't tell me but she said she'd come back if her friends could come and stay with her."

Dianne nodded eagerly. "You said yes, didn't you?"

"I said I was sure it'd be fine but she said I had to check with you to make sure. It seemed as if she didn't believe you'd let her do it. As if she didn't know how worried you were. It was crazy."

341

He'd tried to get a number from her but she'd refused. She was going to call again in an hour. She didn't want to talk to Eddie or Dianne or Nadine, she'd reminded him. He was the only one she could talk to, the others didn't really care about her, they just pretended because they thought they were supposed to.

We shook our heads.

Amos went back to the other house right away. Daisy and Philip were alone there but more important, we were afraid he'd miss her call if it came early. A little while later we followed him. When we tried to talk we cried and when we cried we asked each other how we could be crying when Carly was safe. When the phone finally rang again we all jumped out of our seats except Amos, who got up in his normal way but walked to it quickly.

"Hello," he said, "yuh, Carly, it's me. No, it's not your father, it's Amos. . . . You'll have to take my word for it. Unless you want me to put your fath— NO! Hold it!" We all held our breaths, terrified that she'd hang up and we'd lose her. "No, I won't unless you want me to."

Dianne and Eddie looked at each other and shook their heads.

"Yuh. Uh-yuh. When will you get here? Where are you coming from? Do you need any money?" He asked the questions Eddie had told him to ask and waited with relative calm for the answers. "What?" He was startled. "You didn't say that—no, I'm not saying it's not, but I didn't—hold on. Hold on, damn it, I have to— just hold for a second while I check." He covered the receiver with his hand. "What they want is to stay in the apartment over the shop."

"Oh, Jesus," I moaned.

"But there's nothing in it," Dianne cried out.

"Tell her okay," Eddie said. "Just tell her whatever they want they can have. We can talk about it when she gets here."

My mind, rapidly and reluctantly, jumped to a moment when Carly was refused something she'd been promised and took off again. Yet there was no alternative now, certainly. No way to take a chance on having that connection broken.

"They say you can do whatever you want. . . . Huh? No. I think it's stupid. There's plenty of room at the house and we'll be heating the whole upstairs for nothing. You *do* need heat."

Dianne and I looked at each other, terrified that his bluntness, his *uncaringness*, would make her hang up. Except, I reminded myself, he was the one of the four of us who'd always cared least for her, and he was the one she wanted to talk to now.

"Yuh. Okay. We'll do it. Right." He paused. "You know that. You know they're gonna give you whatever you want." Pause. The three of us held our breaths. "Yuh. When will you be there?"

When? When? When can we *see* you, Carly? When can we believe it? When can we fill up our eyes against the time of your next disappearance? Will Daisy do this someday? Or Philip?

As he listened Amos groped for a chair and sat down. His voice changed. His expression was difficult to fathom.

"Yuh," he said. "Yuh. Okay but they want to see you." His voice was flatter. More neutral. "Okay. Fine." He hung up and looked at us. "They're in there already."

"What? Where? In the apartment?"

Eddie and Dianne stood up as though they were going to run down through the snowy field to the shop without stopping to find the path or put on boots.

"They were there the whole time," Amos said flatly. "Two of 'em just went down to the shop to make the phone calls."

Eddie and Dianne sat down again. Dianne began to weep softly. I thought of the week we'd just gone through but I didn't cry.

The shop was two stories high in the front of the building to accommodate the car lift. The apartment windows faced back into the woods. Lights could be on there for weeks in the winter without anyone's ever noticing. The men might have heard sounds if they'd been in the shop but they hadn't gone to the shop all week because they'd been out looking for Carly. Fucking little Carly had had us all tied up in knots while she and her funny little friends flopped out in an empty room a few hundred yards away.

Dianne was still weeping. I wondered if a little rage hadn't

343

moved in with her misery, as it had with mine, but decided this wasn't the time to ask. Eddie was frozen in position like a character in one of those flashy new TV serials where they stuck on the last frame. He looked as though he'd never move again but a minute later he did—to the cabinet where I kept whatever liquor we had in the house. He poured himself a stiff shot of bourbon, drank it and poured another. I looked at Dianne uneasily but she didn't seem to have noticed.

"What now?" I asked.

"She said she wants to see me first," Amos said. He was embarrassed. "Then she said she'd see Eddie and Dianne just for long enough so they'll know she's all right." He couldn't say it directly to them. "She says if anyone hassles her she'll really take off."

"Why you?" Eddie demanded. "Did she say why she suddenly trusts you?"

Amos shook his head.

"Maybe it's just that he isn't her parent in any way," I said to Eddie. "Maybe she needed a neutral party and he was the most neutral of the four of us."

Eddie didn't respond. I couldn't tell if he was at all comforted by the idea that it was love, not lack of it, that made Carly need to stay away from them. I wanted to hug him and reassure him. He seemed so much more lovable to me, more vulnerable, more *human* than he'd seemed before Carly's disappearance. But it was Dianne not Eddie who asked anxiously if I'd come back to the shop, too.

"I don't think she wants me there," I said.

"Please," Dianne begged. "You don't have to go up and talk to her, but please just come back with me."

Bootville was very beautiful, with the winter's snow piled along the sides of the road and a thin new layer whitening the road and lightly lining the tree branches. When we'd first come to Bootville the huge old maples and ashes along the road had been in full leaf but I'd never noticed what was around me in those days, so intent had I been on bringing to a successful conclusion the

344

dilemmas of my young life. Now I noticed, but sadly, the beauty of the black night and the white-frame houses, the scruffiness of the more ancient paint jobs hidden in the darkness. It was a scene on a Christmas card.

Unfortunately you couldn't make a life on a Christmas card.

We had to bring Carly back because Carly was a child but what was there to bring her back to, really? This was where her parents were. Where your parents were was the center of order, in some sense, even if there was precious little order at that center or the order was invisible or perverse. But what was here if there was no unspoken agreement that it was where Carly belonged for now? From the sound of that phone conversation she hadn't returned to family or town—if she could be said to have returned at all, since she hadn't left. She appeared to have returned for convenience' sake. Of course, that might be why kids always thought they came home. I remembered the regularity with which the grown son of the Singletons in the general store, now working for a car dealer in Claremont, brought home his laundry to be done in the apartment over the store although there were half a dozen laundromats in Claremont.

But she's a child.

She just got her period for the first time a few months ago and it seemed too early. Dianne told me she'd flatly refused to ask questions or discuss it except to ask Dianne to buy her sanitary napkins. She was quite certain it was napkins she wanted.

We turned off the main road and onto the dirt road that led to the path through the woods. We were walking through several inches of snow because it had snowed earlier that week and this road hadn't been cleared since Carly's disappearance. My heart skipped a beat when I saw the buildings looming ahead of us in the night; I hadn't been back there since they were completed. A two-story, white-stucco cube joined by a covered bridge that was elevated from the ground to a surrealistic-looking glass dome. The freakoseum. I shuddered.

"From here you can see that the lights are on upstairs," Amos said. It was the first time anyone had spoken since we left the

345

house. The lights in the dome were also on, although they hadn't been before. If they had we might have seen them from the back windows of Dianne's house.

Amos opened the locked front door. He turned on the lights. I looked around. From this vantage point it was possible to believe in the sanity of the enterprise. Shelves lined two unpainted pine walls of the huge room; the floor was poured concrete. A third wall was covered with the pegboard they used for hanging tools and jars. The fourth wall was the retractable door which raised to admit cars and trucks. The men were still waiting for a permit to put in the road that would allow cars and trucks to reach the building. There was a problem because at some point along the path other people's property was involved, but Amos was confident of working it all out by spring and they couldn't put down the road before then anyway.

The three of us sat down on the bench at a worktable. Amos went upstairs but came down immediately. The signs of their occupancy were there but they weren't. I began to get furious and then thought of the lights on in the pool.

"Maybe they're swimming," I said.

Eddie looked stolidly at the poured-concrete floor. Dianne looked at me. Amos disappeared through the passageway, came back just to signify with a nod that they were there, and then disappeared again. When he came out again it was with an attempt at levity.

"Well," he said grimly, "the heat's workin' real good in there."

"Amos!" Dianne wailed. "Tell us."

"All right," Amos said. "They're swimming." He paused. "No clothes on."

Eddie rose from his seat as though he'd been kicked out of it. "WHAT?"

"I asked her," Amos went on, "did she think she should be doing that, and she said, 'Tell 'em I'm not into fucking, if that's what they're worried about.'"

"Oh, my God!" Dianne began crying again.

Eddie sat down and looked at the floor.

346

"What else?" I asked.

Amos shrugged. "That's about it. They want to stay there, they said they had no idea how long, and they don't want to be hassled. They don't have any money left. They need some food. . . . They said" (to Dianne and Eddie), "you can go in and talk for a couple of minutes if you want to."

"I'm not goin' in there if she's naked," Eddie said angrily.

Dianne cried softly.

"Maybe she should know," I said to Eddie, "that you don't approve of what she's doing."

"No please," Dianne sighed. "I'm afraid she'll just vanish again."

Eddie sat down.

"I can't go in alone," Dianne said after a while. "Nady, will you come in with me?"

"She doesn't want Nady in there at all," Amos said.

"That kid's really got us tied up in knots, hasn't she," I muttered, hurt and angry but willing to confess only to the latter.

Dianne and Eddie looked at me as though Carly were going to hear me and take off for wherever they'd thought she was in the first place.

I told Dianne that if it would make her feel any better I'd go around on the outside to the dome and keep an eye on her while she talked to Carly. She was grateful but still scared. She walked to the passageway, hesitated, and waited for me to go out and make my way around the building. I crept stealthily through the snow, like a thief in the night, and looked in, confident they couldn't see me in the darkness with the lights on inside.

Dianne stood at the edge of the pool in her sheepskin winter coat, the scarf still around her neck, high boots covering her legs, her arms folded across her chest, her mittens on, looking as though she were freezing in that room whose temperature had to be seventy or eighty degrees.

In the middle of the pool Carly treaded water. Her friends circled her, prepared to protect her at any moment that Dianne decided to attack. They were all treading water but once in a

347

while the two boys, as though by prearrangement, would flip onto their backs. The first time my heart skipped a beat at the sight of their grown-up penises and dark bushes. Kids! We'd been talking about kids but these were the kind of kids who could get your twelve-year-old daughter pregnant!

I'm not into fucking, if that's what they're worried about.

Dianne's face was distorted with the effort to keep from crying.

That's what *I'd* be worried about, I decided. That and everything else, too. I'd be—I *was*—worried, *frightened* by those faces that registered indolence and contempt even as the bodies under them moved easily in the water, those faces that suggested you could work out a set of the best and most reasonable and benevolent rules in the world and it wouldn't matter, they'd still be there only to be broken.

Dianne threw Carly a kiss and moved heavily toward the door. I trudged back around the building to the shop door. She was waiting there for me.

"They don't want beds," she said. "They like sleeping on the floor. They don't want anything but food."

"And heat and shelter," I pointed out automatically.

Dianne glanced at me to see if I checked out resentful but I didn't.

"I ought to get back to the house," I said. "Nobody told Daisy and Philip we might be out." They were asleep, of course, but I wanted to see them lying there in their beds. I might not be able to fool myself that they'd always be there but I had an urgent need to see them there now.

Amos locked the shop door and we trudged back through the snow on the path. At the juncture of the path and the dirt road I turned to look back at the buildings. Which would be worse—to raise children who took this gigantic insanity for granted or to raise children whose guts churned in perpetual rebellion against our insanity? My life was tolerable now for several reasons, not the least of which was the fact that Philip had managed to incorporate Amos's dislike of him into the assumptions of his daily life, but aside from the matter of my own convenience, why should I want—how could I *bear*—that my beloved son take such a condition for granted, perhaps assume that it was justified? Now the buildings, too, were part of his existence, this monument to our joint infancy. Did I want Philip—either of my kids—to incorporate this idea of life as a kind of arcade where you went from the home shop to the workshop to the swim shop with as little time as possible spent in the world outside?

I ran to catch up with the others but my brain wouldn't stop hacking at me. Which would be worse, to raise children capable of remaining in this town or to raise children sufficiently intelligent and sensitive to go out of their minds here when they were swamped with the first restless urges of adolescence? And who was I kidding, pretending I didn't already know the answers to all these questions? Pretending I didn't know already that there was no way in the world that my children would be in Bootville when Philip reached the age that Carly was now.

At home I went up to the kids' rooms without even taking off my boots, kissed and covered each one, came downstairs again. Eddie had poured himself a tall glass of straight whiskey and Amos had put up a kettle of water for tea. We sat around the kitchen table, barely speaking. Eddie looked like a wounded animal who would lick the place where it hurt if only he could find it. Dianne was wasted. I was upset in a different way than before. Earlier my central concern had been for Carly, then it had been for me and my kids, now I just hurt for Eddie and Dianne.

"I don't know how long they'll let her stay out of school," Dianne said hopefully. "Once they know she's here."

"I doubt they care," I said. "Maybe she'll just get bored and go back on her own."

I didn't believe it.

"They don't really seem like such bad kids, her friends," Dianne said.

I stared at her, finding it difficult to believe that her voluntary blindness could triumph over such odds.

"They weren't rude," she said defensively. "They never really are. They're just a little lost."

Eddie gave her a dirty look.

Amos suggested that what we all really needed was a decent night's sleep. I considered accusing him of indifference and then remembered that he was the one Carly trusted. He was waiting for me. I told him to go on up, I'd be there in a few minutes.

Would I have to tiptoe around Amos now, as well as Carly? He was our link to her. What quality did Carly perceive in her Uncle Amos that I failed to appreciate? Aside from his attentiveness to me, which seemed to stem from little more than a desire to get fed during the day and get off in something warm at night, he seemed to me cold, indifferent and quite out of touch with the realities that pressed in on us. If he wasn't a total liar and hypocrite it was probably just because his life didn't happen to offer him any bonus for those qualities. He lied without difficulty or regret when the occasion presented itself. If I'd chosen not to make a continuing issue out of his lies to me that first night in the new house, it wasn't because I'd forgiven him but because I could no more ask him to apologize than I could ask him to apologize for being Amos, a man who could not or would not understand what was wrong with lying or why that was a particularly deadly kind of lie.

Maybe Carly loved Amos best because she knew him the least. Certainly that had been true of me. Certainly it was when the reality of Amos had been too weak to create static in my fantasies that I had been happiest with him.

I glanced at Eddie. His hurt, angry love for his daughter made him more appealing to me than he'd ever been. I wanted to hold him, to cuddle him, to reassure him. I wanted more than that.

Stop the cunt-think, Nadine, the man's married to your best and only friend. And to your husband. Fucking him would be like being back in bed with all of them!

But it was difficult to force myself to stop. He needed someone like me right now. And I was in the mood for someone like him. A man who could be hurt by his children.

THE immediate fear was gone but nothing was solved or even improved, really. We couldn't do anything until we knew where we were and we couldn't know where we were until we knew what was going to happen with Carly. I told the kids that Carly was safe and staying with friends. There was no word from the little fugitives except an occasional shopping list slipped under the door to the workshop: 4 boxes Captain Crunch, 2 gallons milk, a dozen oranges.

This state lasted for about a week, during which time the men started working in the shop again but Dianne remained on leave from her job. She said she wanted to be around if Carly needed her. She spent most of the time at my house and was attentive to my kids for the first time in their lives.

At the end of the week Carly appeared one morning at the door of the shop and hung around for a while, talking to Amos, asking how Daisy and Philip were and so on. Eddie got tenser

351

and madder and began dropping tools and banging his own fingers and making mistakes in measurement of a kind he never made, drunk or sober. If Eddie asked her a question she answered Amos. On the third day Eddie asked her where her friends were and she told Amos they'd all split. Then she burst into tears and threw her arms around Amos, sobbing against his chest while Eddie looked on helplessly. She'd been alone there for two nights and one day. She missed Daisy and Philip terribly, she sobbed, and she wanted to live at home and go back to school. Only there was no way, she cried, that she could live with Eddie and Dianne, as she now called them. She wanted to live with Amos and Daisy and Philip.

Amos told me when he came home for lunch. The Carly business had created a rift between the men and now, instead of disappearing for the day, each came to his own house for lunch.

"Oh, Jesus," I exclaimed. "Did she say that in front of Eddie?"

"Uh-yuh. Eddie stormed out of the shop."

"Poor Eddie."

Amos didn't say anything. He didn't particularly get off on Carly's new fixation and deemed it doubly unfair that Eddie should be as angry with him as though he were encouraging her.

"Poor Dianne," I added.

"Poor *us*," Amos said. "It'll be a real pain in the ass if we let her do it."

"We have to let her do it," I said quickly. "No matter what kind of pain in the ass it is."

"Why?"

"Because—because—because of *everything*." *How could you not see that?* "Because of our lives. Because she might run away again. Because we love her, or at least I do. I don't know about you."

"I love *you*," he said.

But how can your love have any value to me if you're not capable of loving anyone else? If you love only me then you really love only yourself and just think you need me to live.

"Then don't ask me why Carly should be allowed to live here

352

if she needs to," I said. "I love Carly as much as I love Daisy and Philip." *More than I've ever loved you.*

Suddenly I was struck by the hilarity of my position; I was the one person in the household with whom Carly would have nothing to do. I laughed shortly. "Don't ask me what this all has to do with her coming here," I said. "It's you she wants, not me."

"You'll have the extra work," he said.

"We'll tell her she has to help." Not that I was sure I'd need help. I seemed to have forgotten for now about a job. About moving out. I seemed to have somewhat more time than I needed to worry about the future.

"It's not just that we *have* to," I told Dianne when she came over. "We *want* to. We're her family, too." Many kids at that age, I told her, would probably be happier living away from home, if only they had another home available.

Dianne sighed. "I guess I'll just wander around the house all day and worry about her."

"You can go back to work," I pointed out. "Now you won't have to worry that nobody's there when Carly comes home."

"Do you mean that?" she asked, her poorly concealed eagerness telling me what I hadn't realized before, that it was exactly the idea that had been in her mind.

"Yes," I said, mildly resentful but knowing there was no way to go back on it now. "Of course. There's no point at all in your staying home if she's living here with us."

"Oh, Nady," she said, tears of gratitude in her eyes, "I really don't think I could have lived through this without you."

Carly came back the next day at the lunch hour, with Amos, her knapsack on her back, her eyes suspicious, her hair uncombed. She seemed taller than I remembered. She also looked more like Dianne than she ever had before, so that I was taken aback for a moment and didn't know what to say. Not that it mattered; she didn't want to hear anything from me. Philip and Daisy were both at school and I missed them. I wanted them standing on

353

either side of me, two pillars to support me and to tell Carly by their affectionate presence that what her eyes said about me could not be true.

"Hi," I finally said. I wanted to give her a hug and a kiss but there was no way to get around the invisible wall. "I fixed up the back room so you could use it."

She walked past me, through the kitchen, and out to the back room, where she closed the door behind her, not opening it again until the kids came home from school.

"Did she come?" Philip asked, bursting into the house at a record-breaking early moment. "Where is she? Is she here? Did she come?"

I smiled. "She's here. Where's Daisy?"

He'd forgotten his standing instructions to wait at the school bus stop until Daisy got off and escort her across the road.

"She's coming," he said. "Where's Carly?"

"In the spare room."

He pushed past me and ran to the back of the house. I heard him knock at the door and say his name. The door opened. I was dying to follow him but knew I couldn't, so I stood as far to the back of the kitchen as I could, pretending to do something or other, trying to hear what they were saying, which was futile, particularly since the door had immediately closed again.

Daisy walked in a minute later.

"Philip didn't wait for me," she said matter-of-factly. She didn't particularly care, she was just reporting in.

"He wanted to see Carly," I told her.

"Where is she?"

"In the back room."

Daisy hesitated.

"It's all right," I said. "You can go back there."

"Take me," she said shyly.

I laughed. "It's just Philip and Carly. Your brother Philip and your sister Carly. They're waiting for you."

"Please take me, Mommy." Urgently. She held up her hand. Irritably I took her hand and led her back to the room.

"Knock," I whispered to her in front of the closed door.

"You," she said, clutching my hand more tightly.

I knocked and the door opened on Carly.

"I'm sorry," I said uncomfortably (then got furious with myself for apologizing). "Daisy wanted me to bring her." A likely story. "She seems to feel shy."

Carly held out her arms and Daisy ran into them, as though to make sure I was branded a liar. Carly drew back into the room with Daisy and closed the door gently in my face.

"YOU HAVE TO TALK TO ME!" I yelled when, at the end of dinner, I asked if she'd rather clear and wash or dry and put away and she told Amos that she would do it all. "You can't live here and not speak to me!" I was fighting back tears. "You don't have to like me and you don't have to be grateful for anything but you have to speak to me when I speak to you! Is that clear?"

"Yes," she said quietly. "I'll take care of the dishes. I don't mind."

"Fine!" Then the dam burst and I ran upstairs because I felt much too vulnerable to let them see me cry.

I remained in the bedroom for the rest of the evening. The kids didn't come up and I assumed Amos had gotten them to bed but when he came upstairs he told me that Carly had done it. She'd washed the dishes, watched TV with the kids and read them the fourth chapter of *The Phantom Tollbooth*, where my place mark had been. Then she'd come down and watched the TV news with Amos, kissed him good night and gone to her room.

"It's good you told her off," Amos said. "She took it just fine. She'd be better off if Dianne did it sometimes."

"Mmm," I said. "You're probably right."

But if I had provided Carly with a measure of relief by forcing her to be civilized, I was slow to feel any comparable relief myself. As a matter of fact, the weather in my head got worse and worse.

355

Carly's demeanor around me was Model Prisoner. An unfortunate combination of circumstances had forced her to put in time with a warden she loathed, but she was going to make the best of matters. She made herself Extremely Useful. She cleaned up after meals, was outright motherly with the children and straightened up the house if she came home from school and I hadn't done it already. I began doing it as soon as everyone left in the morning. I also started cooking meals in advance because most afternoons she offered to make dinner. If I said I'd prepared it already she baked cookies with the children.

She never seemed to go to anyone else's house or bring home friends from school. I asked if she knew she was welcome to have school friends to the house and she said, "Yes." Period.

I started to think about looking for a job in the fall and then remembered that it was when Carly had been asked to run the house while Dianne worked that the shit hit the fan. I could see that my being there while she took over was partly what she was grooving on; every time she managed to smooth over some silly squabble between Daisy and Philip she'd glance at me out of the corner of her eye to see if I was noticing how much better than I she was with my children. She would only do the mother number if I was there to witness.

I became increasingly resentful. *I* was the prisoner, really—locked into a role whose only actual function was to allow a thirteen-year-old to perpetually prove that there was no part of my job that she couldn't do.

Dianne and Eddie had dinner with us two or three nights a week but Carly never spoke while they were there. Amos was the only one she talked to.

"Ask her," I told him one evening when I was going up to read and the two of them were going to watch television, "ask her why she never brings home any friends from school."

"Did you ask?" I inquired when he'd come up to the bedroom and was getting undressed.

"Uh-yuh."

"What'd she say?"

356

"The kids in school won't talk to her."

"Oh, my God! The poor kid!" I was stricken.

"I guess she's having a rough time," Amos conceded.

"But why?" I wailed. "Do you really mean that? That they don't talk to her *at all?*"

"That's what she says."

"But why? Since when?"

"Since she got back."

"What's wrong with them? Did she scare them? That must be it. They all want to get away from this shitty town and they're afraid it's contagious!"

"It's not this town, it's Pomstead," he pointed out. Brilliantly.

"Same thing. They're all the same."

I was treading on dangerous ground now. The ground whereon we stood. And lived. The ground wherefrom I would need to move in the not-too-distant future. Maybe Amos would come with me, maybe if I waited until the novelty of the building had worn off, and until . . . Probably Amos would not come with me. Probably that would be just as well.

"What else did Carly say?" I asked, switching to a safer topic. I felt I needed to tell Dianne and Eddie what was happening to Carly but I wanted to know as much as possible before I talked to them.

"I dunno," he said. "She talks all the time when we're watching TV."

"But what does she say?"

He laughed. "I don't remember."

I looked at him incredulously.

"Most of the time I'm half listening to her and half to the TV," he explained.

The lip of my mind curled. It wasn't that I'd believed for a long time that he was any nicer than he was . . . or more understanding . . . it was just—I was flooded by a sense of *déjà vu. Déjà* and *déjà* and *déjà, vu* and *vu* and *vu.* I stood up and began to get into my clothes.

"What's the matter?" he asked.

357

"Nothing," I said. "Haven't I seen you someplace before?"

He laughed and beckoned me back to the bed but it was unreality time again and I wasn't about to lie down for it. I ran my fingers through my hair to make sure my head was still there. I pulled on my socks.

"You mad at me?"

"Not really."

"Yes, you are."

"How come you weren't curious? Didn't you want to know what's been going on with her?"

"She's only a kid," he said. "You think I love being the only one she talks to? It never occurred to me you'd want to hear what she said. It's not interesting. She's a kid and she's not even our kid."

Carly. The kid.

Why bother?

Don't bug me, kid.

Alex.

Alex and Amos.

Alex and Amos and Shlomo and Tumulty.

It must be you, Nadine. It must be the men you find. After all, anyone who spends her whole life trying to wring blood from stones has to be suspected of loving blood less than she loves stones!

I pulled on my boots. It was mud season. I had the fleeting thought that from here on it would all be mud season.

"Where you going?" Amos asked.

"No place," I said. "I just feel like taking a walk."

"Want company?"

"No," I said. "I want to be alone."

I walked down the road past Dianne's house. A dim light was still on in the living room. The light that was on when no one was doing anything except watching TV. In the only house beyond theirs on the road, the same kind of light was on. Forty watts, folks. This is a town full of forty-watt bulbs.

It occurred to me now for the first time that for all her jobs and all my years of jealousy, in terms of potential Dianne was as unrealized as I. She'd been a genius when she was young. You could knock it, mock it or forget it for twenty years but the truth was that she should have been writing symphonies or arguing cases in the Supreme Court, not defending thirty-year-old dopers, then coming home at night to a town of fifty semiliterates and a husband who made his twin brother's reasonable intelligence look like brilliance. What had happened to Dianne? I was willing to take a part of the blame but basically she'd already been on the wrong track when I got her racked up on the twins.

Dianne had told Ken McDougall if she hadn't met the twins she would have lived a monastic life in a book-lined study; there was so much hypocrisy in that statement that I'd failed to realize that there was truth in it, too. If it wasn't what she would have done, it was probably what she should have done. A mind like Dianne's should have continued making its own music.

When had her intellectual growth ceased? It seemed to me that it had been almost as soon as she came East to college. It sounded funny to make that connection because she had a brilliant record at Radcliffe, but that was essentially a record of how well she'd absorbed *other people's* ideas. When I thought back to our conversations in Los Angeles, I remembered talk of politics, of literature, of music. Dianne had first found Marx and Engels in her father's library and Nietzsche in the library of Elizabeth Irwin High School. What she'd understood of them had excited her in some very direct way and she'd communicated that excitement to me. I could still remember the way her voice shook with excitement as she read me a paper she'd done for some undeserving idiot at Beverly High on the subject of Marx vs. Freud in which she proved conclusively, that is to her own satisfaction and that of her worshipful disciple Nadine, that the former rendered the latter irrelevant—or worse. The numerous objections that might have been found to her argument had I the sophistication weren't to the point; the point was she'd discovered the issue on her own and then thought it out. She'd read the books and drawn from them and added something by contrasting them.

While from the time she left home Dianne's letters, still intellectual, were full of praise for Professor So-and-So's wonderful thesis that, or Berry's poem which was the epitome of, and so on. As though at some point she'd made an almost conscious decision to stop digging around at the roots of knowledge. To seek wisdom only at the head of a penis.

I reached the road bridge that was a kind of southern boundary for Bootville. I sat down on the top rail and looked at the creek that ran under the road. Melting snow was still running down from the mountains and the creek was high; icy clear water swirled around the big rocks and ran over the pebbles. Hundreds of tall firs and pines bordered the creek. Their beauty made me ache.

I turned back toward town, filled with a sweet sadness. I should tell Dianne what was happening to Carly but I didn't want to intrude if she and Eddie had already gone to bed. If they seemed to be upstairs I would go home, perhaps read for a while. I hoped Amos would be asleep because I had nothing to say to him. I was finished with asking him to be his true self and asking him to be loving with the children; I'd finally noticed that the two requests were contradictory.

The whole issue was a trap, anyway, designed to lull me into believing that under the proper circumstances (whatever the proper circumstances might be that week) I could live with a man I didn't know and couldn't respect.

I knocked at the porch door because the kitchen light was still on. There was no answer but that was probably because they hadn't heard my knock over the TV. I pushed open the door. I could hear the set droning. I walked through.

In the living room Dianne and Eddie stood facing each other. Dianne had been crying and her expression reflected anguish— and fear. Eddie's face was red with rage and his arm was raised as though he'd been about to strike her when some invisible force had grabbed hold of his hand to make it impossible.

Oh, God. I started to back away, half hoping that they wouldn't even notice I'd come in, but they both looked at me.

"I—I'm sorry. I didn't mean to . . ."

She looked away. Slowly Eddie's arm came down to his side. Dianne brushed past me and ran upstairs. There were tears in Eddie's eyes, too, I saw now. It must be about Carly; Carly was the only one who could make him cry. I went to him and hugged him; he put his arms around me and began to sob. I led him to the love seat and we sat down without letting go of each other. When his sobs had subsided somewhat, I got up and turned off the TV set and came back to him.

361

"What is it, Eddie?"

"She wants to take Carly to California."

"For a vacation. To see her parents."

"That's what she says."

"Has she talked to Carly about it?" She hadn't mentioned it to me.

"She wants to look for a job out there," he continued, ignoring me. "I listened on the phone when she was talking to her mother."

I stared at him. Had there been room for doubt I would have disbelieved him. I started to ask why but before the words came I could think of three good reasons: she was finding the situation with Carly less bearable than she could admit to me; she was sick of her job, which tended to be boring at times when there was no attractive man to save; she wanted OUT—from Bootville, from Eddie, from me.

"You told her you'd heard."

He nodded. "She said she wasn't trying to run away. She said she wanted us all to go out there."

"Then why didn't she discuss it with us?"

"'Cause she wanted—" his face was screwed up in concentrated effort at mimicry "—to get a sense of the possibilities first."

"Mmm," I said. "It could be true."

"Bullshit," he said fiercely. "She knows we're never leaving here."

He reached for the bottle of bourbon.

"I think I could use a drink." I laughed nervously.

He gave me the filled glass and took a swig from the bottle. I sipped slowly. Eddie drank it straight, without water or ice, slowly but surely. I didn't really like the strong taste but tonight I was distracted and it went down without difficulty.

"Amos told me something upsetting," I said after a while. "Carly's apparently having a terrible time in school. Not with the teachers. But the other kids aren't talking to her."

His head, which had been bowed in dejection, snapped up.

"It seems to be since she ran away and came back," I continued.

362

"Does *she* know?" he demanded, looking up in the direction of their bedroom.

I shook my head. "We just found out. That's why I came over. To tell you."

He was silent.

"I do think," I said, slowly and carefully, "that Dianne's been more unhappy than she's admitted over the situation with Carly. And now she's trying to find some solutions." I kept sipping at the bourbon. I wasn't intentionally getting drunk; I was just trying to take the edge off my anxiety. The rage between Dianne and Eddie had upset me more than the tension between Amos and me, maybe just because it was in the open.

"She doesn't care about Carly," he said. "And she doesn't care about me. Some people from Pomstead just bought a house near Davis's. Regans. They have three girls, one Carly's age. I tried to tell her. She don't care."

"I'm sure that's not true." I wasn't sure but the bourbon's warmth was spreading through me, helping me to see matters in the best possible light. "She does care." *She just cares more for herself.* I didn't know if that was all right or not. "Do you mind when she talks about a vacation?" I asked after a moment. "Or just when she talks about a job and staying out there?"

"She's not just leaving me alone here," he said, tears returning to his eyes, his manner at once forceful and pathetic. I hadn't realized until that moment that he'd never stayed alone in a house; the last time Di and Carly had gone to California we'd all been together here. It seemed a hundred years ago.

"That's no problem," I said. "You can stay with us. Carly's room'll be empty."

"You mean it?"

"Of course. Why not?"

"Will *he* mind?"

"I don't think so," I said. "He hasn't been mad at you, Eddie. He feels bad about the whole business with Carly. He doesn't do anything to encourage her, you know."

"Then why is she there?"

363

I sighed. "Who knows?" I was making rather large inroads in the bourbon, I noticed. I grinned. "Anyway, I'll talk to him. I bet he'd *want* you to stay with us. I don't know if I'll talk to him tonight because I'll prob'ly be too drunk by the time I get home. But I'll talk to him. I *want* you to stay with us. I'll enjoy it, Eddie. You know I've always been . . . very fond of you."

We hugged again. I kissed his cheek and before I knew it he was kissing my mouth and I was responding to him. As soon as I felt what was happening I pushed him away (but gently) and stood up.

"Mmm." I laughed nervously. "Sex rears its lovely head."

He looked up at me.

"I can't, Eddie," I said, draining the last of the bourbon in my glass. "How can I face Dianne if . . . I have to talk to her about Carly, now. How could I talk to her if . . ." I trailed off. Dianne was standing in the doorway. In my less charitable moments I sometimes think she was hoping to catch us in the act.

"Did you come over to talk, Nady?" she asked quietly.

"Yes," I said. "But how can we talk about anything that matters? You haven't even told me you were thinking of splitting for California?"

"I'm not," she said. "Not seriously, anyway."

At that point Eddie grabbed the bottle of bourbon and walked out of the room.

"You could have told me and also told me you weren't serious."

My head was pretty muzzy by now but I was trying.

"I was afraid you'd get hysterical."

"Well," I said slowly, "that's no good either. It's no good my having grown up and calmed down and your still treating me as though I were a hysterical teenager."

She smiled. There was condescension in it but she was trying to keep it muted. "Are you upset because you think I can't see that you've changed?"

"I'm not upset. I wasn't upset even before I started getting drunk, except I was upset about seeing you and Eddie fighting." And about Carly. But this didn't seem like the moment to tell her about Carly. "And I don't even know what change means,

364

when you talk about it. All I'm saying is that I'm not on a short fuse anymore."

Again that smile. "Now you're on a long fuse."

"Oh, shit." But I wasn't really mad. "Maybe the whole fucking fuse is in your mind, Dianne, not in mine." Dianne wasn't mad either because she was so sure it wasn't true. "Anyway, I want another drink." I went into the kitchen, where Eddie sat at the table, drinking and reading the *Pennysaver*. I took a glass and poured some bourbon, leaning over to kiss the top of his head, then walked back to the living room.

"I told Eddie he was welcome to stay with us when you and Carly went to California," I said. "For your vacation."

"You're very sweet, Nady," she said.

I sipped at the bourbon. Waited.

"I've wanted to talk to you about the future," she said, "but I needed to get my own thoughts together first. And talk to my mother. We've become very close, you know. I talk to her a couple of times a week on the phone."

A moment of jealousy; I'd been replaced by the woman I'd once replaced.

"Anyway," she said, "it's true that my mother thinks we should move out there and it's true that she's lined up a couple of job interviews. But it's not true that I'm seriously considering taking one, certainly not without discussing it with everyone. And even then I wouldn't take it until . . . I mean, in my wildest dreams I wouldn't think of taking Carly out of Pomstead two months before the end of the school year. Not that I'm seriously considering doing it even then."

"Mmmm."

"What does that mean?"

"I'll tell you what it means, Dianne. It means I think you know as well as I do that the men will never leave here. Maybe if you'd caught them before they put up their goddamn building. Not now."

Her lips quivered. "I can't stay here forever, Nady. It doesn't work for Carly."

"It doesn't work for you, either. Or for me, for that matter. Not

365

for much longer. But at least if we can be a little straight about it . . ."

Silence.

"If we're straight about it then maybe when it's all over we can be friends."

She smiled. "I thought we were friends now."

More or less. More and less. Friends who have to hide important plans from each other.

"You certainly act like my friend, Nady. You have my daughter living with you. And now you're taking Eddie."

"I'm not taking Eddie for your sake. I'm taking him for his. And for mine. I want to have him. I feel very close to him right now because of what he's been going through with Carly." *You were the one who said we had to be straight, Nadine.* "I also sometimes feel like climbing into bed with him."

"I think you should if you want to," Dianne said promptly.

"Wait a minute," I said automatically. "What are we talking about? Climbing or fucking?"

"We're talking about your feeling free to do whatever will make you feel better."

"Better than what?"

She sighed.

"Look, Dianne, I'm not exactly madly in love with my own husband and half the time when he's making love to me I wish he was someplace else. But I wouldn't want that someplace else to be you."

"Don't worry. It won't be." Her voice was saying she wouldn't do it for my sake but her face was reminding me she'd never wanted to anyway.

"If you were fucking Amos I'd feel as if I was getting fucked." My head was pretty fuzzy but I needed to clear the air between us. On the other hand, I still seemed to be drinking bourbon.

"I can understand that, but I don't feel the same way," Dianne assured me. "I'd just like everyone to be comfortable. I haven't wanted Eddie in . . . I don't know how long. And he doesn't really care; he just wants *someone.* He'd just as leave it were you. He said as much. He said you were sexier than I am."

366

"He *did?*"

She nodded. She looked almost conspiratorial; she wanted me to do this.

"When was that?" I asked.

She shrugged. "One of our arguments."

If I were sober I wouldn't have liked that. Still, tainted appreciation was better than none. And I wasn't sober. I was able to focus on our conversation but with each minute it became more difficult. It was even more difficult to remember why I was here in the first place. It was about Carly. I'd wanted to tell them how unhappy Carly was. Now Carly's needs were getting lost in the dark swirls of the grown-ups' feelings.

The phone rang. That would be Amos. Eddie picked it up in the kitchen and came to the living room to tell me. He didn't look at Dianne.

"It's Amos," he said.

"Tell him I'm not here," I said. "Tell him . . . I went swimming. As a matter of fact, that's a lovely idea. Let's go swimming."

"I told him you were here already," Eddie said.

With some difficulty I got out of the love seat, which felt as though it were attached to my bottom and wanted to come with me, and made my way—lurched, actually—into the kitchen where I picked up the receiver but didn't speak. Eddie followed me into the kitchen; I grinned at him wickedly.

"Hello? Hello?" Amos's voice called finally.

"Nadine isn't here," I said. "She went swimming. She just left her voice here."

"Hi, Nady," Amos said softly. "You coming home?"

"No," I said. "I'm going swimming."

"How come?" he asked. "You never go back there."

"I feel like it," I said. "I'm drunk. I'm trying to talk Dianne and Eddie into going with me. Eddie, anyway."

"I wish you'd come home," he said. His voice was wistful and for a moment I almost relented, but I was too far gone, and besides, I'd gotten drunk so I wouldn't feel how sad I was. Why should I feel Amos's sadness instead?

367

"I don't feel like it," I said. "I feel like being drunk. And I feel like going swimming. . . . And I feel like fucking Eddie."

"That's not funny," Amos said.

Eddie was grinning.

"It wasn't meant to be," I said.

"Why are you doing this, Nady?"

Because I want you to leave me. He sounded so sad, so human. If I wasn't careful I was going to relent and act human myself.

"I seem to want to make you angry."

"Why?"

"Because I want you to leave me." *I want out of this mess and it'll be easier for me if you're the bad guy.*

"Don't be crazy, Nadine."

"All right." I hung up the phone, which began ringing again almost immediately.

"Were you serious?" Eddie asked me.

I leered at him. "About swimming? I definitely want to go swimming." I looked around me as though I weren't sure just where I was. "Where's Dianne? Does she want to go swimming? Do you?"

He nodded eagerly.

"Dianne!" I called. "We're going swimming! Wanna come?"

"No thanks," she called serenely. "I have a brief to read."

The phone stopped ringing. I patted the receiver.

"Let's bring the bottle with us," I suggested.

"We don't have to," he said. "There's plenty back there."

"Let's get out of here fast," I said. "Before the phone starts ringing again."

Through my drunken haze the night was even more beautiful than it had been before. The sky was full of stars. The ground was still muddy but the road was dry and it was warm for the beginning of April. When we got to the path we took off our shoes and socks and walked barefoot. By this time I could feel that the air itself wasn't quite as warm as I'd thought, but it didn't seem to matter. Eddie walked ahead and held aside the brambles so they

368

wouldn't stick into my flannel shirt. The building—the buildings
—looked just as garish in the spring moonlight as they had on
that clouded, snowy night in February, but after a brief glance I
kept my eyes on the ground as we made our way to the shop,
unlocked the door and went in. Eddie turned on the lights. The
shop was beginning to look used but it was no warmer than it had
been outdoors. My feet felt the cold first.

"Brrrr."

"No heat on in here," Eddie said. "The pool's warm."

We walked through the passageway and opened the door to the
pool; warm air touched my face.

"Mmmm. That feels nice." Then I giggled into the quiet glass
cavern. My giggle echoed, then died away. More beautifully than
it had begun.

There was an eerie quality to the whole domed space, now. The
moonlight was shining in so that shapes were clear but there
were no colors. You felt as you stood inside that all the light in
the world was in that space and outside there was nothing but
darkness. Eddie went to turn on the lights but I called to him
not to.

"It's too beautiful. The light will ruin it."

He nodded.

I kneeled at the edge of the pool and dipped in a finger; it was
perfect, just a little warmer than the air. I sat down. I wanted to
take off my clothes but I felt I had no strength. Besides, I was
self-conscious. No, it wasn't my self I was uncomfortably conscious of now. It was Amos. And Dianne, who'd given me *carte
blanche* to screw her husband but hadn't entirely succeeded in
blanching my brain as well, even with the help of some whiskey.
I shook my head and without standing up I unbuttoned the loose
flannel shirt under which my breasts were bare, then squirmed out
of my jeans and pants. I looked around. Eddie was naked already.
He grinned at me. Was he self-conscious or Amos-conscious and
if both, where did one end and the other begin? I shook my head,
stood up and was about to dive in, but then my head was so heavy
I was scared so I walked around instead to the shallow end of the

369

pool, where I waded in up to my knees and then sat down so that I was in warm water up to my shoulders. At the other end of the pool Eddie seemed to be waiting for some signal from me. I raised one arm; he dived into the water and swam under it toward me. My heart was beating wildly; my mouth was terribly dry. I leaned forward and let my face rest gently on the water, wetting my tongue; a moment later Eddie's head touched mine and we came up kissing each other.

The phone was ringing.

"Wait a minute," I said, moving back from him.

"What's the matter?" He didn't seem to notice the phone. His body was still straight out behind his head in the water. He moved toward me on his elbows.

"Nothing," I said. But I was frightened. The whole room was swimming now and the phone was still ringing. *Hang up, Amos! Disappear, Dianne!* I laughed nervously. "There are too many people in this water bed."

The phone stopped ringing. I rested back on my elbows and let my legs trail out in front of me. Apart. I smiled tentatively. Eddie's head ducked beneath the water and moved between my legs, burrowing up against me. Mmmmm. I leaned back so far that I fell and my head went under. I was struggling to the surface when the phone began ringing again.

Fuck off, Amos! I'm willing to understand what I'm doing but not until after I've done it!

We edged back so I could lie back on the bottom of the pool but with my face above the water. Eddie moved so that he was over me. We kissed again. He'd become a sensational kisser somewhere during the years since his mouth had last been on mine, and I couldn't get too much of him—if only he could have blotted out the telephone screaming at me.

"Eddie," I whispered, "do something so I don't hear the phone."

He slid into me and my body began coming almost immediately except it never carried away my mind, which barreled along in its own frantic, drunken way, arguing, holding back, fighting, reacting to a phone that it heard even after the ringing finally stopped.

You haven't changed at all, Nadine, you're still a crazy—

No, no, it's not true! I have changed! I just haven't changed enough. I'm a mutant, but I'm a dumb mutant!

Not even dumb, exactly. My brain worked but it worked weakly; it didn't have the strength to affect my life but it wasn't weak enough to let me go along living in superficial harmony with a husband who professed to love me and countless other blessings I couldn't put my finger on!

"Eddie! Wait a minute!"

"What's happening?"

What's happening is that I've learned the limits but I'm still overstepping them. Like the cracks in the sidewalk.

He was halfway out of me between strokes and I tried to pull back, but he wasn't having any; he pushed right back into me and pumped until he came, probably never noticing because we were underwater, certainly not caring, that my insides had gone completely dry.

Afterwards we toweled ourselves dry on the outsides and Eddie got a bottle of whiskey from the shop, as well as a beer six-pack from the ledge where he stored them. We stretched out on towels next to the pool and drank boilermakers. Then I covered myself with a large towel. The weight of my head drew me quickly down into sleep.

I was in a very cold place. A phone was ringing but there were hundreds of phones and I couldn't tell which one it was. Every time I picked up a receiver I got a click or a busy signal or utter silence. It was very important that I talk to the person on the other end, who had information without which I would soon die of the cold. Frantically I tripped over wires and slammed down receivers, trying to find the correct phone.

I opened my eyes and after a moment knew where I was, and that I was really cold. Through the passageway to the shop I could hear the phone ringing. I stood up but nearly toppled back

371

to the cement floor. Cautiously, holding my throbbing head between my hands, I made my way into the shop and picked up the phone.

"Nady," the voice said, "what are you doing there? It's three o'clock in the morning."

"Sleeping," I said. "Before that we were fucking." My head could not possibly continue to throb this way without exploding.

"You're not being funny."

"Mmmmm."

Silence. Then, "Come home. It's after three in the morning."

"In a while. I want to take another swim." Maybe I could kill my headache in the water. I hung up the phone and walked carefully back to the pool. Eddie was still sound asleep near the apron, curled up on his left side on the towel. I held my head and looked around. The whole place looked spectacularly ordinary, somehow. Not ugly but not magical, either.

The magic was gone.

Holding my head I jumped in and did a few laps, feeling my temples throb with each stroke. I would've come out sooner except that I didn't want to go home. As it was, Amos appeared at the doorway a few minutes later. I was prepared for anything. Almost anything. What he said was:

"I missed you."

"Maybe your feet were just cold."

"No. I felt like talking to you. Can I come into the pool?"

"No. I'll come out."

I climbed out, wrapped a towel around myself, another around my hair. What I needed was some aspirin. I began to shiver. He held out his arms.

"I have a horrible headache, Amos. What did you want to talk about?"

"I don't know, I just wanted to talk. You're the only one I can really talk to."

"What about Eddie?"

"Eddie doesn't understand me."

"What doesn't he understand?"

"Me." Quite emphatic. "He doesn't see who I am. He doesn't—When he makes me mad it's because he's being stupid. When you make me mad it's because you want to."

There is a hint of insanity in this statement yet there is more than a hint of the truth.

"Like on the phone."

He nods. Smiles. He's really so sweet. So loving. A year or two ago—whenever it was—right after the surgery, it was enough for me to be loved like that. Now being loved isn't enough to do for the rest of my life.

Again he reaches out to embrace me.

"And like the fact that I really was fucking Eddie."

He withdraws. "Are you saying it now just to make me mad?"

"I'm saying it because I don't want you to touch me. And one of the reasons I don't want you to touch me is that I was just fucking your brother." *And vice versa.*

Silence. Then, "Whose idea was that?"

It had to be one or the other of us. If it was mutual consent he had no one.

"Mine, Amos. It was entirely my idea."

I walked around to the other side of the pool, where my clothes were, and began to get dressed.

"Nady?" he calls to me. "Did Eddie tell you about Wycliffe? Is that why you're mad?"

I say nothing. Amos has been alone with the children and his thoughts for several hours the way I've been alone with the children and my thoughts for so many days of every year. People thought it was the children who were the problem, but it wasn't the children, it was the thoughts.

"Because I want you to know that whole business was a big nothing!"

Aha. Nothing like being alone with your children and thoughts to make you start feeling guilty.

"Which whole business?"

"If he told you it meant something he's full of shit. We didn't even start it, she did. Robyn. At first she just wanted to see how, you know, how we did it then . . . I think she was turned on by, you know, the two of us."

"How crass," I murmured, buttoning up my flannel shirt.

"What? I can't hear you."

"I said I only go for one or the other!" *These days it's the Other. . . . Why? Well, because he's not the One.*

Why?

Well because I didn't respect the One.

Of course I didn't respect the Other, either, but you didn't have to respect your husband's twin to feel like fucking him. You only had to want to get far away and stay close at the same time.

And by the time I'd done it I hadn't even wanted to anymore.

"Nady? I hope this whole crazy business is over now."

"Which?"

"This . . . I hope we're even. You're my wife."

Even. An interesting concept.

I was tired almost beyond belief but wide awake with the pressure of my headache. I opened a beer. Over near Amos, Eddie stirred, then sat up. He saw Amos, shook his head, got up and dived into the pool. Amos watched him. I watched Amos. My legs felt less as if they'd kicked water for a few laps than as if they'd walked a hundred miles. Or were going to. I sat down. Amos looked at me, then he looked back at Eddie. I knew that he was going to dive in, too. He looked at that moment as though he'd been in the desert for weeks. He glanced back at me. His last words rested in the room someplace, like flour that's too stale to use but not rancid enough to get thrown away.

"I'll take you home in a couple of minutes," he promised. "I just want to take a fast dip . . . as long as I'm here."

I sipped at the beer. He got undressed and dived in. He and Eddie never spoke. Or looked at each other. But in a minute they were in rhythm, each doing the sidestroke at opposite sides of the long pool, one on his left side, the other on his right. When they moved away from each other the effect was of two parts of the

374

same being pulling at opposite ends of an invisible elastic string. Or two ends of an accordion.

How could I ever have believed that it was possible to get into the space between them?

I shivered.

I stood up, wandered into the shop, pulled on my socks and boots. Found my jacket and put that on, too. I was still horribly thirsty but I was afraid to drink more beer because it might make my hangover worse. I decided to tell Amos I was going back to the house because if I walked out I might upset him all over again. But when I went back to the pool, they were already getting dressed. They weren't speaking but the air around them didn't seem angry, either. In silence we trudged back into town, Eddie leaving us at his driveway, Amos and I heading toward our house.

I took some aspirin and got into my flannel nightgown. Not just my head but every limb ached. My hair was still wet but I was too cold to stay out of bed. I spread a towel across my pillow and lay down, feeling Amos's eyes upon me as he lay wide awake, his hands cradling his head on the pillow. I lay on my side, my back to him. He leaned over and kissed my cheek.

"I love you so much, Nady."

So much more than he had before he'd known I was capable of hurting him.

"You're not angry at me?" I didn't care, I was just curious.

"No," he said after a moment. "I'm hurt but I'm not angry."

"What about Eddie? Are you mad at him?"

"No. I don't want him to . . . do what he did. But I can understand that he wanted to make love to you when you asked him. I would have, if it was me."

I turn to look at him. Encouraged, he presses his mouth against mine, which cannot open because I'm made of stone. Amos doesn't mind that I'm made of stone. He loves me.

Indeed, in the days that follow, when I am dominated by depression, Amos is more loving to me than he has ever been. Not just affectionate. Loving. *Turned on.* Turned on to his turned-off wife. The sexuality whose full blossoming she had once eagerly awaited has turned out to be not a hothouse flower requiring dampness and warmth, but rather one that flourishes in the cold, dry atmosphere of the new Nadine. The mere sight of her lying there in bed, limp with indifference, is enough to give Amos an erection. And having to work his fingers to the bone to get her damp enough to be entered turns him on beyond belief. He makes love to her for interminable periods of time. Those minutes for which she would once have paid in blood or gold now drag on as though she herself had to push the hands of the world's timepiece. After he has an orgasm she thinks, Why couldn't we reverse the whole process? Now that I'm wet inside it wouldn't hurt so much. But she thinks it in the most objective way and of course lacks the will to voice such thoughts. After he makes love to her Amos is a pussycat, purring at her his satisfaction in their love life.

"Do you know what you make me feel like, Nady? Nobody's ever made me feel the way you do."

"Me now or me before?" I asked absently, knowing the answer.

"What do you mean?"

"Well . . ." tiptoeing through my lips, "am I the same for you now as I used to be?"

"Not really. You've changed a lot, Nady. You're much more of a woman than you used to be. Much more feminine."

I gazed at him with cool distaste. It was too easy to say that everything he'd ever learned about women he'd read in the ladies' magazines. What was going on now in our bed had nothing to do with anything he'd ever read, it was much more basic than that. Not only was it more basic, but I couldn't be absolutely certain that he was wrong. If I'd been certain that he was wrong—certain that being too depressed to need anything and too passive to act if I did *wasn't* the same as being a real woman, then I might

376

not have been so depressed in the first place. Or I might have been able to mobilize sooner to leave. As it was I had to wait for events on the outside to move me. As it was I had to wait for a large load of the Other Mrs. Smith's electromagnetic bullshit to galvanize me into action.

THE movie—*Born Chained, The Story of Amos and Eddie*—
turned out, as you know if you've seen it, to be the heartwarming
tale of a couple of Olivers (a little Twist and a lot of Wendell
Holmes) with their own special cross to bear who, through luck
and pluck (not to speak of some suck and fuck because Hollywood has thrown itself into the seventies) and the love of two
good women (one a big-titted Florence Nightingale and the other
a flower child left over from the summer of '69), eventually triumph over the special hell which their parents have created for
them.

The shit begins flowing even before the titles. In the bottom
center of a black screen a small, shapeless, flesh-colored blob
stretches and expands and molds itself until it is visibly two intertwined humans who, in the course of the next minute grow into
handsome, well-muscled young cartoon figures, each with a hand-
cuff around the wrist adjacent to the other's, the handcuffs

joined by a large heavy chain. At the end of the sequence we see two young supermen, by Zeus out of Daisy Mae, who at this point pull apart so far that the chain between them breaks neatly in the middle, thus freeing them to fly up to the right and left corners of the screen, respectively, from which they unfurl from the remaining links the banners that read BORN CHAINED.

The screen has been silent but as the credits unfold we hear the now familiar theme song from *Born Chained* with its banjo accompaniment:

> Think of how it feels to be-e bor-orn chained
> Think of how it feels to be in con-stant pain
> Growing big and strong but never able to do
> The things red-blooded boys like us just wanted to do
> Prisoners of each other in a world we never made
> Can't walk or run or work alone or go to get—paid

And so on. I don't know how much more of this stuff you can take. Or maybe you've seen it. The slight pause in the last line between get and paid was indicative of the schizophrenic spirit of the geniuses who produced it. Their heads were pure Disney and their hearts were in their deep throats, but there was no way they could go for the jerk-off segment of the moviegoing population without making hash of the movie's tenet that these two boys had gone through thirty-seven years of hell. Their solution to this problem was to do the sex scenes in slow motion with some kind of haze-making filter on the camera. The haze and the slow motion allowed them to deny the physical difficulties of sexual congress among four large people without losing any of the clinical detail that the dull-witted feed upon. The Hardy Boys meet and eat Elvira Madigan. The first clear clinch was in the happy ending, when the doctors tell the men they're fine and can lead normal happy lives. At the hospital doors each man turns to his loving wife and embraces her.

What's important about all this is that Dianne came home from California humming the theme song.

She was so high when I picked her and Carly up at the airport at the end of Easter vacation that at first I assumed she'd gotten the job she wanted. Carly was silent in the back of the Volks as Dianne rattled on about Los Angeles, about conspicuous consumption as exemplified by Hollywood, about the preview of the movie, which had turned out to be absolutely delightful, a delightful myth I'd get a real kick out of. She was looking forward to all of us flying out there in June for the opening. Sel really wanted us to come out, it would be wonderful for the press, and she hoped we could do it although for now she was utterly contented to be back in Bootville. She was really ready for Bootville, was the way she put it.

"Oh?"

She nodded. "You lose all sense of proportion in that place."

In a few days? I'd talked to her once in the middle of the week and she'd been ready to swallow the whole package.

"Has anything happened since I last talked to you?"

"What do you mean?"

"You were pretty high on moving there the last time I talked to you," I said. "On L.A. in general."

"I've never been high on L.A.," she said, her tone gently reproving me. "You know that, Nady. It's just a place where I can see living under certain circumstances." She turned to see if Carly was listening to our conversation, then turned back to me and said, in a lower voice, "If I could get a good enough job to forget the values out there. And if I could get Carly into some kind of therapy."

"What about the job situation?" I asked carefully.

"The one I wanted," she said, the lilt in her voice breaking for a moment, "they gave to a twenty-four-year-old glamour girl just out of law school. No experience at all."

Aha. Nothing like having a veritable teenybopper snatch away your job, so to speak, to make you detest the values of L.A.

380

"The other one I'll probably get but I won't know until summer and I don't think I'm going to take it anyway."

This time she wouldn't admit to wanting it until she knew she could have it.

"How does Carly feel about being out there?" I asked in a low voice.

"She loved it," Dianne said promptly. "She loves being with my mother. If it were up to her she'd move in with them. But . . ." She trailed off.

"But?"

Dianne shrugged. "My mother doesn't seem to feel it would work. A little sympathy is one thing, actually living with a young girl in the house is something she's not prepared to cope with. She never was. My mother's so much better than she used to be that sometimes I forget her limitations."

Her limitation at the moment being that she didn't want to raise her daughter's daughter. The pieces were beginning to come together now. If only I were in better shape and could do something with them.

No, there was no need to do anything, really. What Dianne wanted was for me to sit still until she found a way to leave. While this seemed unfair in theory, the facts were that I would just as leave let Dianne be the first villain in the breakup of our families, and that I had neither the will nor the energy to do anything at this time.

"How's Eddie?" Dianne asked jovially. "How's Bootville? Honestly, Nady, you don't know how glad I am to be back. I missed Eddie. Maybe it sounds funny but it's true. I'm looking forward to seeing him . . . being with him. I thought about Eddie a lot in California. The truth is, I really love him when I can accept him for the person he is. The fact is, I chose not to marry some turned-off intellectual type and I wouldn't have been happy if I had. I married a very strong, solid, unpretentious, working-class . . ."

She continued mining this rich new vein of fantasy until I let her and Carly off at their house. It was understood that we would bring a picnic lunch back to the building where the men

381

were working. Dianne thought that would be a real treat. She was going to see if there was a bottle of jug wine around the house and bring that back, too. I wouldn't have believed it was Dianne talking if I hadn't been in a condition where I could believe anything because none of it mattered.

I kept wondering if she'd ask if I'd taken her up on her declaration of open season on her husband, but this was a woman who didn't remember that two weeks before she'd been passing out engraved invitations with Eddie's name on them, much less consider the possibility that I'd picked up one.

At the shop Dianne threw her arms around her surprised, new, blue, working-class husband and kissed his cheek. He responded with obvious pleasure but not with the intensity with which he reacted a moment later when Carly followed us into the shop and said, shyly, "Hi, Daddy. I'm ready to come home."

He looked at her with tears in his eyes. He wanted to hug her but he was afraid she'd shy away. She took the basket with the food from Dianne and brought it out to spread on the grass. I went back to the pool, where Daisy and Philip were playing with a few other kids at the shallow end. I told the other kids to go home for lunch and we all had a picnic. The high point of which occurred when Dianne whispered in Eddie's ear and they disappeared into the freakoseum for a while, Dianne giggling in such a way as to signal that her intentions were sexual.

"Does anyone mind," giggle giggle, "if Eddie shows me the apartment upstairs? I've never seen it since it was furnished."

I minded. Or I would have if I'd had feelings. It wasn't that I thought for a moment Dianne didn't have the right to screw her own husband. What she didn't have the right to do was to maneuver me into screwing him and then pretend it hadn't happened. Her denial left me as the sole perpetrator of the vile deed.

Carly moved home after lunch. The next day she went back to school and met the youngest of the Regan daughters, who was exactly her age. Within three days they were the closest of friends. Carly began smiling occasionally; I'd forgotten what she looked like when she smiled.

The weather got warmer. The men succeeded in renting the apartment over the garage to a young couple with an income. Even better, the couple had fallen in love with Bootville and were going to have Eddie and Amos contract for them on the house they wanted to build. Other jobs were coming their way. Philip and Daisy were turning into spectacular swimmers. The men worked hard and were contented at night. Amos took me for granted in a way that was dangerous for him but convenient for me. Dianne talked a few times to Sternheim on the phone. His office made arrangements for all of us to come out to Hollywood for the premiere of the movie, now put off until the end of summer. I told Amos I had no intention of going but it didn't seem necessary yet to tell that to Dianne. He said that if I wanted to go the four of us would go and otherwise we'd all stay home. I said, "Mmmm."

In our two families Philip is the only person who is upset by my continuing depression. When he comes home after school he sees my face and asks, "What's the matter?"

"Nothing," I say.

Nothing is wrong and nothing is right.

He gets crazy. He keeps asking what he did to make me angry and no power in heaven or earth can convince him that he's done nothing.

"You and Daisy are the ones who make me *happy*," I say with as much force as I can muster. "I love you so much, Philip."

But my telling him I love him can't make up for the fact that I'm not really there.

On the other hand there is no act of mine that Amos would not countenance (again) in order to hear those same words from me.

"Is there anything I can do to make you happy?" he asks.

"I doubt it," I say truthfully.

"We could rent out everything and move someplace else for a while."

"No," I say. "I've thought of that but I don't think it would

383

work." The time when I could settle for unloading the symbol, or fancied that I could, is past. It's the realities I have to deal with now. The invisible, twisted passageway between my house and Dianne's. The lack of any real reason in the present or the future for my life to be joined to Amos's aside from the fact that they are already joined. There is the welfare of the children, of course, but it is difficult to see how the children's welfare is served by this endless depression and more difficult to see how I will climb out of this depression if I can't get away from Amos, the representation of my childish needs, and make an adult life for myself.

And of course it is most difficult to see how I can do that when I can barely find the energy to breathe, much less to eat or engage in more strenuous activities. At night I lie in bed in my seersucker nightgown like a lump of suet in cheesecloth waiting to be pecked at by the birds. At dinner I eat a few bites of food lest I have to endure another conversation with Amos about my health. Aside from that I run on coffee. The twenty or thirty pounds accumulated in my housewife's life have fallen away. I'm still losing, but more gradually, because there's no excess flesh left on me. I take no pleasure at all in my new skinniness, in the fact that warm weather is here and I can easily fit into the cotton clothes that have been in cartons since I shipped them from California.

Over at the other house the euphoria was gradually wearing off, although Dianne faked it for a while. Like his brother, Eddie was contented in his family life. His daughter was back with him where she belonged (although she spent half of her free time at Louisa Regan's house and Louisa spent the other half at hers); his wife was sleeping with him; and his and Amos's reputation for car work, now that their road was in, had spread so far that people from towns twenty and thirty miles away were bringing in cars and trucks. Finally, a friend of the young couple who'd rented the apartment had bought about a hundred acres of land in Pomstead and was getting the approval of the zoning com-

384

mission for a development he wanted the men to contract for. Amos said he was so busy he was glad I didn't want to go to California for the premiere.

One night in July Dianne came over to chat. I'd barely seen her in the weeks after her return but now she was dropping by occasionally. If she'd noticed that I wasn't inhabiting my own life, she hadn't seen fit to comment on that fact. Now I could see that she was uneasy about something but my antennae were withdrawn, like the rest of me, so I had no feeling for what she might be about to say. I watched her flutter around it like a butterfly in a net. Another butterfly in another net. Another butterfly in the same net.

"The office is ghastly," she finally said. "I seem to be spending all my time drawing up leases."

"Maybe we should exchange for a few days," I said without rancor.

"Oh, Nady," she sighed, "believe it or not there are times when I would if I could."

Silence.

"How're things with Eddie?" When the men in her life were okay the job was tolerable. What good did all her brilliance do if it left her in the same place? Poor Dianne.

She shrugged. "It's not terrible the way it used to be. It's just . . . nothing. We have nothing in common. Nothing to talk about. Even if he didn't fall asleep from drinking he'd still be watching TV every night and we'd still have nothing to talk about."

"It's amazing, isn't it?" I murmured.

"What's amazing?"

"Oh . . . it's amazing that we married them, amazing that we lived with them for so long . . ." (I heard myself talking in the past tense but it didn't seem an error worth correcting.) "Amazing that we never really thought about all these trifling factors like whether we had anything in common . . . until we'd had children and gotten them through the early years. It's as though

385

that was all that was ever important. But now it's done and we want something else."

She shook her head. "Stop, Nady. I can't stand what you're doing."

"I didn't mean to do anything."

"You're making it sound different than it was."

"How?"

"When we were young and we were in love," she said, "the rest of it didn't seem to make any difference."

"When we were young," I said, "we were desperate to be in love, so we didn't allow anything to make any difference."

She stood up. "I don't think I can talk to you anymore, Nady."

As though she'd once freely confided in me. She was making up a new Dianne-Nadine just as she'd made up a new Dianne-Eddie.

"Why don't you sit down?" I said wearily. "And tell me what you meant to tell me when you came in?"

She wavered. It was important or she'd have left already.

She sat. "I've been offered the other job."

"Are you going to take it?" I didn't much care. It didn't feel as though a chasm yawned before me but more as though I'd been trudging through the chasm for ages and was coming to a place where the scenery might be different.

"I don't know," she said. "It's very appealing in some ways."

"I thought that one wasn't so appealing."

"I was too flip about it. The other one sounded more stimulating but it was really just more glamorous, you know, the movie business. So I tended to underestimate the possibilities of this one."

Including the possibility of breaking out of a used-up marriage. I didn't bother to quiz her to get some sense of whether "the possibilities" were just another set of the rationalizations that Dianne used to make her way through life's compromises. It didn't matter. We were separating now and her lies to herself didn't matter to me anymore.

"Have you told Eddie?"

"There's no point until I decide for sure."

"It sounds as though you've really decided."

"No. There's one problem. I talked to Carly last night and she says she won't go no matter what. If I force her to go she'll run away and come back here." A wry smile. "To Louisa Regan, I tried to convince her she'd make plenty of friends out there but it was useless. She wouldn't listen for a minute. She got *hysterical,* Nady. It was *frightening.* I've never seen anything like it."

Not from Carly, anyway.

She seemed to be waiting for me to speak so I cast around for some appropriate question to ask her.

"How long do you have to make up your mind?"

"A couple of days."

"Mmm. Rough. If you had some time maybe you could convince her. Maybe she'll have a fight with Louisa and she'll see she can't order her whole life on someone else's—"

"The job will be gone by then. . . . Help me, Nady, I'm desperate! I don't know what I can do!"

And then I realize for the first time what it is Dianne wants from me. And at the moment of realization I say:

"No."

Her body starts, as though from an electric shock.

"No no no no no. I can't do it. I won't do it. I can't live that way any more."

A bunch of blobs that have been slopping around in my head for months have come together and in so doing turned me into a person again.

"It wasn't my idea," Dianne said, at once tearful, sullen and defensive.

"It doesn't matter whose idea it was. I have my own kids and my own life to live, I can't take on yours anymore."

"I wouldn't even have broached it," she said, "if I'd thought of her as some huge burden. I thought it would be natural. Easy. Maybe you'd all live together again."

"Natural and easy for whom?" There she was moving pieces

around the board as usual. Now that I was a person again I was getting angry.

"To tell you the truth, Nady, I thought of it as a . . . I thought Carly would be a comfort to you after I was gone."

I mustn't explode. I mustn't throw her down on the floor and try to choke her to death. After all, in some strange way Dianne was fighting for her life and if I really tried to kill her it would lend weight to her conviction that it was me she had to fight for it. Anyway, maybe she really believed what she was saying. After all, once *I'd* thought that privacy was what you got when you were bad.

Now I needed space to breathe, even if I didn't know yet what else I'd do with that space.

I was about to explain this to Dianne when I decided I didn't actually need her to know.

"You're so full of shit, Dianne," I said instead. "Comfort. Bullshit. You're still trying to move us around like a bunch of fucking hand puppets."

She stood up. She sighed.

"You don't want to sleep with the Eddie puppet so you move it into the Nadine puppet's bed, then you decide you want the Eddie puppet after all so you pretend it never happened when it did. Now the Carly puppet's keeping you from doing what you want to do so you try to move it into the Nadine puppet's house and tell the Nadine puppet you're comforting her for the huge loss of the Dianne puppet."

"I'd hoped," she said, her voice quivering, "that it would be possible to do this in a civilized fashion."

"Do what in a civilized fashion?" I demanded. "Break up two marriages and put everyone through God only knows what kind of awful shit and make believe the whole time nothing's happening?"

"Please don't shout at me," she said. (I hadn't realized I was shouting.) "I didn't know we were talking about both marriages."

"The reason you didn't know is that you never ask! The reason you didn't know is that we hardly ever talk, we're barely friends!

Our friendship long ago got lost in our marriage! I've been in the most godawful depression of my life, just like the one when my parents died, and you haven't noticed! My marriage is ending, and you haven't noticed! I don't have a life and you haven't noticed!"

"I'm sorry, Nady."

"I am, too."

Her expression changed. She was looking at someplace in back of me. Amos was there. I didn't turn to look at him.

"I'd better go," Dianne said. "I still think . . . there's no harm in trying to do this in a civilized way."

No, I was about to cry after her. *It's not right for it to be quiet and civilized. It should be . . .* what? As ugly as possible? Full of fights we don't really want to have with men we aren't even close enough to for a good fight? Fights that rip the children's guts in two without ever really solving anything?

I looked down and saw that with the index finger of my left hand I was lightly caressing the brow of the Stern Old Judge, and then I thought for the first time in years of how when I was little and my mother's health always seemed precarious, my parents would throw a big Saturday night party and death and illness would vanish for the duration. My mother was beautiful and gay; other men flirted with her but she looked with adoration only at my father. He drank more than ever but it was all right for him to be drinking because it was a party. Allergies—to grapefruits, to avocados, to everyday life—disappeared. Everyone danced. My parents danced beautifully together; they had met at a dance and come together almost without words. At some point in the party's progress, often during a tango, everyone else would clear off from the center of the terrace to let them do their formal yet sensuous routine, a performance which ended when they disappeared up the lemon-tree-lined path which led around to the front of the house.

Applause.

In the morning they both had headaches and life—tenuous, boring, frightening daily life—returned to normal.

"You're right," I said to Dianne's back. "I mean, we'll have to

389

be straight about it. The children will have to have reasons. A divorce isn't a party. You can't just dance out of a marriage and make believe nothing's dying. On the other hand . . . we can be as decent as possible."

She didn't turn again before she left. I don't know whether it was me she didn't want to face. Or Amos.

Silence. Once silence had frightened me. I talked for no reason but to fill the silences between my mother and me. My father and me. Dianne and me. Eddie-Amos and me. Now I waited. Amos came around and stood facing me across the round table.

"Why, Nadine?" His teeth were clenched, his voice shaky.

He'd never asked me why anything before. Not through all the years of decisions or the months of depression. What should he do, what did I want, but never Why? The answer would have to be honest, then. You couldn't respond with a lie the first time someone ever asked why you'd done something.

"I need to make a life for myself, Amos."

"I'm not stopping you. I want you to be happy."

"I need to be on my own. I need to find a job to do that needs to be done."

"Why can't you do that and be married?"

"I don't know. I can't." Our marriage is a weight that pulls me down with the memory of who I was and the knowledge of who I am now and the realization that the difference between them is at once enormous and not nearly great enough. "I feel as if our marriage is a solid weight, Amos, pulling me down every time I try to find out who I am."

Now that's a lie, Nadine; identity has never been your crisis.

"No, that's not really what I mean, Amos. It's not that I don't know who I am, it's that I don't know what to *do* with who I am. I'm thirty-eight years old. If this were a hundred years ago I'd have one foot in the grave and it wouldn't bother me that my hands were the only part of my body that were fully employed. I'd bake a few more loaves and patch a few more quilts and then I'd look up in this gray, wrinkled way and notice that the other foot had slipped in, too. Now I might live for another twenty, thirty, forty, even, years. The kids are in school full time. *There's absolutely nothing I have to do!* Do you realize that all this time that I've been depressed I've hardly done anything *and it hasn't mattered to anybody?"*

"That's not true," he said. "You matter to all of us."

"But I'm just this *thing* that's *here." A true product of the twentieth century, all form and no function.* "You may like me but you don't need me." *Besides, I don't like you. Usually. Right now I like you because I'm leaving, but usually I don't.*

"The children need you," he said.

"Of course they do," I said.

"Then you can't just talk about going off and leaving them."

"I never thought of leaving them," I said truthfully. "They're like pieces of me. How could I leave them?"

Amos made the transition with ease—from you can't leave them to you can't take them.

"You mean you think you're just going to run off and take them with you?"

I nodded. I stood up and put the coffee cups in the sink and wiped off the kitchen table. I felt as though I were making preparations to leave.

"Where will you go?"

"New York, I think. I have to figure things out. New York seems like the only place."

"It costs a lot of money to live in New York."

Money. It had taken a good five or ten minutes for money to enter the conversation. (It would never leave again.) A milestone, I thought.

"There's my parents' money; that'll keep us going for a while. I'll work. There'll be money from the movie."

"Maybe you won't get it if you don't stick around!" he shouted suddenly.

"I'll sue you for it."

"Maybe we won't even get it, maybe it won't do well if there's no promotion, maybe—"

"It's you they really want," I said patiently. I felt kind toward him. And sad. "You and Eddie'll be fine. You'll be celebrities without being freaks. You'll have hundreds of women flocking after you. You'll have no trouble finding another wife, if that's what you want."

"You're just saying that because you—"

"Not true. You're a nice man, Amos, and you're going to be rich and famous. You'll have your pick. It's going to be much harder for me to find someone than for you. I don't even want to." Not right away, certainly. If I find someone right away the same thing will happen all over again.

Amos sits, clasps his hands on the table, stares at them.

"Just when our lives are getting good," he says slowly, "you're fucking everything up. Why can't you give it a chance? Why can't you wait for the movie?"

"Even if I stayed with you I wouldn't have anything to do with the movie." Or the book. The movie would be a book which wouldn't quickly disappear. "I hate the fucking movie."

"How can you hate it when you haven't even seen it?"

"Where it's a lie," I said, "I hate it because I hate lies. And when it's the truth . . . if it shows me as I really am . . . as we really are . . . were . . . then I'll hate it because I hate the way we were."

This time it takes Amos even longer to speak. His face goes through a series of contortions. He's in such pain that I have to keep myself from running to him, holding him, trying to comfort him. When he looks up there are tears in his eyes. At first his mouth moves but no sounds come out. But, finally, he says what he has to say:

"You only loved us when we were freaks."

Then he buries his head in his arms and cries.

And I cry, too, not only for the part of what he's saying that's true, but also for the far more painful truth:

Not even then.

Thanks to Frederick Karl
Helen Puner
Jean Rossner